Miriam Halahmy

Miriam Halahmy was born in London in 1952. She lives in Golders Green with her husband and their son and daughter. Her three great passions are reading, writing and History. Research for this novel took her to the Imperial War Museum and the homes of former members of the Irgun in London. She has written and published short stories, articles and two poetry collections. A teacher of children with Special Needs for 25 years she now enjoys painting, gentle exercise, travel and leading Creative Writing workshops. At the heart of her inspiration for this novel and future work, are the activities of various Jewish Groups in post-war London.

First published by Citron Press, 1999.
Reprinted in 2003 by Bookchase (U.K.) Ltd in the UK.

ISBN 978-0-7544-0064-6

Printed and bound in Great Britain by Biddles

Cover design by David Hyams.

A copy of this book is held at the British Library.

Secret Territory
Miriam Halahmy

By the same author

Stir Crazy, Hub Editions, 1994, second edition, 1999
Cutting Pomegranates, David Paul Press, 2003

For Rafael

Author's note

All characters in this book are fictitious.
Kibbutz Kfar Gilead is an imaginary kibbutz.
Moshav Nevae Ativ is a real settlement on the Golan Heights.
Information about the Irgun's activities in London in the 1940s was gathered from interviews with former Irgunists, and the events described are based on fact.

Part One

Kibbutz

CHAPTER ONE

October 1975.

'It would never work. You're Jewish.'

Like a slap the words went on stinging and stinging.

The no-smoking sign flicked off. Eve released her seatbelt and leaned back. Four and a half hours to go. Then I'll be in Israel. Wonder if Andy's left for Greece yet? It was automatic to think of what Andy was doing. But immediately she remembered and the ache poured back in. His final words in Montpellier at Patrice's house rang in her ears.

Suddenly being Jewish had meant more to her than at any other time in her life. If it meant that much to him. Enough to break the love bond they had sealed a thousand times. He had left for Paris an hour later, the rucksack his dad had given him from his mountaineering days, sagging sadly as the front door closed and she was left alone.

The Air hostess smiled over her, 'Would you like any drinks?'

'Yes please. Coca Cola. With some ice.' The drink was cool and refreshing. She hated flying. She felt squashed and hot. Her long hair lay heavy and sweaty on her neck.

After the drink she went to freshen up. The plane rocked in bumpy air as she was drying her hands. She gripped the hand basin and stared in the mirror picking strands of hair from her blue T-shirt .

Blue was her favourite colour, the colour of the sky and the sea. When she was little all her paintings were blue.

'Even the grass?' Mrs Plummer had questioned in Class Two, her rouged cheeks dimpled as she smiled.

'Yes,' Eve said firmly, furiously stirring the brush in the palette.

Only the top half of her body showed in the mirror. Thick dark hair hanging almost to her waist, clear skin, nose not quite straight, white teeth.

Good teeth, she thought. I'll never have falsies.

Her skin was always dark. She tanned quicker and deeper than anyone else in school.

'Wish I was Jewish,' Susan Parker had said one summer and everyone laughed. Eve didn't like the quality of the laughter, but Susan was her best friend.

On tiptoe she could see below her waist. Hips too wide and legs too short. I'll never be a runner.

Susan Parker had whizzed to victory down the hundred yard sprint every sports day. Eve was usually sixth or seventh.

'But you are fast darling,' her mother always comforted. 'Look at poor Derek.'

Derek was fat and wobbled in twentieth every year.

'I want to be first,' Eve would scowl.

She brushed her hair and pulled it back in a band, feeling its silky weight in her hand. Andy used to brush it for hours as they sat up in bed in the flat. The memory prickled in her tear ducts. She threw one last look in the mirror and went back to her seat. It's over, she told herself firmly and flipped open a magazine.

She had met Andy at a party at the end of her second year at Manchester University on a History degree. He was twenty-one, in his third year studying English. A little taller than Eve's five foot three, Andy had blond hair that straggled his narrow shoulders. He wore denim shirts and jeans and drove a beat up old A 40, 'only because I know how to fix it,' he smiled apologetically, as if worried she might think him a capitalist.

It was Sally's twentieth birthday party. She had just moved in with her boyfriend, Pete, and Eve missed her. They had shared a room since the first day.

'We'll have to fix you up with someone,' Sally laughed as she stuck a bottle of wine between her legs and pulled the cork. 'Enough of your roving eye my girl!'

The party was small and intimate. Eve noticed Andy early on as they all rocked to David Bowie, shouting out the words, a joint passing from mouth to mouth. Then the record changed to a slow one and he asked her to dance, his body warm and soft in her arms.

The no-smoking sign had flashed on again. They were approaching Tel Aviv airport. Excited chatter broke out all over the plane. Someone shook her hand.

'Eretz Yisrael.'

She nodded, bewildered.

As she stood in the crowded aisle after landing a woman said in a hushed voice, as if in church, 'Isn't it marvellous?' Eve smiled politely but all she could think about as she struggled through customs was getting to Tel Aviv. It was past midnight and too late for buses.

I'll just have to sleep at the airport, she thought wearily and was relieved to see several sleeping bags dotted about on the floor.

She settled herself down on a bench and rested her head on her rucksack.

My first time in Israel, the Promised Land, *eretz ha vad v halav,* land of milk and honey, But the old clichés from her Zionist Movement days failed to rouse a thrill.

She tried to picture her mother and father crossing the shiny floor, trolley piled with suitcases, heads turning as they drank in the lettering for Coca Cola in Hebrew, the sullen guards with their sub-machine guns, the velvet night beyond the automatic doors.

Eve had grown up with an echo in her ear, 'You could have been born in Israel.' With the sound of knocking on doors on backstreet alleys, the scent of illicit meetings in musty synagogue halls, the faded route maps, the boats silent and dark on the shoreline.

That was how her mother told the story. In the evenings after homework as they sat together waiting for the sound of her father's car, the headlamps flaring at the living-room window.

'I was a nurse, trained in the Navy. Most of the other girls were just shop assistants or typists. They snapped me up.'

Sometimes her mother would sing the Zionist songs she learnt at camp as a child, sleeping on straw mattresses in a muddy field. She showed Eve a photograph of herself at thirteen, her long dark hair tangled in the wind. She seemed a wild tough figure, not easily subdued.

She would have made a good pioneer, thought Eve.

But they didn't go. Her father never added anything to the stories. Her mother never answered her questions, 'Why mum? Why didn't you go?'

Eve hungered for details. But it was her father, she sensed, who held the key to the truth.

Eve went to camp and learnt the songs of the Zionist pioneers. They dug trenches round the bell tents while rain poured relentlessly. Everyone wore shorts and boots, the uniform of the kibbutznik.

Some of the leaders had khefiyas brought back from holidays in Israel. Sometimes Sarah, Eve's leader would lend Eve her white khefiya. Draping it around her neck, still warm from Sarah's fragrant skin, Eve would close her eyes and feel transported.

The heat would be terrible, worse than last summer when the temperature hit eighty and everyone wished it would rain. They would rise before dawn, singing as they walked out to the fields. Wearing her shorts and boots, white khefiya hanging down her back, she would dig the land. At the end of the day, beneath a starry sky, they would hold hands and dance, hoping the fedayeen would stay away.

God I'm tired, thought Eve, pushing aside the sinking feelings, which were rising as she stretched out on the bench. It's just because there's no one to chat to, have a joke with. I'll feel better when I get to the kibbutz. Her last thought was, If Sally were here we'd be giggling and swigging wine by now.

'Ok. Now you must to wake up.' A guard was nudging her gently with his boot, the barrel of his gun tilted back, away from her face. Eve had never been close to a weapon before. A strange thrill went through her. The guard had liquid black eyes and tight black curls. His jeans hugged his bottom into neat curves as he turned and strolled away. She looked at her watch. A boy in a sleeping bag near the bench was lighting a cigarette. He grinned and offered her one.

'No thanks.' Eve ran a hand through her hair. 'God, what time do they call this?'

'They always wake everyone at five.' He had a South African accent. 'Watching for the kamikazes. Remember the massacre in '72 by the Japanese? They're careful now. Lots of guards and no-one's encouraged to take root.'

Eve yawned and stretched. 'Might have been safer to sleep in the street. I'm Eve.'

'Ben.' He nodded and smiled, neatly rolling up his sleeping bag and tying it to the bottom of an orange rucksack. Ben had high frizzy hair, which accentuated his long suntanned face. He wore cut-off jeans and a white T-shirt. A string of beads hung round his neck.

'You going to a kibbutz?'

'Yes,' nodded Eve.' Somewhere called Kfar Gilead. I'm a volunteer, here for a few months. I have to get a bus from Tel Aviv.'

They left the airport together. Outside the sun was already warm. Ben flagged down a sherout, a shared taxi, and they sat squeezed in the corner next to a family from Argentina who spoke Spanish and Hebrew. Tall palms reached to the sky along the airport forecourt . Eve felt a delicious sense of distance from England, the October gales, the rain.

'This is lovely Ben. I'm dying to see the sea. I could have been born here you know.'

He laughed.'Couldn't we all!'

The Argentineans, spurred on by the excitement in their voices, began to talk even louder.

'This is a very noisy country,' cried Ben.

Eve broke into helpless laughter, flooded with a sense of relief. I'm here now, she thought. There's no turning back.

The car set them down at the beach. A concrete promenade topped by high rise hotels lined a wide stretch of golden sand.

'You want to go for a swim? The water's warm,' said Ben.

'At six o'clock in the morning?'

'You're in Israel now. This is the Med., not the North Sea!'

They were shouting at each other.

Like two kids on a day trip to Brighton, thought Eve, as she ran down some steps and sank into the sand, her rucksack bumping on her back.

Ben sat by their packs as she went to change and then threw herself into the sea rolling on her back to float and stare into the deep blue sky. She thought of yesterday and England. Then as if to purge the memory of the colour grey forever, she rolled onto her front and swam fast for several minutes in a line parallel to the beach. The water was so warm. She relaxed and floated on her back again.

Is Andy in the sea now? she couldn't help wondering.

Swimming round some Greek island. 'You're Jewish, it wouldn't work.' The words stabbed a little less hard now. That night in Montpellier it was almost too much to bear.

'What do you mean I'm Jewish? How can you say such a thing after two years?'

What is this? she blazed inside her head.

'Come on Eve, you've always known. Why do you think I never took you home?'

'You said you hated your parents, you didn't want me to meet them.'

Take me in your arms for God's sake! she cried silently. I want to smell your hair, kiss you in my special place behind your ear. This isn't happening Andy, tell me it isn't.

'I'm sorry Eve. But it's over.' His face was drawn and pale. Sadness she had thought then. Later she realised it was guilt. Two years of sharing the same bed, graduating together, travelling round France. She felt so unprepared for this.

His words drove her back years. To her childhood when she was the only Jewish child in school.

To her teens and the overwhelming discovery of the concentration camps. All that anger and nowhere to vent it, no one to go out and thump. What happened to the six million she felt in every fibre of her body, but there was no one to scream at. It was over.

When had she drifted away from it all, lost interest? Probably after the Six Day War when she was too young to go to Israel as a volunteer. Studying took over and then the all consuming desire to escape the suffocation of her home. At University she steered clear of Jewish groups telling herself she wanted to mix, not be categorised.

Her love for Andy, who was neither Jewish nor Christian, but just Andy seemed to affirm her loss of commitment. She was Eve. She lived with Andy. They were a unit.

She shook herself mentally, waded out of the sea and ran up to Ben.

He handed her a towel. 'Use mine. My mother will sort out the washing. I live a bus ride from here.'

They had rolls and coffee in a pavement cafe and then he took her to the bus station and showed her the right bus stop. 'We'll meet again,' he grinned.

'How do you know?'

'Israel's like that. It's just a neighbourhood really. You'll see.' Then he was gone into the dense crowds that filled up the narrow pavements.

Simon had had curly hair like Ben but he was taller with a strong muscular body, in his khaki shorts and half-laced work boots. She wondered if she would recognise him now. But she never did ask Sarah which kibbutz they had gone to.

It had been the spring of '67. Eve was fourteen years old. Simon was seventeen , one of the leaders in the Zionist Movement. She had found him in Grandma Stone's flat one Sunday morning, stopping over to visit before the group met that afternoon.

'Come in darling, someone is here.' Her grandmother's Yiddish accent grated in the doorway.

The living room was strewn with fur coats, silk linings, ends of black thread snaking the carpet, a tin of assorted buttons open on the coffee table. Her grandmother lined fur coats at home.

Simon, balancing a tea cup, serviette and china plate, sat on the sofa his long legs folded awkwardly under the crockery. Eve felt lightheaded. Here he was, subject of all her dreams, amongst the fur coats and the heavy furniture. 'I know his mother darling,' said her grandmother. 'Sometimes he comes to visit me'.

Simon, a quick shadow of something on his face too, but afterwards Eve decided just imagined said,'Hello Eve.'

The fateful spring of '67, the Easter holiday, her fourteenth birthday. The Group went to camp in the week after bank holiday. Sarah lent Eve her white khefiya for the last night. Outside the tents a huge bonfire was lit. Everyone was singing and dancing, their voices carrying over the black wet fields.

Eve was standing next to Simon. She felt his arm encircle her shoulders. Several other couples had begun to slip away from the main group.

Eve felt the fragility of standing with Simon's arm around her. She felt caught in a moment when time must surely stand still for her, if only long enough to feel that the memory would remain. She reached up to his fingers resting on her shoulder. Almost imperceptibly his thumb began to stroke the inside of her palm.

Then he bent down to kiss her, his muscular legs pressing a bulge in his groin against her tingling body.

The evenings grew lighter. Simon was studying hard. His father was strict, he said. They could only meet on Sundays. Eve knew it was she and not Simon who cared. June began rainy. Nothing seemed inevitable except end of term exams.

When it came no one seemed ready. WARSHIP OPENS FIRE ON TEL-AVIV, screamed *The Times*. Eve stood in her school uniform watching television. Simon filled the screen, battered rucksack on the smooth floor of the airport, Sarah in her white khefiya speaking into the microphone, ' We're going because we're needed. The men have gone to war and the crops are rotting in the fields.' Then they all linked hands and danced, singing songs of the old Jewish freedom fighters. Eve, her school tie loose around her neck, face running with tears, begged and begged.

'You're too young. They wouldn't even consider you,' her father smiled gently.

'I'll lie about my age. Everyone says I look older than fourteen.' Inside she was screaming, Simon, Israel, kibbutz, her mind a whirl of confusion.

Her mother dished up dinner. The newsreader spoke excitedly, showed film of Israeli tanks, the blue and white flag streaming across the screen.

'They need me. The kibbutzim are empty. Who's going to bring in the crops?' She knew it was hopeless.

'Do you understand there is a war?' Her father's voice was suddenly sharp. 'This isn't a night game at camp. The Arabs could overrun the country any day.'

Her mother's eyes wide with fear, the steaming dishes on the table, her books open in her bedroom. If she walked out, thumbed a lift to the airport, what then? Simon's group had already left, boarding cards trampled on the cabin floor. They were probably singing, sharing a cigarette, relacing their boots for the work ahead. She would be here, in this house, at this table, watching it happen on television.

'What if I'd been born there,' she cried.

'You weren't!' Her father's voice almost broke with the force of his words. Gunfire rattled on the television, the living room door swung decisively as Eve flung herself upstairs.

She never saw Simon again. Sarah came back in August, sunburnt, a brand new khefiya for Eve, ' Because you couldn't come with.' She gazed into Eve's dark eyes. 'He's living with an Israeli girl now.' Eve turned back into her tent and wound the soft white khefiya round and round her neck, tucking the ends in carefully at her throat.

Her head jerked. She had fallen asleep on the kerb, the bus wheels arriving to a halt inches from her feet. She climbed aboard and fell back into a deep sleep her dreams racing between London and the beach.

She changed buses at Ashkelon. The ride was stuffy and slow. She sat next to an American called Harvey. Eve thought she had never seen anyone look so miserable. A paunch hung over the waistband of his shorts. But not a beer paunch, thought Eve. Probably an indulgent mother. Harvey didn't look married.

Eve gazed out of the window at the flat kibbutz fields. Everything was in straight lines. The crops, the trees, the roads leading between fields. The sky was a uniform colour, powder blue from end to end.

After a while, her eyes tired by the glare of the sun, she turned to Harvey and said, 'Volunteer or just visiting friends?'

He blinked behind large framed glasses. 'I guess I'm a volunteer but it sounds kinda heroic doesn't it. I'm not the heroic type.' Quite, thought Eve, glancing at the teenage soldiers opposite, carelessly balancing rifles between their legs.

'What did you do in America?'

'I was a manager in a shoe store. Then my mother died and I came out here.' He made it sound like Indian country.

He offered her a cigarette.

Marlborough, the red packet, thought Eve and they smoked in silence until they reached Kfar Gilead.

The road to the kibbutz ended in the low roofs of the cowsheds. Eve jumped down from the bus and pulled on her rucksack. 'Where is everybody?' said Harvey looking slowly around him.

'I shouldn't think they send out a welcoming committee,' said Eve and she set off along a dusty track. Harvey padded along beside her, feet turned out, a large suitcase on wheels bumping along behind and two cameras knocking in and out on his T-shirt.

In the distance Eve could see a girl in army uniform. They caught up with her by some huts. Doors stood open onto rough wooden verandas and a radio was playing. Frayed shorts hung dripping on string washing lines.

'Hello,' she said to the girl soldier.

The girl turned and smiled. 'Hi, you have just come? Dutch or American?'

Eve smiled.' English. Is this where the volunteers live?'

'Yes. Ok. I will show you somebody.' They walked between rows of dilapidated huts, the soldier nodding to people as she went.

'Hey Rivka. What's new?' a tall blond boy called out.

'Hey Bud. Nothing. Army, army.'

Eve found it hard to keep up with the soldier, her rucksack like an ironbar on her neck. Harvey had already given up, collapsed in a sweating heap on one of the verandas.

'You are tired?' asked Rivka. 'Now we stop and drink something.'

She turned off the path and through the open doorway of one of the huts. The room was dark after the bright sunshine, but only slightly cooler. On the bed a boy with long shaggy hair lay sprawled asleep, dressed only in blue underpants. A girl sat beside him painting her toenails. She wore shorts and a singlet. 'Make yourself comfortable. I won't be a minute. My name's Lou-Ann,' the girl smiled.

'She is new,' Rivka explained, pouring some water from a metal jug on the table. She handed a cup to Eve. 'First you must to drink. Then Lou-Ann will show you Irit.'

The boy woke up. 'Is it dinnertime?'

'No,' said Lou-Ann smiling. 'It's only 2.30. We have a visitor.' She nodded in the direction of Eve.

The boy pushed his hair out of his eyes and stared sleepily at Eve. 'Hi I'm Rick.'

'Eve.'

'Oh you're British. Not many British people here. Lot of Americans.'

'And French,' said Lou-Ann smiling again.

'Don't remind me,' groaned Rick.

Harvey appeared in the doorway. ' I wondered where you'd got to.'

'Jeez, another American.' Rick rolled over closing his eyes.

Eve sat on the floor listening to the buzzing of flies, the steady beat of the radio outside.

Well I made it, she thought. I'm on a kibbutz. She tried to remember how much she had longed to be a kibbutznik when she was at school. It seemed the only real option. At least that's how they made us feel in the Movement, she thought dryly.

It was after the Six Day War that her Zionist feelings had begun to fade. As though she had gone off the boil. She felt she had missed the crest of the wave, the whole purpose of her life until then, the struggle to come to terms with the holocaust, her mother's voice repeating, 'You could have been born in Israel.' Everything had suddenly side-stepped her, rushed on past and she was left to be just a schoolgirl.

Then why am I here? she thought.

Lou-Ann looked up from her toes and smiled at Harvey and then Eve. She seemed to have an endless supply of smiles. 'I wonder who you'll share with?'

It suddenly occurred to Eve that she may have to share with a man and that could be Harvey. But in the end it was Myra, who had the last hut before the swimming pool and Franck lived next door. Franck was an electrician from Lyons who only spoke French.

'But he's ok because he always fixes the lights when they go. Oh and hey, watch the kettle. You get a shock if you touch it when it's plugged in. Everyone gets them but it's ok.'

Myra was seventeen and weighed fifteen and a half stone. 'Two hundred and eighteen pounds but I had my jaw wired up for two months so it was worse.'

Eve had never seen anyone as wide as Myra. On the wall she had pinned up a towel which read, I CAN'T BELIEVE I ATE THE WHOLE THING.

'Back home in Florida we all get our jaws wired up now. Mom, my big sister. Dad was going to but then he chickened out. That was just before I left. I've been here a week already. Don't you think it's just great?'

'I'll tell you after a week,' said Eve.

Suddenly there was shouting and yelling outside and a loud rattling on the end wall of the hut. A crowd of children were throwing stones. One flew through the hole in the mosquito net above Eve's bed.

'What the hell...' Eve ran outside. The children fled through the volunteer section to the bungalows jeering and laughing over their shoulders.

'It's a kind of initiation test. They stop after a while.' Myra shrugged her shoulders and went back into the hut.

But Eve was furious and stormed over to the little office near the dining hall to find Irit. Irit shrugged her shoulders. 'Ok Eve.'

'Ok. What the hell does ok mean?' Eve almost yelled.

'It means ok. Calm down Eve. You have to get used to kibbutz.' Irit carried on stamping some papers.

'Isn't anyone in charge of those kids? If they were mine...'

'Well for one thing they are not. And for another thing did you know you are working in the laundry tomorrow? Be there at seven please.'

CHAPTER TWO

'No Eve. Water. Put water.'

The laundry was filled with a nightmare of Jewish grandmothers. Eve grabbed the squeezy bottle and sprayed, writing her name on the frayed cotton.

This lot are going to drive me up the wall, she thought. I won't last a week.

'Gut. Now you press.' The blue tattooed number on Leah's left forearm waved past Eve's face as she pressed her husband's best trousers. 'My second husband,' she told Eve. 'Auschwitz,' and she tapped the faded number.

The laundry was in a long low hut. Only women worked there. On kibbutz the men drove the tractors, Bedouin harvested the cotton and the women did women's work.

'Why can't I work in the fields?' Eve demanded after a week, when she met Irit in the dining room.

'It is finished now. Wait for the oranges,' said Irit spooning yoghurt into her children as they clambered round.

'When will the oranges be ready?'

'*Od mayat,* soon.'

Eve stalked off and sat down on the volunteer's table. 'Everything's *od mayat* in this place. What the hell does it mean anyway?'

'It means, hang around baby and mebbe one day....' grinned Bud.

'I didn't come to hang around.'

'What did you come for?'

Eve was silent. Then Rick yelled from the end of the table,' Definitely not tomatoes! Jeez, when I get home if mom ever serves tomatoes...'

'To get thin,' put in Myra.

'*Les femmes,*' grated Franck.

Bud gave a loud hoot, 'Well whadya know. I thought you didn't speak

English!'

Franck shrugged his shoulders and gathered some crockery on a tray. Pushing his chair back he said, 'I come to be Israelien.' He walked off his slight figure stooped over the tray.

'The army'd have to be desperate,' muttered Rick.

'He can always wire up all the borders and electrocute the bloody lot,' said Eve grinning. 'And what's wrong with tomatoes?' She prodded the mound of food on Rick's plate. He shook his head mournfully and began eating.

Eve and Bud walked back to the huts together.

'Feeling a bit edgy?' Bud asked.

'No, just Tom. Yesterday everyone was wasting water. Today it's food. Tomorrow we'll probably be talking too much and wasting oxygen. ' She shook her head. 'He's more Israeli than the Israelis.'

Bud smiled wryly. ' Yeah, right. I'm the non-Jewish volunteer from England who stayed, converted and became a kibbutznik. So howzat!'

'Something like that,' laughed Eve.

Bud grinned and spat out the end of his cigarette like a wadge of chewing tobacco. 'Coffee?'

She sat down on a crate in Bud's hut. 'How long have you been here?'

'Two months. I quit school in June. Not my scene, I guess. I'm thinking of joining an Ulpan to learn Hebrew. He paused. 'Maybe I'll stay.'

'Go on *Aliyah* you mean, become a citizen?'

He nodded. 'How about you?'

'I was nearly born here. My parents were supposed to come in '48. But it didn't work out and they never tried again.'

Bud was crouched on the floor by the kettle his body huge under the window. Eve felt an overwhelming desire to talk about Andy, to evoke a response to his name in this hot and foreign place. 'I had a boyfriend... Andy. He isn't Jewish.' The words felt displaced in the shabby hut.

'So what happened?'

The sharp prick of tears as she pictured Andy, blond hair straggling his face as he lay in bed in the flat in Manchester. She lit a cigarette and watched the smoke drift towards the door. To have never heard his words, 'You're Jewish, it wouldn't work.'

'We went to France after college. Then we split up. I thought I'd give Israel a try.'

Music filtered in through the open doorway. Eve could see Lou-Anne hanging out Rick's shorts on the opposite veranda. Myra was probably sleeping now, her huge form beached on the narrow bed, a towel over her face against insects. She would mutter in her sleep, disconnected words about food, clothes and the beaches in Miami. The Israelis would be sleeping too, in their neat bungalows, the sprinklers freshening the thick green lawns. In the children's houses the women would be singing, pleading with the children to lie down.

What did it matter about Andy now? He'd made it clear. After two years together he'd said it all in one sentence. Time I put it all behind me, she thought as she stubbed out the cigarette on Bud's floor. Meet a sexy soldier!

Bud had lit another cigarette. 'I was thinking last night about coming over here. Seeing what's really going down in this country. I guess I have to make some kind of decision.'

'You mean about *Aliyah?*'

'Right. I feel as though I've been kinda pushed. They know how to put on the pressure.'

'Oh yes. The fellas from the *Suknut*, all dressed up in shirts and ties to impress the foreigners.' They laughed.

But Bud was getting indignant. 'Why can't they leave us alone? I mean, we're here aren't we? At least we're trying. Why do they have to make us feel so goddam guilty because...'

'Because we weren't born here,' finished Eve. 'That's what it's really all about underneath the ties and the offers of flats and cars. Our parents should have clawed their way to Palestine in '48 and dug in for victory. Then we would have been sabres and built the Promised Land,' she ended sarcastically.

Bud smiled grimly, ' Well it would've saved a lot of confusion. Think of all the Jews since then who've sat around asking who the hell they are, where they really belong.'

'I don't think we'll ever make up our minds. If we go back home or stay, the questions will always be there. It's only an idea that brings us here.'

'That's not enough Eve,' blasted Bud suddenly. 'What about history, identity, language, all ours and no-one else's!'

'Do you really feel you belong that much?'

Bud kept a chameleon in the corner of his hut. To catch the flies, he said. When Eve came to visit they would watch it together. Its stillness, the bulging eyes moving independently, the tongue shooting out half the length of its body to catch a fly. Stickier than Sellotape, stronger than a fishing line.

Bud worked in the loul with Harvey. 'He won't last long,' Bud would say. 'Don't like the smell of chicken shit.' His Texan drawl echoed in the half empty dining hall, the Israelis already at home watching television. Harvey his back to them two tables away could hear him.

One afternoon Bud brought back a newborn chick to his hut, fluffy and yellow like a clockwork toy. The volunteers crowded round, watching its soft feathers, its tiny movements.

'What're you going to do with it Bud?' Harvey, crouched on his knees, seemed almost animated to Eve before such helplessness.

'Keep it I guess,' said Bud.

Franck sneered from the doorway of his hut. *'Bah oui, comment tu le garderais?* It will die very soon.' He turned and closed his door abruptly.

Bud said nothing. Too silent really, thought Eve. For Bud.

Two days later the chick was dead. 'I had to do it Eve,' Bud said. 'Couldn't put it back with no injections. It would've diseased the others. And I couldn't keep the damn thing could I!' Then seeing the look on her face he had stomped off yelling 'Christ!'

There were no more chicks but the chameleon stayed and in the long hot afternoons, while the kibbutz slept, Eve and Bud would lie on the bed and watch the chameleon's gigantic tongue sweep the flies from the mosquito net.

Sometimes the radio played and rock ballads would fire Bud with a wild energy. He would leap to his feet and stalk round the room kibbutz cigarette clamped between his teeth, roaring out the words. The chameleon would hang motionless in the afternoon light and when the song was over Bud would reach over and switch off. Silence. Not even leaves rustled, the hot air was so still.

One afternoon Bud said,' It's not background which makes them change colour. It's emotions…fright, defeat, victory.' Then he leaned over and kissed her lips. Eve's blouse was open, half a breast, the line of her bikini top above the diaphragm.

She felt the rush of blood from the centre down and then she said, 'No it's not what I want.' He rolled back nodding, disappointed.

'I'm nearly twenty, Eve. Only two years younger. Is that the problem?'

'I see us as friends Bud. That's all,' and she sat up buttoning the neck of her blouse. 'We all live close together here. Sometimes we get confused.'

In the laundry Leah and the other women grumbled and sighed.

'Have you nearly finished Eve. The coffee is coming.'

'Od mayat.'

When she spoke Hebrew the women would laugh and shout to each other in Yiddish. She felt at home then.

Steam filled the air around her head, the irons slapped on the heavy cotton. Like the workshop in the backroom of her grandfather's house. Her parents last line of retreat after the end to their pioneer dreams. 'Filling her head with nonsense, ' grandma would say when her mother told the stories of their plans.

'I don't think it was nonsense,' Eve would defend fiercely. 'Why didn't you go later. It would have been…' words failed her. 'Well smashing, wouldn't it.'

'Run along to the workshop lovey and see if grandpa wants a cup of tea.'

Eve stood up defiantly, ' One day I'll go and build the land. Then you can come and visit me.' Her grandmother shook her head, her mother's eyes fixed on the needle in her hand. Eve turned and marched out to the corridor.

Looking back, the workbench was always chin high. Grandpa, tape measure round his neck, would pace the length of the room, marking huge tacking stitches on the smooth black cloth. Like the broken white lines on new tarmac. Sometimes he would hand Eve a piece of tailor's chalk to play with. Thin and flat, concave on the side where the manufacurer's lettering was printed, tailor's chalk only worked on cloth. Eve would run outside to the kitchen step but it was useless for a hopscotch grid or graffiti, EVE IS 9, I LUV MY MUM. The letters barely showed before the chalk broke in two and Eve would have to wait for another piece.

'No trouble, no trouble at all,' her grandmother would say when friends came for tea. 'They've lived with us since before she was born. One big happy family.'

Eve would help to set the Noritaki cups and saucers. She knew how to arrange the tea plates, with a serviette between each one, which side to stand when offering cake.

'A quiet little girl, rather serious.'

'How about a smile lovey?' Eve would oblige with her brilliant smile that showed her large white teeth. People always complemented her on her good teeth.

The hiss of the gas in the workshop. Her grandfather heated the flatirons on a long rectangular gas ring. After he had marked the cloth with chalk he would start again, pacing the bench, sewing huge tacking stitches. Her grandfather made cassocks for Rome. He would parcel up the finished garments and a van collected them for the big tailoring firms in the West End. But that was in the fifties, when he was already an old man. Too old to cope with delivering, too skilled to be dropped. In the thirties he would have to deliver every day.

'Dad would meet us after school,' Eve's mother told her. 'We would have to take the parcel on the bus to the West End. My sister and I took turns.'

'That must have been fun,' Eve said. 'A bus ride after school right into town.'

'We never liked it very much.'

Ceremonial robes in bright coloured silks, deep reds, blues and purples, hung in the workshop, shots of light streaming down the wall. Eve collected the little pieces of cut-offs for her rag bag. The cool bright silk against her skin, the different layers of colour in her bag, the hiss of the gas, the rattle of the sewing machine.

As grandpa pressed the cloth, great clouds of steam, the smell of damp material, would filter down to Eve as she sat on the floor playing. A huge block of wood damped down the cloth with thuds which echoed round the dreams inside her head. Grandpa was a tailor. He made cassocks for the Vatican. Eve was a little girl playing amongst the long black threads on the floor.

When he died she was sent away to stay with grown-up cousins. Her mother had to spend the week of the shiva with grandmother as she cried and cried. All through the long dark nights and cold winter days. In the evenings they sat on little hard chairs brought specially from the synagogue for the mourners and listened to the wail of the Rabbi's prayers.

Eve was ten. She had to share a bed with Cousin Sharon who was nineteen and worked in a hairdresser's. Cousin Sharon had long bony legs. Eve had never shared a bed before. Lying awake through the nights of the shiva week, she wondered about the funeral, what her grandfather's face looked like now and whether Susan Parker had taken her place as inkwell monitor in 4A.

Sharon's mother Dianne tried hard to amuse Eve. 'Shall we do some baking?' 'How about a walk to the park?'

Before the war, the sisters had slept in the big bedroom above the workshop, Eve's bedroom now, the rattle of the sewing machine lulling them to sleep at night.

'There were a lot of cousins,' Dianne said as she beat eggs and sugar for cakes.' We went to school together and on Shabbos morning we would meet in the street and walk across the park to the synagogue.'

Eve could imagine them all, stiff in their best homemade dresses and short white socks, the boys in their school caps.

'I wish I had just one cousin my age, ' Eve said, scraping the bowl with a teaspoon.

'They all live in Australia,' Auntie Dianne nodded sympathetically.

On Saturday afternoons all the cousins and aunts would meet in the park for a picnic. Grandpa stayed at the sewing machine, all through Shabbos, his foot working the wide metal pedal close to the floor. The black cloth skimmed under the racing needle, the bobbin spun like a top, the French windows open onto the scent of summer roses. In the evenings grandmother made button holes, a hundred to each cassock.

Eve was named after her mother's grandmother whose photograph hung on the living room wall. Grandmother Eve came from Poland and never spoke a word of English.

'She had a very sweet smile,' said her mother.

Eve would look at her photograph sometimes and wonder why she never learnt English. How did she do the shopping and speak on the telephone?

'They had servants,' her mother told her. 'The telephone hadn't been invented.'

Grandpa died when he was seventy-two, falling onto a pile of material in his work room. 'Three score years and ten. Then its borrowed time. That's what he used to say,' Eve's mother was fond of murmuring. Eve had nothing from her grandfather. But when grandma died, three years later, her mother wrapped up the Noritake tea set in tissue paper and put it in the loft. 'For Eve when she has her own home.' Then Eve forgot about it.

In the laundry Leah chattered all the time, in Hebrew, Yiddish and English. Her words catapulted round the room to land in Eve's ears as she daydreamed in the steamy heat.

'Now, coffee. Then we start again. You still in that room Eve with fat Myra?'

Eve smiled,' Yes, she's o.k.'

'What, o.k.? A girl that age, so fat. *Zeh loh bari.* It's not healthy. Did you tell her?'

'It's not my business.'

'Listen to me. You would be better with someone else. *Nu,* Eve? That trouser is no good. Again please.'

Eve sighed and sprayed more water. Leah would have been at home in Grandma Stone's living room, she thought. On Sunday afternoons the room was filled with 'the widows'as her father called them.

'Are the widows coming today?' he would ask wickedly on his weekly phone call, her grandmother's voice scolding down the line.

All the refugees from Poland, Austria, Germany seemed to gather in the little flat. Cups and saucers on the glass-topped table, sliced cakes and biscuits, and sometimes, the outspread hands of cards. The air was thick with Yiddish.

In the laundry Leah never wore shorts or a dress. 'Aren't you hot?' Eve asked her one day. Leah's left arm wiped sweat across her camp number.

'*Nu,* it's a hot country.'

'Why don't you wear a skirt sometimes? I can hardly bear to wear anything, especially indoors.'

The laundry suddenly went very quiet. The faces of the women loomed round her, like wolves on the scent of pain.

Then Leah bent down and pulled up her trousers to the knee. Her legs were cratered with scars. 'My sister they injected with petrol,' she said quietly.

Grunts and clicking noises from the women filled the air, as they sighed, shuffled round again, picking up clothes, scraping chairs.

Eve looked into Leah's face. For the first time it seemed tangible. She had seen her mother, the faces of her grandmothers, Auntie Dianne and Cousin Sharon, in the faces on the newsreels of the holocaust. They all looked like her relatives. But this time she could actually touch one.

She knew it like a prayer, like a nursery rhyme. Yellow stars flat on their winter coats, waiting patiently in the lines for selection. To the left or right, the men had already disappeared. She knew it from the age of twelve when she read her first book about the camps. She had gone to check with her father.

'It isn't true is it? No-one could actually do that.'

In his face she could see how he had dreaded this moment. Like most parents dread the first questions about sex.

'Remember, every German was a Nazi. There were no exceptions.'

His words lived with her for years, but she couldn't close her eyes as she read more and more. Later she tried to reach him.

'What about the Germans who resisted, who hid Jews, fed people in the camps?'

It was all meaningless to him. He just shook his head. 'Every last one of them was a Nazi. That's why we have to have Israel.'

She had a dream that recurred through her teens. She was in a concentration camp with her mother. They were standing next to a tier of bunk beds in a hut.

Her mother's face, broken into chunks of misery, tears falling in a constant stream, as she said, 'I can stand anything but being separated from your Dad.'

The words sliced Eve's heart like a knife, the pain radiating outwards until she woke sobbing.

CHAPTER THREE

Eve glanced at her watch as she stumbled out to the concrete toilet block. A cold sliver of moon skulked above the eucalyptus grove. Starlight pricked the sky through the hole in the roof as she sat shivering. It was December and she hardly wore shorts any more. But the rains hadn't started. 4 am. Her shift started at seven.

Irit had suddenly moved her to the kitchen and she missed Leah and the other women. Tom ruled in the kitchen, when Chaim wasn't around.

'Just do your work. And don't waste the bloody water. There's a shortage in this country!'

Tom was thin and bony and wore long sleeved shirts rolled up to the elbow.

Like a miner, thought Eve. What the hell is he doing here? Must have got lost on his way to Bognor!

Her legs ached after the brief bout of *shil shul*. Walking slowly back to her hut, a blanket wrapped round her shoulders, Eve could see across to Anneka's hut. Outside the door swathed in a blue sleeping bag, like a New York vigilante, stood Harvey. It struck Eve that he could have been there all night. She hesitated and then shrugging her shoulders she hurried back to bed and fell asleep. In her dreams Harvey floated above the toilet block, dry even though it was raining, begging her to open the door.

Later that morning Eve sat on a stool chopping a crateful of aubergine. It was peaceful in the kitchen. Tom had gone into Ashkelon. If Chaim was in a good mood there would be cake.

Cake was almost a status symbol on kibbutz. Eve smiled when she thought what Harvey was prepared to do for cake. Come running from the shower if he sensed the slicing through buttercream. But then Harvey hungered for luxuries like the kibbutzniks hungered for personal things.

Two or three of the women had come into the kitchen that morning to bake cakes for their families. There was something sad it seemed to Eve about the way they stood mixing cakes in a corner of Chaim's vast stainless steel empire. Hugging secret wishes tight as the mixing bowls they held to their bodies.

'Ok Eve. You can go now.' Chaim stood over her surveying the huge colinders bursting with vegetables, the wooden crates empty on the floor.

'Same time tomorrow, then?' She lingered, still hoping there would be cake.

'Ok.' Chaim turned abruptly and walked off.

Eve pulled on her denim jacket and wandered off downstairs. Hands in her pockets she strolled through the kibbutz to the volunteer huts. Passing Anneka's hut she saw the veranda was empty and realised she had expected to see Harvey still standing there.

Harvey had fallen madly, crazily in love with Anneka, had longed for her and followed her, while she studiously ignored him. Anneka, who was part of the Dutch group, was tall and slender with long frizzy blond hair that had bleached almost white in the fierce Israeli sun. She had a wonderful clip to her English which entranced Harvey.

'Please say that again, Anneka,' Harvey would beg as he stood by her chair in the dining room, his work trousers stained with chicken shit. But Anneka never spoke to Harvey.

In the dining room, the blue smoke from their kibbutz cigarettes winding towards the pristine kitchen, Eve never felt she could ask Harvey about Anneka. They talked about the chickens and the food and how bored everyone was. Harvey made Eve feel she was coping. He was talking about going home for Christmas.

'What for?' asked Eve.

'It's just a point to stick a pin on. Like a map reference. And I can't stand the chicken shit much longer.'

Harvey took to visiting Anneka's hut. The first time he knocked on the door she had opened it, stared out at him disdainfully and then firmly closed the door again. After that she seemed to know instinctively when it was him and never opened the door again.

That morning as Eve passed Anneka's hut and stopped for a minute she heard Bud's voice call out, ' Want to know what happened?'

'What do you mean?'

'Harvey's gone. Packed up and left.' Bud gave a short sarcastic blast. 'Cracked up more likely over that stupid bitch, Anneka.'

Eve felt bewildered. Harvey would have said goodbye to her surely.

'He stood outside her hut all night. She wouldn't open the door once. Not even to see if he was ok. So he packed his gear and left. Took a lift into Ashkelon with Sammy at five this morning. ' Bud lit two cigarettes and gave one to Eve.

Harvey was gone and perhaps she should have gone over to him early this morning instead of climbing back into bed. But probably by then it was too late. Eve drew on her cigarette. Kibbutz was not for everyone.

The kibbutz battened down for the winter, closing in on itself. The vast dining hall was almost empty in the evenings, just a couple of the more committed families, the volunteers and one or two young people. The gap between the volunteers and the kibbutzniks widened as rows of empty trestle tables stretched between the little group and the silent munching Israelis.

When the food was ready the women would hurry in, heads wrapped in woolen scarves, arms piled high with plastic containers. Quickly filling up with food they would hurry away again to their tiny bungalows. Hunched over their plates, the kibbutz families would sit watching television until it was time for the children to return to the children's houses and the men to take a turn at guard duty.

Sometimes Eve could not face the cold trek to the dining hall. Huddled in her thin denim jacket she would walk over to Rahel's bungalow.

Rahel, short and dark, from Iraq, would open the door and smile with eyes that always seemed to brim with tears. She hated kibbutz, but mostly she hated the children's houses.

'They are dirty, very dirty,' she would whisper to Eve in a mixture of English and French. More and more frequently Carmella, her daughter, slept over in the bungalow. Brushing the child's long dark hair, in the evenings, Rahel would whisper to her of their new life to come.

Rahel's husband Benny, a huge wreck of a man, humped in a chair chain smoking, would stare blankly at the television. Rahel casting nervous glances towards him would confide in Eve, 'Next year, I will go to Paris, with my daughter and live with my brother.' Her eyes would fill with tears. Benny only spoke Hebrew but Eve detected in his expression the knowledge that he was losing.

Benny watched television, Carmella coloured in pictures and Rahel served three kinds of cake. Eve, eating and looking up words in her French dictionary, could almost hear Rahel gasp for air, a landed fish on a steep riverbank.

Rahel's family had come to Israel from Iraq, in 1950, two years after Independence. Rahel was fifteen. They brought nothing with them but the *Suknot* provided everything. Even the tents. They lived in a tent in the immigrant camp for four years. In Iraq her Uncle Nuradin had been a rich man. He and his family put gold between the soles of their shoes, hidden from the Iraqis and the Israelis. After three months they left the camp and bought a big house in Jaffa. Still like Rahel's father Uncle Nuradin could only get a job on the roads. They dug roads for twenty five years, unable to read or write Hebrew to the day they died.

'In Iraq my father was a lawyer. In the tent he would put bread and onion together and say, 'There, I have food. It's enough.'

But inside she could hear his heart breaking. Lost in a foreign land, lured by promises and threats, he had been abandoned to sink without hope. 'It was us they wanted,'Rahel breathed fiercely to Eve. 'To work on the land and go to war.'

Trying to read by the uncertain light of the kerosene lamp, while the little ones squabbled and her father click clicked his worry beads, Rahel felt as though her head was bursting. The pathways were a quagmire in the winter rains, her mother was trying to arrange a marriage with the boy in the next tent. If she stayed she would never escape the drudgery and the mud. Her only route out was kibbutz.

She met Benny on her first day at Kfar Gilead. He was a sabre, already over six feet tall at seventeen, with mouse coloured hair and small pale eyes. They became lovers, lying on the floor of the children's house, while the kibbutzniks picked oranges and the children were at school. Gradually the rest of her group and then the kibbutzniks found out but by then it was too late. Rahel had found the way to cut all ties with the immigrant camp for ever. They could never send her back with 'their' baby inside and the boy in the next tent would never look at her now.

At sixteen, wearing a white cotton dress and sandals, she was married outdoors under the bridal canopy. A burden slipped from her shoulders as she and Benny walked home to their bungalow, Three days later she miscarried.

In hospital her mother weeping and whispering at her bedside, Rahel lay in a dream of disbelief.

'Come back to us now,' begged her mother. 'Soon they will give us an apartment. The have promised. You can live with your family again, not among strangers. What else do we have but each other?'

Staring at the cracks in the whitewashed ceiling Rahel could see the emptiness of life without Benny. She knew the promises of the Suknot were handfuls of sand, without substance. She would never return to the camp. She belonged in the clean neat world of kibbutz, slotted in next to Benny.

'I am Benny's wife, ' she breathed to her mother and closed her eyes.

Rahel did not conceive again until she was in her thirties, just before the Six Day War. Benny, his tall frame and broad shoulders comfortably encased in army fatigues, waved goodbye from the back of an army truck, crying, 'Kiss the baby for me if I'm not home in time.'

The baby was born on the sixth day of war as the victorious army swept the Arabs aside. But Benny, caught in a final crossfire, was hit in a tank attack. Three of his closest friends were killed.

The next time Rahel saw him he had shrunk, encased in a white sheet as if under a surrender flag, his shattered jaw held together with wire.

Benny never spoke properly again although his face was hardly scarred. Inside he felt disfigured, ugly to his wife, his child, ugly to the families of the men who had died. Everyone said he was feeling guilty for surviving. But inside he believed it was the scars which made him feel too bad to cuddle Carmella, make love to his wife.

Benny's nerves finally broke down completely. Now he sat silent, somewhere else inside his head, away from his wife and daughter. When he worked it was in the fields and always alone.

For Rahel kibbutz had become the final trap since the flight from Baghdad all those crazy mismanaged years ago. Her parents were dead, two of her brothers had been killed in wars, one brother had married a fanatical American Jewess and lived surrounded by prayer in Jerusalem. A fourth brother had married a French Catholic and immigrated to New York.

But Eli, her beloved Eli who had denounced everyone and finally stormed out of Israel because the Iraqi Jew, 'does not and will not ever have anything under this goddamned Ashkenazi rule,' had gone to Paris.

So finally, at almost forty and well past any prime she may once have had, Rahel had decided to pack up and leave. To bring up her daughter herself far away from Benny and kibbutz.

Was Eli looking forward to Rahel coming to settle with him? Eve had inquired cautiously. Of course, Rahel had almost laughed aloud. I am family. Iraqis never turn anyone away, especially family.

What is considered normal in one's homeland can be seen in a different light abroad, thought Eve. Eli had a French wife. But it was clear that Rahel had no intention of suffering kibbutz and Benny much longer.

Dreams. Everybody had them. But in Eve's experience if they meant too much then they broke. Or broke you. Her father had written her a letter, mostly news about the family. But at the end, almost as an after thought he had put, 'Remember Noah, our Ark who sunk us all. Don't let anything sink your plans.'

She carried the letter round with her for days, bewildered by the urgency of his words. Why had he written that suddenly? Why now, after all these years, commit to paper the memory of their first child, the baby who died years before she was born.

Her mother's voice resonated in the creaky wooden hut , 'If we'd gone to be *chalutzim,* pioneers, you would have been a sabre. You would have been able to say you had been there from the start.'

As a child Eve would ask, ' Why didn't we go. We could have gone later?' But her mother never replied. Eve knew if she kept asking her mother's face would grow sad and a headache would start. Then grandma would put her to bed. Not that she didn't love grandma, but she was strict and she didn't like stories about pioneers.

'Noah. The Ark who sunk us all.' In her father's words Eve heard all the power of the broken dream.

She would discuss dreams sometimes with her imaginary friend, Kitty-in-the-corner, who lived at the top of the stairs and spoke to no-one but Eve. They agreed that bad dreams were to be avoided but it was difficult to know in advance whether a dream would turn out good or bad.

One day when Eve was seven she was sent up to get a book from her mother's bedside table. It had a drawer which was slightly open. Something red, tantalising, caught her eye. She stored it up. Saved it for the right moment, like the best sweet in the bag. Later that afternoon, everyone busy, she crept up to the bedroom and slid open the drawer. She could feel the hair on her neck rising as she knelt on the floor. What if someone came? What if it were grandma with words harder then a smack. But she wanted a secret, needed one, to share only with Kitty-in-the –corner.

First the lipstick. It smelt of her mother's good dress. She put some on her wrist and looked in terror at the bright red mark. No matter how hard she rubbed it wouldn't clean off. In the end she pulled her cardigan sleeve down to her palm. She should stop now. But curiosity burned in her. There was a tiny comb, some pens, an old address book and a silver handbag. At the back was a brown envelope. She didn't touch the envelope for a year. Every time she opened the drawer she took each thing out carefully, smelt it, ran its surface along her cheek and put it back exactly in the same place.

Sometimes a new thing appeared in the drawer, a different lipstick or a photograph. Her mother didn't have many personal possessions. But each item she treasured in the same way as though by checking and caring for the contents of the drawer she was keeping her place inside her mother. She was also looking for something. Kitty-in-the-corner thought it was a present.

Then just as Eve turned eight the brown envelope shifted its place into the centre of the drawer. 'Her' drawer. It had decided to invade 'her' secret territory. Eve had never opened an envelope before. But, she reasoned, it had moved from the back, almost as if it wanted to be noticed. Just like the other things. She reached down, picked up the envelope and opened it. She read the paper inside.

Noah Henry Stone. Born 1.15am NOV.10th 1948. Died 1.20am NOV.10th 1948. Cause of death : birth asphyxia.

She was kneeling on the floor by the bed, holding the death certificate in her hand, as her father walked in.

Silence, worse than words, worse than smacks, followed the opening of the brown envelope. The only words spoken were by her mother. 'What were you looking for darling?' Eve didn't answer. But she told Kitty-in-the-corner she had been wrong. About the present. It wasn't a present Eve had found in 'her' drawer.

Later that evening she hid on the stairs and listened to the adults talking in the kitchen.

'I thought you'd put it away in the hat box.' That was her father.

'I turned that old thing out ages ago. I never thought she'd look in my drawer.'

'We should tell her. He was her brother. '

What brother, Eve almost called out.

'She's not old enough yet.' That was grandma.

'Don't be so sure.' Her mother's voice sounded strange.

How can you be born and die on the same day? When would you have your birthday party? Noah built the Ark and saved lots of animals. How could he do that if he only lived for one day? The words of a song were going round in her head. ''The animals went in two by two...' She was falling and someone caught her. It was raining and they weren't wearing their boots. A little boy held her hand. Rain soaked his hair and poured down his tiny unformed face. Grandma said, 'You'll catch your death.' Eve tried to keep hold of his hand. But he slipped away and was gone.

As she walked home from school the next day with Susan Parker Eve said, 'I've got a brother.' The word felt strange in her mouth.

'No you haven't. Don't be stupid.' They were jumping cracks in the pavement but Eve wasn't concentrating. 'You stepped on that one. You'll marry a spider.'

Eve didn't care. 'I have got a brother. His name's Noah.'

'It can't be. Noah built the Ark. No-one's called Noah. Anyway when's his birthday.'

Eve couldn't answer. She wanted to take Susan home, show her the paper, prove that there was a brother. At least, there had been. Once. But Susan was already through the park gates. 'Bye. See you tomorrow. You can ask Miss Aspinall if your brother can come.' Eve watched Susan's thin legs disappear up the hill. They looked good in her white ankle socks. Like a runner's legs. Eve wanted to have long thin legs, to be best at running.

She walked across the road and arrived at her front door breathless. She often felt short of breath as she got to the house. Mr. and Mrs. Jones, the deaf and dumb couple next door, were in their front garden. ''Lo Eve. 'Ome fom school?' Eve smiled and nodded. 'Swimming today.' She pointed to her duffle bag. She'd learnt as a small child that it didn't matter if they understood her or not. They loved her attention. Most people couldn't be bothered.

Her grandmother opened the front door.

'Hello darling. Your mother's lying down. Headache. Change out of your school things and come down for a piece of cake.' The hall was dark. Like a large mouth ready to swallow her up. The breathlessness lasted until she reached her bedroom. Lying on her bed, her school shoes adrift on the rug, she concentrated on the whir of the sewing machine in the workshop below and gulped air.

'You know what is *chalutz* Eve?' Leah had invited her to tea on Saturday afternoon.

Eve nodded. Her parents had wanted to be *chalutzim,* pioneers. Until Noah launched his Ark into their lives.

'My husband was *chalutz*.'

Eve looked across at Jan, her eyes flicking instinctively to his left arm. There was no blue number. Jan shook his head. 'I wasn't in the camps.' Eve felt herself redden but Jan didn't seem to notice. 'I am a founder member of Kfar Gilead. My group came from Holland in 1936. The rest of my family...' He shrugged his shoulders and sipped some coffee .

There were so many subjects to avoid here. Like at home when she was a child. Eve could feel her chest tighten as Leah and Jan plied her with food. The table was crammed with home-made cakes, avocado dip, yoghurt and sour cream, fresh challa bread, jam, honey and chocolate spread. There were dates, sunflower seeds and nuts. The food tasted wonderful to Eve after the bland kibbutz meals.

'But now *chalutzim* is finished. No more. Kaput. Before '67 this country was fantastic.' Jan spoke slowly as if testing each word for its sound quality. 'We did everything ourselves. We accepted what we had. Worked together more. It was the way it had to be, there was no choice. You felt part of something new exciting.'

Eve felt a stirring of her old Zionist feelings as she listened to Jan talk. This is what I missed, she thought enviously.

Jan had long sensitive fingers, worn and swollen from years of hard work. A pianist, thought Eve, in the life before, when there was nothing to avoid.

Leah poured more coffee. She was chain smoking a packet of Time cigarettes Eve had brought.

'After'67 every kibbutznik want television.' Leah's voice was hoarse from the smoke. 'So the ideas begin to die. Now they want to bring the children home and close the children's houses. You know Rahel, Eve? She works with me.' Eve nodded. 'You see how she brings Carmella to her house almost every night.'

'But maybe things have to change if the kibbutz is going to survive. You can't expect things to stay the same. Rahel is tired of the kibbutz life. She wants to leave.'

'Sure we must to change. But not to die.'

No, thought Eve. There's been enough of that.

'Do you ever think about leaving?' she asked cautiously.

'Never,' Leah said firmly. 'But you never know when the next war will be. In Israel everyone lives for today.' She laughed her shrill loud laugh.

'You should stay Eve.' Jan was smiling now, more relaxed. 'We need young people like you on kibbutz and you are a Jew. Israel is your home.'

I already have a home, thought Eve.

CHAPTER FOUR

The letter from her father kept turning round in Eve's mind, as she wandered the perimeters of the kibbutz in the cool dry weather or sat for long hours in the kitchen.

Why had he suddenly decided to write to her? He had never written before, when she was at college, or away in France with Andy.

It wasn't only the fact he had written. Right at the end he had thrown in that startling reference to Noah. As if they had spoken about it all her life.

We never spoke about it, she thought bitterly. They shut me out completely. As though it was nothing to do with me.

All her life she had longed for a brother, even before she had found the death certificate. As if she instinctively knew her mother's womb had been used before. But not a sister, she remembered, that was Kitty-in-the-corner. Someone made up. What I wanted was a brother. She wanted to explain all this to Bud. But she didn't know where to start.

That's the problem she thought. I don't know, I don't actually know a damn thing.

It was then she decided to write back.

December 2nd.

Dear Dad,

Thanks for your letter. It's great to hear all your news. Look, you don't have to tell Grandma Stone this, but I haven't looked up her cousins in Herzlia. Well what would I have to say to a bunch of ancient Polish refugees. They probably don't even speak English. And Yiddish never was my strong point!

There's a woman here called Leah who would really fit in with the widows' tea parties. Except she's married. He's her second husband actually. The first died in Auschwitz. You really see that here. In England it's as though it never happened. But here you're always seeing people with blue tatooed numbers on their arms. One of the volunteers, a Swedish girl who isn't Jewish, asked Leah what the number was for. She actually didn't know. Can you believe it? I was horrified.

You said something at the end of your letter dad that I'm curious about. Being here in Israel, the first one to get here out of the three of us makes me think a lot about you and mum. All the stories mum told me about your plans to come in 1948. But I never really understood why you didn't come. What did you mean in your letter when you said Noah sunk all your plans? What happened around his birth and death? Why didn't you go later? Please write and tell me more. I really do want to know.

I miss England and everyone at home sometimes. I feel I must stay here for a while and give it a chance. But it's not how I imagined it would be, even though I knew it had changed since the old pioneering days. It's sort of like living on a rather claustrophobic housing estate. Modern and streamlined and rather sterile.

My hut is one of the original houses the founder members built when they were living in tents. It's very basic. There's grass growing through cracks in the floor and you get an electric shock every time you plug in the kettle. They haven't tarmacked this far yet and they say it'll be a quagmire when the rains come. But as Bud, my American friend says, who wants to play at being chalutzim?

The kibbutzniks all have telly and fridges and some of them are dying to shut the children's houses. Everyone's very depressed about the Yom Kippur war. They feel so vulnerable now. All the young people say they want to leave. They've been through one war . They don't want to die in the next one.

We all really enjoyed the cigarettes and chocolate. It hadn't melted. Bud says, send more!

Write soon dad. Love to mum.

All my love Eve.

*

Eve's father had been born Johnathan Henry Stone in 1922 in the East End of London within the sound of Bow Bells. Everyone called him Jack. His first language was Yiddish. He had one brother, David, who was two years older than him.

His father had come to England twice . The first time was in 1910. He had stepped off the train at Waterloo, taken one look at the fog and gone straight back to Poland. He joined the Russian army, but left in 1913, 'just in time!' and walked down through Europe, landing in England as the first shots of the War were fired.

Grandpa Stone was a barber and a gambler. He was a short stocky man, with a mass of dark hair and a handsome distinguished face. Gambling made and lost him several fortunes through most of Jack's young life.

'We lived all over London,' Eve's father told her. 'Sometimes in beautiful houses, often in two rooms above a shop. When David and I came home from school we never knew if the handcart would be there to move us on. Your grandmother worked her fingers to the bone, lining furs.'

Grandpa Stone was a card player and he knew all the tricks. He taught Eve to play Pontoon when she was six, gambling with piles of matchsticks. Twice a week, right until his death, Grandpa Stone played cards at his club. All the old men, in their neat dark suits, shell pink shirts and silk ties, competed with each other to play him.

Walking through the streets of the East End, hand in hand with his brother, Jack's mother would pronounce, 'This is a Jewish house, this one, not this one.'

'How do you know?' the boys would ask.

'By the curtains.'

His mother was the power behind the family, pushing the boys through school, snapping at them when they lapsed into Yiddish. 'You get English good. You don't want people to think you are a filthy Pole.'

She hated Poles with the vehemence of a tigress. 'Now I am a British citizen. I don't want to die a filthy Pole.' She almost spat on the table as she made noodles, finer than strands of wool, for chicken soup.

Jack was good with his hands, fixing clocks and bicycles for everyone in the street. David inherited his father's taste for risk. He folded several businesses before he was called up in 1939. Three months after he was demobbed he took the ten pound boat to Australia and married the daughter of a sheep farmer. With a more certain instinct for profit than his father he made a fortune in swimming pools.

'David invited us over so many times. I think he would have made me a partner,' Eve's father told her once. 'Must be lovely in Australia. All that sunshine and fruit.'

In the autumn of 1946 Jack returned home to the flat his father had managed to keep for the last year of the war. 'It's no *meziah*,' his mother said, her hands deep in flour as he walked into the kitchen and lowered his kit bag to the floor.

She was right. Three rooms over a second-hand furniture shop on the Willesden High Street in North London. 'But it's home. Drink your tea and then take out the dust for me.'

He could never get her to say rubbish. One day after school he had yelled,' It's not dust, it's rubbish! Rubbish! You came here when you were sixteen. You should have learnt by now for God's sakes!'

She had stood looking up at him from the table, her hands slicing beetroot for borscht, his tall boy's body awkward at thirteen in the striped school cap.

'Look at me Jack. What am I doing?'

Her tone, surprisingly gentle, bewildered him. She rarely spoke gently to him. Often he felt like a race horse and his mother was the jockey spurring him on with words like sticks. 'Doing? I dunno. Cooking dinner.'

'I am working Jack. I started work when I was twelve. My mother took me from school and put me with a milliner. We lived in Paris. Every morning at seven o'clock I walked across the Place de la Concorde and worked until six in the evening making flowers to put in the ladies hats. There was no time to learn.'

Jack and David shared a tiny room overlooking the back yard. David had been demobbed two weeks earlier. 'Still not used to it. But I'm not bloody staying here.' He nodded out the window at the bombed out buildings opposite, an American cigarette hanging from his thin mouth.

To Jack being home again felt as though he had suddenly, violently been tugged back by a rope and tied to a post in the ground. The flat, the barber's shop where the men still gathered and challenged his father to a game, the buildings torn from their roots, everything seemed small, narrow, suffocating. The war had been too big, the adrenalin too plentiful. All he had now was a ration book and a gun he hung on to, not quite certain he no longer needed it.

One evening he sat up late drinking beer with David. 'We've got to get out,' his brother suddenly said.'Did you see the Belsen newsreel!'

Jack nodded taken aback at this sudden show of passion . 'This bloody world. What we have to do is leave,' David's words were slurring now as he thumped the beer bottle on the floor. ' Bugger off! Who wants to stay in a place where they could let that happen. Come to Australia with me. Make a new life.'

'Not Australia for God's sake! We should go to Palestine, get the land, build a fence. Then let them bloody well come for us. We'll be ready next time!' Jack's arms ached for the work.

'Another war! Another damn bloody war! Is that all you want!' David was screaming now. 'I never want to see another gun as long as I live!' He flung himself from the tiny bedroom.

David would go his own way, Jack knew. He always looked after himself. But something dragged Jack in another direction. Some urge or desire. Or was it simple revenge?

At the synagogue that Sunday night there was a talk by The Hammers, a Zionist group. When Jack arrived the speaker had already started. The hall was half empty. In the front row sat a line of boys in their late teens. Spoiling for a show of their own, thought Jack.

The speaker was a tall broad-shouldered man in his thirties. He wore a well-tailored grey suit.

Educated bloke, thought Jack and not short of a bob or two either. He looked round the room. Most people were local, working-class Jews, tailors, shop assistants.

The speaker had a deep resonate voice and as Jack sat down he launched into an attack on Ben Gurion and the Haganah.

'Does Ben Gurion imagine we are queuing up for the privilege of joining his 'defence league'?'

Why not? thought Jack. We have to do something. He looked into the face of the man at the front of the room. He had deep set blue eyes, wide and almost as passionate as his voice which hammered on and on.

The face of a man who won't compromise, thought Jack.

'What does he tell us we are striving for? One more watch tower, one more strip of desert, one more goat.'

'Nothing wrong with the kibbutz movement,' cried out a middle aged man. Several people nodded in approval.

'Nothing at all,' the speaker smiled. 'But what use is a kibbutz without a homeland. No my friends, a homeland is never given. It must be taken. It must be won!' Roars from the boys in the front row.

'From the British!' boomed out the speaker. There was angry muttering and shuffling around Jack. Two people got up and left, banging the door behind them.

A woman in a fur coat stood up to speak. There were cries of Shush! 'This is all very well, ' she launched,' but you boys are crazy if you think we can get away with it. I mean, we're British aren't we? I'm warning you,' she shook a heavily varnished fingernail in the direction of the platform,'it won't go well for Yiddishe people if you go on like this. Nacht tig a tog, like turning night into day. Crazy!'

The speaker shook his head. 'It is Ben Gurion and the Jewish Agency who are crazy if they think they can persuade the British to leave. And even if they do, what will they agree to in their stupidity? Partition! The slicing of our ancient homelands into a tiny strip. A ghetto , my friends. That's what you will have. A tiny fragment of a country unable to defend its borders, unable to take the few survivors of the camps, the Remnant of our once great communities, squeezed of its very life blood.'

His eyes fixed on the boys in the front row. They're the ones he wants, thought Jack and leaned forward in his chair, more excited and alive than he had felt since being demobbed.

'We demand the whole of Palestine and we demand it now. Not half a loaf, but every single crumb! The Haganah is the watchword for self defence. Sit behind barbed wire and wait for them to come and get you. We've seen all that and we Jews know better than anyone, that gets you nowhere. It is our dedicated underground fighters, the Irgun Zvai Leumi who have taken up the offensive on behalf of World Jewry. By their actions in Palestine today, they will force the British out, make no mistake. Our organisation is committed to the complete withdrawal of the British from Palestine and we will use any means at our diposal to achieve this end.

Our motto is *RACH CACH!* Only this way! Join us now and pledge support to your future!'

The meeting broke up and people left talking and arguing noisily. Jack walked over to the speaker. He had to wait until a crowd of teenage boys and girls had plied him with questions. Then, as they moved away Jack put out his hand and said quietly, ' Jack Stone. I think you could use a bloke like me. I was in the commandoes.'

The speaker took his hand and shook it. 'Michael Levy.' He paused and looked at Jack, his eyes wary.

Then Michael spoke, his voice even, cool. 'Why don't you wait while I gather up my things and then we could go for coffee at my flat.'

Michael lived a twenty minute walk from the synagogue in West End Lane. He had an elegant first floor apartment in a large block. In the living room were wall-to-ceiling bookcases filled with books. Two deep leather armchairs stood round a walnut coffee table. Blackout curtains still hung at the window and a couple of crates marked Government Surplus stood behind the door.

When they had settled down with a pot of coffee between them Michael asked, ' Where are you from?'

'I live with my parents in Willesden.'

Michael nodded and heaped sugar into his coffee. 'What about your parents?'

The room was very quiet. Jack could hear the steady tick of a clock , but he couldn't see one. Must be in the kitchen, he thought. Hasn't this bloke got a wife?

'They're from Poland , Lodz. Came over before the war. The first one that is,' and he grinned.'

'And you're Jewish?'

Jack was taken aback. He hadn't expected that.

'Yes, I'm Jewish,' he answered.

'Can you say something in Hebrew?' Michael's blue eyes stared at Jack.

The words came naturally, flowing from his childhood as he chanted, ' *Shema Yisrael, adonai elohaynu, adanai ehad. Baruch shem cvod....*' He continued until the end of the short prayer.

Michael gave a satisfied nod. 'What have you been doing with yourself since you were demobbed?'

'Not much. I work in a small electrical shop, fixing radios.' Jack lit a cigarette. His body felt tense with energy. 'Not easy to know what to do now it's all over.'

'I quite agree, ' said Michael softly. 'Look why don't you come up to the office. I'll give you the address. It's in Avery Row, near Hyde Park Corner. Give a hand on the newspaper. There's always something to do. Help you to feel involved a bit.'

'Fine,' said Jack. 'I'll do that.'

During the next two weeks Jack spent every spare minute in The Hammer's office. They produced a weekly newspaper called The Vanguard and sold it at Speaker's Corner every Sunday morning, while Michael spoke to the crowd about the struggle for Palestine. Jack addressed envelopes, roneoed articles, made coffee and helped with the typing. He began to meet other members of the group, ex-servicemen like himself, unsettled, angry, looking for another war. They argued, speculated on the moves of the British, followed avidly the exploits of the Irgun.

After a couple of weeks Jack invited Michael to dinner with his family.

'I'd like that very much,' said Michael.

Jack sensed that Michael had been ready for an invitation. To check me out? To be sure that I'm not a spy, an infiltrator from MI5? They're clever those blokes. They hear Michael's speeches in Hyde Park, ranting against the British. They're sure to keep a close eye on him. Even a Jew could be in MI5, why not? The thought chilled him.

Jack's mother was delighted. She had been to one of the meetings in the synagogue. 'Lieutenant Michael Levy? Coming here? *Oy va voy*, wait till I tell Daisy at the Friendship Club.'

'No need for that mum. Just make one of your big dinners.'

Jack smiled to himself. His mother was a fierce Zionist. He'd said to Michael once, If the British knew what they were up against in my mum, they'd quit tonight!

When Michael arrived the following evening Jack's mother wore her black cocktail dress with the cameo brooch from Poland pinned above her right breast. His father was dressed in his dark suit, his hair slicked down with barber's oil. A rich, thick smell of chicken soup warmed the air.

'Offer Lieutenant Levy a glass of sherry Jack.' His mother fussed round, plumping cushions, smiling brightly.

'Interesting photos Mr. Stone,' said Michael as he stood near the fire sipping sherry.

'Yes, my family,' said Jack's father. 'This is Zvi, my grandfather. Now he was very privileged. He was a distiller to the Czar. Had a pass to live in Moscow. Not many Jews could do that, *Nu*?'

'That's right,' nodded Michael.

'Next to him is my grandmother and then these are my parents and myself, four brothers, three sisters.'

'And are some of them living here now?'

Jack's father laughed. '*Oy*, you must be joking. Some are in Paris, some in Belgium. Some are dead.' He shook his head. 'We don't know. The bloody Nazis got them. But we have something.'

The Red Cross letter, thought Jack. From Uncle Marc. 'It's in the sideboard dad. I'll get it.'

'Yes, here it is. 1942. Paris. He says they are all well and safe.' His father looked up into Michael's blue eyes. They were staring at him intently. 'Nothing more. We heard nothing more.'

'Enough Solly, dinner's ready.' His mother's face was beaming above a huge pot of steaming soup, the noodles already heaped into bowls on the table. For an instant Jack felt a sense of pride that his parents were the people he had described to Michael.

As they sat round the table in the tiny living room Jack's mother asked, 'And what about you Michael, not married, a nice young man like you.'

Jack frowned in embarrassment, 'Mum!'

'Haven't met the right girl yet,' smiled Michael.

Jack's mother clicked her tongue and dished up chicken and potatoes. Michael ate with relish. 'Haven't had a meal like this in years,' he said as he held out his plate for more vegetables.

'You got a profession?' asked Jack's father, his voice gruff as he gnawed at a chicken leg. Jack looked sharply at Michael, but he showed no signs of being put out.

'Law. I was at Oxford before the war. Do a bit in my father's firm now. You might have heard of them, Levy, Cohen and Finkelstein? They have offices in the Strand.'

Jack's parents shook their heads, his mother's face a mixture of awe and envy.

THen his father said,' And what do they think about all this work you do, in your group? They get annoyed?'

Michael gave a short laugh. 'Actually they don't know. They'd be horrified I think, give all sorts of arguments why I'm wasting my time. They think I'm a bit of a playboy and that's why they don't see much of me.'

His face changed, his eyes sinking back into the hollows of their sockets, the blue centres deepening. 'They are rich, comfortable. The Jews who died in the war are not their Jews. They are from distant foreign places. They don't understand their sufferings. I've given up on them actually.' He shook his head wearily. 'I just use them to keep me afloat while we fight for the cause, right Jack?' Jack nodded.

Then his mother served up *lokshen* pudding and they all laughed as Michael told them about some of his court cases. He's from a different world, thought Jack. But it doesn't seem to matter.

After the meeting with his family Jack noticed a deeper feeling of trust between himself and Michael, as though he had seen enough now to be convinced he was genuine. One evening about ten days later Jack was licking down envelopes in the office when Michael said, 'What are you doing Monday night?'

'Nothing. Why?'

'I want you to go and hear a chap called Shlomo Fitz speak. Make a few notes and we'll put together something for the newspaper. It's a closed meeting, invitation only. You'll needs this card.' He handed Jack a small white card.

'Who is Shlomo Fitz?'

'He's a Palestinian Jew, over here as a student.'

As soon as Jack arrived at the synagogue in Hackney he could feel that the evening would be different from other meetings. His invitation was scrutinized carefully at the door. When he entered the hall it was almost full. There was a hushed air of expectancy. He sat down near the front.

The speaker was a short bald man in his thirties, with staring eyes and thick glasses. Like a caricature of a terroist, thought Jack. He felt an immediate attraction to Fitz as he began speaking. He spoke good English but with a heavy accent. The audience sat riveted.

'There is only one way to see the Haganah, running boys of the British. They have nothing to give to our struggle. It is the Irgun who are the true freedom fighters of the Jewish people.

The Irgun have people working in every D.P. camp in Europe. We know the mood of the survivors. They hate the Haganah, who tell them come, work the land, watch the British and one day if we ask them kindly they will leave.'

Fitz's voice was rising as if the anger would spurt from his throat. Jack could feel the adrenalin run in his muscles.

'We know what the survivors want. They want to fight. They want weapons, they want to run the British out of Palestine and take a homeland for themselves so they will never suffer again. The Irgun will get a boat soon and fill it with its supporters from the camps and send it to Palestine to carry on the struggle for freedom, for liberty.'

A buzz raced through the hall. Jack stood up. 'I want to ask Mr. Speaker. What if the Haganah tries to stop them?'

'Then we will fight them!' Cries of, That's right, came from all around Jack. 'Remember our motto, *Rach Cach!* Only this way. We will fight and we will win. Not just the little strip the Jewish Agency would be happy with, but both sides of the Jordan!' More cries from the audience. 'We will not stop until we have run the British and the Arabs off our ancient homelands!'

The following day Jack handed Michael a ten page typed transcript of the

Palestinian's speech. Michael looked at him in surprise. 'What's this?'

'Fitz's speech.'

'The whole thing?'

'Yes.'

'How did you manage that? Did he show you a copy?'

Jack grinned. 'No. I have a photographic memory. Came in useful in the commandoes.'

Michael was looking at him carefully. 'I'm sure it did.'

At the weekend Michael asked Jack to come to his flat in West End Lane. 'Shlomo wants to meet you.'

At last, thought Jack. He was fed up with typing envelopes.

*

CHAPTER FIVE

Eve sat on the veranda outside her hut and watched the cacti in her little garden. Squat and solid, with huge poised spikes, they never swayed in the wind like plants in England. She had soaked the ground for three days, pouring buckets and buckets of water, before she could dig deep enough for the cacti. 'You English, you go crazy over your gardens!' Myra had shook her head in disbelief as she sat on a chair and watched. 'You could help,' Eve had muttered grimly as she hauled water from a nearby tap.

'Are you kidding! C'mon. I got better things to do.' Myra opened up a week old copy of Newsweek and reached for a box of dates.

It was nearly Christmas but the winter rains hadn't started. 'There's a drought, turn the bloody tap off,' grumbled Tom every morning in the kitchen. Eve had never felt so dry. Her skin, her hands, her clothes, the soil in her garden all felt sterile. She needed the rain, needed to be replenished, soaked, touched. Rain changed the landscape, the daily routine, the smell of the air. She longed to feel moist again.

The Dutch group were organising a Christmas party. Anneka was the main force behind it. She had a new boyfriend, a young kibbutznik home on leave, his tight army trousers hugging his groin, his olive skin gleaming below the rolled up sleeves of his khaki shirt. Uri shone on the outdoor basketball court his long slender hands pulling the ball from nowhere and pitching straight into the net. Anneka and Uri seemed to be everywhere, entwined firmly in each other's arms, as they patrolled the lawns in front of the dining room , or walked the moonlit track between the volunteers huts. As she turned her lovely head from side to side, Anneka's eyes searched out admiration and envy. This is all it means to her, thought Eve.

Bud was furious at the idea of the party. 'What the hell did I come all the way to Israel for to celebrate Christmas!' Even some of the Israelis turned their heads.

'Come on Bud. Don't be so boring,' Rick drawled laconically.

Lou-Ann flashed one of her frequent smiles. 'We're going, aren't we Rick? ' She twined her arm round Rick's neck and began stroking his chin. He didn't move. ' It's just a bit of fun. God knows we get little enough of that here.'

'*Et toi, Franck? Qu'est ce que tu pense?*' Eve asked 'Will you come to a Christmas party?'

'*Bof!* ' Franck tidied his knife and fork. ' *Merde*. This is Israel. I do not need Christmas.'

Eve pushed away her plate and opened up a letter which had arrived that morning from Sally.

'*Andy's back from Greece and he's going out with blond Janey from the Art School. Pete says he's changed since you split up, more morose. No fun any more.*'

Does she have to keep me up to date with Andy? Eve groused to herself. But it hurt to see his name on paper. Rather Andy than that mindless Uri.

'*Israel looks great. I've started teaching but maybe I'll pop over in the holidays. We could have a laugh. What are the soldiers like ?!? Have you met any nice blokes yet? Write soon and don't leave out the juicy bits. I'm really pining for you, there's no-one to talk to anymore.*'

I miss you too, thought Eve miserably. She looked round at the volunteers; Anneka and Uri slung together like Siamese twins, Franck with two chairs between him and the Americans; Lou-Ann fawning over Rick.

There was a smudged postscript, '*P.S. Pete and I are unofficially engaged!*'

Eve felt a sharp pang of envy and then immediately one of guilt. I should be pleased for Sal, she thought and stood up, pushing her chair in irritably.

The party took place in a large room below the dining hall. Eve arrived late. The room was packed, the lights and the music turned up full. God! she thought, I won't be able to stand much of this. So many Israelis, not like them to mix with volunteers.

'Wanna drink?' It was Bud looming over her, his voice distorted by the noise. 'Isn't this disgusting? You staying or splitting?'

Eve shrugged her shoulders. ' What is there to drink?' Her voice broke with the effort of competing with Gary Glitter.

'Coke, coke and coke. What the hell else? C'mon.' In a corner coca cola and bowls of crisps were lined up on a trestle table.

Eve took a bottle just to have something to do. She looked round the room. The Israelis were packed in a tight group, laughing rowdily and dancing. They all wore jeans and T-shirts.

It reminded her of a brochure she had read as a teenager about Israel.

'Even when going out on a heavy date Israeli girls wear jeans and don't put on make-up.'

'Do you like to dance? My name is Max.' Eve looked up into the friendly eyes of an Israeli she hadn't seen before. Not kibbutz, she thought immediately. It was the clothes. He wore faded corduroys and a black shirt open at the neck. No medallion on the hairy chest either.

She smiled back, 'Sure. My name's Eve.'

Max was a good dancer and when the music slowed down, he held Eve close, her head just reaching his shoulder. She felt her body relax against the smell of his skin, the breeze from the open doorway cooling her forehead. Its ages since I did this, she thought. Then she didn't think anymore. Just listened to the music as Max's beard muzzled her cheek.

The music changed to heavy metal, breaking the moment between them.

'Let's get out of here, have a coffee.' Max had to shout to be heard. Eve nodded and they headed for the door. On the way Bud caught her eye. He was dancing with Shula, Chaim's daughter.

Shula sometimes washed the dining room floor with Eve when there was no school and kept Eve up to date with kibbutz gossip, chiefly who was sleeping with who. Her English was awful.

'I must to speaking. My teacher says to must,'Shula was fond of telling Eve with a mischievous grin on her face.

Bud glanced at Max, glanced back at Eve, shook his head and scowled. Thanks for the vote of confidence, thought Eve grimly and raised her hand in a little salute.

Outside the moon was full in a clear sky, flooding the path to the bungalows. Max put his arm round Eve. 'I'm staying with friends for a few days. But usually I live in Tel Aviv.'

'Your English is really good, Max. How come?' She loved the lilt of his American/Hebrew accent.

'I lived in New York for a few years. But I couldn't make it. So I came back to Israel. All my friends and relations are delighted.' He gave a short laugh. 'I'm a painter.'

So that's it, thought Eve. The black shirt, the slightly long hair. Wonder how old he is? His thick black hair and beard showed signs of greying and deep lines scored the face. But his body and manner were that of a young man. Anywhere between thirty and forty, she decided. What if he's married?

'Here we are.' He guided her towards the door of a bungalow. Inside were two Israelis in army uniform. 'Ephraim and Israel, this is Eve.'Smiles all round as they pulled out chairs, broke open packs of cigarettes.

'You like Turkish coffee Eve?' Ephraim asked.

'I don't know, but I'd like to try some.'

'Sit here Eve,' Israel was laughing, banging chairs down. 'It's the best chair. My English she is good?'

Eve laughed. 'I think you all speak really good English. My Hebrew is non- existent, except for *boi regah* and *od mayat*!' Everyone laughed at her accent.

Ephraim clapped Israel on the back, 'Israel has a girlfriend Eve. She is Danish, very beautiful.'

'Is she a volunteer here?' Eve couldn't think of anyone Danish.

'No not here. But now she make a trip, Jerusalem, Haifa, Ramat Ha Golan.' Ephraim slapped Israel again. 'She come back soon, Israel. You must not to worry. Eve is here.' They all raised their coffee glasses to Eve. She glanced at Max and smiled. He gave a small nod of his head and smiled back. They sat close, knees touching in the small room. A little thrill went though her. Did he feel the same?

Suddenly there was a loud crash. Eve jumped, spilling her coffee. An Uzi sub-machine gun had slid to the floor, its barrel pointing straight at her legs. The room bleached white with silence. Then Israel lifted the gun, very gently and took it out of the room.

Eve looked into the worried faces of the other two men. She felt bewildered. Max said in a quiet voice, 'These guns are no good. If you drop them they can fire. It could have shot through both your legs.' Eve shuddered and took the lighted cigarette Max passed her.

Israel returned and said something quietly to Ephraim. He stood up. 'Ok, we go now. *Shalom, lehitrayot.*'

After they had gone the bungalow became very quiet. Eve looked across at Max. She became aware that her heart was beating fast. Should she go now, before he made his next move? Or should she stay, let things just happen. Sally's letter rang in her ears. 'Don't leave out the juicy bits.'

Max stood up. 'My room is through there. I've got some wine in the fridge. Let's make ourselves more comfortable.' He held out his hand to her. His face was relaxed, open.

In the next room there was a bed. Eve sat down with her back resting against the wall. Max brought the wine and sat down next to her. The wine was delicious and cool. Max's body felt firm and comforting against her shoulder.

He began to talk about his work as a painter, his failure to break into the art world in America. They drank more wine, the alcohol breaking the tension in Eve's muscles. She loved the sound of his voice, his eyes following her closely, smiling, seeking her response.

Then she was pouring out all her anger about Andy, reliving the hurt at being thrown over because she was Jewish.

'Maybe he just used it as an excuse because he felt he didn't love you anymore,' Max said quietly.

Although she had said the same thing to herself so many times and once Sally had said it too, his calm voice soothed her, made the anger feel contained.

He began to stroke her neck, his fingers straying into her open blouse. Their conversation died away. Eve couldn't remember who had spoken last. Nothing mattered except this stroking and the hot blood filling her skin. His hands were massaging her abdomen. He pulled at the zip on her jeans. 'Is it ok?'

She nodded. This was no longer a risk, an adventure, it felt right. They began removing clothes, their own, each others'. Then she was entering again that dark flowing river and although she knew the strokes, had practised them so many times before, the banks had moved and all the landscape changed.

On the morning after the party Bud came into the kitchen. 'How're things.' He looked morose.

'Fine.' Eve felt high, filled with energy and warmth after the early morning with Max.

'Bit old for you, isn't he?'

'He's thirty-five, lives alone in Tel-Aviv and he's a painter. Anything else the grapevine needs to know?' Bud scowled. She smiled up at him. 'What about Shula? You looked as though you were having a good time last night.'

'She's just a kid.' Bud growled. He eyed her guardedly. 'I prefer older women.'

Irit came in with the post and thrust a letter into Eve's hand. With a thrill she saw it was from her father.

'Letter from home?' Bud was gazing at her mournfully.

'Just mum and dad. Don't you have any work to do Bud?' She pulled open a drawer and raked through for a knife.

'Ok, I can take a hint. But don't come crying to me when he ditches you. Seen his type before,' and he stomped off.

'I can take care of myself,' she called after him, but a cold shiver ran through her. Stay cool, she told herself firmly. This is not a lifetime's commitment. Max and I are just having fun, for as long as it lasts.

After her shift Eve went back to the bungalow. Max was sitting up in bed when she opened the door of the bedroom. She flung herself down beside him and they kissed. Then she pulled away, brushing her hair back from her face.

'I love it when you do that,' murmured Max. She smiled and snuggled down on his shoulder.

'I've got a letter from my father I've been waiting for. I just want to read it.' She ripped open the envelope.

'Well don't take too long. I've been waiting for you all morning. ' He blew gently in her ear.

Eve started to read the letter.

Dear Eve,

Glad you liked the parcel. Your mother's getting ready a few things to send again. Helps her to stop missing you. But never mind about that. The important thing is that you're doing what you want to do.

Am I? Eve thought.

You ask in your letter about Noah. I don't think your mum and I ever realised how curious you were about him. Even when you found the death certificate. You can't have been more than seven or eight. We didn't think you would understand.

Why not for God's sake! They always behaved as though I was too young. You could never ask a direct question in my house.

But perhaps we should have said something to you. I remember I was very angry at your mother for leaving such an important piece of paper lying around.

She didn't, thought Eve, with a stab of guilt. Maybe they never knew I used to go through the drawer.

Your grandmother was adamant you were too young to know any better and as usual your mother went along with her. Seemed to think she knew best about everything. I don't mind telling you Eve, now your grandparents are long dead, that I used to get pretty fed-up living with my in-laws. But you have to understand , after Noah's death your mother was never really the same again. She needed grandma and in her own way, well, your grandma needed us. To be in charge, to have people to look after, to control I suppose.

My God! thought Eve. I can't believe he's writing all this stuff to me. It felt like the silence of a lifetime had been broken. She turned the page almost feverishly.

Your grandfather just used to tuck himself away in the workshop and shut his eyes. I could never get through to him. I thought he regarded me as useless because I didn't go out and get my own home. But just before he died he suddenly said one evening, 'It's not your fault Jack. Life's like that.' He must have realised how impossible it was to prise you mother away.

I had a lot of plans Eve. To go to Palestine. Start a new life. Your mother was keen too. But after Noah it all seemed to slip away. I just kept hoping things would improve and we would go later. That's why I say to you get on with your life and take care. You never know what's round the next corner.

Write soon,
Love dad.

Eve folded the letter carefully along the creases and put it back in the envelope. Max was watching her. 'What is it Eve? Bad news from home?'

His voice seemed very distant. She didn't respond. Her mind was filled with a thousand questions like little open wounds. How had her mother changed? Lots of women lost babies, particularly in those days. What was different for her mother? Why couldn't her father get away from that house, buy his own home? If you want something badly enough you go out and get it.

But nothing is ever that simple Eve! Think! Think about Andy and how it all came to nothing. You thought you had him taped. God! They're so far away and all we have between us is the unreliable Israeli post. How can I ever get the whole story? Why the hell didn't they come here later, after mum had recovered? But did she.....'

'Eve?' Max's voice was soft, penetrating. 'Where are you?' He stroked her cheek gently.

She turned and looked into his eyes, suddenly feeling infinitely sad.

'It will be alright Eve. My father always said to me, It changes.' He put his arms round her and murmured in Hebrew, little sponges of comfort which soothed the muscles tensed around her face. Then they were rolling together naked, making love, her mind blank, her body loose, open.

CHAPTER SIX

January 4th, 1976

Dear Dad,

I got your letter last week. You're right, you should have told me more. At least about Noah.

Eve stopped. She could feel the anger rising again. Why didn't they tell me, damn it, why, why? The voice inside her head rose almost to scream and then evened out again. Not even his name. I had to find it out for myself. She could still remember Susan Parker's sneer at the park gates, 'No-one's called Noah.'

She started writing again.

I don't understand why you and mum didn't tell me. God I fell like yelling at you as I'm writing this. Why didn't you tell me something, build up to it, bits and pieces over the years. He was my brother after all Dad.

Parents are so stupid, Eve thought. When I have kids, I'll tell them everything, answer every question, no matter what it is.

I knew much more than you gave me credit for actually. Kids pick up vibes in families. I knew you and grandma didn't get on. And I knew something bad had happened once that no-one wanted to talk about.

Our house was so oppressive. Did you know I found it hard to actually breathe sometimes? As though everyone was holding something in.

Eve stopped again. She felt she could rage on and on and still get nowhere. I must stick to the point, she thought, or he'll just dry up and tell me nothing. I want to know everything now he's started.

A kind of desperation rose in Eve as she looked out of the door of her hut towards the neat bungalows of the kibbutz. The air was very still. It was mid-afternoon. People, animals, leaves hung suspended waiting for the clock to move on. Like a great deep blanket the kibbutz lay around Eve, holding her in. For a moment she felt her chest tighten, as the air refused to inflate her lungs. She picked up her pen and carried on.

What I still don't understand is why you didn't go later, when mum was well and things were safer in Israel. I know it wouldn't have been easy Dad, but you were so keen.

Part of me has always felt guilty I wasn't born in Israel. They're a dab hand here at making you feel you should go on Aliyah. I feel so torn sometimes. Should I stay and do my bit, isn't it selfish to go back home? But I feel the Israelis don't realise what a big decision it is. I've left a lot behind in England. Its not as though I have to escape persecution.

Write again soon Dad. I really look forward to your letters. It's really important to me to understand why you didn't make it.

All my love,
Eve.

Eve licked the envelope and stuck it down. She wished her father were here, thousands of miles from home, released from all the constraints. There's so much I want to know now, she thought impatiently. So much he could tell me. But then again, maybe he needs this distance. He probably wouldn't say anything if we sat opposite each other in this room.

She looked around her hut. She had hardly spent any time there since the party. The cacti in her garden hadn't changed. She remembered how dry, arid she had felt because of the lack of rain. All that seemed far away now since Max.

'I've been looking for you,' Max's face smiled in at the doorway. 'Israel's booked a kibbutz car. We're all going to Jaffa tonight for a pizza.'

'That's fantastic!' She flung her arms around his neck. 'I feel as though I've been in this place for years.'

As the car bumped down the kibbutz road Israel tuned the radio to the Voice of Peace and they all chorused, 'This is Abie Nathan broadcasting to you from somewhere in the Mediterranean.'

'She is a real crazy guy, you know Eve,' shouted Israel over Bruce Springsteen's 'Born to Run' . 'She put all her money to this boat and she give all the people music free.'

'He may be crazy,' Eve shouted back,' but at least he's trying to do something for peace in the Middle East.'

Ephraim began yelling,'Babee we were bo-orn to run! Crazy music, crazy guy. You like pizza, Eve?'

Israel suddenly swerved the car round a van and both drivers leaned on their horns for almost a minute. Eve was thrown heavily against Max who held her in a tight embrace, lips locked together. Everyone's mad in this country, she thought. They kissed, tongues searching deep into each other's mouths. She hoped the car wouldn't swerve again. They might bump teeth next time.

It was a cool dry evening as they pulled into Jaffa. The narrow streets and old stone buildings balanced against a clear sky full of stars were tranquil, half empty. They parked and walked through the artists quarter, peering in at tiny galleries. 'I show here sometimes,' Max murmured quietly and nodded to one or two people.

'Hi Max,' called one, a grey-haired American in a suit and tie.

Max nodded, ' Cyril, this is Eve.'

'Pleased to meet you, come in. Have a coffee. Long time no see.' Eve sensed Max wasn't keen.

He shook his head. 'Just passing through Cyril. Another time.'

They walked on in silence. 'Friend or enemy?' Eve asked after a while.

Max shrugged and laughed. 'I'm not sure.'

They caught up with Ephraim and Israel at the restaurant. Two American boys with long hair tied back in pony tails were kneading dough expertly at the back. Throwing and turning it into perfect circles on the palms of their hands they heaped on toppings, opened and shut oven doors at a rapid professional pace. The restaurant was full of young people.

'Pizza is very popular in Israel. These guys have just opened,' said Max.

'She is the best Eve. Only the best for Eve, ' cried Ephraim, ever romantic. Eve laughed and they all clinked glasses.

'Lehaim!' roared Ephraim and half the restaurant responded.

Suddenly across the crowded restaurant she saw the high frizzy hair of a boy. As he turned she searched for the beads at his neck. It was Ben!

He saw her immediately and waved. Then he began pushing his way between tables towards her. Eve, laughing and waving back, scanned Max's face out of the corner of her eye. His expression was neutral.

'Why am I always holding myself in with men?' she had asked Sally once in despair.

'Because you want them to love only you,' Sally replied. 'Just relax, enjoy yourself.'

'But look at you and Pete,' moaned Eve.' You're committed.'

Sally shook her head. 'Don't open all your doors Eve. Keep them guessing.'

After she had dragged herself back from France miserable, alone, Sally had said to her,' You wanted too much. Andy was ready to finish, move on.'

'He said it was because I was Jewish,' Eve repeated yet again, tears streaming down her face.

'That was only an excuse,' Sally murmured. But the slap kept on stinging and stinging.

'I told you we'd meet again.' Ben put an arm round her and gave her a friendly hug.

'I can't believe it. It's ages since we met in the airport!'

Ephraim pulled out a chair. 'Sit here please. Eve has lots of boyfriends.'

They all laughed and Eve went slightly red. She looked at Max and he smiled at her politely. Am I at all important to him? she thought and then realised Ben was saying something.

'I only came over to say hello again Eve. I've got a couple of cousins here from Jo'burg, so I can't sit down. It's great to see you. Kibbutz o.k.?'

She nodded, 'It's fine.'

He squeezed her shoulder lightly, 'I'll see you then,' and he turned back in the direction of his table.

She watched him go, his South African accent jarring on her senses. South Africans fell into two camps for Eve. Those who stayed and therefore supported apartheid and those who must be absolutely sickened by it and stormed out. Ben and his family belonged to the second in her mind.

She turned back to Max and said enthusiastically. 'At least he doesn't support apartheid. I admire his family being prepared to give everything up for their ideals.'

Max shrugged, 'If that's the real reason why they left. Most people in Israel don't know much about apartheid.'

'Don't they show documentaries on t.v.? We have a lot in England.'

'Israel has to make friends wherever she can to survive. Israelis have their heads turned East Eve. What is happening in Jordan and Iraq is more important to us.'

It's as though he's patiently explaining something to a child, she thought. A tinge of disappointment trickled onto the edges of her feelings.

Max was continuing to talk. 'South Africa has links with Israel. Vorster is due to visit us early next year. We supply them with Uzi sub-machine guns.'

'I didn't know that. ' Eve said, surprised at how betrayed she felt.

'You must understand Eve. This is not safe little England.'

The tone was recognisable now. Eve felt like a resentful teenager.

'It is 1975. Israel has just gone through her fourth war in thirty years. The people are depressed and exhausted. They don't want to go in the army anymore. As many people leave Israel as emigrate here. ' He looked into her large dark eyes, his expression suddenly softer, sympathetic, as if he wanted to protect her.

She felt a sudden rush of warmth for him and squeezed his knee under the table away from the laughing eyes of Ephraim.

'I don't say I like apartheid,' Max said.' Just I know why Israel makes her friends.'

He looked up as the waiter arrived with their pizza. 'Come on Eve. Eat, eat! We must be happy today. Tomorrow we can to be dead!' Ephraim's voice pulled Eve out of her thoughts and they all toasted life again in Hebrew and English along with various other rowdy groups in the room.

Max seemed to relax again, sharing out pizza, joking with the others in Hebrew, translating for Eve . 'It's good isn't? ' he mumbled, mouth full of food and she nodded and smiled.

But Ephraim's words hung in her ears. She had thought coming to Israel would answer questions for her. Instead she was presented with an endless list of new ones.

'You'll burn yourself out with all this emotion,' Andy had said to her once. It was October 1973. The Yom Kippur War was five days old. Eve could think of nothing else. They lay together in their tiny flat in Manchester, the sky outside the window stone grey, uncompromising.

'What should I do?' Eve moaned wearily.

'You have to decide what's best for you. For us.' Andy snuggled down, warm against her naked body.

He wants to make love, she thought. Now. At this time. But she had covered his lips with hers automatically.

The Dean of Studies at the University offered her a month off to go to Israel. 'But not a year dear. I'm sorry but it doesn't work like that.' Eve knew as she walked away down the highly polished corridor that this wasn't what she wanted.

I should have been born there, then there'd be none of this mucking about! I don't feel the same about Israel anymore. The realisation came as a shock. She felt filled with the guilt of betrayal. Her mother's voice echoed in her ears,'You could have been there from the start.' Well I wasn't dammit! I'm here and I want to be with Andy and finish my degree and go to Sally's party and get stoned.

To Eve it seemed that for her parents everything must have been so clearcut. The Germans murdered millions of Jews. The State of Israel must be created. Therefore if you are a Jew you join an underground movement and make your way to Palestine.

*

The blackout curtains were drawn in Michael's flat when Jack arrived, although it was only lunchtime. Fitz was pulling books off shelves, flicking through pages and then snapping them shut. He swung round when Jack entered the room.

'Shlomo Fitz. Please. Sit down.'

Jack held out his hand and Fitz gripped it in a brief handshake. ' Jack Stone.' He sat down opposite Fitz. Michael was moving about in the kitchen.

Cups clinked on a tray. Fitz was staring at him, his eyes wide, penetrating. He had a small, tough body, dense with muscle, his fingers restlessly beating out rhythms on the arms of his chair. Jack wondered what Fitz had been up to in Palestine. Bombs? Assassination?

'You have an excellent memory Jack.'

'That's right.'

Michael came in with the coffee and passed it round.

Then Fitz said, 'We have a few things you could help us with Jack. Would you be interested?'

Jack felt a rise of excitement. 'Certainly.'

'I want to buy a boat. Not a boat for people. A boat for war.'

'I don't know much about boats,' said Jack.

'You don't need,' said Fitz. 'But I can't to buy with my accent. This is a German E boat. Fastest torpedo boat in the war. It's government surplus now. I want to get it and repair it, send it to the Irgun in Palestine.' He spoke in rapid biting tones as if time was short.

'An 'E' boat!' Jack gave a low whistle. 'That's quite a plan! But what if they ask why I want it?'

'You tell them you want to take the boat to South Africa. All the people want to go there now the war is over. Bring it up to the West India Docks. I have a company there ready to do all the work.'

'Does this boat have a name?'

'Lost Horizon.'

Suddenly Jack found himself thrust into the centre of things, working for the Irgun, close to the struggle. It felt like active service again.

On the train to Gillingham in Kent where the boat was harboured, he thought back to the summer and the bombing of the King David Hotel. About a hundred dead, he remembered. And the outcome? Nothing, no increased Jewish immigration, no nearer to a homeland. He hadn't been sure then and anyway he was still in uniform. British uniform. Now he was free and a new war had begun.

The purchase of the boat went smoothly. A Jewish business man, Mr J.G. Cohen agreed to pay for repairs, estimated at around £5,000. Mr. Cohen had a large office overlooking Hyde Park. 'You've got a lot of work ahead of you young man,' he said, when Jack took Fitz to meet him.

'Maybe, but we're going to get there in the end.' Fitz paced in front of the window as Mr. Cohen sat at his desk, a thin man in his sixties, with military short white hair.

He had lost an arm on the Somme , '..and what do the buggers do?' he boomed. 'Give us Jews a bloody hard time. Call that gratitude?' His remaining arm waved a cigar in their direction.

'The British will give us nothing!' Fitz's voice dropped almost to a hiss.

'We take what we want'

Mr. Cohen nodded vigorously. 'Quite right, old chap. Been coming to hear that Lieutenant Levy of yours every week. I'm with you one hundred per cent. I'm not much use these days,' he nodded to the empty sleeve of his jacket. 'But at least I've got a few bob to spare.'

'That's more than most people can give,' said Jack. 'Funds are the backbone of our struggle.'

This war, thought Jack, as he waited for a bus on the Edgeware Road in the pouring rain. It's like a drug, the adrenalin won't go down. He thought of the light in the business man's eyes when he saw a chance to join in. We're all hungry for another war. Just to have gone back to dad's flat and settled down to some ordinary job! He shuddered at the thought. I need all this to be happening, as much as the cause needs me. He pulled a hand through his wet hair. A bus roared by, full. The smell of fish and chips reached his nostrils from a side street. Total dedication, he thought, and shoved his hands deeper into the pockets of his jacket.

Mr Cohen wanted to know about the progress on the boat. 'Give me the details Jack, I like to know the nitty gritty of it all,' he said, his eyes gleaming above the line of cigar smoke.

Jack spent the following weekend supervising the movement of the'Lost Horizon' from Gillingham to the West India Docks. The foreman listed repairs to Jack in a rapid monotone. 'Starboard Auxiliary to be finished, flanche on aft engine to be fixed, starboard running board to be mended.' He paused and shouted something to one of the men running across the deck. The man nodded and shouted back, then lowered himself down an open hatch.

It began to rain but the foreman, adjusting his cap slightly, carried on, ' navigation lights, wash basin waste line got to be cleared.' Without altering his tone he said,' Brought the cheque?'

'Jack nodded,'£1500, right?'

The foreman took the cheque without speaking and tucked it into the top pocket of his overalls. 'That's all right then. See yer tommorrer.'

After several visits Jack wrote to Mr Cohen,

....Up till now I have seen steady progress with the work on the vessel and all three engines and clutches are in order. The steering comunications are working, both from the bridge and if disconnected on the hand tiller.

Once the bearings on the starboard auxiliary have been assembled the vessel will have lights all over, which means that with both auxiliaries working the air flasks can be charged up within twenty minutes to be able to start the main engines. I'm collecting the nife batteries and the portable wireless on Monday. It would be rotten for the crew without any entertain - ment at all.'

Once the work was underway Jack found there was less to do at the docks. He still helped on the newspaper, attended meetings, stood at Speaker's Corner on a Sunday. What he craved was some action.

David wrote from Australia. *'Come over any time you want to Jack. It's so different here. You wouldn't believe it. No rationing, more meat than you've ever seen in your life, mate. We have steak with an egg on top every morning for breakfast. You've never eaten steak like it. Come to think of it, you've never eaten steak! And the sun never stops shining. I go to the beach all the time. Loads of work as well. I've got a job with a bloke who builds swimming pools.'*

Sounds wonderful, thought Jack grimly. His stomach ached for the steak. But it wasn't for him. Working on a building site, lazing on beaches every day. He threw the letter onto David's empty bed opposite. It was Saturday night. The girl he was going to take dancing had a cold. Saturday night in Willesden without a girl. He decided to go and see Michael.

'Jack! Come in, I want you to meet someone. This is Deborah, she's interested in our work. Came to the meeting this evening.'

Deborah was sitting on the sofa, a short girl in her early twenties, with long dark hair and large black eyes. She was dressed in a Fair Isle hand knitted cardigan and a calf length navy blue skirt. She smiled at Jack. 'Hello.'

'Deborah's a nurse Jack. I think we could use her don't you?'

'Definitely,' said Jack with a grin.

It was her bright confidence which drew Jack to her. She was always cheerful, always optimistic. Michael had told her to finish her training, 'Then I'll be more use when I go out there. I do want to go, don't you? I mean there's no alternative, we have to go and fight.'

He took her hand and smiled. They were walking down Willesden High Street looking at the shops. 'There's no other way,' he said.

'I didn't used to see it that way. When I was a child I was in Habonim. We talked about going on a kibbutz all the time. Building the land. But since the war, since Belsen, God! Who can believe the British will give us anything.'

She suddenly stopped and swung round to face him, her cheeks flushed. The pavements were crowded with shoppers. Someone bumped into Jack and he fell against Deborah's body. His hand was on her breast. It felt warm, soft beneath her wool sweater. He could feel the shape of that breast in his hand long after. She looked into his face surprised and then pleased.

Then she cried out, *'Rach Cach!'* People turned to stare. 'That's it isn't it Jack?'

She was almost shouting. Jack looked round worried a policeman might hear. He put his arm round her shoulder. 'That's right Deborah. But not here. Not now. We don't want to be noticed.' She nodded and calmed down. 'They know the Irgun and the Stern Group are active in London. The British are getting jumpy. It won't help anyone if we get arrested.'

'You're right, ' she said quietly. 'Of course you are. I got a bit carried away.' She gazed up into his warm brown eyes. It was Christmas 1946, he had been demobbed for four months. What he wanted more than anything else at this moment was to lie in Deborah's arms and shut out the whole damn mess. The concentration camps, the survivors eyes, the piled up dead.

'Would you like to get engaged?' The words fell out, tumbling from his lips, almost before the thought.

'Jack! Of course! I love you so much. We can go together.'

It took him a minute to take in that she meant Palestine and then he laughed out loud in a storm of relief. He had just realised how much he had dreaded going alone, perhaps dying out there, in that foreign, foreign place, which he must soon think of as his home, and no-one close to mourn him.

*

CHAPTER SEVEN

Eve pushed her way through the tables to the tiny toilet at the back of the restaurant. It was fairly clean with the seat intact. On the wall was graffiti in Hebrew and several other languages. Someone called Ibrahim had scrawled in English capitals, IF NOT NOW WEN? The misspelling took away some of the impact but the tall red letters conveyed a strong blend of impotence, anger and impatience.

Who is Ibrahim? she thought. Where does live? In Gaza, the West Bank? Does he wear a khefiyeh wrapped over his head like Arafat and menace women and children with a Cuban rifle? Her head ached. More questions, she thought wearily.

She felt a terrible longing for Andy and Sally and Pete and the old flat in Manchester. They used to sit up half the night talking about this kind of thing, putting the world to rights. That was supposed to be why you went to University.

But now I'm out here, she thought miserably. Right bang in the middle of this wrong world of ours. And I don't really understand Ibrahim's message. She knew she couldn't talk about it with Max. Not after their exchange about apartheid. That's the difference, she thought. Me and Andy, we would have been able to communicate about all this. But Max just treats me like a kid when I bring up something deeper than sex.

This made her grin. She shook herself, pulled up her pants, zipped up her jeans with a swagger and said out loud, ' Just enjoy yourself! He's not for keeps, God forbid!'

'You want to see the beach?' Max asked her when she returned to their table.

'That would be great'

She felt refreshed and energetic as they strolled along in the night air. The beach was empty. Eve had never seen such calm water. Waves hardly broke the surface as they met the sand. The lights of Jaffa softened the black sky until they walked right to the water's edge. Then she felt surrounded by the night, curiously safe, steady. As if at that moment she was in the right place at the right time. It's not often one feels like this, she thought. Max's arm hung loosely on her shoulder. Ephraim and Israel wandered off.

'Good evening wasn't it?'

'Lovely'

'My apartment is not far. Would you like to see it?'

'I thought you said you lived in Tel Aviv.'

'I didn't think you would know about Jaffa yet.' His hand was gently stroking her face.

She smiled.' I'm not that ignorant. But o.k. I'd love to see your flat.'

Max called over the other two and spoke to them in Hebrew. They nodded. 'O.k. See you Eve. Later. O.k.' Then they were gone, striding and laughing back towards the Jaffa lights.

'They're not going to leave us stranded here, are they, ' asked Eve a little alarmed. 'I have to be at the kibbutz for work in the morning.'

Max's face was shadowed, bent towards her shoulder. 'Come and stay a couple of days Eve, ' and as she began to pull away, shaking her head in protest, he continued, ' No listen, we are two grown-ups. I'm not going to kidnap you.' She laughed. 'I just want us to have some time together.' Sensing he was winning he pressed on, 'Come on Eve.Why not?'

'What would they say at the kibbutz. They might chuck me out if I muck them about.' To herself she was thinking what Bud would say.

And that bastard Tom, 'Too bloody hard for yer was it?'

Irit would give one of her superior sabre smiles, ' You must to tell us Eve. We are not holiday camp.'

Oh to hell with the lot of them! I want to be with Max. Smiling up at him she said, 'I don't really care what they say. Let's do it!'

'Right, come on then,' and Max turned her back towards the city. They walked through narrow streets until Max stopped at a door and let them into a house. He led the way to the top floor to reveal a huge square room, almost empty of furniture. Under a big arched window was a double mattress lying on the floor. It was covered with a brightly patterned blanket. Large thickly padded cushions, richly embroidered lined one wall. The floor was tiled. There were canvases along all the walls, some hung, some just propped. Paints and brushes stood on a beaten copper tray resting on rather rickety-looking wooden legs.

'This way Eve, up here.' Before she had finished taking in the room he had pulled her through a small kitchen at the side and up a flight of worn stone steps to the roof of the house. It was flat and square with a low wall around the edge. Eve caught her breath.

'My God it's beautiful!'

Below them lay Jaffa, dark shadows of palm trees outlined against the white stone towers of minarets. Around the great sweep of the coast, midnight blue in the night, shone the lights of Tel Aviv, the hotels standing rectangular above the apartment blocks. The air was chill now, but Eve was pulling great lungfulls inside her, swallowing the salt on her lips.

She turned to Max and cried, 'This is the most beautiful country I've ever seen.'

'That's good,' he murmured and began kissing her lips, her neck, reaching down to her breasts.

She felt the rhythmn begin again as her hips swayed against his. It's so different, she thought. Never, never did I feel like this with Andy.

They made love standing under the pattern of the night sky. Afterwards her hair falling around her breasts, she hugged him tight, squeezing the breath from his body. Then they fell laughing to the stone floor of the roof and lay there until she said she was cold.

'Would you like a shower?' Max asked. She nodded and he showed her the tiny bathroom. 'Here's a towel,' and he stood for a moment in the doorway watching her undress, her skin tanned dark around the white lines of her bikini.

She felt her knees weaken again. Then he turned and walked away. She stood under the hot shower and let the water pour over her head, her eyes closed, her cheek resting against the smooth wall.

When she had finished he handed her a long white dress. 'It's called a jelabah. The Arabs wear them.' In the main room she sat down on one of the cushions, rubbing her hair with a towel.

'I love this room Max. The ceiling, the arches, all this space. I love space.'

'I can't paint with many things around me. But my wife hated it like this.' He paused carefully for her reaction.

She said nothing.

'I was married for five years. But we never got used to each other. We were too young. She was eighteen and I was twenty-two.'

'What was her name?' Eve wanted to know, felt a burning curiosity as to why all this was coming out now. She glanced casually round the room for a photo, but there were none.

'Natalie. She's married to someone else now. They have two boys.'

His face looks really sad, she thought. She changed the subject. 'Are you a sabre Max?'

'No I was born in Kenya. We came here in '49 and bought a house in Jaffa. Taking this apartment with Natalie was like going back to the beginning for me. My parents moved to Tel Aviv when I was sixteen. When Natalie and I split up I stayed on here and someone looked after the apartment for me when I was in the U.S.'

They were silent then for a while. Max lit a cigarette. Eve carried on drying her hair on the towel. How well do I know him? she thought, looking across at his wiry tough figure, the lines on his face.

All the men in Israel had faces older than their years. It was the war. Max was old enough to have been in two since the sixties. I've never had anything do to with the army before, she reflected. In England we wouldn't have dreamed of going out with a soldier. Here everyone's a soldier. As though the military were more powerful than anything, the government, the people, anything.

Later they lay down on the double mattress, the curtains left open to let in the moonlight.

'I never really noticed the moon in England,' she said. 'Here I'm always looking for it, so big and beautiful. I don't think the skies are ever really clear at home.'

He was stroking her body, tracing the rise and fall of her shape as she lay on her side facing him. 'It is a good body Eve, not thin, but firm, strong and you skin is very beautiful. You know it shines on your face when you laugh.'

She lay drinking in his words. Andy had never spoken like this. He used to say, 'Come on lets fuck,' or 'How about a screw beautiful.' It was a turn on in its own way. But hardly romantic, she thought wrily.

Max was murmuring, ' Look at your hair, it loves to fall over your neck to your breasts. I think your hair loves your body.' She laughed. 'See! In the moonlight. Your cheeks are shining. I'd like to catch that on film. But I think it's impossible.'

They fell asleep eventually and when she woke the next morning he was gone. There was a note propped up against a paint pot. 'Back soon. Max.' The handwriting was thin, untidy, like a schoolboy's. Maybe he can't spell any more than that in English, she thought, pleased to feel superior in something.

She padded to the bathroom, took a quick shower and put on the jelabah again. She loved wearing this long flowing garment in this high ceilinged room, her feet bare on the cool tiles. She felt different, tall and elegant, her legs long and thin like a runner's legs. She had always longed to be a good runner. When you ran you were alone, relying on no-one and nothing. Just the power of your legs to win the race. She hated being dependent. It was one of her main criteria for leaving home as soon as possible.

She went into the kitchen, boiled some water and made tea. It wasn't the fact of dependence she hated, having to rely on her parents for every detail. It was the fear that in 'the long run' (as her Junior school teacher was fond of saying) she wouldn't make it, she wouldn't be able to stand alone. Ever since she was small she had been dogged by this fear. She set herself little tests regularly. At six she could light the gas, boil the kettle and pour from the teapot. Grandma had been horrified, 'What are you doing darling? You'll burn yourself horribly.' But Eve was privately elated. There, she told Kitty-in-the-corner, I can do that. The emotion was one of profound relief.

Eve carried the tea into the main room and began looking at Max's paintings. He worked in curved flowing shapes sometimes covering quite large canvases, working layer upon layer until he achieved the blend of colour he was searching for. Some of the paintings, a group under the windows chiefly, gave her a feeling of content, the artist seemed at peace with himself. But others hanging on the wall gave a sense of chaos. She thought perhaps they were unfinished, but they were signed and framed. It was the colours that seemed chaotic, as though Max hadn't achieved the blend he wanted. She wondered if this was something to do with Natalie, or maybe her children.

At college Eve had been friendly with an Art tutor called Joe. He was a thin, gaunt man of about forty, who held his chest when he spoke and coughed in a haunted way. He dressed in a long tweed overcoat and white collarless shirts. He was always saying he was off to London to visit his friend Lucien Freud. She knew he wanted more than to sit and drink with her in the college bar, but she wasn't interested. Instead she flirted mildly and got him to talk to her about art, a subject which was never mentioned when she lived at home.

'You're different from the other kids here Eve. I mean, look at them.' A crowd of giggling girls passed by, waving their fingers in a dolly bird way, 'Hi Joe!' 'See you at the party tonight!' Eve smiled and looked away.

'See what I mean, ' said Joe, catching the grin on her face. 'You'd never behave like that. Now how's about picking up a crate of beer and coming up to my place. You've never seen my etchings.'

She laughed. She knew his use of the last word meant he understood she wouldn't come. She loved his suggestions, they were always over the top. Even though he was a bit fake, hanging onto his ribs as he coughed. Perhaps he's pretending he has T.B., she thought, and soon he'll start coughing up bits of his lungs.

'We'll give it a miss this time Joe. Have you seen Lucien lately? I saw some of his paintings in a colour supplememt recently. I really liked them.'

Joe smiled,' I'm seeing him on Sunday. Ah, now here comes that lanky boyfriend of yours.'

Andy didn't approve of Joe. 'Trendy yob,' he growled after the first time Eve introduced him. But Eve wouldn't be put off. Dimly she was aware she needed Joe to counter some of her mixed feelings about the intensity of her relationship with Andy. To live with a guy and she was only twenty. Often she wondered, are we married? Should we get married?

'What are we doing?' she asked Andy early one morning, on the end of all these thoughts.

He smiled and then said simply, 'We're fucking.'

When Max returned she was humming to herself in the kitchen, washing glasses in the sink.

'Happy?' He stood behind her and folded his arms over her breasts. 'You sound happy?'

'I feel very carefree all of a sudden. As if I've been given a half day from school.' She swung round, 'I don't miss the kibbutz at all.'

'That surprises you?' He gave her a wry grin.

I hate people who know all the answers, she thought and was amazed at the strength of her feeling against him.

'Yes it does rather,' she replied cooly and turned back to the sink.

Max drew back his arms and shrugged. 'Cyril asked us for coffee at his gallery. Do you remember? He was the American in the suit. He's talking about a new exhibition for me.'

'Fine, but what shall I wear? Will the jelabah do?'

In the end Max brought out a hand embroidered white smock and she wore it over her jeans. 'Natalie's?' she asked with a raised eyebrow.

Max shook his head and mumbled,' It was some American girl's. She was just passing through.'

Great, thought Eve, former lover. But it was washed and ironed and fitted her well.

'You look beautiful!' said Max with a broad grin. 'Let's go.'

When they arrived at the gallery several people stood or sat around the small room talking noisily and calling to Cyril across the room. The women were all heavily made-up and very beautiful. They wore very tight jeans and brightly coloured blouses. The men were older than Max, balding or with grey hair. No-one looked capable of holding a paintbrush.

Max introduced her but after saying hello in broad American accents the conversation continued in Hebrew. Eve stood and sipped her coffee. The walls were hung with Impressionist style paintings of fruit and flowers. She hated still life art.

Is this what it's like to be the artist's girlfriend, she wondered. Dressed up and left to hang out in a corner while the men do business. Stifling a yawn she caught the eye of one of the women.

'I'm Yaffit. You smoke?'

Eve smiled gratefully, 'Thanks. I'd love one.'

'You don't to speak Ivrit.'

'No, just the odd word.'

Yaffit nodded and looked Eve critically up and down. 'You should to put on lipstick. Max like it.'

Christ! thought Eve, she sounds like my grandmother. 'I don't like wearing make-up. I thought Israeli women didn't bother much either.'

Yaffit waved her hand sharply. 'That was before, in the days of the chalutzim. Everybody wear the same clothes and get very dirty. Now its different. You think Israel is backward country?' Her slender eyebrows frowned at Eve.

'No not at all.' Eve felt uncomfortable at being accused.

'We are very modern. Everybody come here and see.'

'Right. Absolutely. Are you an artist?'

'You are not serious,' said Yaffit incredulously. 'I'm his wife.' She nodded at one of the men talking to Max. He was around fifty with a slight stoop. 'He paints pictures of you, me people.'

Eve nodded, 'Portraits.'

'Yes,' said Yaffit and turned abruptly back to talk to one of the other women.

How does she know what Max likes, thought Eve furiously. God! Israelis are so rude! This is worse than the kibbutz.

She put her coffee cup down on a beautiful round table with a mosaic of small coloured tiles and walking over to Max, slid her arm round his narrow waist.

'Eve, hello, enjoying yourself?'

She smiled trying hard to put a warning glint in her eyes. 'Yes, thankyou. I've been chatting to Yaffit.'

There was a hint of confusion in his eyes and then a second thought crossed her mind. Was she wearing Yaffit's blouse? How the hell does she know what Max likes? It was the sort of comment only a former lover would make. I'll kill him if he's brought me here in a blouse she left behind in his flat!

Controlling the shake in her voice she muttered, 'Why not show me around?'

'Ok,' said Max in a measured tone as if she was dragging him away. He spoke a few words in Hebrew to the others and they smiled and nodded, closing up the gap as Eve and Max wandered away.

Out of hearing Eve hissed, 'Who's Yaffit? She seems very familiar with you?'

'What if she is Eve?' His voice was cool. 'What's it to you?'

'Nothing. At least if she's a former lover I don't give a shit. But is this her blouse?' and she tugged at the open neckline.

Max's voice was icy now. She felt a little afraid, but she was angry too. ' No and anyway, what does it matter. You and I are together now and that's all that is important.'

'For crying out loud!' Eve felt like shouting.

Max took her arm. 'Come on Eve, let's talk outside.'

In the streets it was drizzling and the sky was grey. The sea, so clear and calm the evening before, was whipping up, bouncing the Arab fishing boats in the swell.

'I can explain about the blouse Eve if you will stop for one minute.'

Eve was striding ahead hands deep in the pockets of her jeans, shoulders hunched. The streets were crowded, the pavements narrow and she had to stoop and brush past pots and baskets, T-shirts and jelabahs hanging on the walls outside the little shops.

One Arab called out, 'Come inside beautiful lady. We drink coffee and I make you a good price.' His big round face seemed to fill the street.

She felt ridiculous in this blouse, out here at the shops. 'Not now,' she growled and had to sidestep into the gutter to pass him.

His laughter crackled in the air behind her. She felt mocked by the whole town.

Max half ran half strode beside her. 'Come on Eve, come home with me and we'll talk about it.'

She stopped, realising she was lost. Some pans clattered on a wall behind her. 'What is it Max? You want the blouse back so you can give it to the next girl!'

A pained expression crossed his face. God! Why do I feel like crying? she thought angrily. He's the one who's hurt me. But she nodded and let him put an arm round her and guide her back to the apartment.

Once inside Eve picked up her T-shirt and denim jacket and without speaking to Max went into the bathroom to change. She locked the door and stared at her face in the mirror above the sink.

'Don't get worked up,' she muttered under her breath. 'Don't let him think you're heartbroken.'

Because I'm not she thought. That was Andy's prerogative. The slicing through of my love.

She felt better in her own clothes, more in control, on home ground. She found a bent kibbutz cigarette in her pocket lit it and went out to Max. He smiled when he saw her.

'Sit down Eve. Let's talk. Come on.'

She sat down on one of the big cushions and Max sat on the edge of the bed.

'The blouse does not belong to Yaffit. But we were lovers once and then...' His eyes flickered away. 'We stopped, because she got married to Moishe. I met an American girl. The blouse belonged to her.' They were silent. The wail of an Imam filtered through the closed window and some one slammed a door very hard on a rooftop.

'I see,' said Eve, still uncertain.

He looked at her hard, as if seeing her for the first time His eyes were sad.

There's something more, she thought and I know I want to hear it, whatever.

'Yaffit knew this girl, they were friends and she probably recognised the blouse on you today. I'm sorry Eve. ' He reached out and took her hand. She let him.

I should never have worn it, she thought bitterly. That Yaffit has me down for some cheap tart. The word cut though her and she took away her hand.

'So why ..' her voice was shaking a little now. Dammit, I won't cry. ' Why did you say in the gallery it didn't matter who's blouse it was. Of course it mattered. I feel humiliated.' Max stood up as if he'd tired of the conversation and walked over to the stereo. He flicked through a pile of records. His detachment gave Eve a sense of relief.

It's over, she thought and stared out of the window.

'I'm sorry you felt like that. I was just angry because I thought you were asking too many private questions. Natalie never let me have any room. I don't like women who do that.'

This marriage of his sounds like a bloody disaster, thought Eve, not for the first time. 'Right then,' she said brightly, standing up. 'If you would just point me towards my bus stop I'll be on my way.'

He turned swiftly at her tone and crossing the room put his arms round her and smiled down into her face. 'Ok Eve. We can finish, but as good friends. I am sorry and we had fun, Hey?'

She smiled too. 'Of course, but do something for me would you Max?'
'Sure, anything.'

'Get rid of that blouse before you meet someone else.'

He laughed. 'But there will never be anyone like you Eve!'

'Now you sound like Ephraim,' laughed Eve.

'I know,' and going into the bathroom he picked up the blouse and tossed it into the rubbish bin in a corner of the kitchen.

CHAPTER EIGHT

'What do you mean, you're leaving!' exploded Bud. They were walking towards the kitchen. He had been quizzing her about Max. She answered in monosyllables. Bud was annoyed, but she didn't care. 'Christ! You're almost a member!'

'Do me a favour Bud.'

'Hell another six months...'

'Six months!' Eve cried. 'You're joking. I couldn't stand this for another six months.'

'Stand what?'

'This...this...oh Bud. Look, let's just agree to disagree. I need to get out, stretch my wings. I may even go home.'

'Home!'

'Please stop repeating everything I say. I'm not speaking a foreign language.'

'Right, that's another thing. What about the Ulpan. They're gonna start one here next month. We can learn Hebrew.' He was standing in front of her now, waving his arms. Almost pleading , she thought. Because I'm pulling out his rug too. Raising all the doubts again.

'Don't nag me about speaking Hebrew, ' she said more sharply than she felt.

'What do you mean?'

'Forget it. Someone I met in Jaffa. Look Bud, I'm not deserting you. We're good friends, but I'm moving on. It didn't grab me, that's all.'

She strode past him and into the kitchen. Tom stood at the sink peeling onions. Her heart sank. That's all I need, she thought grimly.

'Oh, back are yer. How kind. Well if you could spare a few minutes, chop that little lot down there.' He jerked a thumb at a crate of aubergine on the floor.

Bud growled, 'I'll see you later,' and stomped away.

Eve picked up a knife and wearily began chopping the dark purple vegetable. I could leave now, she thought. Put down my knife and walk out. Does the kibbutz really mean so little? The thought frightened her. Why did I say I was going home?

Leaving had always been a part of her fantasies. Packing a bag and walking out. It went right back to childhood. When she discovered Noah's death certificate and only silence followed from her family, she wanted to leave. One afternoon she put some sweets and a warm jumper in her duffle bag, tipping her swimming things out onto the bed and crept downstairs.

It was five o'clock. Dinner would be ready soon. Grandma was in the kitchen lighting the stove. The sewing machine whirred in the backroom. She let herself out the front door. Mr. and Mrs. Jones were watering their front garden. ' 'Lo Eve. Go to pay in park?'

She smiled and shook her head, She could tell them. 'I'm going to look for my brother.'

Their eyes screwed up, lost, not following the words on her lips. Then they smiled. Eve felt safe, cocooned in the mystery of their deafness. They were always secret people in her games. People who knew everything but would never tell.

She crossed over to the park and walked up the hill. On the right a great expanse of lush green grass stretched out. On the left were dense shrubs. She and Susan Parker made dens here. THey had left a bottle of Tizer in the last den. Eve searched through tunnelling along the back by the fence but she couldn't find the bottle. She settled down finally inside a rhodedendron bush and rummaged in her bag for a pineapple chunk. I'm going to stay here all night, she thought and think about Noah. But it began to rain.

Eve smiled when she remembered the rain.' 'Appy in yer work, are yer?' Tom's voice cut across her thoughts.

She glanced at him. 'Why shouldn't I be?'

'Lots of reasons,' sneered Tom and walked off.

That guy is such a bastard, and Eve wandered into an internal tirade on Tom and all the other people on kibbutz who irritated her.

When she had finished chopping the aubergine someone called, 'Here Eve, eat some cake. Chaim make it!' They all laughed and Tom glared.

'Why you not happy Tom?' cried Sara a huge white-haired woman.

'Eve she is back,' laughed someone else. 'You need her.'

'Like a hole in the head,' said Tom and spoke rapidly in Hebrew to the women, nodding and winking. Everyone laughed.

Eve was furious. 'What's the problem Tom?'

'Problem? I don't have a problem.'

'Then get off my back. So I played truant for a couple of days. For God's sake, this isn't the army.'

Tom's face darkened, his eyes narrow, almost threatening. 'You bloody volunteers, you're all the same. Don't give a damn do you?'

'Oh come on, that's not fair.'

'It's not fair,' mimicked Tom in a squeaky voice. 'Well nothing's fair and if you're looking for that in life you won't get far!'

'Get stuffed!' yelled Eve, her eyes suddenly blind with tears. She ran off to the toilet. I let him see. Oh God, I let him see. How I feel. Dammit. She knew it was because she had widened the chink, let Max in too close. Every goodbye is hard, she told herself. Every single one.

She felt a sudden sadness. All the goodbyes ahead; Leah and Jan, Chaim, Rahel. Bud, Rick and Louanne, the Dutch group. Behind her stood Sally, Andy ((did we actually say goodbye, she wondered) Leila in Paris, Jean and Fabienne on the farm, Patrice in Montpellier.

I was in love with Patrice, she suddenly thought. The first time they had all met, he wouldn't open the door. She had to say she was Lucien's friend.

'Lucien from Paris, ' she called out in French. 'He said you would put us up.'

'Which Lucien?' came the voice from inside the apartment.

'What's he saying?' demanded Andy. They were exhausted and dirty from the long journey. They had left the farm in the Lot valley at six that morning and ridden with a lorry driver most of the way.

'Hang on,' Eve said and then in French she called softly, 'Lucien the anarchist.'

There was the sound of a lock turning and then the face of a young man in his late twenties, with short brown hair, peered out, beaming.

'Come in, come, this way, sorry to be so cautious. The police have been around a lot.'

'The police?' asked Eve. 'Why?'

'They think we are drug addicts. Or that's what they say. It's all politics.' He laughed a cool soft laugh and grabbing both rucksacks, waving aside their protests, he led them into the kitchen.

They spent a week with Patrice, eating enormous meals and drinking a crate of wine. The atmosphere swung between drunken camaraderie and silent stupors. Andy didn't touch her once. His eyes were closed, wary. She couldn't understand why, but he refused to talk, to make love. 'I'm tired,' he muttered every night and rolled over in his sleeping bag. Part of her kept excusing him, part of her was longing for Patrice, as the wine crept along her muscles in the long lonely evenings. He's so good looking, she thought and was surprised and confused at the betrayal after two years with Andy.

Andy left at the end of the week, his words crashing inside her head. Any feeling she had for Patrice evaporated as she struggled with the overwhelming anger and confusion.

But I definitely said goodbye to Patrice, she thought. Because of the kiss.

It was a long soft kiss that seemed to go on for ever. She didn't once think about breathing. She just felt the soft gentleness of his mouth on hers and the light touch of his hands on her shoulders. Then he said, '*Au revoir. Un de ces jours,* ' and walked out of the railway station without a backward glance.

Patrice, Max, Max , Patrice. She turned the names round in her head. Both wanted to take and give, neither wanted to commit, become a fixture. Nor did Andy.

But I thought he did, that was the problem.

She washed her face, redid her pony tail, drawing her hair tightly back from her face and walked back to the kitchen. Tom ignored her for the rest of the morning.

As the next couple of weeks went by. Eve felt in a limbo. The Dutch group threw a party the night before they left. She half hoped Max would be there. But not even Ephraim and Israel appeared.

One bleak windy morning in late January she sat with the volunteers in the dining room. Everyone was bored.

'We could get drunk.

'Eat, sleep and then swim.'

'Too cold,' yawned Rick. 'We'll sleep,' he grinned at Louanne. She smiled back, her slow lick of a smile.

She'd be content whatever Rick said, thought Eve. 'So what are we going to do?' moaned Myra.

'How's about a visit to Yad Mordechai and the museum there?' Bud stuck a cigarette in his mouth and glared round the table.

'Jeez Bud, no more culture,' groaned Rick.

'No, hey Rick, that's a good idea,' smiled Louanne. 'We can all go together.' She put her arm round Rick's neck and pulled him closer to her. 'We'll still have most of the day to rest.'

Tom dropped them at the big kibbutz in the afternoon. Eve enjoyed the trip in the back of the van squashed in between Bud and Franck. Bud put his arm round her silently. Nothing like a body when you're low, she thought snugly.

Yad Mordechai was the largest kibbutz in the area. 'Volunteers get Time cigarettes here,' growled Bud. 'Not that wood chip muck they hand us.'

The kibbutz had been the front line in the '48 war. Thousands of Egyptian soldiers had poured up the Negev desert to this point just north of Gaza. The kibbutzniks had reconstructed a trench with guns used by the pioneers to defend their land. Rifles from all over the world, America, Canada, Czechoslovakia, bought, smuggled or stolen, stood propped on sandbag walls.

'Pathetic ain't it?' muttered Bud. 'Not much of a defence.'

'Dreadful,' nodded Eve. 'My mum and dad could've been here.'

'They must have been real dedicated,' said Bud. 'My parents never even thought about coming. Just wrote out cheques. Couldn't manage without deep pile carpet and air-conditioning.' He gazed into the middle distance.

'Well you're here for them,' smiled Eve.

'Huh.' He pulled a hand through his hair. 'God knows why I'm here.'

They walked around for a little while in silence. Then Bud took her hand and said, 'Have you decided what you're doing yet?'

'I have actually,' and she smiled grasping his big hand with her free one. 'I'm going to Jerusalem. That is the place where we are all supposed to ascend to. So that's where I'll go. Soak up the atmosphere, take in some emotion.'

'Some emotion?'

'Yes. That's what I came for. A strong feeling that this is the place for me. I want Israel to evoke a response in me. Paris did. I still miss it.'

'How long did you live there?'

'A few months. It was so beautiful, the wine, the streets, the feel of French in my throat. It's a very beautiful language.'

'Hell! So's Hebrew!'

Eve shook her head. 'No, Hebrew is hard, it feels harsh in my mouth, it has a strongly accusatory tone. French is ethereal, misty, half the words don't even sound, they just drift on your breath. I want to feel this strongly about Israel, or at least part of Israel before I go home.'

Eve sat down on a rock and looked out over the kibbutz. An air raid shelter stood in the middle of a lawn, its outside walls painted with a bright mural. So the children won't be so scared, she thought.

She had gone down in one of the shelters on Kfar Gilead once with Louanne. It was one of the rare times she was without Rick. They had sat down on the concrete floor and lit cigarettes.

'Kinda scary, isn't it?' Louanne had whispered.

'Yes, ' said Eve in her normal voice. 'But clean.' They had both burst into peals of high-pitched laughter.

Eve turned to Bud, her eyes burning. 'When my mum and dad wanted to come here, it was a passion. A thing I've never experienced. A true ideal. Not like joining the Soc. Soc. at college.'

Bud's face screwed up, ' The what?'

'The Socialist Society,' she brushed aside irritably. 'I mean, just being an armchair something, anything. It doesn't matter what. My parents had a real choice. Sit at home or go out and do it, because the opportunity was there. Even then they didn't go.'

'Nor did most people. Let's face it.'

'No that's right. But they had the chance. It's just they blew it. I don't really know why,' she finished lamely.

She was thinking about the last letter she had written to her father. Pressing him for information. She had sent it weeks ago, but he hadn't replied yet. Maybe I've pushed too hard, she thought anxiously. Frightened him off. But I have to know, I just have to. Did they really mean to come, or were they pleased at the chance of getting off the hook? It's everything, she thought, absolutely everything. To know.

'Maybe they don't really know and that's why they never told you,' Bud shrugged his shoulders and walked off through the narrow trench.

If that's true, thought Eve, then why the hell am I here? It was their dream to build this land, not mine. That damned echo, 'You could have been born in Israel.'

Her mother's face always seemed to her like a mask when she said those words. The smile fixed at exactly the same angle, the slightly lost look in her eyes. As though this had been the last expression on her face before she finally knew they would never go.

In all the years, thought Eve, we never had a proper conversation about it. Only with dad, since he started writing to me here, have any of my questions been answered. She remembered her last letter. But he will write back, she thought desperately. He must!

*

'This is Jack,' Deborah had said simply the first time she brought him home. It was a dark cold afternoon in early January. But a good fire burnt in the front room grate and Betty Freedman had laid high tea. Apple cake, scones the size of saucers, home made plum jam on fresh bread.

Deborah's father, Morris, stood by the mantelpiece, pulling on a pipe. He was a short stout man, with thin black hair, already balding above his forehead. He wore a dark blue waistcoat and trousers. Around his neck hung a tape measure. 'Workroom's through there.' Morris nodded at the wall between the front and back rooms. 'We bought the house before the war. Everyone laughed.' He nodded meaningfully and drew on his pipe.

'Who laughed? Don't be silly,' retorted Betty, her voice loud in the small room.

'Your brother,' muttered Morris and mumbled something about rented rooms and crooked landlords.

'What does Larry know? Couldn't even keep his stripe in the war.' She shook her head and turned to Jack eyeing him up and down.

He stared cooly back. She had Deborah's big dark eyes, but her hair was short and curly. A small dumpy woman, in a hand-knitted woolen dress and carpet slippers.

'What's your trade then, Jack?' she asked in a tone which suggested it couldn't be much. She handed him a cup of tea. Weak, with too much milk.

'I fix things, radios, clocks, anything.' He sipped his tea and looked round the room. The Freedman's were definitely better off then his family, but this was a dull room. Too much brown and the large heavy furniture felt crammed into the limited space. He thought of his mother's lampshades trimmed with lace, the bright curtains at the windows. Not for the first time he appreciated her taste, the continental influences.

Deborah spoke, a little too eagerly. 'Your dad wants to set you up in business, doesn't he Jack?' She smiled into his eyes.

'Perhaps,' said Jack shortly.

He could see the thinly disguised look of scorn in Betty's eyes. 'He can afford that can he?' said Betty as she passed the scones.

'Mum!'

Betty shook her head firmly, her hair bouncing up and down. 'Now, now, Deborah. Jack doesn't mind. We have to ask these questions if you two are going to get married, don't we Morris?'

Morris hurriedly took a pull of his pipe. Then seeing the warning look on his wife's face said resignedly, 'Of course dear.'

'There, you see,' said Betty and she smoothed down the skirt of her dress in hard strong movements. Likes to be in charge, thought Jack and sipped his tea warily.

Morris drew on his pipe. Betty poured more tea without asking. Then Morris suddenly said, 'She's not going Jack. She's not going to Palestine. So you can forget all that nonsense.' His pipe was pointing straight at Jack.

Like a gun being held to my head, he thought. He could almost feel it boring into his brain.

'I don't need your permission dad,' Deborah said quietly, but firmly.

'You're only a girl.'

'I'm 22,' cut in Deborah.

'Just a girl until you're married,' said Betty in a loud domineering tone. 'Already gone behind our backs getting yourselves engaged.' The room went silent. 'What did your parents have to say about that? ' Her tone implied negligence on the Stones' part. Jack bristled.

'They're quite happy mum,' said Deborah quickly before Jack could speak. 'Anyway, it wasn't behind your back. We just sort of went out and did it.' She squeezed Jack's hand for reassurance under the table. He smiled at her.

Betty snorted. Then her voice changed. Sugar sweet, thought Jack. Like her tea.

'Anyway what would we do if you went thousands of miles away to that dangerous place?'

Deborah answered quickly, in hurt tones, 'You wouldn't be left alone mum. What about Diane and Gerry and the kids. You've got grandchildren and Gerry, he's always very happy to see you both. Stop trying to make me feel guilty.'

'Guilty! Me? When do I ever make my children feel guilty. I never heard such nonsense, did you Morris?' Morris hardly had time to shake his head before Betty's tirade continued. Jack found himself switching off. All he could think about was how quickly they could get married and get away from his future in-laws.

'Are you all right love?' Jack's eyes were warm, kind. Deborah settled back as he put his arm round her shoulders. 'You're rather pale.'

'Yes, well it's not surprising is it? She's afraid, but she's too scared to admit it to you.' Morris's pipe threatened to blow his brains out again.

Deborah threw herself to her feet. 'I am not afraid, am I Jack?' she cried.

'No Deborah.' His voice was cool, measured. 'I don't believe you are.' He turned and fixed Betty with his eyes. 'We are going Betty. As soon as Deborah has finished her training . We're going because it's the only way forward now. To take our land and build an army. For the next time. So that we're ready.'

Betty's face was set, the corners of her mouth pulled into a thin angry line, but it was Morris who spoke.

'Why does it have to be you and Deborah?' A look of passion crossed his face for an instant and was gone. 'Let the others go. It's no work for women and what about when you have kids?'

'Well exactly,' Betty's voice was almost exultant. That's torn it, thought Jack. Now she's really in her element. 'All they've got out there are tents. I don't know what you're thinking about. Now let's finish the tea, ' and she banged the cups and saucers about as if to finish the matter once and for all.

Later Deborah walked Jack to his bus stop. 'It's not because they don't like you.'

'I know,' said Jack generously.

'They've always been like that. Didn't want me to become a nurse. Not for a nice Jewish girl,' she laughed, mimicking her mother. ' But they couldn't stop me. They can't stop me going to Palestine if I want to.'

'And you do want to, don't you Deborah?' His voice was cool. In her hesitation he read a world of indecision and uncertainty.

'Yes, but...'

'But what?' His voice was infinitely patient, gentle.

'I don't want to hurt them.'

The bus arrived. Jack climbed to the top and watched Deborah walk away, her coat collar turned up against the first flakes of a snowfall. We are all of us alone and fragile, he thought gloomily. It was the first time he felt a doubt they would get to Palestine.

*

Part Two

Jerusalem

CHAPTER NINE

February 1976.

The Armenian woman remembered her. 'There is a bed by the window.' Eve crossed the tiny walled courtyard and trudged up the stone steps in the corner, her rucksack heavy on her shoulders. The room hadn't changed. Iron bedsteads crammed together, high windows, a wide stone shelf for bags. Everyone slept together in the Armenian woman's hostel.

Eve had come once before with Bud, Rick and Louanne, for a weekend at the end of October. The weather was still hot and the room was crammed with Americans. ' On a Bible cycling tour,' they grinned. ' We cycle round the Holy Land and read the Bible. In appropriate places.' They were very blond.

In a corner at the far end of the room Rick groaned, 'Jeez what a bunch. And there ain't no double beds.'

Eve giggled,' For God's sake Rick...'

'Whadya mean? I need my oats or I get bad-tempered.'

Louanne smiled and rummaged through her bag for her nail varnish. 'We'll manage Rick. I'm sure.'

'So long's you two keep the noise down!' said Bud, his eyes on the Bible cycling group. 'Hell Eve! You remember that time in Haifa?' He nudged her hard. The room had gone very quiet, just the rustling of book pages, turned discreetly. 'I mean for Chrissakes, no grunts you guys.'

The Bible cycling group left the next morning.

But now Eve had plenty of places to choose from. A girl was asleep on a bed by the door, brown hair covering her face. She was long and slim in tight narrow jeans and a chunky sweater. Her feet were bare. Sewn onto her rucksack beside the bed was a badge which said Australia.

Eve lay down and lit a cigarette. The room was chill. Downstairs the Armenian woman would plug in her electric fire and boil water for tea. Eve considered putting on another sweater, but couldn't be bothered to move. Imams began competing for air space inside the high walls of the Old City. One long note rolled through the evening air, pulling at the ears of the faithful, demanding their full attention.

Did people ever talk to the Imams? Eve wondered. Like you do to a vicar. Rabbis had always seemed remote. But she had gone to a Christian Society meeting at college with some friends once. The young preacher was very friendly. Accessible, she had thought. He gave her a book. Her friends had looked at her expectantly, as if she was about to make a miraculous conversion. But it hadn't made sense to Eve to take on another religion.

'Freeze your bum off in here.' The Australian girl had woken up and was rubbing her arms furiously. 'Got a light?'

'Yes of course.' Eve smiled and walked over with her matches.

'Jenny's the name. How about you?' She held the cigarette around her cupped hand as if to gain maximum warmth and drew on it deeply.

'I'm Eve. Are you a volunteer?'

'Me? Never volunteer for anything.' The girl laughed, a brief harsh sound in the high room. 'Been here almost six months. Nothing to do is there.'

'Depends what you want.'

'Yi, well, night life's better in the bush and if you get onto one of those kibbutzes, shit, they really are the pits. Wanna go out for a beer?' Jenny had leapt to her feet and was vigorously brushing down her hair. She slid her feet into a pair of sandals and stood smiling at Eve.

'Ok. Where on earth do you get a beer around here?'

'Just follow Auntie Jenny.'

They walked across the yard and Jenny called, 'Coo-ee,' into the Armenian woman's doorway. 'See you later. Just going out for a beer.' The woman came to the door and waved to them, one hand in the pocket of a floral pinafore.

It was almost dark outside and most of the market stalls had closed up. Groups of men stood around laughing and shouting to each other. Suddenly a loud clattering of boots began higher up the street. Eve looked round. A squad of Israeli soldiers, rifles held across their chests, were moving through the market, running down the wide shallow steps. The Arabs stepped back slowly against the wall and regrouped after they'd gone.

'Just kids,' laughed Jenny.

'What do you mean?'

'Did you see their faces? Eighteen year olds, new conscripts. It's just an exercise. Not much to do round here.' She nodded down the narrow winding streets.

Eve couldn't help herself. 'How old are you Jenny?'

The girl flashed her a cocky smile. 'Nineteen. I grew up quickly.'

They walked on into wider streets and then out of the Old City through

Damascus Gate. 'Know where you are?'

Eve nodded. She had walked most of Jerusalem two or three times. She loved it. Like everyone, she thought. A walled city with proper gates. Even the beggars had a place, terrible though that seemed. David's City. Where the Jews fought and made a great kingdom. So what happened to us? Even if you don't want to be a Jew you can't let go. You know you are part of the Remnant.

'Sammy'll give us a beer.' Jenny's pace was faster now. A deep dry wind blew through their clothes. Winter in Jerusalem, the cold rolling in from the desert hills beyond the city. Not even a heater in the room, moaned Eve to herself. They were walking along a wide street that sloped upwards away from the Old City. On either side were small cafes and open doorways with hostel signs above them. Jenny turned off into one. A bright neon light over the door said BEDS.

Three boys, one of them Japanese, were sitting around a paraffin heater in a large square hall. Jenny called out to a man in his thirties, wearing a denim jacket and jeans. He said something back. It took Eve a minute or two to realise they were speaking Arabic.

Then Jenny said, 'This is Sammy. Do you want a Maccabi?'

Eve gazed into the thin pretty face, brown eyes that matched the shoulder length hair. She wore no make- up. There was a look of coy innocence as she smiled back at Eve, holding out the bottle.

'Sure. Anything.' Sammy offered her an American cigarette. Marlborough, the red pack, Eve registered automatically and remembered that first time on the bus to the kibbutz, when Harvey gave her a Marlborough. I haven't even started to miss them all, she thought. Not as much as I'm going to. If Bud were here he'd ask her how the bloody hell she mastered Arabic in under six months.

They perched on stools drinking beer. The boys round the fire were playing cards, making small bets cigarettes. The Japanese boy in immaculate Levi's and a white sweater kept losing. The others were stripping him. Sammy and Jenny began talking rapidly in Arabic again, their voices a low rhythmic hum behind the laughter of the card players.

When there was a pause Eve turned and said to Jenny, 'I thought you'd only been here six months.'

Jenny laughed. '*Yi*, that's right. I pick up languages like a parrot.'

A knowing grin spread across Sammy's face and Jenny laughed again. Eve got off her stool and went nearer to the fire to warm her hands.

'Want to play?' One of the boys spoke. He was English. She opened her mouth to say no, but he caught sight of Jenny. 'Hey! Jenny. Long time no see. Give us a game.'

Jenny hooted with laughter, her face alive. 'You joking you bloody bastard

Steve. I'm not wasting Sammy's Marlboroughs on you crooks.'

The Japanese boy looked round uncertainly, shook his head, gathered up his jacket and left.

'Anyone got anything to smoke?' inquired Steve. Sammy pulled out a tin and began rolling joints. Eve smoked a little. No-one seemed concerned that the street door was open and the police could walk by at any moment. A thick sweet smell filled the air.

Sammy was muttering to Steve. 'Good stuff. Not rubbish. Jenny gets you some.' Steve nodded and said something to the other boy.

Eve suddenly asked, 'How long did you say you'd been here Jenny?'

'Five years.' It was Steve who spoke. 'She came with her mum and dad when she was fourteen. Proper little sabre aren't you Jenny love?'

Jenny laughed and said something short, harsh, in Arabic to Sammy. He sneered and pulled on a joint.

'Shouldn't you be in the army or something?' Eve pressed.

This time everyone laughed, a loud echoing splutter of laughter that finished abruptly. The joke was obviously an old one. 'I wasn't fit enough for them,' said Jenny mockingly.

You look fit enough to me, thought Eve. She looked at her watch. It was nine o'clock. With some relief she heard Sammy offer to walk them back to the hostel.

Eve didn't see Jenny for two days. But her rucksack remained on the floor of the dormitory. Several people came and went. Eve took to undressing in the bathroom.

In the mornings she wandered round the shouk looking for bargains. There were less tourists than in the summer, fewer trolleys pushed by urchins yelling ' 'Allo, allo!' as they hacked a path though the crowds. Stall holders competed to offer her coffee.

'Beautiful lady, come inside. Uncle Abdul will serve you. Ali! Coffee! Quickly! ' She would sit down, grinning knowingly. 'What do you buy from my good friend, Ibrahim? A dress?'

Click, click of the worry beads, a hookah pipe bubbling in the corner. 'I have dress. Beautiful dress. Good price.' Uncle Abdul would lean towards her, khefiyah dangling from his head, teeth wide in a blackened grin. 'Better price than Ibrahim.'

The coffee came in tiny white cups, beamingly presented by Ali in torn jeans and a ragged polo neck jumper. She hated Turkish coffee. But she loved to drink it with the Arabs in their cramped open-fronted shops. The air was awash with sweat, the scent of cardomin in the coffee, the smell of hung carcasses from the butcher's stall opposite.

'They tell such wonderful lies,' she had said to Max once.

'It's business here,' he smiled. 'They lie, you lie, everyone haggles and usually they get the best price.'

'So what's the point?' Eve had laughed.

'It's a game. Don't they play games in your country?'

'The whole bloody set up's a game,' she remarked.

On the third morning Eve walked up to Jaffa Gate. Through a cafe doorway she caught sight of Jenny huddled in a corner. Steve sat next to her. They were sharing a cigarette and talking quietly. As she moved away Eve saw Jenny pass a small packet to Steve. Hash, she thought automatically. She wondered again why Jenny hadn't told her she lived in Israel. And what was so wrong with her the army wouldn't take her? Terminal cancer?

Jenny came back to the hostel that evening. 'Wanna go to a party?'

Eve looked at her, cautiously. 'What kind of party? Where?'

'It's some students I know in Uni. They got a batch up in the new city.'

Eve wasn't sure what a batch was but the idea of a party with some Israeli students appealed to her after two days on her own. 'Ok. Can we get back in if we're late.'

'No worries,' smiled Jenny dangling a large key from her hand.

The party was a short bus ride away. Jenny was quiet on the journey, almost subdued, thought Eve. She noted the bus number carefully. If they're all spaced out on drugs I'm not staying, she decided. She felt a sharp longing for Sally and a bottle of harsh French wine. We could get plastered in a corner and not give a damn.

They could here music from the party as they got off the bus. The Beatles were blaring from an upstairs window, almost drowned by the noise of the crowd shouting out the words. Everyone was dancing when they got inside. Jenny seemed to come alive and pilled Eve into the middle. 'Come on. Let yourself go!' she yelled.

'Ok, ok, laughed Eve, relieved that it seemed an ordinary sort of party. She saw Steve and hailed him like an old friend.

'Eve? Oh right, we met a few days ago.' He had to shout over the noise. The record ended. Everyone started clapping hands and shouting, 'Rolling Stones, Rolling Stones!' The opening chords of Brown Sugar blasted out from the record player in the corner.

Someone offered Eve a joint. She shook her head and joined in singing the words with everyone else. Israelis really have a wild side to them, she thought. When she paused for breath someone cried, '*Yallah! Yallah!* Sing, you must to sing, everybody sing!'

'They're a bit mad this lot!' Steve shouted in her ear. She nodded and smiled. 'How about a drink?'

'Have they got anything worth drinking?' she yelled back doubtfully.

By way of response he took her hand and led her through the crowd to a small bedroom at the back of the apartment. With the door closed they could talk in normal tones.

'I always bring something. They're a useless bloody lot when it comes to booze.' He pulled out a paper bag from under the bed. Inside there were six bottles of Maccabi beer, a bottle of whisky and two glasses. Steve poured them both an inch of whisky and leaned back against the wall.

Sipping her drink Eve asked, 'Are you studying in Jerusalem?' He's very young she thought. Maybe only seventeen. Steve grinned. 'Me? No. I left school at sixteen. I came over here with a couple of mates last summer. Bummed around a bit, did a few kibbutzes. I'm between things at the moment. How about you?'

'I was on a kibbutz for a few months. But I got fed up. I'm not sure what to do now.'

'I know a good place where you can go skiing.'

'Really,' Eve perked up. 'Tell me about it.'

'It's a place on the Golan Heights. They run a ski lodge. You work in the kitchen or the hotel and you can go skiing for free.'

'Sounds great. What's the name of this place?'

'I'll write it down. Its called Nevae Ativ. It's a new place.'

He handed her the slip of paper. She tucked it carefully into the pocket of her jacket. It made her think of her father's letter. If she went to this place she would have a forwarding address. She decided to ring the kibbutz the next day and find out if there was any mail for her.

'How long have you known Jenny?' Steve interrupted her thoughts.

'Just a couple of days,' smiled Eve. 'She's a bit weird, kidding me she's only been here six months.'

Steve took a swig of the beer. 'You want to watch her, she can be a little cow.'

Eve said nothing, wary of the tone in his voice.

'She can't stand living here.' Steve went on. 'Her mum and dad dragged her over when she was fourteen. She was really pissed off. Had to leave all her friends behind. But she's a clever little bitch. Fluent in Hebrew, Arabic and Spanish.' There was a sneer in his voice.

You're jealous, thought Eve. No 'O' levels and precious little chance of getting a job back in England.

'What happened about the army then?' Eve asked.

Steve's face closed down. Forbidden territory, thought Eve. He began packing up the drink. 'I dunno. Let's go back to the party.'

*

CHAPTER TEN

The music suddenly stopped. People began pulling on jackets and pushing noisily towards the door. Someone shrieked with laughter in the street below. Eve looked round bewildered. There was no sign of Steve or Jenny. She grabbed the arm of a boy with long blond hair. 'What's happening? Where's everyone going?'

He laughed and shook his head, 'No English, no American.'

Oh hell! thought Eve and made her way back through the living-room. A pile of records spilled over the floor, record sleeves strewn everywhere. The carpet was littered with bits of food and coke bottles. You feel so out of it if you don't know the rules, she fumed to herself. No-one seems to wind down in this crazy country. Like Ephraim said, Tomorrow we could die.

'Thank God that lot's over!' Jenny poked her head out of the kitchen as the last person left, slamming the front door. The flat suddenly seemed very quiet. 'You and Steve make out o.k.?'

'Come off it Jenny. We had a drink, that's all.' Eve was annoyed at the grin on Jenny's face.

'Yi? Save any for me? I could stand a beer right now.' She walked into the room and flopped down on a chair, her long legs sprawled out if front of her.

'Steve packed it all up. I suppose he's gone by now.'

Jenny nodded, her eyes closed. Her face looked drawn. As if it's all been a strain, not fun, thought Eve. 'Should we go for our bus,' she asked gently. Jenny didn't answer.

'Hey Jenny.' Eve patted her arm. 'Wakey, wakey. Time to go home.'

'We can't. Missed the last bus.' Jenny opened her eyes and stared at Eve. 'We'll have to stay here.'

Eve sank down, suddenly tired. 'Great! That's all I need. I haven't even met the inhabitants of this pad.'

Jenny shook her head, her eyes still wide with fatigue. 'No worries.

They've gone off with some friends. I asked them. It's ok.'

'Well you could've asked me!' So bloody sure of yourself. And of me! 'I suppose we're clearing up.' Her tone was cold but Jenny didn't seem to notice.

'It won't take long. We'll just pick up some of the garbage.'

Jenny was surprisingly efficient, scooping up armfuls of rubbish and tipping them into a basket. Twice she dashed down to the dustbins in the street. Eve could hear the clattering of the metal lid through the open window. God knows what the neighbours must think, she grinned to herself as she washed up in the tiny kitchen. She found some bread and toasted it with cheese.

'Shit! that's smells good,' Jenny cried, on her way back from the bins. They took the food into the living room. Eve started to sort through the records, putting them back in their sleeves.

'Hey, Moondance. Van Morrison. Put it on Eve please,' Jenny begged. Eve nodded and put the record on at low volume. Bud used to play the track every evening on his tape recorder. She could hear it as far as the dining room when the wind was in the right direction. 'Music to make love by!' he would roar between verses. Eve felt very lonely. If I ring tomorrow at six maybe Bud will answer on his way into dinner, she thought. He would understand about the letter. If it's there by now. If dad wrote back.

Jenny cut across her thoughts. 'I'm so angry with Steve.' Her voice was very low.

'Why's that?'

Jenny shrugged. 'It doesn't matter. Just he promised me something and he's let me down.'

'Have you told him you're angry?'

'No, well....I'd never do that.'

'Why not?' Eve wasn't really interested. But she was curious to see how far Jenny would confide in her.

'I never show someone I'm angry.' She reached behind a cushion and pulled out a bottle of vodka. 'Ever been pissed in this bloody country?' She rocked the bottle in her hand.

Eve shook her head. 'No.'

'Let's do it tonight.' She scrambled to her feet. ' I'm going to.' She went into the kitchen, banged about in the cupboards and came back with two glasses. 'Mine's a bit chipped but I won't notice in a while.' She poured them both some vodka and drank quickly. 'That's better. One or two more then I'll reach the click.'

'Then what?' asked Eve. She felt cautious as though alone with some dangerous unidentified creature.

'Then it's ok. I feel good.' There was a silence.

Eve began thinking about what she would do the next day, Friday. She wanted to go to the Wailing Wall and light the *Shabbat* candles. But she couldn't remember the prayer. At home all that had stopped when her grandparents died, leaving the three of them alone for the first time.

She had been thirteen. What she remembered most, after the last mourners had left at the end of *shiva* week, was the fear. But she couldn't say why she was afraid. The next morning, Saturday, she'd left home early, before her exhausted parents had got up. She ran across the park, the grass still thick with dew and knocked on Angela's door.

Angela was her best friend now. Ever since Susan Parker had failed the eleven plus and ended up in the secondary modern.

'Come out Ange,' Eve's long hair hung in a tangled mess down her back.

Angela was in her dressing gown. She looked nervously over her shoulder. 'I can't Eve. Honestly. I'm not even dressed.'

'Please. Look, you've got to.' Eve felt desperate to be with her friend, blot out the fear. 'I saw Graham's scooter on the High Street.'

'Graham Stevens? Are you sure?' Angela's face lit up. 'Ok, won't be a sec.'

They spent the morning tracking Graham Stevens, sipping coffee in the snack bar next to the hairdressers, talking non- stop. As Eve left Angela's door at lunchtime and walked home, feet dragging, hands deep in the pockets of her slacks, she thought, just me and mum and dad now. A chasm seemed to open in front of her. As she reached the house her lungs heaved for air.

Jenny broke the silence. 'Were your mum and dad born in England?' Her voice was low, as if inside she was beginning to tighten a screw.

Eve nodded. 'Both of them.'

'My mum was born in Germany. Her parents shipped her out on the Kindertransporte in '38. She was twelve. Her whole family wiped off the map. Kaput!' Jenny snapped her fingers and poured some more vodka. Her eyes seemed to fill the narrow lines of her face.

Eve felt a chill creep over her body. The level in the bottle had dropped alarmlingly. Who's drunk all that? she thought, almost fearfully. Perhaps it's me and I'm very drunk. If it's Jenny has she reached the click? What happens then? The night outside the room seemed very dark .

'She went to Australia after the war and got married. In our house no-one ever got angry. Shit!' This last breathed so low Eve almost missed it.

'If you said anything to my mum like, That's stupid, or, Why don't you bake chocolate cake like Marjory's mum? she'd stare at you and say in her special voice, You don't know how lucky you are to have a mother. I grew up without anyone to care for me.

Then her anger and my anger would sort of lock horns across the table. But without any noise. No noise at all. '

Jenny shook her head and took another gulp of vodka. A trail of liquid seeped down the side of her mouth. But she didn't wipe it away.

'Then I would get up and go out of the room very quietly and close the door. But without any noise. No-one ever slammed a door in our house. Not me, or my dad, or my sisters.'

To never raise your voice, thought Eve, say what you feel, slam a door. But then you couldn't. Because once you took the lid off, how would you ever cope? All that charred , bone shredded pain. Your entire family enslaved and murdered. Who could keep a lid on that lot?

'They made me come here.' Jenny's voice was so quiet Eve had to strain to catch the words. 'I never wanted it. They didn't even ask me. I hate this piss of a country. Everyone in uniform. The kibbutz was terrible. You had to muck in or they hated you. I didn't want to be in their gang.' Her voice was mocking now.

'So what did you do?' asked Eve.

'Walked out. I was fifteen. The Armenian woman?' Eve nodded. 'She took me in. I move around a lot, but most of the time I stay there.'

The record finished and there was just the whir of the turntable. Footsteps sounded in the street running steadily past the window. The smell of toast lingered in the air.

'Do you ever feel guilty you weren't in it?' Jenny asked.

'The concentration camps?' The girl nodded. Eve sipped her vodka slowly. A familiar finger pressed hard against her chest. 'When I found out about it I thought it was amazing, quite unbelievable really that I wasn't in it. I couldn't understand how I escaped. I've always felt like a survivor.'

'I've felt guilty all my life.' Jenny put her glass down and began drinking from the bottle.

'Hey Jenny. Slow down,' Eve laughed gently.

Jenny ignored Eve and carried on drinking. When she put down the bottle, almost empty now, her face was flushed and wet. 'Shit! Wasn't my fucking fault. I wasn't even born!'

Eve felt desperate to say something comforting. 'You're very clever Jenny, picking up all those languages. Why don't you go to college, take up interpreting or something?'

But Jenny's eyes were closed. Her chin dropped to her chest. That's it, thought Eve. The click. She's out for the count. Eve pulled a blanket off the sofa and draped it over Jenny's slumped body. Then she went into the bedroom, lay down on one of the beds and pulling a quilt over her shoulders, fell into an exhausted sleep.

Eve woke late the next morning. The flat was empty. She made coffee and listened to records for an hour. But Jenny didn't return. 'That's it then,' she said aloud. 'I'm splitting. You can come looking for me.' She pulled on her jacket and ran downstairs slamming the front door behind her.

At the hostel she asked the Armenian woman if Jenny had been back. 'Little Jenny? No,' the woman laughed, as if Jenny was an errant schoolgirl. 'Tomorrow maybe. I don't ask her.' Eve shrugged and went to take a shower.

The water was hot on her tired body. She looked down and watched it run through her breasts and stream off the spread of her pubic hair. She remembered Max watching her stand naked. A hot rush enveloped her thighs.

Andy had loved to shower with her. The foreplay, the act, the aftermath. It's the small things you remember, she thought. The way he dried so carefully between his toes. Like an old man.

At about six that evening Eve walked through the Old City to a phone box just beyond Damascus Gate. She was in luck. Bud answered the phone.

'Evie baby! Where ya been?'

'Hey Bud, how are you? I've been all over. I'm in the Armenian woman's hostel.' She felt elated to hear his warm gruff voice. God I've missed you, you bastard, she thought.

'No Bibles on bikes, I hope.' They laughed. 'When're you coming back? Your hut's empty. Myra split two weeks ago. Lonely without you.'

Her voice dropped slightly. 'I'm not coming back Bud. That's the whole point. I left. I'm probably going north, to a *moshav* on the Golan Heights.'

'You're joking!' His voice vibrated down the line. 'What the hell for? It's dangerous up there Eve. Too near the border.'

'Oh don't be so wet Bud. The whole bloody country's dangerous. There was a bomb blast outside Jaffa Gate last week. The IRA Christmas bombing campaign in London sounded much worse.'

Bud grunted and changed the subject. 'Rick and Louanne are still here. I swear, they'll spend the whole winter in bed, fucking.'

Eve laughed more relaxed now. 'I miss you all ever such a lot. You'll have to come and visit me on the Golan.' Then more seriously, she said, 'Look Bud, I'm ringing to see if there are any letters for me.'

'Right, I'll check it out.' She could hear him calling to Irit in the dining hall. His Hebrew's really good, she thought with a pang.

'Hello Eve? You still there?'

'Yes, right here Bud. God, you sound almost fluent.'

He was embarrassed, but she could tell he was pleased. 'Yeah, ok, cut the crap. You got two letters, one from Sally and one from your dad.'

Her heart leapt. 'You're sure Bud, from dad?'

'Yep, says on the back, Mr. J. Stone and it's from London. So you coming to collect it?'

She hesitated. She was too late for transport now. *Shabbat* was in, no buses until the following evening. She wouldn't be able to go until Sunday. She made up her mind.

'No I'll be settled somewhere in the next few days. You can send it on then Bud. Look after it for me.'

'But look Eve...'

'Sorry Bud, my *assimonim* just ran out. I'll see you Bye.' She put down the phone. Dad's written back! The letter must say something, even if it wasn't what she wanted to know. The point was she hadn't scared him off, cut the lines of communication. She realised how scared she'd been that he wouldn't write back.

In her pocket she could feel the stub ends of two candles. It was very dark. The Wailing Wall would be filled with people now. She walked through narrow streets until she was standing above the great square at the foot of the El Aqsa mosque.

It was the height of the Wall and the size of the stones that always moved her. It must have been so big. Beyond imagination, a Jewish building that had made such an impact on the land.

She always thought about Jewish things as small. Little synagogues, dwindling congregations, five or six Jewish kids in the whole school, one kosher butcher within a five mile radius. The only big thing it seemed to her were the six million.

She remembered at college sitting in the bar discussing a new soft drink advert. It said 6,000,000 with a bottle top in one of the zeros. Ben, who was Jewish, said, 'That only means one thing to me.'

'What?' Sally had asked.

Eve chilled to the bone. How could she ask that?

Ben had looked at Sally, his eyes narrow, slid back into his head. '6,000,000 Jews.'

The silence that followed felt almost threatening to Eve. We are alone, she thought. No-one cares.

A small room led off from the women's section at the Wall. Dozens of pairs of candles had already been lit. There were one or two women still bending over, shading their eyes, their heads covered in scarves or shawls. She felt self-conscious as she pulled the candles from her pocket and stood them in a corner. She struck a match and melted them to the floor. Then she struck another and lit the wicks, watching them flame.

Someone said something to her in Hebrew and she turned and smiled apologetically. 'I don't understand.'

The woman changed to fluent English, with a strong New York accent. 'Aren't you going to say the prayer?'

'I can't remember the words.'

The woman who was in her fifties and smartly dressed, shook her head disapprovingly. She held her hands up above the candle light, as if she were warming them and recited rapidly in Hebrew. Eve recognised the beginning,

'Blessed Art Thou O Lord Our God....' and the ending, '*shel Shabbat*.' Then with a curt '*Shabbat Shalom,*' and a nod of her head the woman left.

'*Shabbat Shalom,*' Eve called after her.

Outside she went up close to the Wall and put her hands on the big stones, tracing their shapes. Thousands of tiny pieces of paper were stuffed in the cracks. Messages to God, she thought cynically. What would I write?

She turned and walked back to the hostel. I would ask about Jerusalem, she thought. Why it feels so foreign. An Arabic city in the Middle East, everyone squeezed together behind high walls for safety. It's medieval, its smelly, its exciting, mysterious and its about as far away from a London suburb as any Jew could get.

Yet this is the pinnacle of Judaism, the point we must all strive to ascend to. It's the most wonderful city I've ever known, she though with a sudden rush of passion. But is it mine?

CHAPTER ELEVEN

Eve woke cold on Saturday morning, her head throbbing, throat dry. Her bladder was full but she lay for a few minutes clutching the last patches of warmth from the blanket. When she swung her legs to the floor the room swayed. Sitting on the toilet with her head in her hands she saw someone had written something in pencil at the foot of the door. She had to squint to make it out. JESUS LIVES! JEE- SUS!

When Eve got back to the room the Armenian woman was sweeping under the beds. 'You are sick?'

Eve nodded. 'I feel all achy, might be the flu.' The woman clicked her tongue sympathetically. Eve climbed back into bed. No- one else was staying in the hostel. Wouldn't have hurt Jenny to show up, she thought resentfully. The rucksack still stood in the opposite corner.

Eve closed her eyes soothed by the presence of the woman quietly working round her. She dozed off and when she woke there was a steaming bowl of soup and a plate of warm pita bread next to her bed.

'Drink it while it's hot,' the woman smiled from the doorway.

'Thankyou,' called Eve. The soup comforted her. When she had finished she pulled the army grey blanket around her shoulders and fell into a restless sleep.

Steve appeared. He handed her a paper bag. 'You have to take this when you visit Jenny in Tasmania,' he said.

But Jenny lives in London, not in Tasmania, thought Eve. 'I can't take it, they'll ask me if anyone gave me anything before I get on the plane.'

'Tell them it's a bomb,' said Steve.

She took the paper bag. It was full of large white pills marked DRUGS. That's o.k. then, she thought. But I have to get to Tasmania. The rest of the dream was a long struggle to board the plane. When she woke, for a few seconds, Eve wasn't sure where she was.

She lay in bed all afternoon, listening to the changing noises in the street below. The Armenian woman brought her cups of mint tea and sweet biscuits.

When she was ill as a child her mother had looked after her. Never grandma. It had been our special time, thought Eve. Mum never had headaches when I was ill.

How long did she mourn for Noah? Why couldn't she put it behind her? Something her father had said once suddenly fell into place.

'Right little surprise you were in 1953.' She was nine and he had laughed when he said it. Then they had raced to the top of the hill in the park and it had begun to rain.

But now she thought, I was a mistake. Mum never meant to have another. Did she feel angry, or was it guilt because she hadn't realised Noah was in danger?

Eve suddenly longed to be home, with both of them again. To sit around the kitchen table. And talk, she thought furiously. Like we never have. As a proper family, not... not... unwilling guests of her grandparents. It felt like a betrayal. Just one more in a long line, she thought wearily.

*

'We must not betray the Remnant. The D.P. camps are still full of our people, desperate people, who have nowhere else on earth to go but Palestine. We must keep up a constant pressure on the British Government to remove the Mandate and grant Independence so that the Jewish people can finally return to their homeland and build their future.'

The crowd shuffled and muttered in approval. One or two people clapped. Jack looked over his shoulder. The Blackshirts had arrived and taken up their usual place. He looked back at Michael, tall on his orange box, his voice carrying across Speaker's Corner.

'We have to keep chipping away at their consciences.' Michael had told him. ' They went out and fought the Fascists. Now they have to realise their responsibility to the Jewish people, to the survivors. The Allies could have bombed the lines to Auschwitz as early as 1944.'

His dedication sent the adrenalin running down Jack's veins.

Tucked under Jack's arm was a pile of newspapers, The Vanguard. He put the newspapers on the ground and held one up. As he straightened he could see some of his group bunched round the Blackshirts. There was some shoving.

Someone called out, 'Aven't yer got enough room?'

Jack's group closed ranks. There was more protest.

'Get out the bleeding way!' Two policemen were patrolling near the grass.

Keep your tempers boys, Jack thought. Don't give the coppers the excuse.

The policemen slowed down and stared across at the group around the Blackshirts. Everyone quietened down, muttering, shuffling boots. One of the Blackshirts tried to hold up a copy on his newspaper but there was no space.

Jack looked at his watch. It usually took them about ten minutes to get the message. A young woman came up and bought a newspaper from him.

Suddenly one of the Blackshirts called out, 'Let's land 'em one!'

There was a swell of noise and movement. Jack stiffened ready to run over. Then a big man in overalls pushed through from the back.

'Not 'ere. We're moving on. ' He turned round, his face full of hate, 'Why don't yer get back to Belsen, bleeding Yid scum!'

As the Blackshirts left the Square one of the crowd shouted out, 'Good riddance!'

Jack blew on his hands in the freezing February air. He had to catch up on paper work after lunch. There were problems with the boat. Technical failures meant they were behind schedule and the bills were mounting. Mr. Cohen was pressing for a deadline, threatening to withdraw his financial support. Fitz wanted to sail in May but Jack couldn't see how they would be ready on time.

In Palestine the Irgun were hungry for weapons. Dov Gruner was under sentence of death. The revolt against the British was deepening.

Deborah appeared at the far corner of the square, hands in the pockets of her coat, her long hair piled neatly on the top of her head. Her face broke into a smile as she saw Jack and waved. That smile, he thought. Fills every bit of her.

'Seen them off again?' she tossed her head towards the road.

'Yes,' he said and kissed her on the cheek. It's not enough, he thought as he drew away. 'Are we still going to your parents for lunch?'

'Of course. You want to, don't you?' She brushed a hair off his cheek. Her finger was soft against his skin. He could feel its warmth go deep inside him.

What I want... he thought. Then he stopped. At least there is this.

'I'll have to go about three.'

'Oh.' Her eyes were searching his face. 'I thought we could go out later. Are you busy?'

'Yes,' he said shortly.

'I see.' They stood together in silence. Two young men came up and bought a newspaper from Jack. The wind whipped up. Deborah drew her coat collar round her ears. 'How about tomorrow night then?'

'Fine,' he said relieved she hadn't asked more. He hated lying to her. But if she knew she would tell him to carry on.

Fitz had called Jack to his house at the beginning of January to talk about the 'Lost Horizon'. He lived behind Kilburn High Road near the station in a small terraced house. When Jack arrived Fitz took him to a small room at the back. Several upright chairs were grouped round an old kitchen table. There was no central light, just a small standard lamp by the window. The curtains were closed and the room was lit by sunlight which filtered through the thin grey material giving a washed out pallor to the walls.

On the wall behind the table was a large map of Palestine, stretching both sides of the Jordan. In the middle was a clenched fist holding a rifle.

Fitz fired question after question as Jack pulled papers from files, described repairs, tried to keep up with Fitz's restless energy. All the time Jack felt the questions were just a front, that behind them Fitz had another reason for calling him round.

'So Jack what happened about the trials?' Fitz had lit a cigarette and was pacing the room, occasionally flicking the curtain back to stare into the yard below.

'The engineer wouldn't take the boat out. His name's Harry and I think he's slightly deaf.' Fitz snorted as if he had no time for disabilities. The work took supreme place. 'Anyway he muttered something which sounded like 'engine not fit' and then walked off the dock side. We didn't see him again.'

Fitz flicked the curtain back impatiently and strode over to the table. He picked up one or two papers and dropped them again. 'Can we get someone else?'

'Oh yes, no problem. The company down at West India Docks will get someone in, but I'm still not happy about the generator. I think there was a short when they were repairing some electrical cabling.' Jack stopped. Fitz was staring into space, cigarette ash falling onto the bare floor.

Then he said,'I want you to join the training cell. Michael does the recruiting for us and we train the groups.'

Jack's heart leapt. Action! he thought. He could hardly trust himself to speak, but when he did his voice was calm, 'Train in what?'

Fitz's eyes were bulbous behind the thick glasses, his bald head glistening in a stray beam of thin winter sunlight. He stared hard at Jack, as if pinning him to the chair like a specimen. A man without humour, thought Jack.

'We take them in groups of twenty,' said Fitz. 'Talk to them about our aims, our work. When they go to Palestine we have to be sure they don't go to the Haganah.'

'Brainwash them.'

'*Bidouk*, exactly. We take them out to the woods, teach them Hebrew commands. Then they are ready for the Irgun when they get there.'

'You want me to train a group?'

'Several groups Jack.'

Jack met the groups in a synagogue hall. Michael lent him his car. Jack kept an automatic pistol under the seat. When the youngsters had gathered he would take the gun out, teach them to strip it down, clean it. Most were only seventeen or eighteen years old, the generation who had missed the war. They listened hungrily as he talked about operations and night attacks in the war.

'One place, I remember, everything went wrong. Had to fight our way out. Ended up running through gardens, houses. I went head first through someone's kitchen window and there was the table laid for breakfast, table cloth and everything.'

The teenagers leaned forward, Jack turned over the pieces of the gun. He picked up the barrel, hefted it in his hand. 'Ours is a military objective. We want soldiers, not farmers. ' He looked at the young faces perched on tables, leaning against the wall. 'Ben Gurion tells us to negotiate. Defend what we have. Buy land, build a kibbutz. Buy another piece of land. Build another kibbutz. Stuff and bloody nonsense! We have to train, train hard, become soldiers, build an army and go and throw the bloody British out of Palestine!'

The air in the hall was stiff with energy as Jack stared into their eyes, welding them to the cause.

'If we want a homeland to save what is left of our people,' he pointed the gun barrel around the group, 'then you and you and you will have to fight for it. There's no other way!'

He could tell Deborah nothing. He would sit through lunch with her parents in the dreary living room and then he would have to make some excuse to leave, Betty's eyes piercing his skin accusingly. He congratulated himself through the dessert for keeping his temper.

'Busy again this afternoon Jack. Can't stand our company until the evening?' Betty gave her short pretend laugh.

Like a strangled owl, Jack thought and wiped his mouth to hide a grin.

'Lot of people have radios these days Mrs Freedman.'

'Time you had promotion then, isn't it?' Betty always fired the last arrow.

After lunch he walked with Deborah across the park opposite the house. The air was white, heavy with snow. No-one else was about. They sat down on a park bench. Jack put his arm round Deborah and squeezed her tight. 'Warm enough?'

'Mm. What are you going to do this afternoon?'

'Oh, catch up on some work for the Vanguard and then I have to go and see Michael. I thought you had some studying to do.'

She nodded vaguely. 'It can wait. You don't have to tell me everything you're doing Jack.' Her face was shadowed and she turned away from him. 'And I won't ask any questions. I just couldn't bear it if.....' She stopped and turned to face him, eyes full of fear. 'Promise me something Jack!'

'Of course, anything.'

His arm clenched more tightly round her shoulder. She wriggled and he relaxed the muscles.

'Don't let Michael drag you into going without me?'

He turned to her, astonished. 'Is that what you thought? God! Palestine without you? How the hell would I manage!'

Then they were both laughing, kissing , fumbling. If it were summer, he thought, there would only be the lightest of cottons between me and her breasts. His mind swelled with images of Deborah, naked, on top of him, her breasts falling to his chest. Their natural resting place, he thought as his hand penetrated her winter clothing to find a curve of flesh. A thrill went though his body, her mouth closed over his and then she pulled away gently, brushing the hair back from her face.

'Jack, ' she whispered and then she stood up, smoothing down her coat, her face turned away.

'You're not sorry?' he said quietly and she turned back, smiling, shaking her head and took his hand to walk back.

It was very dark when they arrived in the woods. Jack led the way to the clearing. He had about four weeks to train each group and then they'd be off to Dover, their bags weighed down with equipment.

'Each of you can take something with, a radio transmitter, walkie talkie. We buy stuff from Government Surplus and issue it to you when you're leaving date is near,' he had told the group.

'They might ask us at Dover what it's for,' said a girl.

'So what?' smiled Jack. 'You say it's for fun. Anyone can buy this stuff. They'll probably tell you to hang onto your passports.'

'What else would we do?'

'Give them to an illegal immigrant once you get to Marseilles.'

The girl thought for a minute. 'If we did that, how would we ever get back to England?'

'Who said anything about coming back?' said Jack.

He drilled them for two hours, marching, turning, standing to attention, at ease. The sky was black, clouds deep across the moon. In the clearing, too far from the road to be heard, Jack barked out the Hebrew commands.

'Amod dom! Amod noach! Kadimah! Yamina, smoalah, yamina, smolah!'

He watched as the teenagers, dressed in a collection of jackets, overcoats and mufflers, stamped their feet, their heads filled with dreams of glory on a battlefield not of grass but dust, the hot sun beating against their pale skins.

How many of us will make it, he thought, when this war really gets underway. One thing he knew, he would not be here, but in Palestine, at the head of a unit. Hopefully armed to the teeth, he thought grimly.

*

When Eve woke her head had cleared. She felt warm and cosy in bed. It was early morning, a cool grey light had begun to spread across the sky outside the curtainless window. Her head filled with plans.

Finish sightseeing. Might be a long time before you come back. If ever. All those places I didn't bother about in France.

Do some shopping. I doubt if they have a shop on this *moshav.*

It was almost with surprise that she heard the word in her head. As if she hadn't quite made up her mind before. That she would travel north, so far away from the kibbutz. From Bud, she thought.

Take a shower, wash my hair. Tip out my rucksack, chuck away anything heavy and repack it for long walks. The thought made her feel tired and she snuggled back down again.

When she opened her eyes once more the Armenian woman was standing over her, 'You are better?'

'Yes, thank you,' said Eve sitting up and swinging her legs out of bed.

'Little Jenny was here last night. She left you a message. She will be at Sammy's tonight if you want to go to dinner.'

Eve nodded. 'Thanks.' Trust Jenny to show up and then push off again, just because I wasn't well. She could have shown some interest. Strange that Jenny had decided to confide in her. Her thoughts were interrupted by some boys noisily arriving in the dormitory. After a few brief hellos she collected up her clothes and went to take a shower.

I'm sick of being friendly to every weary volunteer who flops out here, she thought as she tried to get the water to mix. She thought of Jenny again. Now there's a mysterious person. Tells blatant lies, keen to get you in on some fun and then gets blind drunk and delivers her whole life story.

She threw back her head and let the water soak into her hair. The first thing I'll do, she decided is find out how to get to the Golan Heights. Think snow!

CHAPTER TWELVE

Someone called her name. She looked round. It was Steve. 'Hi, what's new?'

She was sitting at a pavement cafe near Jaffa Gate eating falafel. 'Nothing much, ' she shrugged.

'I saw Jenny this morning. She was looking for you. She thought you were going to Sammy's last night.'

Typical! thought Eve. 'I didn't feel like it.'

Steve sat down and ordered coffee and baklava. 'What you been doing?'

'Sight-seeing, shopping. I found out about the buses to that moshav on the Golan Heights.'

'Should be a gas up there, skiing. Couple of mates and I thought about going, so we might see you.'

'Great,' said Eve, but she didn't feel it.

'Wanna go over to Sammy's for a beer later on?' Steve bit into his cake.

Eve watched him for a minute. 'O.k. but there's a couple of things I want to get in the market.'

'Fine, I'll come with you.'

They wandered off through the Arab quarter. Steve was good company. He didn't seem to mind how often she stopped, fingered things, asked about prices. He was a master at haggling.

'My God you knocked him down over that sweater,' Eve said admiringly.

'Play them at their own game, then they get confused, ' said Steve grinning.

'Honestly, it's beyond me. Give me Marks and Sparks any day.'

Steve groaned and put his arm loosely round her shoulders. He had a broad comfortable frame.

'It's a great place, the Old City. There's nothing like it where I come from.'

'Where's that?' asked Eve.

'Watford!' They both laughed. ' It's just boring there, school was boring, work was boring, parties were boring.'

'What did you like to do?'

'Screw.'

They bumped into two nuns who apologised profusely in a language neither of them recognised.

'Outer Mongolian?' suggested Steve laughing.

'Upper Silesian?'

'Christ knows! You meet all sorts here.'

The light began to fade. Steve said it was time for a beer. They walked back up to Damascus Gate and along the main road to Sammy's hostel.

A card game was going on near the heater. Steve joined in. A black boy was playing, a huge stack of cigarettes in front of him.

He seems to have got the measure of that lot, thought Eve.

Sammy and Jenny were huddled in a corner, passing a joint between them. Beer bottles stood on the floor around their feet.

Eve walked over. Jenny didn't look up. Sammy opened a bottle of Maccabee and offered it.

'Sit down.' He held out the joint. Eve shook her head, but took the beer.

'Hi Jenny, ' she nodded in Jenny's direction.

Jenny looked into Eve's eyes as though she didn't recognise her. Then her face split into a broad grin. 'Bit late for dinner aren't you?'

Eve nodded. 'Couldn't make it. Why didn't you come in and see me? I was ill.' She kept her voice deliberately cool.

'Yi, well I was busy. You know how it is.' She turned back towards Sammy and gently drew the joint out of his mouth.

She's embarrassed, thought Eve. After the party, because she opened up. Maybe she thinks I told Steve.

Sammy and Jenny ignored her, talking in Arabic in low tones. Eve began to think about the journey north. She felt excited, ready to move on.

That was why Andy had been so good.

'When we get fed up, we'll just stuff everything in our bags and move on, ' he'd said, on their last night in Manchester. She gazed round the flat, at the faded patch where her Bob Dylan poster had hung, the table empty of books, both chairs tucked in neatly. A whole year, she thought. If we'd stayed much longer it would have become a marriage.

In Paris they had moved a lot until they found a room in the *Quartorzieme*. There was a street market nearby. And Oscar the Duck. He belonged to the fishmonger and floated about on the stream of water in the Paris gutters. Andy would pull the end off a baguette and throw it to Oscar.

'Greedy little bugger aren't you? ' he'd yell and the fishmonger would shout back in French, laughing.

Lucien and Leila lived in the apartment next door. Leila's father was a famous mathematician in Iran. His photograph, blown up to poster size, filled the kitchen wall. Leila had big dark circles under her eyes. Partly from smoking opium and partly because her sister had committed suicide the previous winter.

'Do you know why, Leila?' Eve had asked, refusing the opium. The thought terrified her.

'My sister was not of this world,' was all Leila would say.

Lucien informed them early on that he was an anarchist. 'Is that why he has a new stereo?' muttered Andy. But Eve felt excited as though anything might happen in Lucien's company. After a couple of months she realised nothing would.

Lucien showed them how to use the student cafes dotted around the centre of Paris.

'You go up to someone in the queue and ask to buy a ticket. The students get them by the book. They cost two francs fifty each. '

At night Lucien's apartment was filled with friends, smoking opium and listening to Leila's Iranian records.

'They've certainly got stamina, this lot,' Eve said after a week.

'Maybe it's time we suggest they turn the music down. I'm knackered,' growled Andy.

When they left Lucien gave them thirty francs. 'God no! We couldn't,' Eve had protested.

'You must. We're all in this together,'Lucien said with a smile. 'If you get as far as Montpellier look up my friend Patrice. ' He handed them a piece of paper with the address. The circles under Leila's eyes deepened.

As they walked off to the metro Eve whispered to Andy, 'I just hope to God he looks after her.' Andy threw a last glance over his shoulder and nodded grimly.

The card game had finished. The black boy scooped up the pile of cigarettes. 'You guys around tomorrow?' No-one answered. As he strode out to the street he almost collided with two Arabs in the doorway.

Eve lit a cigarette. She caught Steve's eye. 'Cleaned you out did he?' she grinned.

'Who the hell cares. Just passes the time.'

'We'll get him tomorrow, ' one of the other boys said. He had a Scots accent, and was very tall.

The two Arabs squatted down to talk to Sammy. Sammy listened intently, nodding his head. Then he stood up and leant against the wall.

'O.k. everybody. Please to listen.'

The boys round the heater turned their heads. Eve looked across at Jenny.

She hadn't moved , the joint between her fingers almost finished.

'Their mother is sick,' he nodded at the two Arabs. ' She needs an operation. Blood. But here you have to give blood before you can take from the blood bank. Because of the war. Who can give their blood tonight?'

Eve sat very still. She felt cold but she didn't want to get up, move nearer to the heater. In case they think I'll go. Though I would. But not on my own.

'*Yeah*, o.k.' Jenny stood up, pulling on her jacket.

Of all people, thought Eve.

'Me too,' said Steve. He nudged the Scots boy. 'Why not? You coming?'

'Must be bloody joking you bastard,' grinned the Scot.

'How about you Eve?' Steve was staring at her.

Eve hesitated. Then she said, 'If you're sure you're both going. No dropping out and leaving me on my own.' She glared at Jenny.

Jenny laughed. 'No worries. We'll hold your hand.'

The Arabs smiled and shook hands all round. '*Shukran, shukran*. Please, here.'

They led the way to the street where a battered car was parked. The two Arabs squeezed into the front seat. Eve sat between Jenny and Steve in the back. The driver wore a black and white checked khefiyah covering his face and neck. He turned round and grinned broadly at them.

As though we're in his clutches now, thought Eve. Those scarves make anyone look like a PLO terrorist. She wondered what her father would think if he could see her now. In the hands of the enemy. Living and moving amongst them, travelling in their cars, giving blood for their sick.

Because even if these men aren't really my enemies, they belong to the side who've sworn to throw the Jews into the sea. It's no different to when the British were the enemy and dad went on fixing their radios and spending money in their shops. The British didn't care about the Jewish survivors who just wanted their own homeland.

The Jews were terrorists once. What else could they have done in the face of such indifference? I would have done the same, she thought. But now the tables are turned. It's the Palestinians who have the cause and the Jews who are the oppressors. Is that where the old idealism went? How can you build the land and sing until dawn if you occupy the villages of another people and then employ them to do all your skivvying?

They entered the Old City, along streets too narrow for cars to pass. 'Any one know where we are?' asked Eve.

'No idea,' said Jenny with a grin. 'Getting cold feet?'

When I get scared, Eve thought, you'll be the last person to know.

Steve spoke, ' Sammy said the blood bank is behind the *shouk*.'

Eve suddenly realised with a jolt she was the only Jew in the car. They turned left sharply and came to a halt with a screech of brakes.

Everyone climbed out. Unpainted doors of houses opened on to the narrow road. A thin wild-looking cat snarled from an alley-way and slunk off. It was very dark. Clouds covered the moon. A sour smell, like the smell from the meat stalls in the *shouk* blew into her nostrils. The scent of the Middle East, thought Eve.

'This is it,' said Jenny pointing to a sign above an open door. She read aloud BLOOD BANK in English, Hebrew and Arabic. The word for bank was almost the same.

'Hope they clean the needles,' said Steve grinning.

'That's the least of our problems,' muttered Eve, but no-one heard her.

They followed the Arabs inside. There were some chairs in a corridor which opened into a square hall at the end. One of the Arabs spoke to Jenny and pointed towards the hallway.

'Toilet's that way,' she said. 'But it's just a Turkish one.' She sat down and lit a cigarette.

Eve could smell the toilet as she entered the hallway but it was quite clean. Just the awful plumbing, she told herself firmly as she stood on the corrugated foot rests. It was no better in Paris. Her hands began to shake as she pulled up her jeans. This is crazy, she thought, nothing's happened. It's just a blood bank.

As she walked back down the corridor she could see an Arab in a long black coat talking to Jenny and Steve. His head was smooth and bald with thick neatly cropped hair at the sides and back.

'Good evening English lady. My name is Doctor Aziz. And now will you please come this way.' His voice had almost no trace of an accent.

Steve and Jenny followed behind Eve as she walked down the corridor. She could see the low slit in the doctor's black coat open and close slightly as he walked. She counted her paces. When she reached fifteen they entered another room. There was no-one inside. No terrorists. No guns.

A bare light bulb hung from the ceiling. Steve said something she couldn't hear and Jenny laughed. At me? Do I look that scared?

'The English lady first,' said Doctor Aziz quietly but firmly. 'Lie down and put your arm through there.' He pointed to a small square hole in a wooden wall.

Eve looked at Jenny and Steve. They seemed very distant, giggling quietly near the door.

They know something, she thought. Why don't they tell me and get it over and done with?

As she lay down the doctor stood at the end of the bed, smiling. Like the Arab in the car? She couldn't move at all now. She felt numb.

'Just put your arm through the hole. That's right. I am going to the other side now.' He disappeared through a doorway in the wall.

I'm going mad, she thought. He'll chop it off or something. Steve and Jenny had moved out of her line of vision. Or was it just she couldn't move her head?

The doctor said something but she couldn't make it out over the roar in her head. Then there was familiar sensation of a needle entering her vein and the heat as blood started to pump out.

She could have shouted with relief. She knew this, had done it a dozen times before. She turned her head, caught Jenny's eye and grinned, 'You're next.'

Jenny grimaced back.'I hate blood. Good thing we don't have to look.'

'Eve laughed, her abdominal muscles shaking as she relaxed. The doctor came out and smiled. He had a handsome face, his skin radiating a warm olive glow.

'You are very brave, English lady. Have you done this before?' He gave a wry grin.

'Loads of times.' Her voice still shook slightly.

'So you are experienced. We will be finished soon.'

After taking out the needle he told her to lie still on another bed. Eve felt pleasantly warm and relaxed. Last time I gave blood, she thought, was in the '73 war. So this evens things up.

She felt guilty now that she had distrusted the Arabs. Judged them by their grins and their head scarves. They hadn't judged her. They knew she was Jewish. They were just ordinary people who needed help, like people anywhere, she thought.

Like the Germans who fed Jews in the camps. We are all caught up in situations. Who can be sure they will keep their integrity?

'I would never do that!' she had shouted at her father when she was thirteen. 'Just stand in a line. I'd jump on one of the guards and kill him. I'd rather die fighting than like a sheep!'

He had smiled, a mixture of guilt and sadness. 'That's what the young sabres, the young Israelis shout at the camp survivors. Why didn't you fight back? We would. They forget we Jews had no country, no government, no American high velocity rifles, no flag.'

'Well it's different now,' she had said sullenly. 'Won't happen again.' Her father didn't reply.

In the fight to make sure if doesn't, thought Eve, do we have to grind the Palestinians into the desert first? I must write to dad, tell him about Doctor Aziz and the other Arabs with their sick mother.

When they were finished they drove to a cafe.

'They want us to have an Arabic winter drink,' said Jenny.

The cafe was warm and cosy. Eve sat between the driver and Steve, knees squashed under the low table. The Arabs were laughing and kept thanking everyone in English and Arabic.

Eve said to Jenny, 'Tell them it's nothing, we were glad to help.'

Jenny spoke rapidly in Arabic, her fluency never ceasing to astonish Eve. She's so talented, she thought. What a waste. The Arabs smiled and shook both of Eve's hands.

'They keep saying how grateful they are,' laughed Jenny.

The winter drink was boiled milk sprinkled with cinnamon and coconut. There was also humus and warm pita bread. Eve was starving and as she ate the Arabs kept filling her plate.

'You've made their night eating that muck,' grinned Steve.

They drove back to the hostel past Jaffa Gate glowing under spotlights. The sky had cleared and a full moon lit the uneven skyline, mosques, apartment blocks, the high wall of the Old City. 'Let's stay at Sammy's tonight. I've got a sleeping bag you can borrow,' said Jenny. Her arm was entwined with Steve's.

Eve felt a rush of warmth towards them both. 'No worries,' she said. Jenny laughed.

At the hostel Eve said goodbye first. As she walked towards the doorway she looked back over her shoulder. Jenny was deep in conversation with the two Arabs. What now? thought Eve but then the group broke up , the Arabs jumped in the car and drove off.

The hallway was empty, although the heater burned cheerfully in the middle. Eve held her hands out rubbing them together in the heat. Jenny and Steve came in arms loosely round each other. Jenny had some notes in her hand. She handed them to Eve.

'Here you are. Sixty lire. I managed to get twice the normal rate.'

Eve was stunned. 'Where did you get that?'

'Where do you think you bloody pommie? The Arabs. Don't get something for nothing.' She exchanged raised eyebrows with Steve.

'No-one said anything about getting paid. I did it for free!' yelled Eve stuffing the money back in Jenny's hands.

'You must be joking,' sneered Jenny. ' I don't do anything for free! Nice little earner donating blood. I do it every three months.'

Eve felt numb. Jenny stared cooly into her eyes and turned on her heel. 'I'll get the sleeping bag.' She disappeared up the stairs.

'You still don't get her do you Eve?'

Eve turned, poised like a hunting cat. 'Get what? She's a bloody cow! I would never have asked for money from those people. My God! to ask for it after we'd sat together like friends!'

Steve shrugged, 'That's Jenny's style. She'd nick it if she could. She's cunning, she knows how to get what she wants. That's why...' He stopped.

'Why what Steve?' Eve's voice was filled with menace. She was shocked at the depth of her anger towards him. If I had claws they'd be unfurled, she thought.

'Why the army wouldn't take her. She's delinquent, she lives by nicking, or conning people. She's known, the army won't touch kids like her.' His face darkened. 'I warned you didn't I?'

'But after the party.... she cried...told me everything....'

'No, ' Steve cut in. 'Jenny never tells everything. It's like a jigsaw. You keep putting it together but there's always a piece missing. There are loads of things I don't know.'

They could hear Jenny's footsteps on the stairs. As they both stood looking up she appeared round a corner, her face composed, sleeping bag in her arms.

'This do?' she smiled down at Eve.

Part Three

The Mountain

CHAPTER THIRTEEN

March 1976

'What do you do when you stop?'

'What do you mean?' Eve laughed.

'When you stop? You go and go, America, France, India. But one day you have to stop. What do you do?' Zoar's face was serious.

It was after midnight. She had drunk too much. One of the American boys, Luke, was mixing tequila sunrise in the bar and she was on her fourth. Her limbs felt weak. She wanted sex, she wanted to be held, but she didn't want Zoar.

'You don't just stop, wherever you are. You sort of decide to go home. Then you get a job I suppose.'

I'll finish this one slowly and then I'll tell Luke that's it. If I have another one they'll have to carry me home.

She liked Luke, he was tall and blond, a huge Californian. But only seventeen, she reminded herself. Not that desperate yet.

Zoar tipped up his coke bottle, finished the last inch and stood up. 'I'm too old.'

'Too old!' Eve cried. 'At 26. Do me a favour.'

'I'm going to sleep.' He turned and walked out the door. The bar was empty except for Luke drying glasses.

Eve pulled on her anorak and zipped it to the neck. 'Sleep tight,' she called.

Outside a dense mist had settled around the *moshav*. She could hardly see her hand in front of her face as she stomped down the rough perimeter road.

Suddenly a torch shone in her face and a voice shouted in Hebrew, 'Who's that?'

'Me, Eve, I'm a volunteer.'

The soldier lowered his torch and eased back his rifle. His voice seemed nervous. 'The night she is dark.' He gave a short laugh and walked off.

At the volunteers' house everyone was asleep. Everyone except me and Luke and Zoar. Must be drunk reeling off names. Her toe stubbed painfully on the door and she almost fell onto her bed. Judy, asleep on the other side of the room, rolled over and groaned. 'Sorry,' Eve whispered. She pulled her duvet over her head and lay in the dark, not yet ready to sleep.

Zoar had said it before, about being too old. He was sick of Israel, but afraid to leave. He couldn't understand why people travelled around the world.

'It's a challenge,' Eve said, but it sounded hollow on the side of this mountain, tucked in a triangle between Lebanon and Syria.

Zoar had laughed. 'You want a challenge. It is the army. Even if you don't want. I tell them I am a pacifist, I don't want go to the army. They don't to listen. I did five hundred ambushes in three years on the Golan. We fire into bushes for terrorists.

'His pale delicate hands covered in a fine blond down closed around the coke bottle.

Not the warrior type, thought Eve. They can't all be heroes.

'Everytime you pull the trigger maybe you kill somebody.' He shook his head and took a swig of the coke. 'I never see even one terrorist in three years.'

'You should go abroad, Zoar. I think it's really important. To go outside your own country, see how other people live.'

'I've been abroad. I've been to Jordan and to Egypt!' He grinned at her.

She laughed. All the Israelis said that.

'You know what I mean.'

'Sure, o.k. I know. Living in Israel is like waiting for the next war. All you know is you survive the last one.'

Lying in bed listening to Judy breathe, remembering Zoar's thin face upturned to the coke bottle, Eve thought, I've been here a fortnight and I love it. Then sleep covered her in darkness like mist rolling down from the mountain.

The first thing she loved about the Golan was the water. She could feel the tension on her skin release in the cool damp air.

I'm a rain and wind person, she thought on the bus up the mountain from Qyriat Shemona.

She sat next to a Druze woman with a chicken in a cage. Apart from a couple of soldiers and a few Israelis the bus was empty. Rain lashed against the windows darkening the late afternoon sky. She could feel the air outside grow colder as they pulled away from the valley. There's nothing except rocks and water, she thought. No villages, kibbutzim, not even cars.

The road curved on past a Crusader castle on the left, winding up the steep slopes. She began to wonder if they would ever reach the *moshav* when the bus suddenly stopped and the soldiers stood up.

'Is this Nevae Ativ?' she asked.

One of the soldiers nodded brusquely and said, 'Yes.' He helped her down with her rucksack. When the bus had pulled away she was alone on the unmade track. A huge dog began to bark. She peered up through the weakening daylight and saw he was chained at the top of a wall. The wind was blowing hard now and she had to struggle up the road with her pack. A long low building appeared on a rise. Two soldiers in army Parkas and boots pushed into a brightly lit doorway. Pop music blared out.

Well I'm somewhere, she thought and followed them inside.

The heat hit her first. She lowered her pack and unzipped her anorak. A tall girl with short brown hair in jeans and a red T-shirt came over. 'Hello, I'm Judy. Are you a new volunteer?'

'I hope so,' said Eve. 'It's a long way back down that road.'

Judy laughed. 'They'll take you. They're desperate. There's some Americans, Dutch, usual crowd. Oh and of course, the Israelis.'

The volunteers' house was at the bottom of the road, the last house on the moshav. Two soldiers stood on the doorstep. They were much older than the soldiers in the bar.

'They're in the *miluim,* reservists. Getting a few weeks away from the wife and kids. They're a real pain,' said Judy, 'tramping through here at all hours, making coffee. Oh God! Not again.'

They had entered the house and were on a wide platform above an open area used as a living room. At the end of the platform was a step down into a corridor which lead to the back of the house. A girl was down on her hands and knees mopping a flood of greyish water.

'Toilet or shower?' demanded Judy.

'Shower. Shit! what a nightmare! Drain's always getting blocked. ' She nodded to Eve. 'Hi, I'm Robin.' She had an American accent.

Judy picked up Eve's pack, sloshed down the corridor and kicked open the door of a bedroom. 'This is where we sleep, but your bed will have about an inch of water under it now.'

'This place been open long?'

'Just a few months,' said Judy.

It was a crazy spring that year on the Golan. Two days of sunshine and the snow was almost gone. Then they would close the mountain and the guests would sit around the bar on the *moshav*, ski jackets unzipped, smoking and grumbling. Young executives and their families, up from Tel Aviv , used to the city streets, the beach. They slept in guest rooms in the *moshavniks* houses and ate in the restaurant next to the bar. The wheels of their fast cars would skid and slip on the mountain road spraying mud onto shining hub caps as they took off looking for amusement.

Then the skies would whiten and within hours the slopes had recovered. On *Shabbat* scores of buses would block the road bringing thousands of kibbutzniks for their first taste of snow. They tobogganed on plastic bags. Soldiers skied down the nursery slopes with rifles slung round their backs. From the top of the ski lift the Mediterranean Sea hung a blue line on the far distant horizon.

Eve began work in the kiosk at the foot of the ski slope. Judy introduced her to Herzl who was in charge of the volunteers.

'Ok Eve. You work here with Judy and Mick.' He nodded into the narrow corridor of the kiosk. 'We have no water...'

'What do you mean no water!'

'It's ok. You get snow in a bucket.' He pointed to the bucket as if she was an imbecile. 'Then you take it to the gas and you melt it.'

Eve stared incredulously at Herzl, big in his snow boots and parka. He had large blue eyes and looked over her shoulder as he spoke. Someone more beautiful behind me, she thought sarcastically.

'He's a prat,' Judy had informed her as they hitched a lift up the mountain. 'You can always tell them. They're the ones who stick pistols down the backs of their jeans. Ruin their married lives if they're not careful.'

The kiosk was a chaotic place to work. Everyone shouted ; for snow, for coffee, for falafel.

'No falafel,' Judy would shout back as the crowd pushed and shoved, tipping over sauce bottles on the counter.

'Bring another bucket of snow,' yelled Mick.

Eve hauled snow, filled sandwiches, took orders. They worked until mid-afternoon. Then Herzl and a Druze boy called Nidar took over. Everything appeared calmer once Nidar arrived. 'He works twice as hard as the lot of us and speaks fluent Hebrew and Arabic,' said Judy.

'And he's too well-mannered to shout,' put in Mick.

'Even the Israelis calm down when Nidar pops up behind the counter. Now for our skis.'

Fitted out with boots, skis and poles Eve grinned,' Haven't done this for years.' Sixth form trip to Austria, 1969, she thought. Before college, before Andy, France, Israel.

They skied for two hours taking the lift to the first station for an easy run down. Eve felt the same thrill as in Austria years ago ; the speed, the feeling of flying, the control over her body as she zipped downwards. Her jeans were soaked, her hands numb without gloves, but she felt exhilarated. As they handed in their skis at five o'clock she said to Mick,' Can we do this every day?'

Mick nodded. 'If you can wangle the skis.'

They stood on the road hitching a lift back to the *moshav*. There were less cars now, most people had already gone home. Then a car honked and slid to a halt in front of them. A young man was driving. Mick and Judy climbed in the back, Eve in the front. The driver grinned and said in an American accent, 'Ok, here goes.'

Sounds like a fairground assistant on the dodgems, thought Eve.

The driver let out the handbrake and headed straight for a hairpin bend. There were no barriers. The mountain fell away steeply to their right. Eve clutched the edge of her seat. 'Have you done this before?' she asked in a quiet voice.

'Nope,' he grinned. 'I've been up but never down. We don't have roads like this in Israel.' The car whipped round two bends, skidding on gravel at the edge.

'Would you like me to drive?' offered Judy.

'No, it's ok,' shrugged the driver. 'I'll manage.'

Eve shut her eyes for the rest of the journey.

Apart from the water the beauty of the Golan felt like an addiction after only a few days. She couldn't imagine ever leaving. From her balcony the view was unbroken right down to the Huleh Valley, lines of the big fish ponds on the kibbutzim glinting in the early morning sunlight. The nearest settlement was a Druze village an hour's walk away down the mountain through ancient olive groves.

On a clear night there were more stars than black in the sky. Walking back from the bar down the perimeter road, full moon hanging on a ridge, she felt as though she were outside of it all, watching a film. When I go back to England there'll only be neon against the London sky. It made her ache to think of what she would be missing.

Her days were filled with melting snow and skiing. In the evenings they sat in the bar drinking. She learnt the difference between the *moshavniks* who lived in the houses and shared the profits and the *garin*, conscripted soldiers helping on new settlements. Zoar often came into the bar in the early evening. He liked to sit with the volunteers.

'To practise my English. For when I live in New York,' he would grin.

Eve asked one evening,' How long has this been a *moshav*?'

'After the '73 war a group of us stayed. We wanted to make something here. All this, the bar the restaurant, reception, it was a Syrian outpost. We lived here and the government said o.k. and slowly, slowly, we build the houses.'

'When the women came up they said it stank,' laughed Judy.

'Sure it stink, but it was warm,' said Zoar.

'What about the Arabs who lived here?' asked Eve.

'There are no Arabs, just Druze. They are happy the Syrians go. Now they all have trucks. Business is good. The *moshav* want to send one Druze boy to university, but he don't want.

'Why not?'

'He say he don't want leave his village,' shrugged Zoar.

'Do the Israelis think they'll stay forever?'

'I don't know. I only know if I have a big gun and I put it at the bottom of the road, I can hit every kibbutznik in the Huleh Valley. I don't want the Syrians do this again. Little childrens growing up in bomb shelters.'

'This place gets in your blood so quickly,' said Judy. 'It must have been fantastic at the beginning, starting something new. Like the old pioneers. All packed into one place together, working, sharing.'

Is she getting carried away? thought Eve. But then I am too. After a couple of weeks I feel like this. Six months on kibbutz and I left without a backward glance.

Zoar gave a short laugh. 'It's like this for everybody. Everybody come, want to stay. We are all escaping from the city. But don't be fooled.' He finished his drink and left.

'What did he mean?' asked Eve.

'Politics,' said Judy. ' It's the same everywhere. But this is the closest to the pioneer dream I've ever been.'

'Me too, ' said Eve and she knew she wanted to be carried along on Judy's enthusiasm, to be infected and not to think too many questions.

A sudden vivid picture of her parents came into her head. The old dreams, the echo of her mother's voice telling their story.

'So we'll stay until the end of the season,' laughed Judy.

'Definitely!' and they shook hands expansively as a ripple of laughter coursed through the bar.

There was another *moshav* further along the Golan, newer than Nevae Ativ.

'Just the *garin* and half a dozen *moshavniks*,' Judy told her. 'We should go and visit. '

The only way to get to Har Odem was by army truck. They went with Shula, one of the soldiers, late one afternoon. Shula was eighteen, a tall girl with a mass of black hair piled on her head. She was very self-assured.

'Ok, you must to stand here. We wait and the soldiers are coming.' She pulled the hood of her parka over her head as a flurry of snow blew down in the cold wind.

The road was empty. All the guests were home, taking showers before dinner, the moshavniks in front of the television. 'How far is it?' asked Eve.

Shula didn't answer, her face aloof, staring fixedly down the road.

Judy stamped her feet. 'Hope someone comes soon. I'm freezing.'

After about twenty minutes, when Eve had almost decided to give up, an army truck appeared at the bottom of the *moshav*. Shula held up a limp hand. They'll never see that, thought Eve and stepped out into the middle of the road.

'Come back!' Shula jerked her arm and pulled her to the side. 'They see, don't make accident please.'

The truck ground to a halt in front of them. Shula called out in Hebrew. Several soldiers jumped down laughing and shouting. 'Ok, they take us,' she said abruptly and climbed onto the truck.

Eve and Judy scrambled up behind and sat on a bench opposite Shula. The soldiers passed cigarettes and tried out their English.

'At least they're friendly,' muttered Judy, nodding her head in Shula's direction.

'Christ! she made me feel about four years old back there on the road,' Eve laughed. '*Rak b'eretz*, only in Israel as Mick constantly reminds us.'

'You're not kidding. My mother'd have a fit in this country. In fact she'd be in a permanent state of fit.'

'My mum would find it tough too. But they'd cope.'

'Not my mum,' said Judy. 'Lived all her life in Golders Green, except for the regulation package to Spain. Her idea of religion is keeping up with the Cohens. Kosher chicken sandwiches in my lunch box and park the car two streets away from the synagogue on Yom Kippur.

My dad's an electrician. He spends *Shabbos* morning dodging the neighbours and doesn't come back until after dark in case they guess he's been working. I used to feel like the daughter of a Russian spy, the cover-up job I had to do!'

She shook her head as Eve laughed even harder. ' You sound like a really normal family to me. Mine covered up all the time.'

Judy looked at her curiously but just then the truck hit a pothole and everyone was thrown against each other. When they had regained their seats Judy seemed to have forgotten Eve's words.

'The Israelis are like an extreme version of Golders Green. They're completely crazy! They keep you further than arm's length and then are astounded that you won't make *Aliyah*. I mean...' Judy's voice rose in indignation, ' why on earth should I make the effort!'

'It's different on the *moshav* though,' said Eve.

'Oh, without a doubt, no comparison to kibbutz, or the city. I feel it's the first time I've really sat down and talked to young Israelis. I think they're great. They really let you in up here, make you feel you're part of it all. They couldn't run the kiosk without us.'

The journey seemed endless. Out of the back of the truck the wide flat plain of the Golan stretched out on either side, Syria on the horizon. Behind them they could see the huge fist of Mount Hermon, snow covering its sides.

The far end of the Great African Rift, thought Eve. All that geography and politics for thousands of miles. Just for a finger of land.

It was very cold. The soldiers passed round parkas.

'This must be some kind of delivery truck,' said Judy. 'We seem to be going the whole length of the Golan.' They stopped at outposts every few miles. Eve dozed off snuggled down in her parka. The grey wintry sky grew dark.

After nearly two hours she was shaken awake by Judy. The truck stopped and the three girls jumped down. A thick mist had descended and Eve could hardly see the nearby fence of the *moshav*.

Shula spoke. Her voice seemed less confident than before. 'We are very late. The gate is closed. I know a hole.'

They followed her around the fence until they saw the hole. As they climbed through Shula whispered,' There is the guard. He can shoot now if he wants.'

My God! thought Eve. He'll think we're terrorists. She could just make out his shape through the trees, the length of his gun across his body. Judy gripped her hand.

They started to walk slowly forward towards the soldier. Suddenly he stopped, pointed his rifle straight at them and called out in Hebrew, 'Who's that?'

'Shula,' came the soft reply. '*Garin*.' Shula had stopped still. To give him time to recognise her, thought Eve.

'Shula?'

There was a pause. Water dripped onto Eve's neck from a branch. But she didn't move away. Then a stream of angry Hebrew broke out. Relief flooded Eve's knees.

'Close thing,' grinned Judy. ' Not one for the postcard home.'

Har Odem was much smaller than Nevae Ativ, just a communal dining room and bedrooms in a long low building. Shula took them into the dining room which was filled with young soldiers.

'We can eat something,' she said her aloofness restored after the incident at the fence.

Someone brought them soup and bread. The room was very noisy, people shouting from one end to the next. A lot of guns lay on floors and tables or propped against walls.

Suddenly two of the biggest boys began wrestling in the space before the door. In the dim light of the room they seemed huge to Eve, moving slowly like bears as they tumbled and struggled, leaping on each other. There were smiles on their faces, but she sensed the grim determination between them. They both wanted to win.

'They do it to keep in practice,' said a girl near Eve.

'How far is the Syrian border from here?' asked Eve.

'Half an hour. But everyone would get here very soon if they attacked.'

'What a comforting thought,' grinned Judy. She turned to Eve and said in a low voice, ' Don't you think they enjoy being on the edge of it all like this? Gives me a thrill.'

Eve nodded. 'It's just impossible to imagine anything happening.'

Shula took them to her room after dinner. 'You can sleep here. I go next door with my friend.'

Judy fell asleep immediately. But Eve was restless in the strange bed.

Which one is Shula's boyfriend? she thought. Perhaps one of the boys in the wrestling match. The big blond lad who forced the red-haired boy to surrender, one arm bent stiff behind his back. She could imagine Shula and the blond boy in the next room, whispering intimacies in Hebrew, as he slipped his khaki fatigues to the floor.

It's been ages, she thought. Maybe I can't do it anymore. She thought about her first time with Andy, her first time ever. It had made her laugh.

When Eve woke the next morning sunlight blinded her eyes. They had breakfast in the dining room and then two soldiers, Saul and his girlfriend Natalie, a tiny dark-haired girl, offered to show them around. They walked to an old watchtower beyond the quadrangle of buildings and climbed to the top.

Eve looked all round her. 'Nothing,' she said. ' Trees, clouds, horizon, nothing else. No roads, houses, telephone wires, electric pylons. It's like the real hippie dream.'

'Get back to the land man,' laughed Judy. 'Why do you think all these people are up here?'

'Well,' demanded Eve, looking at Saul and Natalie. 'Why are you here?'

'Because it's so beautiful,' said Natalie. She had her arm round Saul's back but it didn't reach to his hip.

What on earth could she do in a war? thought Eve. Her gun must be longer than she is.

They climbed down and wandered around the buildings. The sun was very bright, filling the air with a harsh yellow light. Saul stopped by some rocks and offered cigarettes. On the ground lay two poles each about three feet long. He picked one up and kicked the other. It rolled towards Eve. Saul started to swipe the air slowly with his pole. Eve reached out and touched the other pole with her shoe.

If I pick it up we'll engage, she thought. A sudden urge filled her. She picked up the pole, leant forward slightly and looked up at Saul. He grinned and threw away his cigarette.

Eve took the pole in both hands and lunged. Saul caught the pole neatly and flipped it back. She could feel the weight of his body shudder through her hands. They lunged and swiped, cracking on the wood, careful to avoid fingers. Eve didn't think about anything but the struggle, the other pole, the position of the sun to keep her eyes clear. They began to circle faster. Saul had the edge, bigger, stronger, quicker on his feet. She knew he was holding back, she felt desperate to out-manoevre him. She wanted to win. Then her ankle gave way and he was on her, his pole stretched across her chest, her hair loose in the dust. For a second she saw red in his eyes. Blood? How does it feel to meet the enemy? Maybe he is thinking that too.

Then he was pulling her up, brushing her down and they were all laughing. 'Soon you will be a *Golani*,' said Saul.

'Don't be crazy Saul,' said Natalie. 'Come on Eve, I have something for your hair.'

Eve followed Natalie's small slim legs to her bedroom.

CHAPTER FOURTEEN

The letter from her father was waiting for her when she arrived back at Nevae Ativ. She had almost given up. She had written to Bud with her address and then phoned when she heard nothing after a week.

'I sent it Eve, soon as I got your letter. Days ago.'

'Well it hasn't arrived Bud. Where is it?'

'How the hell should I know? Efficiency is not one of Israel's strengths. Especially with the mail. Chrissakes it takes weeks to get letters from the States.'

'Oh come on Bud! We're talking about a couple of hundred miles on the country's internal post. Are you sure you sent it?' She knew Bud wouldn't let her down but it was weeks since her father had written to her. He would be looking for her reply.

'Of course I'm sure! Look Eve, give it a bit more time. It'll find it's way to you. My mother sent me some socks in November and ....' but her *assimonim* had run out.

January 5th.

Dear Eve,

Happy New Year! I got your letter a while ago but it's been difficult to find the time to reply. We've both had flue and the weather's been dreadful. Enjoy the sunshine. I hear they've had a drought in Israel this winter.

In your letter you ask again why your mother and I didn't go to Israel later. Well Eve, it all seems so long ago now. Perhaps you just have to accept that we didn't and all your mother's stories about how you could have been a sabre came to nothing.

It seems to me, going back through your letters, that you have gone to Israel looking for some meaning to your life. Not just as a Jew, but as an individual also. All I can say is I hope you find what you are looking for because in the end you're the only one who can. Nothing I tell you will change that for you.

When you come home we'll find some time to talk. I'll be very interested to hear all about your experiences. Take lots of photos. Keep writing. Mum has stuck your postcards up all over the kitchen wall.

Love dad.

Eve leaned back against the balcony wall.

Why did it take him so long to write? But she knew, had guessed long before. He didn't want to answer anymore questions. She read the letter through once more with a rising sense of freedom. This is the first time he's recognised I'm independent with my own life to lead. I don't need his letters anymore, she thought. My reasons for being here are my own and not driven by mum and dad's dreams.

'Robin's gone.' Judy was standing in front of her blocking out the sunlight.

Eve looked up. Judy was wearing a pair of khaki army trousers. She's joined up, Eve thought. 'Got a gun as well?'

'What? Oh.' Judy looked down. ' Zoar was throwing them out.' She shoved her hands self consciously into the big thigh pockets. 'Did you know about Robin?'

'No.'

'Honestly Eve!' Judy sounded annoyed. 'She was the first volunteer here. Came right at the beginning. Apparently Herzl made a pass at her yesterday morning.'

'Stupid bastard.' Eve pulled herself up and went into the kitchen. 'Coffee?'

Judy followed. ' Anyway, Robin never complains or anything. Mick said she just packed her stuff and took the first ride down the mountain.

"How does Mick know?'

'Nidar saw her. She didn't even say goodbye. I'll miss her.' Judy took the mug Eve held out. 'You'll have to look out for Herzl. I think you're next.'

Eve grinned. 'God help him! You could always scare him with a war whoop.'

Judy laughed. 'All the members have to have weapons training up here. Even the women.'

'Beats the dole queue back home.'

They fell silent watching the evening sunlight. Not even a photograph would hold this, Eve thought. I'll have to keep it all inside my head when I go. She began to wonder if Judy ever intended leaving.

'Moishe and Etty asked us to go to dinner tonight,' said Judy. 'I can practise my Hebrew.'

They walked up to Moishe's house at eight. It was already dark. The night patrol were prowling the perimeter road, chewing gum, flashing torches into the bushes opposite the houses.

They knocked on Moishe's door which opened silently. Moishe had his finger to his lips as he beckoned them inside. 'The children, they just go to sleep now,' he whispered. In the living room the lights were dimmed. A jug and some glasses stood on a low glass coffee table in the middle of the room. They all sat down in silence.

Do we have to stay like this all evening? thought Eve. She tried to catch Judy's eye, but she seemed to be staring at a bookcase trying to read titles. They were all in Hebrew.

Then Etty appeared. 'It's ok now. They sleep.' Everyone relaxed and Moishe poured Martini from the jug. Etty was a tall woman with long blond hair in tight jeans and a loose sweat-shirt. She smiled at the two girls on the sofa. 'My English is not good.'

'You should hear my Hebrew,' said Eve. She leaned back on the sofa. It was brand new, like most of the furniture in the room. A bit sterile, she thought. But on the opposite wall hung an Arabic style dress, beautifully embroidered, the arms stretched out and nailed down. 'That's a lovely dress. Where did you get it?'

'It's a Bedouin wedding dress,' said Etty. 'Everything is done with hand. A lot of work. I look a long time for this one. You like? Maybe I can to get you one.'

'That'd be great,' said Eve.

Etty served warm pita bread, falafel and salad, with black olives and feta cheese. 'You eat this in England?'

'God, no,' said Judy. 'It's all chips and spaghetti these days.'

'Together?' asked Moishe and everyone laughed. 'In England it rain everyday and all the peoples drink tea, tea, tea.'

'Good, you know about England. There's a bit more but you'll have to come and see for yourself,' said Judy.

'I like very much. One day but first I have to join the *moshav.*' He was a big man, sleeves rolled up on thick forearms overlaid with long dark hairs.

He has such beautiful eyes, thought Eve. Like liquid brown, very sensitive. Must be hard to be a soldier with eyes like that.

'Is it difficult to join the *moshav*?' she asked.

'Sometimes the peoples make problems. They want to keep everything for themselves so they don't take new members.' Moishe broke a piece of pita bread in half and pushed in salad and olives.

'We hear about that sometimes. Mafia, mafia,' said Judy.

'Yes,' said Etty, pushing back her hair with her hand. 'But we can make something good here. We don't to give up easily.'

'We want to begin something new for our children,' said Moishe. 'And for us. My father was chalutz.' He looked at Judy.

She nodded,' Pioneer.'

'Yes pioneer. Now it my turn. I grow up in the city. My mother, she don't to like kibbutz. Now I come to the mountain. Up here it is very clean. We have a place to be free,' he finished simply.

If he had said that in England, thought Eve, he would have been laughed at. A pseudo hippy. But here, on the *moshav*, it rings true. They're ideal pioneers. She looked across at Judy. There was a distant look on her face, a forgotten piece of bread between her fingers.

'So do you think they'll take you?'.

Moishe looked at her steadily, his eyes large in the dim light. 'They must to take us. We work hard. Somebody have to work here.'

They left just before eleven. Outside a thick mist blotted out the other houses. They stumbled over walls towards the road, clutching each other and giggling.

'Oh God! That was a hole,' cried Eve.

'You ok?"

'No, let's take a rain check.' Eve sat down and pulled out a cigarette. ' I love this place so much. Even in the mist.'

'It's so exciting. All the different colours and shapes. Nothing's recognisable. Didn't you think they were great?'

'Yes,' said Eve thoughtfully. 'I did. This place is amazing. Crazy, but amazing.'

They stumbled on through the powerful Golan night.

The following week when they returned from work a soldier had moved into Robin's room.

'Hi, I'm Meni.'

Meni was a dropout. His shirt was always half out of his trousers. He grew his hair below the collar and tried not to shave. But even dropouts had to join the army in Israel.

'So they put me on the Golan,' he told Eve and Judy. 'Make me a border guard. All by myself.'

'Where's your *garin*?' asked Judy.

Meni lay stretched out on his bed, boots unlaced, cigarette perpetually hung from his lips. 'I am a *garin*.'

'Just you?'

'Just me.'

Meni kept his kaloshnikov rifle under his bed with the dust. His record collection lay in pristine condition in the wardrobe. Meni was a Communist. 'What's mine is yours,' he would shrug sleepily.

Anyone could go into Meni's room and put on a record. Even if he was asleep. Nothing woke him.

'Christ knows what he'd do if terrorists showed up,' said Mick.

'Go on sleeping,' grinned Judy. 'I seriously doubt that gun of his would fire. Have you seen it?'

They were sitting in Meni's bedroom listening to Jefferson Airplane. Meni was on the mountain digging the new toilet trench. It was a warm afternoon at the end of March. The moshav was getting ready for Passover. The mountain was closed from lack of snow and the volunteers were bored.

'Let's get it out,' said Mick. He dug around under the bed and pulled out the gun. A ripple of excitement permeated the little group.

'He never cleans it,' said Mick in a low almost reverent voice. He put the gun to his shoulder and squinted down the sights.

He looks like the real thing, thought Eve.

'Want a go?'

Judy took the gun. Startled by the weight she almost dropped it. Eve felt the sharp prickle of sweat in her armpits.

They passed the gun round, felt the weight of the metal, smell of grease, jerk of the trigger. The music pumped louder into the small hot room.

Then the record stopped. The volunteers looked round at each other. Eve pushed the gun back under the bed. She felt strange, half guilty, half thrilled. Judy had a streak of gun grease on her army trousers. We're getting in deeper, thought Eve. As though we're not volunteers anymore.

Meni had his own opinion of the *moshav.*

'You know the stories from Chelm. That crazy Jewish village in Poland where nobody gets things right? Well here is my story. Only it is from the *moshav.*

They were pushing the mountain. It gets hot. They take off their shirts. A Druze truck come on the road and pick up the shirts. The men still push the mountain. When they turn around and see the shirts not there they say, 'Oh! We must have pushed the mountain really a long way.'

Judy laughed. 'We have a saying in England, Too big for their boots.'

Meni thought for a minute and then he laughed and nodded. He reached out and changed the record. Janis Joplin, thought Eve. Now she was really crazy.

It snowed hard five days before Passover. The ski slope was packed. Eve was sent to work in the ski shop with Moishe. This was better than the kiosk and it meant she could talk to Moishe while they watched the Israelis careering down the slope.

Moishe told her he had dreamt since childhood of living on the mountain.

'Before we go to the city we live on kibbutz in the valley. Every morning I look up and see the Hermon, with snow, or cloud or covered in sunshine. I know one day I come here to live. After the Yom Kippur war my friend Herzl start the *moshav* with some other guys. I come and say I want to join.'

'Do you think the *moshav* will grow?' asked Eve watching the rise and fall of his eyebrows as he spoke.

'I think. And I think it will be a big place one day. This is only the first season and look at all the peoples.'

'It's so different from the rest of Israel. More like the way I thought Israel would be.'

'You know what Nevae Ativ means?' Eve shook her head. 'Nevae in Hebrew is oasis. But also a house. A house for shepherds. In ancient days they bring their sheep to oasis and they make a house. Ativ is the initials of four soldiers who were killed here.'

'An oasis,' said Eve thoughtfully. 'A place to build your house.'

'Like Israel for the Jews. But still they don't to come.' He sounded resentful.

She wanted to reach out and touch the line deepening between his eyes.

'The ones who need to come are here. The ones who don't are like people everywhere. They stay where they feel comfortable. It's not easy to think about Aliyah when you come from London.'

'You never know where Hitler will be next.'

Eve sat in the bar that night with Zoar, Judy and Mick. Luke was mixing cocktails. Some soldiers were standing near the juke box changing records, drinking coke, their guns propped near the door.

Eve wondered what she would feel if Moishe came in. Into this warm smoky atmosphere, asked her to dance, with two of Luke's cocktails already flowing inside her.

But he won't, she thought. Because he is a good man and he is in love with his wife who is beautiful and kind. Maybe I should tell Herzl I want to go back to the kiosk.

'Dance?' Mick was smiling over her. Judy and Zoar were already in each other's arms, moving slowly to the music. She stood up and out her arms round Mick's neck, let them hang down his back.

'Do you like working in the ski shop?' Mick pushed his hips gently against hers. She pulled back slightly.

'It's ok. ' Keep talking, she thought. He'll get the message. 'I heard the Druzim from Magdal Shams are coming here for Passover.'

'Zoar told me the Druze want to show their support for the Israelis and the moshav. They're terrified the Syrians will come back.' He leaned forward to brush her lips with his. She laughed and threw back her hair. 'Ok Eve. But don't get involved in anything you can't handle.'

'Meaning?' she said softly.

'Nothing. Just that.'

Everyone's a mind reader on these bloody Israeli settlements, she thought visciously. I'll definitely ask for a transfer. The whole place will be gossiping soon and nothing's happened. Yet.

But Herzl told her to stay in the ski shop. She began to take her coffee outside when business was slow. Moishe didn't say anything. He's guessed, she thought and he's keeping clear. Sensible. But then that was what drew her to him in the first place. A steady serious guy . With ideals. Not many of them about, even up here.

Oh God where did it all go? Being a pioneer, living together, sharing. Did it ever exist and maybe it was only momentary, while they all tried to survive in those terrible conditions. Like the Blitz.

But I still love it here, she thought. No tarmac on the road, nothing but rocks and snow for miles. It's so raw, so unplanned.

Two days later it began to snow hard again. She sat indoors with Moishe.

'It snow enough to cover Switzerland,' he laughed. 'Crazy winter, crazy spring. Tomorrow will be rain, everywhere a river. Then another one hour and sunshine.' He threw his hands up in the air. 'Everything dry, the road hard as rock.'

Eve smiled. 'Are you and Etty coming tonight?'

'Of course. The Druze make a big feast for us. They kill a sheep.' He looked at her for a minute. 'You have a boyfriend in England Eve?'

'No.' She lit a cigarette. Moishe was quiet, waiting for her to say more. 'I did have but we parted. Fell out of love. At least he did.'

'You still love him?'

'I don't think so. It was last summer. But he wasn't Jewish. He used that to finish with me.'

'It hurt?'

No, she thought. This is too intimate with you so close and that sweet smell from you skin in the air.

She gulped back her coffee and stood up. 'All goodbyes hurt. I'll see you tonight.'

The guest house was packed that evening, *moshavniks*, guests, Druzim all standing in the centre of the dining room, chairs and tables stacked against the walls. Nidar, the Druze boy who worked on the mountain, moved through the crowd carrying a small stainless steel tray.

'Coffee?' he smiled as he reached Eve.

He was sixteen years old, with a long thin body and ears that stuck out of the side of his head. His hair was cropped too short and he always wore a knitted hat.

On the tray was a small coffee pot and two tiny white china cups. Great, thought Eve. Two cups for the whole room. But she took a cup, gulped the coffee and put it back on the tray. 'Thankyou,' she smiled.

'Zank you, zank you,' grinned Nidar cheekily and pushed through the crowd calling, "Allo,'Allo,' like the barrow boys in the *shouk*.

Eve looked around for Judy and pushed through the crowds to her. 'Seen the sheep?'

'Not yet. They've already cooked it hopefully. Try this it's Druze bread.' She handed Eve a large flat sheet of bread. Eve pulled off a piece and put it in her mouth.

'It's awful, like chewing parchment.'

'And it's Passover.'

Eve groaned and shook her head in mock horror.

The room began to quieten down. Everyone turned to the far end. Three Druze men wearing jackets and ties, the white Druze scarf draped around their heads, were waiting for silence. Herzl stood next to them with two other founder members of the moshav. That's the group, thought Eve. The guys Moishe has to impress so they'll let him join. She had never seen them together before.

Herzl , in charge of the mountain, was the best skier amongst the Israelis, his eyes always on the next pair of lovely legs, never on the girl he was with.

Avram, a tall elegant man, wore a silk tie, practically unheard of for an Israeli. A Tel Aviv socialite and a fortune hunter according to Meni.

And Ezra who looked after the horses and wanted to go to America, 'because if I stay in this crazy country I will to be dead.'

Eve wasn't sure if he meant dead from a war, or just every day life in Israel.

Herzl put up his hand and as the room fell silent he began speaking. Judy translated for Eve. 'He says hello and he welcomes the Druze. He hopes for peace and that we can all work together.'

When Herzl had finished everyone clapped, the Druze nodding their heads gravely. Then one of the Druze stepped forward, sweeeping the long ends of his scarf from his shoulders and spoke in Hebrew.

'His accent is difficult to follow,' said Judy. 'Something about peace. He's glad we are all here together and friends and she should stay that way. ' She shook her head. 'I can't follow the rest.'

'It's o.k.,' said Eve. She was thinking about the mountain and the Druze. Moishe had said to her,' Their religion is a *sod*. You know what is *sod*?'

Eve laughed. 'I know what it is in English. ' She loved the puzzled look on his face.

'Something funny?'

She shook her head. She didn't want to explain.

'In Hebrew *sod* is secret.'

'Oh I see.'

'The Mount Hermon, it is very important. The holy place. Their religion is secret. They learn as they become older, little by little. The old men know it all. But they don't tell anybody. All the Druze live round the mountain, in

Lebanon, Syria, Israel. Where they are they make friends.'

As the voice of the Druze rose and fell in the dining room Eve thought, I can see how you could make a religion out of this mountain. Out of such a high, quiet, beautiful place. A solitary mountain, not lost in a giant range like the Alps. She felt a rush of love for the Golan, the *moshav*, the Druze in their villages. I was lucky to get here, she thought. I might have gone home without ever knowing.

The speaker had finished, the crowd clapped respectfully and everyone was moving again, calling to friends, laughing, drinking Nidar's coffee. Then above the noise Eve heard a familiar voice.

'There's that bloody pommie!'

Oh no! she thought. She turned, praying she was wrong. Jenny and Steve were pushing their way to her. They wore denim jackets and jeans, covered in frayed patches. The bottom of Jenny's jeans were torn and muddy. Steve carried a beer bottle in each hand.

'Who's that?' asked Judy, a slight frown on her face.

Eve didn't answer, refusing to introduce them as friends. Instead she grabbed Jenny's arm and pulled her into a corner. 'What the hell are you doing here?'

Jenny tipped up a wine bottle and took a long swig. 'Free country cobber,' she said after a minute, her face flushed.

Christ! she's drunk, thought Eve. 'Come on.'

'Where?'

'You'd better sleep at my house. It's too late to do anything now.' Eve picked up the small bag Jenny had dropped to the floor. Steve had disappeared.

'Hang on.' Jenny tugged the bag out of Eve's hand. 'I wanna enjoy the party. Why aren't you pleased to see us? Came all this way to keep in touch.'

'LIke hell you did. Look Jenny...'

'Don't worry about me. Two days on the road. We're knackered. Need a good party. Where's that bloody Steve. Gone walkabout.' Swinging her bag over her shoulder Jenny pushed back into the crowd.

'Friend?' Judy was at her side.

'No,' said Eve. 'Well I knew them in Jerusalem.' She sighed and pulled her hand through her hair. 'Hopefully they won't stay long.'

The next morning Eve walked up to the guest house to find Jenny washing up and helping with breakfast.

'She is a good worker, your friend,' said Herzl running a hand lazily down Jenny's back. Jenny curved her long body towards him.

They slept together last night, thought Eve.

'They've given me a job in the kitchen,' said Jenny, pushing away Herzl's hand as it reached the curve of her bottom, tight, tantalising in the ragged jeans. 'So where do you work Eve?'

'Not here,' said Eve abruptly and turned away.

As she stood out on the road, waiting for a lift up the mountain, she saw Steve ride out of the stables behind Ezra. The horses were supposed to be the summer attraction after the snow had gone.

They're certainly getting their feet under the table, thought Eve angrily, remembering how Ezra wouldn't let her or Judy ride.

She worked silently all day in the ski shop. Moishe didn't seem to notice her change of mood. It made her feel isolated, marginalised.

In the bar that evening Jenny sat between Herzl and Mick, drinking beer.

'Why don't you try a tequila sunrise?' said Mick. 'Luke's getting a dab hand at mixing cocktails.'

Jenny, her expression innocent, so familiar to Eve, said, 'I take my drink seriously. Can't have kids like that playing about with it.'

Eve flushed in anger.

Mick laughed. 'What's up Eve? She's just joking.'

'Jenny likes a joke, don't you Jenny?' said Steve. 'Anyone for a game?' He flipped a pack of cards.

'For god's sake Steve,' snapped Eve.

'Shut up Eve,' smiled Steve, his voice deliberately casual. Herzl and Mick snickered.

Eve felt Judy's hand on her arm. 'Early night?'

Eve felt close to tears. She nodded and they left together. As they walked back to the volunteers' house Judy said, 'She's a little cow. Why don't you ask Avram to get rid of her?'

Eve was silent, her mind crammed with words; Jenny and Herzl, Jenny and Mick, Jenny and Steve, Jenny drunk, half mad, pouring out her story.

'Eve?'

'Sorry. Look, Jenny won't stay long. They're just here for a holiday. They'll soon miss the shouk. It's not my business to tell the moshav what to do. Just keep clear for a bit.' She shoved her hands into her anorak pockets and trudged on down through the rain.

'O.k ok, but don't let her get you down. She's only a kid.'

Only a kid, thought Eve. I wish. Only a kid.

The words echoed round her head for the next few days as she worked, sat apart from the volunteers for meals, Judy keeping her company. Jenny showed her best side. She worked hard in the kitchen, inventing new salads for the guests. They loved her accent.

'Speak Jenny,' they would say as she wafted into the dining room with loaded trays for the buffet.

'Speak what?' she would laugh, broadening her accent for the audience.

'Anything. We love to hear your voice.'

She'll be here for ever, thought Eve in despair. Maybe I should think about leaving.

It became clear that Mick had fallen for Jenny. Eve watched his small round face as she entered a room, his skin redden as he watched her loop her body around Herzl. Mick was older than Jenny at twenty-one but he seemed raw, unformed next to her.

Grammar school, a Lower Second in Geography from Bath University, and then a trip to Israel as a present from his parents.

'They said I could go anywhere. Always wanted to try kibbutz. It's my first time abroad,' he had told Eve shyly.

Jenny will grind him to a powder, thought Eve. When she realises. If she hasn't already.

Eve avoided the bar for most of the week but on Friday evening she decided she'd felt left out for long enough. She saw Mick standing near Luke drinking what looked like whisky, as she walked in. Then she heard Jenny call out, 'Who're you dancing with Mick?'

Mick lurched towards her, drunk. 'You Jenny. I wanna dance..... with you.' He put his hands on her shoulders, partly to steady himself. Herzl was standing behind Jenny laughing. God, I'd like to smack his face, thought Eve.

Instead she said,'Come on Mick. Dance with me.'

'No, not with you...with her. She wants me to.'

Jenny threw back her head and laughed. Then prising his hands off her shoulders she snarled,' You think I'd dance with a limp prick like you.' She turned to Herzl, her hips swaying towards his pelvis. 'Give me an Israeli soldier any day.'

'Jenny!' Eve was horrified. 'What a lousy thing to say!' But Mick was gone, running out of the bar, his face streaked with tears.

'I wish to God she'd split,' said Judy.

They looked around the bar. Herzl and Jenny were mauling each other, lips locked together, hips grinding in time to the music. Steve was playing cards with two soldiers, a huge pile of cigarettes in front of him. Luke was calmly drying glasses.

'I'm sick of this place. Let's go.' Judy turned and left. Eve followed miserably. It's all my fault, she thought. I'll speak to Avram in the morning.

She was asleep and a terrible struggle was going on. Blood, legs, eyes were flying everywhere. The moon was falling from the sky. As she wrenched open her eyes she could hear Judy calling to Mick. He said something back but she couldn't make it out. Then the front door slammed and it went quiet. What's happening for God's sake? After a few minutes she heard the door slam again and footsteps in the living-room. Judy's back , she thought.

The door opened. It was Jenny. She was carrying a bottle. In the light from the hall she seemed huge, hair tangled round her shoulders, eyes wide.

Drunk, thought Eve.

'He's gone.'

'Who?' asked Eve, getting up and pulling on her clothes.

'Mick. Just as well really. Can't stand schoolboy crushes.'

'What do you mean Jenny?' Eve's voice was harsh.

'He tried it on with me out there on there road. I'm not having that. Got Herzl to make things clear.' There was an ugly edge to her voice as she clenched her fist and then laughed, swaying against the door.

Eve felt the anger rise beyond control. 'That's it Jenny. I've had enough of you and your bloody tricks. Worm your way in here and then screw everyone up. You get out of here tonight or I'm going to Avram, telling him all about you.'

A scream, high pitched like an animal, split the air. Eve stopped, shaken, scared.

'Fuck you, you bitch! No-one tells me what to do or when to go!'

Eve was never sure if Jenny meant to but suddenly the bottle was smashed against the wall and the broken end was coming down towards her. She raised her arm in defence and felt the sharp jagged razor of glass as it slashed the back of her hand. All this in the dark, giant shadows thrown on the wall from the hall light. Eve clutched her wrist and fell to her knees, rigid with pain and shock. The front door slammed. She rolled over onto the floor cursing with every word she could think of.

When Judy found her she had a T-shirt wrapped round her hand, blood gently seeping through.

'You were right Judy,' was all she could say.

Judy fussed round, wrapping her in a blanket, supporting her gently to her feet. They stumbled up through driving rain to Avram's house.

'Don't say anything,' whispered Eve at the door.

'Oh God Eve,' said Judy. But seeing the look on Eve's face she just nodded.

Avram pulled them inside, his face full of concern, not seeming to notice the blood splashed onto his tie, He organised a car and they drove off deep into the Golan. When they came to a halt Eve saw huge searchlights , machine guns mounted on walls. 'We're at an army camp,' said Judy. 'There's a doctor here."

They led her into a room lit only by a table lamp. Soldiers sat or lay asleep on bunks. A man in his thirties, in crumpled fatigues, his hair falling across his eyes and a thick black moustache clouding his upper lip, pulled himself sullenly to his feet. Avram spoke to him in Hebrew. He shrugged his shoulders and turned to Eve. She swayed slightly.

'Show me,' he said.

She didn't want to then, afraid he would be rough.

The doctor passed a hand across sleepy eyes and then said more gently, 'It's ok. I won't to hurt you. Show me your hand.'

She held out her arm and he carefully unwrapped the T-shirt. 'There is glass in it. How did you do it?'

The room seemed full of uniforms. She swayed again and shook her head. 'I fell onto some broken glass.'

He stared hard into her face. She felt he could see into her mind, was calmly watching all the pictures of that evening as they raced round. Change the channel, she kept thinking, change the channel. She was very tired.

Then they were walking just the two of them down a corridor. 'What is your name?' His voice was kinder now, away from the other soldiers.

'Eve.'

'I am Nimrod.' They entered a room. He led her to a couch. 'Lie down here please. '

Eve lay down exhausted. Nimrod moved quietly round the room pulling on rubber gloves, opening plastic packages, filling a syringe.

'Something for the pain,' he said quietly. He took off the T-shirt and dropped it in a bin. Then he gave her an injection in her hand. She lay with her eyes closed while Nimrod worked on her hand. He removed pieces of glass, cleaned the wound endlessly, stitched it up and covered it with a thick dressing.

'You can get up now,' he smiled. 'But slowly. Come and sit in this chair Eve.'

She felt weak as she crossed the room, struggling to hold back tears. She sat down her head heavy with fatigue.

'Why don't you tell me how it happened Eve. Maybe I can to help you.'

Then the tears broke, streaming uncontrollably down her face. As she cried images blew through her mind, Jenny, that terrible scream, Max, Andy, 'It would never work Eve. You're Jewish.' Her parents, the echo of Israel though her childhood. All the way back to the death certificate. Noah.

She felt swept with loneliness, in this remote outpost, on a bleak mountain side, in a country she couldn't understand and was supposed to regard as home.

Nimrod sat quietly until she had stopped crying. Then he said,' Do you want to tell me something?'

Something? she thought. The something is everything and the one thing at the back of it all is Noah.

'I had a brother who died.' The words sounded strange, yet familiar.

'That is very sad. How old was he?'

'He wasn't.'

'I don't understand.'

'He didn't have an age. He died when he was born.'

An only child, she thought. No-one to share childhood with, to whisper secrets about the adults. Just a dead baby no-one ever spoke about.

It was the first time she had cried for him. Beneath the heavy weight of pain, a strong complete feeling began to emerge.

'We go back to your friends now Eve. Come back in five days. I take out the stitches.' He stood over her, big in the narrow room. She nodded and walked to the door.

CHAPTER FIFTEEN

It was the end of April and the season was declared officially over. For each day of snow there was two days of rain washing the slopes to a pulp. Herzl and two Swiss volunteers pushed higher up the mountain to ski on the remaining ice sheet. 'Maybe they ski to Syria,' Meni grinned. 'Say Hi to our neighbours.'

The ski shop was packed up, the kiosk closed and the heavy flow of traffic up and down the mountain road ceased completely. The moshav appeared deserted.

A tennis court was set up near the stables and two of the mosahv wives, neat in matching tennis whites, played every morning.

'Wouldn't hurt them to do some work, ' grumbled Judy. 'How do they think this place keeps going?'

'Volunteers,' laughed Meni 'How do you think Israel keep going? Volunteer work. Volunteer dollars.'

A week after Jenny's attack Avram had taken Eve back to the doctor. Eve felt shy and nervous about seeing him again. Will he remember about Noah, she thought, a strange chill in her spine as they entered the base. It was mid-morning and soldiers were everywhere, starting up jeeps, running between buildings.

They found Nimrod in his surgery. He looked up and smiled when he saw Eve. She smiled back in relief. He looked very different, in a clean pressed uniform, his hair neatly combed, eyes alert, professional.

'How is the hand?'

'Fine.' She held it out and he took off the dressing, looked carefully at the wound.

'Good. You heal well. Sit down Eve. I take out the stitches now. No pain this time.'

As he gently snipped and pulled, they chatted about Israel, the *moshav*, her work as a volunteer.

He's a real sabre, she thought. Lousy on first meeting and then really deep and interesting once you cut through the prickles.

'And your family Eve. You hear from them this week?'

She flinched slightly. Of course he remembers. He was just being tactful. But I'm fine. Everything's fine. Now Jenny's gone.

'We write every week,' she said calmly. 'My parents are well thank you.'

He looked at her steadily for a few seconds and then smiled and nodded, 'Good.'

Eve had slept late the morning after her argument with Jenny. When she woke Judy was sitting on the opposite bed reading. She looked up. 'How are you?'

'Bit woozy, hand's hurting.' Eve's mouth felt furry from sleep.

Judy went out and came back with a glass of water and a tablet. 'The doctor said you can take this for pain.'

When Eve had taken the tablet Judy said,' The good news or the bad?'

Eve groaned. 'Come on, tell me all.'

'Well,' Judy settled herself on her bed,' Jenny and Steve have gone.'

'Thank God,' said Eve softly.

'And....they've ripped off everything they could carry. Snow boots, parkas, a typewriter from the office....'

'A typewriter! How the hell...'

'God knows. Avram is furious. He and Herzl had a yelling match you could hear in Damascus. Herzl is really in the doghouse.'

'Stupid bastard.'

'They brought up about you....'

'What about me?' cut in Eve defensively.

'Oh just that you obviously knew them but I made it clear they weren't friends. You'd just met them in a hostel in Jerusalem. You didn't like them and would be glad they'd gone.'

Eve was quiet for a moment. Then she said, 'Did they say anything about my hand?'

'No, they didn't seem to make the connection. But they knew about Mick. Maybe he'll come back. I miss him.'

'Mm, me too.'

The Golan changed rapidly as spring moved back the snow line. Wild flowers appeared on the hill sides, spreading deep colours beneath the clear blue sky. The weather settled into days of sunshine, nights when the moon hung white and huge beneath the stars.

Meni's window stayed open as the volunteers sat up late with the reservist guards, drinking coffee and changing records. Jefferson Airplane, Janis

Joplin, the Stones beat out through clouds of cigarette smoke drifting through the air like slowboats into the night. The moon was bright enough to read by. Meni rolled joints and made them laugh with stories from the army.

'In my first week they put me in prison.'

'Come on Meni. Don't be crazy,' grinned Luke. ' This isn't Nazi Germany.'

Meni shook his head. 'It true,' he said in his lazy gentle voice. 'I was asleep, very asleep, deep, deep. The sergeant come in and shout, Get up! I didn't think, I put down my hand, pick up my shoe and throw it. It hit his nose.' Everyone laughed. 'Two weeks in prison they give me.'

He shrugged. 'Everyone go to prison sometimes from the army. All the boys. They get tired, angry. Three years. It a long time. No fun for three years. Get up! Do this! Do that! So they make trouble and go to prison. They have a change.'

The volunteers began to leave. The Swiss boys first followed by the Dutch group. Judy and Eve were alone in the volunteers' house with Meni. Luke had a room in a house further up the moshav. Eve thought he was sleeping with one of the moshav wives, although she wasn't sure who.

'What happens now?' said Eve one morning to Judy. They were sitting in the dining room waiting to clear breakfast. 'We stayed until the end of the season.'

'I know,' said Judy, 'But I don't feel ready to leave.' Her voice dropped. She looked cautiously at Eve. 'I thought of perhaps staying until next winter.'

Eve stared at Judy. She's changed a lot, she thought. The army trousers looked worn now, professional. Judy's skin was tanned a deep ,nut brown. She looked strong and fit from the winter's skiing. Ezra allowed her to ride occasionally, although he said no to Eve. 'Not yet Eve. I don't want accidents.' She was disappointed but glad for Judy. Eve wondered again if Judy would ever leave. And while she stays, I couldn't bear to go and think of what I was missing.

She grinned broadly and put out her hand. 'We'll stay until the end of the summer, right?'

Judy's face broke into a relieved smile. 'Right,' and they shook hands, laughing delightedly. You need a good friend in this life, thought Eve.

Once the decision had been taken the *moshavniks* seemed to change towards them. Ezra offered to give Eve riding lessons. Avram asked Judy to be the housekeeper, looking after the guest rooms. They were both given a rise.

'They're letting us in,' said Judy thrilled.

'Soon they give you a house,' said Meni. 'Tell them you want number 16. It the best.'

'Next week,' grinned Judy.

To herself Eve felt less certain. They need us, she thought. Of course they're pleased we're staying. Who else would work in this deserted settlement in the middle of summer. They haven't even got a swimming pool. But she was also excited, glad to be more involved.

Eve was asked to work in the kitchen. Sometimes waking early she would walk up the mountain road, the sun already bright at five, the night patrol about to finish their shift. The guest house would be deserted. The only way in was through the big kitchen window. She knew how to prise it open and climb in. By the time Avram came up with the key she would be stirring coffee, toast browning under the grill.

'You sleep here?' Avram would laugh.

One morning he handed her the key. 'You're in charge now Eve.' She slipped it into the pocket of her shorts. Have to stay now, she thought.

On a still, hot morning in May Eve walked into reception to find a young couple in shorts and singlets talking to Etty.

Etty smiled when she saw Eve. 'Good. You can to help me Eve. This is Norbert and Hilary. They sleep in your house. You can to take them now?' Eve nodded as Etty went on,' and don't forget our house is number eleven. You don't to visit for some weeks. Come with Judy for coffee.'

Eve smiled at the warmth in Etty's voice. Can't have been that obvious how I felt about Moishe, she thought with relief. 'We'll come tonight.' Then turning to the volunteers, she said, 'Nice to meet you.'

Norbert nodded, a friendly smile on his square tanned face. He had long blond hair tied back in a pony tail. His arms and legs were a deep golden brown , his feet bare in worn leather sandals.

'We are very tired,' he said. His accent was German. 'We had to walk about four kilometres in the sun. Hilary isn't used to it.'

'You're not joking,' said Hilary. She was a tiny gutsy figure with a broad cockney accent. Long black hair hung round her shoulders and her wrists were hung with bangles. Eve also counted six rings, three gold chains at her neck and long silver earrings. Must take her forever to get undressed, she thought amused.

Eve shouldered Hilary's rucksack and they walked down the mountain. Hilary talked all the way.

'Blimey it's a bloody long way up that 'ill. I said to Norby this is bloody mad, but there weren't no cars. Except them Druze. But they never stop. They told us that on kibbutz. Was you on a kibbutz?'

'For a while,' said Eve,' and...'

'Well we was for about three weeks weren't we Norby? Anyway we got fed up and Norby wanted to move on. So here we are. Mind you,' she looked about disdainfully,' Gawd knows where this place is. Couldn't even find it on the bleeding map.'

'They probably haven't got round to gridding it yet,' said Eve and Norbert laughed. He's bright, thought Eve. Good English. They're going to be a laugh these two. Meni will love Hilary.

Norbert and Hilary settled in quickly. Norbert had grown up on a farm and at nineteen seemed to have an enormous knowledge of horses. Ezra commandeered him that evening in the bar. Hilary was two years younger, but she made all the decisions. 'Right, we'll stay for three weeks. See 'ow it goes,' she said as Norbert looked at her with a querying eyebrow. 'I don't mind what I do. Cosy little place this ain't it?' She looked round contentedly at the group of volunteers and *moshavniks*.

'Sure,' Norbert said. 'That's good.'

'Where are you from Norbert?' asked Meni.

'South Germany. Near a little town, you won't know it.'

'You work there or student.'

'I have left,' said Norbert simply.

'Travelling,' said Hilary.' We were in Greece, on Spetze. But it was very Club Mediteranee. Not our style was it Norby?' He shook his head gravely. 'So we decided to come 'ere. Tracy, my mate from Bat'ersea, she come last year wiv 'er boyfriend. Said it was very nice. So we come, but kibbutz was a bit dead. You know,' she jabbed Judy on the arm who laughed out loud.

'Yes, right Hilary. Of course,' and Judy subsided into giggles.

'Wot's the matter wiv 'er?'

'Nothing. Honestly Hilary, she's always like that. We're very glad you came. It's lovely to have new faces.' Eve turned to Judy and gave her a hard stare. 'We're supposed to be seeing Etty and Moishe tonight, for coffee. Time we were going.'

Norbert and Hilary slept in the room next to Eve and Judy. They were passionate and athletic lovers. Norbert seemed to talk more when alone with Hilary, his cool voice murmuring on and on through the night.

Perhaps he's shy, thought Eve. Hilary's so full of life. She doesn't seem to worry about anything.

But Norbert often looked strained, his face creased in a frown as he sat with the others in the bar. He barely spoke unless directly questioned.

One night Eve sat late on the balcony after everyone had gone to bed. She heard a movement behind her and turned to see Norbert.

'Can't sleep,' he grinned apologetically.

'Come and sit down,' Eve said. 'It's a lovely night.'

'Every night is beautiful in Israel.'

She nodded in agreement. They sat quietly for a while. Then Norbert said,' Are you a student?'

'I was. History. I went to France with my boyfriend afterwards. We split up and I came here. How about you?'

Norbert's face was pale under the moon, lined with thought.

As though he were engaged in some struggle. It's not easy being a nineteen old German in Israel, she thought. Perhaps Hilary doesn't understand.

'I was studying to be a doctor.' He stopped.

'What happened?' she prompted gently.

'I left.' He didn't say anymore. Eve offered a cigarette. They smoked in silence.

Maybe he prefers horses, she thought and his father pushed him into medicine. She began to build a fantasy of Norbert the country boy, happy on the farm, in love with horses, his one passion and a tyrannical father always pushing him to study. Mother's probably dead, she thought.

'All my life I wanted to be a doctor,' Norbert suddenly said. 'My parents were very proud when I got my place. I was away from home for most of the year. Then I went back for a holiday at Easter.' His voice had dropped, his face tense, sad lines drawn downwards from his mouth.

A chill went through Eve.

'My parents were talking late one night. I woke up. I don't know why. I went out to the bathroom. It's opposite their room. Their door was open. Something made me stop and listen. Some word which hit my subconscious mind, like a trigger. They were talking about the war.'

He turned to Eve, his face hard, intense. 'They never talked about the war with me. I always thought it was because they felt too sad.

Then I heard my father say, 'When I was a guard at Mauthausen Rolf was my sergeant.

'Mauthausen! He said Mauthausen Eve! You know what that was?'

She nodded, her mouth dry, her back stiff with tension. Concentration camp shot repeatedly through her mind.

'That word hit me like a punch. I wanted to die, Eve. Really, to die. ' He rubbed a hand across his eyes wearily.

'I walked into their room. My parents looked at me in surprise. 'What is it Norbert?' my father said. In the exact same voice as when I was small and had nightmares. 'What is it son?'

I said, ' You were a concentration camp guard?' Neither of them of spoke, not in defence, not in shame, not in explanation. Just nothing.

Then I left. I left Germany. Everything. Now I am here.'

Norbert looked at Eve, his eyes washed with uncertainty, fear. Her heart went out to him in his misery.

'Tell me Eve. You are Jewish. I am not. You tell me Eve, should I go back, or not?'

She almost couldn't stand it. Another question, alongside all the others. How much responsibility are we all supposed to bear?

She thought of Jenny's agonised cry, 'Wasn't my fucking fault! I wasn't even born! ' Of Leah's scars, of her own words to her father all those years ago, 'I would never do that, just stand in a line, like a sheep.'

And now here was the worst nightmare, a blood relation of one of them. Appealing to her for advice. What would my father say she thought? My father who so badly wanted to fight back, who never even made it to the War of Independence.

*

'It is written in the Talmud,' Know ye not that there is a prince and a great man fallen in Israel today.' A shudder blew through the crowd, five thousand strong, as they stood in Trafalgar Square to hear Michael's speech. It was the end of April 1947. Dov Gruner had been hung in Palestine. The Irgun posted up warnings all over the Mandate threatening a hanging for a hanging.

'The British Government say our young Irgunists are merely hooligans, murderers, aimless criminals. ' Michael's voice carried across the square as the crowd stood in respectful silence. 'But this is not true my friends. Gruner was a hero who spent five years in the Jewish Brigade of the British army. He was wounded twice in the war against Facism. ' He paused to allow this to sink in.

'No these brave young men are not delinquents, but dedicated freedom fighters and underground soldiers, fighting for the same reasons they fought Hitler. For their nation and their beliefs.'

'I tell you my friends this is a black day for the British people. We say to the Government now, before any more blood is shed, Quit Palestine! Give up the Mandate! Allow the Jewish people the peace and freedom they deserve!'

For a moment there was silence and then spontaneous clapping spread through the crowd, banked up to the far steps. Jack looked down at the mass of faces as he stood next to Michael on the platform. This must be the beginning of the end, he thought. They will go soon, they must.

He shaded his eyes and scanned the front rows for Deborah. She caught sight of him and waved and then held her arms high as she clapped, twisting and turning to those around her, calling to friends to keep clapping.

Jack was filled with a tremendous longing for her, as he watched her body move in the crowd, crying out to people who were turning to go, demanding more from them. Her long hair moved with her, lifting in a great wave and then settling, curling round her face as she laughed up at him from time to time. 'She's a lovely girl. You're a lucky man,' came Michael's voice in his ear.

Jack brought Deborah home to his parents' flat that evening. Her face was flushed with the success of the day as they all squeezed into the tiny kitchen. Jack's mother served up schnitzel and fried potatoes.

'There must have been at least five thousand Mrs Stone, what do you think Jack?'

'Could have been more,' he mumbled, his mouth full of peas. 'Another piece of schnitzel?' May Stone leaned across Jack to fill up Deborah's plate. Jack and Deborah exchanged grins. 'Now go on, I want to hear it all. Oy! Terrible thing hanging that young man.'

'They loved Michael's speech, ' Debroah continued. ' You could see it really moved them. An old woman burst into tears behind me, leaning on a policeman's shoulder.'

Jack's mother laughed. '*Nu*, this should make them think twice. Solly, help Deborah to some potatoes.'

Solly reached forward grumbling to himself as Deborah covered her plate with her hands, 'No really I'm full .'

'You see,' frowned Solly. 'The girl's had enough.'

'Meshugganah!' snapped May. 'Give me the plate.'

Solly lapsed into a stream of Yiddish, as May shoved plates across the table. Deborah suppressed a giggling fit behind her serviette.

'I'm sorry Deborah. But you'd better get used to it,' grinned Jack apologetically. 'This is a crazy household.'

'At least you all say what you think, even if I can't understand. My mum and dad do it all with raised eyebrows and prolonged silences.'

Jack nodded and then went to answer the telephone which was ringing in the hall.

A voice he didn't recognise said, 'Fitz wants to meet you, Friday, 10.am.' Then the line went dead.

Back in the kitchen order had been restored. Deborah was peeling an apple and chatting to Solly about the ward she was working on. May was stacking plates in the sink. They had pushed the table back against the wall to give more space. On the stove the kettle was working itself up into a loud whistle.

'Who was it Jack?' Solly asked.

'Wrong number.'

Deborah stared at him, eyes quizzical. Then she said, 'Phone hasn't been the same since the war.'

She stood up to turn down the gas.

'I eat enough for a week at your mum's,' Deborah said as they walked to the bus stop after dinner.

Jack was silent, thinking of the message to meet Fitz. Would this be his chance to get deeper into the struggle? He felt taut, ready for action, his resolve hardened by Gruner's death. Michael's words echoed in his head, 'Quit now or suffer the consequences!' Would he be part of those consequences?

'Can you tell me about it Jack?' Deborah stood in front of him, smoothing down his shirt collar, her fingers soft at his neck.

He felt a shudder of desire travel the length of his body. Saw it reflected in her large dark eyes. It was so hard to have secrets from her. He felt it was imperative she understand it was not from choice. He'd tell her everything right now. If he could. But that's no way to conduct an underground war, he told himself sharply.

'When there is something to tell love, you'll be the first to hear.'

She dropped her eyes, rummaged in her handbag for the bus fare. Then she looked up and said simply, 'I'll be there if you need me.'

The following Friday Jack went to Kilburn to see Fitz. It was some time since they had met. The 'Lost Horizon' was still not ready. Jack wondered if Fitz was running out of time. Or money?

Fitz led him into the small square back room. The air was stale. An ashtray on the wooden table was overflowing with stub ends and the curtains remained closed. He never opens them, thought Jack.

Fitz sat down behind the table and indicated a chair. For a moment they sat quietly looking at each other. Fitz was wearing a thick brown sweater under a grey flannel jacket, even though it was a warm day. Jack was wearing a short sleeved shirt.

But I never feel the cold, thought Jack. Must be chilly here for him, after Palestine.

Fitz seemed calmer than on other occasions, more focussed. Only his hands moved, pushing a cigarette pack in geometric lines across the table. His eyes were wide behind the thick glasses, gazing steadily at Jack.

Reading my mind? thought Jack. He felt keyed up, ready for anything Fitz was planning.

'I need to ask some questions now. To know you better,' Fitz suddenly said. Jack nodded.

Fitz questioned Jack for an hour, covering the tiniest details, about his family, their lives in Poland, why they came to England.

'But I don't know which street in Lodz.'

'Are you sure Jack? They didn't say it even once.'

'No never. Why should they? My mother went to Paris when she was twelve.'

The afternoon wore on. He didn't dare look at his watch in case Fitz thought he was tired. Suddenly the questions switched. 'What did you do in the war?'

'I was a commando.'

'Operations?'

He listed the main ones. What would they mean to a Palestinian Jew shut away in the Middle East for the duration?

'What weapons did you use?'

Jack gave a short laugh.'Just about everything I should think. Thompson, .45 Colt, Browning, Vickers K Gun. We had demolition training too. Incendaries, anti-tank grenades, percussion caps, TNT, plastics, strikers, shrapnel mines.'

There was a pause. Jack's throat ached. How much more for God's sake?

'Who was your commanding officer?'

The interrogation started up again, his regiment, the names of the rest of his unit, who was killed, wounded decorated.

'I'm not sure if he was wounded in the leg or the hip. I'm really not sure.' His mind was beginning to whirl. Where was all this leading?

'All right Jack. We can to stop.' Fitz relaxed in his chair, uncrossed his legs.

'So what now?' asked Jack.

Fitz didn't move. 'We will see. Maybe nothing. Go home Jack. Goodbye.'

Jack stood up, feeling uncertain. Then he shrugged and strode out of the room. He walked through the lunchtime streets smoking cigarette after cigarette, his mind turning over the meeting. Are they planning something? Do they want me? Do they trust me? How do you prove you're not MI5?

He thought back to the previous Friday. He had been in the office in Avery Row when two men in dark suits came in. They started talking to Michael, asking about the newspaper.

'It comes out every Friday, in time for *Shabbos*,' said Michael. 'We can put you on the subscription list if you like.' He turned to Jack and gave him a slow wink.

Snoopers, thought Jack. Special Branch maybe?

One of the men was studying a large map of Palestine on the wall. Stuck into many places were small red flags. 'What are these for?' he asked in a public school accent.

Michael grinned. 'Those mark all the recorded attacks made on the British. Coffee?'

The men exchanged blank glances. 'No. We'll see you again.'

As they left Michael called out cheerily, 'Anytime. We're open office hours.'

After they had gone he turned to Jack, 'MI5 on our tails again.'

'Blind as bats the pair of them.'

A week after the meeting with Fitz, Jack had a message to meet at the Palestinian's house again, this time in the evening. The front of the house was dark when he arrived. In the back room the lamp was lit, casting a soft white light over the table. In the room with Fitz were two other men.

Fitz introduced them. 'Jack, this is Harry and Simon.'

Harry nodded curtly. He was a tall man built like a boxer with a square red face.

An experienced soldier, thought Jack with interest.

Simon was much younger, around twenty, long and thin with delicate pale hands. He smiled at Jack and said, 'Hello.'

'I tell you to come,' said Fitz,' because we want that you join our cell. We are four, like all Irgun cells. We are an active cell.'

'Active?' said Jack. 'In what way?'

'We're the blokes that plant the bombs,' cut in Harry. He had a low growl of a voice. Bit of a sergeant major, thought Jack. But he liked his direct manner. Someone to trust in a tight spot.

Jack nodded and said in a cool voice,' I have done this kind of work before.'

Simon grinned, 'So have I. In the school lab.'

There was a silence as everyone looked at Simon.

Then Jack said, 'Been in the army?'

'No.' Simon stopped, his round face reddening. 'After grammar school I was at university. Then the war ended...' he tailed off.

'Simon is a good boy,' said Fitz sharply. 'He fooled the army so he don't have to do National Service. Instead he is with us, in the Irgun.'

Jack nodded. 'What did you study at this university?'

'Chemistry.'

Harry gave Jack a triumphant grin.

Jack smiled. 'I suppose that'll come in handy.'

'We ask you because of your experience Jack' said Fitz.' And because we know we trust you.' There was a pause.

Jack could hear a train rumble over the bridge above the High Street. They checked me out then, he thought. To be sure.

'You can trust me,' he said. 'God knows I'm ready for some action.'

'Ok,' said Fitz and he smiled. They all shook hands and a smile slipped for a second from Harry's lips too.

'In the cell everything is very secret Jack. We look for a long time to make four. You only know us. You don't know nobody else in another cell. They don't know you. Then, if you are taken, there is not much you can to say.'

'I understand.'

'Good. Now we have some work. We have a plan to blow up some trucks in an M.O.D. yard. Harry?'

They all looked at Harry who began to speak in short broken off sentences.

'Right. The British said they won't give weapons. Not to the Arabs. Not to the Jews. Bloody liars, aren't they?' He looked round the room at the three men who waited expectantly. 'We've had a tip off. They're fitting out armoured cars. To send to Jordan. This is our plan. You, Simon. You've got the innocent face. Buy up some sodium chlorate, lots of it. If anyone asks, say it's to kill the weeds on your uncle's farm in Kent.'

Simon nodded, running a hand backwards through his smooth brown hair in short excited movements. 'I can keep it in the garage. We don't use it anymore. It's filled with rubbish. I think mum's got a key somewhere.'

'Whatever, but keep it locked. Me and Fitz'll make the bomb.'

'What about me?' said Jack.

'Right, you.' Harry stabbed a short stubby finger at Jack. The top was missing above the last joint.

Maybe he lost that making bombs, thought Jack, suddenly worried he was stuck with a bunch of amateurs.

'You get down to the yard. I'll give you the address. Take photos. Use that memory of yours. I want to know about guards, dogs, lights. The lot. Got it?'

Harry handed him a camera and a roll of film. 'If we get it right and set fire to the trucks it'll be in every newspaper. That'll show the British it's not clever to lie.'

Fitz disappeared to make coffee. Jack lit a cigarette and offered the pack round. Harry took one and went over to stand by the window. Jack eyed him for a moment and then said, 'Army or navy?'

'Army,' grunted Harry. An awkward silence fell over the room.

Then Simon turned to Jack and said, 'How long have you known Fitz?' Without waiting for Jack to reply he went on, 'He doesn't give much away does he? I mean, I don't even know if he's married.'

'Maybe he prefers it that way,' said Jack, staring at Harry.

The silence deepened. It was a relief when Fitz arrived with the coffee.

In the next few days Jack felt himself move back into familiarity, senses alert, body tight in his clothes, his mind ready to absorb detail, mark out territory. He knew how to spend the minimum time for the maximum information, remain unnoticed.

He visited the depot several times, on different days, in the morning, evening and late at night. He took photographs from every angle and used up the role of film. After his parents had gone to bed one evening, he spent the night in the bathroom developing photographs.

They met at Fitz's house ten days later. The walls of the back room were lined with crates marked Government Surplus. Jack could see radio parts in one. Fitz and Harry were deep in conversation when Simon led the way into the room. Harry's face was creased with concentration his hand gripped to Fitz's shoulder.

Then Fitz turned and nodded brusquely at Jack and Simon. He shrugged Harry aside and said, 'Ok. Let's do some work.'

'Everything ok?' asked Jack.

'You have the photos?' said Harry gruffly, ignoring his question.

Jack nodded and pulled open his coat, taking out a large envelope hidden in the lining.

'I managed to take photos from all round. You can see the guards.'

Harry took the photos and scrutinised them carefully. He handed them on to Fitz and Simon.

'There are no dog patrols and the yard is not that well lit. I think they're a bit lax personally. They don't actually leave the trucks unguarded. But they're casual. You could easily nip out unseen.'

He pulled out a photograph from the pile. 'On the corner, just here,' he pointed to the fence, 'the wire is a bit lower and I think it's loose at the edge. You could be through that in seconds.'

'They look young, the soldiers,' said Fitz.

'Definitely not veterans,' said Jack and Simon gave a short laugh.

Harry nodded sharply, ' Thorough job mate. What about you Simon?'

'Oh everything's fine. I've got the stuff. It's all padlocked in the garage. You can come round anytime.'

In the dim light of the standard lamp they stared at each other, tense with energy and expectation. Jack saw reflected in their faces his own desire to strike back. How could his brother bear to miss this? he thought with a pang.

'We'll meet on Sunday night, eleven o'clock, Simon's garage. Make the bomb and take it to the yard.' Harry pulled on a thick black coat. His shoulders seemed massive in the shadows.

He's no amateur, thought Jack. He went home and slept deeply, the photos inside his pillow case.

The telephone rang early the next morning. Jack was still half asleep as he groped into the kitchen to answer it. 'Jack darling. Deborah. Were you asleep?'

Jack mumbled 'No, not really.'

'Michael wants to see us. At his flat in an hour.'

Jack looked at his watch. It was seven thirty. 'Did he say what it was about. It's not even eight for God's sake.'

Deborah spoke in a low tense voice, 'I don't know Jack. But I think something has happened. He sounded rather serious.'

It's time we went out, had some fun, thought Jack as he shaved.

Fitz had warned him it would be difficult in the cell. 'You say nothing Jack. Not to you girlfriend, your mother, not even you dead grandmother. The police have ears everywhere. You keep stom! Say nothing. Understand?'

Jack had understood. But to keep anything from Deborah felt like a deliberate betrayal of his love for her. My God ! What if she had some awful secret from him. A tiny voice whispered in his ear, Like someone else.

He shook his head to clear it, Not a time for stupid thoughts. Deborah is in the Hammers. She understands there is different work, some of it secret.

It'll be all right.

Several members of The Hammers were in Michael's flat when he arrived. Deborah pulled him onto the sofa, her perfume filling his nostrils as he relaxed next to the warmth of her body. It'll be all right, he told himself again.

Michael began speaking, 'I have some bad news I'm afraid. Simon Block's been arrested.'

Jack's head jerked up in stunned amazement. His eyes met Michael's blue stare. For a second Michael looked steadily into Jack's eyes and them turned away. Give nothing away, thought Jack. Say nothing! Remember the cell.

'Apparently he'd been buying large quantities of sodium chlorate to make a bomb. Stored it in his garage. The chemist he bought the stuff from tipped off the police and MI5 put a watch on the house. Saw him go in with the chemicals a few days ago. Nabbed him last night. His mother phoned me at two this morning.'

Jack's mind was racing, trying to sort information, regain control.

We all could have been caught last night, he realised. MI5 were onto Simon as we were planning the attack. Damn! Damn!. This could blow open the whole cell. He's only a kid, maybe he'll talk. I wasn't completely wrong about the amateurs, but maybe we were all bloody amateurs, letting Simon buy all the stuff alone.

Michael was speaking again,' Naturally it's essential no connexion is made between our organisation and Simon. We must maintain our perfectly legitimate front otherwise we will be accused of being terrorists.'

'So we're just going to leave him to rot,' cried Deborah. 'I was at school with Simon.'

'No of course not Deborah, 'smiled Michael. 'But it is very important we categorically deny this young man had anything to do with the Hammers. Just attended a couple of meetings. Meanwhile we put up the best lawyer in town and give him the brief that Simon, who after all is only twenty, was lead astray by older men.'

'That's not good enough. He'll go to prison. Alone. We must stand by him.'

'Come on Deborah,' Jack put his arms around her shoulders. 'This is England. He's not going to be tortured or put to death. He'll get a prison sentence, but he'll get out early for good behaviour.'

Deborah wrenched Jack's arm away and threw herself to her feet, her long hair flowing round her shoulders.

He thought of the first time he met her parents, when she had jumped up to defy her father. She's tough, he thought and felt a warm rush of pride.

'For Heaven's sake Jack, what if it was you they'd caught!'

'If it were me, ' he snapped back, ' my priority would be the work of the Hammers. The Irgun needs our funds and it needs our propaganda war against the British and against the blind stupidity of Ben Gurion's mob. Our cause must be protected. We can't be implicated.'

Inside he was pleading, please understand my sweet, don't push me to reveal something we'll both regret. It was the first time they had raised their voices to each other.

They met at Fitz's house the following evening. The room seemed hollow, empty without Simon.

'He'll get years for carrying explosives,' said Harry his voice gruffer than ever.

Fitz nodded and looked at Jack. 'About the boat.'

'What about it?' said Jack, suddenly afraid.

'It may be difficult to go on Jack. We need the money to pay lawyer's fees for Simon.'

The room was very quiet, each man full of his own thoughts, his own despair.

'There will be another chance,' said Fitz, his large eyes staring at the other two. 'We'll be in touch.

The death of Dov Gruner, the arrest of Simon, the threatened loss of the boat.

Jack felt the weight of failure. His failure, the failure of the cell to take proper care, the failure of the British to understand that the cause of the Jewish people is a just one. God! where will it end ? he thought as he walked home.

*

CHAPTER SIXTEEN

'Close your windows, close your windows.' The voice was soft, dreamy, floating through the open door.

Eve woke up slowly, reaching for consciousness through clouds of sleep. Two figures stood in the doorway, the outline of their rifles clear in a shaft of moonlight.

'Close your windows, close your windows.' She saw now it was Herzl speaking, Zoar standing beside him. 'There will be a terrorist attack soon.'

Then why close the windows, thought Eve, her eyes sticky, her mind still trying to surface. They could come in through the doors.

Suddenly Judy sat bolt upright in the opposite bed and screamed, 'Oh my God!' She reached for her jumper and looked at her watch. Then in a perfectly calm voice she said, 'Ok. It's 1.15. What time are they due?'

Right, thought Eve. They can't say we panicked. But her insides churned. She threw back her bedcovers, wide awake now, forgetting she was naked in the hot summer night. Herzl grinned approvingly. Blast! she thought and pulled on a T-shirt and jeans. When she looked up Zoar and Herzl had disappeared.

'Bloody Hell Judy! What do we do?' She struggled with the zip on her jeans. Her hands refused to work properly.

'Christ knows! You'd better wake Norbert and Hilary. I'll go and find those two jerks and tell them we expect protection.' Judy strode out of the room and banged on Meni's door.

Fat lot of use he'll be, thought Eve as she approached Norbert's door. Hilary will go mad. She tapped gingerly on the door. 'Norbert, Hilary, wake up.'

Hilary answered, her voice slurred, far away, 'What is it?'

'Er...Herzl came over, said something about a terrorist attack....'

Before she could say anymore high pitched screaming came ffom the other side of the door. Eve decided to leave Norbert to cope.

She went back into the living room. As she went past Meni's room she could hear Judy speaking in a low voice. Someone was rummaging about under the bed.

The balcony doors were awkward to close and as she grappled with them a voice thundered behind her, 'Just let those bastards try anything!'

Eve spun round to see Judy in her army trousers, Meni's Kaloshnikov raised to her shoulder, right leg in front of the left, eyes glued to the sights. For a split second Eve felt a thrill of envy shoot through her. Then she cried, 'For Christ's sake Judy, is that thing loaded?'

'Dunno, shall I try and see?'

Before Eve could say anything Judy leapt out onto the balcony and pressed the trigger. A huge crack of gunfire shattered the night air. Eve watched in horror as a long orange flame streaked towards the olive grove.

'Have you gone raving mad?'

Herzl and Zoar appeared from the kitchen, coffee slopping in cups, mouths open wide in shock. The room suddenly filled up. Reservist guards from the doorstep jumped over the balcony wall, yelling in Hebrew, guns held out in front of them. From all round the moshav behind them came shouts and cries as the *moshavniks* awoke in terror. More and more people pushed their way into the uproar in the living room.

Meni walked out of his room dressed only in his underpants. His small hairy body jerked up and down like a comic in a silent film. 'O.k, where they are? Where they are?' he shouted, his eyes creased with sleep. He's stoned, thought Eve. What an army!

It took hours to explain that Herzl and Zoar had only been joking. In the middle of it all Avram's wife came in with two huge chocolate cakes. A small party broke out.

Hilary packed twice, sobbing, 'Get me out of this bloody place, Norby, they're all bonkers. ' Norbert soothed her, unpacked her rucksack each time and finally gently peeling off her clothes, laid her on the bed and folded himself carefully on top of her tiny soft body. Eve pulled their door shut, her eyes flickering over the slim white moons of Norbert's buttocks as they moved rhythmically in the early morning light.

As the sun peaked above the distant hills Chava, Avram's wife, collected the empty plates and left with Moishe and Etty. 'Next time give us more notice,' she laughed. 'We make kebab.'

Avram remained in the living room. He was wearing a crisp white suit and chain smoked a box of very thin cigars. He should be in a five star hotel, thought Eve .

Meni had been hauled off by soldiers who looked like military police. 'It's not his fault,' Judy kept protesting.'

Herzl and Zoar sat on the floor against the wall.

'What happen Eve?' Avram asked quietly as she sat down on a cushion on the floor.

'Things got a bit out of hand' she shrugged and ran a hand through her hair.

Herzl began talking in rapid Hebrew. Avram listened for a while and then put up his hand, shaking his head. 'Crazy, all of you. Eve, if there are terrorists, you go to the shelter, ok?'

She nodded, awed by the serious look on his face.

Judy came in with coffee and handed it round. Avram continued, 'And you Judy, we don't want you to play war please. You are not to touch the guns, any guns. Ok Judy?'

Judy's face was sullen. 'What will happen to Meni?'

'Nothing. He come back tomorrow.' Avram stood up and ran his fingers down the immaculate creases of his trousers. 'No more trouble you guys. Ok?' Everyone except Judy nodded. 'The guests are very frightened. I have to tell them not to speak to the newspaper. This is very bad for the *moshav*.'

Avram strode out. There was a silence while everyone sipped coffee. Eve thought, Maybe they'll ask us to leave. I couldn't bear it. Not yet!

Then Herzl spoke, his voice low. 'You want we come back tonight. Play the game again.'

Judy let out a scream of rage, her face bright red. Then suddenly she started laughing and they all joined in until the guards put their heads round the door to see what was going on.

There became less to do on the moshav as the visitors drifted away. Occasionally coach tours filled with American women from Chicago or Philadelphia would make a photo stop outside reception. In the kitchen and the guest house there was little work and long coffee breaks.

One morning the volunteers were taken to fields at the bottom of the Golan. 'They don't know what to do with you now the snows all gone away,' laughed Meni. 'But one thing for sure, they never tell you to go.'

The field were next to the Banias, a series of pools where the source of the Jordan river rose. It was raining when they jumped down from the truck. The pools and the riverbanks were deserted. In fine weather the Druze gathered, the boys splashing in the cold clear water, the elders in white headdresses and long black robes brushing fingertips in greeting, the women cutting fruit for children.

The field was very muddy. Eve took off her shoes and rolled up her trousers. She picked up a bowl of melon seed to sprinkle on the ground. Herzl gave her his army parka and she sank into its warm comfortable folds.

She set off along the ploughed rows ankle deep in mud. The steady spring rain soaked the seeds as they lay on the surface. There was no wind, just the rain falling and the squelch of mud and the swish of Herzl's parka as she cast the seeds from her bowl. Searching in the pockets for a handkerchief she found a packet of condoms and a bullet, discarded like a five pence piece, a chipped marble. She didn't say anything to Herzl, but replaced them in his pocket and walked on, wiping her nose on the sleeve of his parka.

The rain falling, the muddy field. In France she and Andy had worked for a week on a smallholding, a hundred miles north of Montpelier. Jean and Fabienne, she remembered with a warm glow. They were open, friendly people, offering a room and food in exchange for their work. It was like a holiday. Jean had asked her to weed the potato field as they sat drinking coffee on the first morning in the big dusty farmhouse.

'I like potatoes very much,' smiled Jean. She had gone out for three days, pulling weeds from the sodden ground and dropping them into an old enamel bowl. She had felt herself set apart. The grey sky, the rain that never really cleared, the bark of a dog in the distance. It was as though she were some slow moving speck on the wide damp horizon.

Andy and Jean dug the field later in the week. Andy in a wide-brimmed straw hat, small next to Jean's tall but fragile figure. From the top vegetable patch Eve stared down on them. How to narrow the distance spreading between her and Andy? The rain suddenly became heavier. Everyone ran for the house. Jean cried out, 'Tomorrow we go to Bernard's to help with a fence.'

For once it was a sunny day. The ground was soaked and each time they dug a post hole it filled with water. Bernard had so much energy, digging a hole frantically, laughing and gabbling to Jean all the time. Then running to help Andy ram a post home. Afterwards they all clattered into the vast farmhouse kitchen. Bernard, a big red-faced man, stood at the table carving a French loaf thicker than his arm. Duck pate in huge tubs appeared, farm butter and currant jam. From a barrell in an alcove large jugs of frothy red wine were drawn.

'Cigarette?' Herzl caught up with her as the last of her melon seeds flew down to stick on the dark brown mud. Eve took one from the damp packet. Herzl's hair was sticking to his forehead.

'Wouldn't you like your coat back?'

'No, no, it's ok.' He waved his hand at her and attempted to light a match but the box was too wet. 'Wait. I have matches here. ' Here reached into the inside pocket of the parka his hand deliberately smoothing her breast and cried, 'Ok. Here. He lit her cigarette with a flourish. On his face was a look, half crude, half impish.

She pulled deep on the cigarette and blew smoke across his face as she turned. Pick on someone your own level, she thought. Then, as if it were now a sweet memory instead of just pain she thought, Andy would never do that.

Norbert and Hilary suddenly announced they were going to India. 'It's been smashing ain't it Norby,' said Hilary as they sat in front of the guest house one warm June evening. The rain had finally cleared and the weather had settled into a promised Israeli summer, hot and dry. 'Everyone's so bleeding friendly and that, but let's face it cock, their ain't much doing'ere. I mean, 'oos going to trek up 'ere just cause of them 'orses. Not even a bleeding pool.'

The *moshavniks* had set up a barbecue on the flat patch of grass and bare earth outside reception. As the sun sank across the Huleh valley the huge white orb of the moon slid up over the far ridge. Sun and moon together, thought Eve. This place is so massively beautifully. But she knew Hilary was right. She looked at Judy, her long slim legs stretched out in cut- off jeans, frayed at the edges. She seems so at home here. Maybe I need more time.

Zoar had a friend, Dani, staying with him. Dani was from Tel Avi, 'But I just spent a year in America doing Business Studies,' he told them as Zoar collected kebabs from the barbecue, passed them around. Dan's father owned a chain of restaurants in Tel Aviv and Jerusalem.

'Wealthy guy,' murmured Judy.

Eve nodded as she chewed on a kebab. Dani was a tall, thin young man. He wore soft blue American jeans turned up at the bottom and expensive white leather tennis shoes. Eve loved American clothes. 'Did you get those in the States?' she pointed to the jeans.

Dani, serious behind black narrow framed glasses, smiled and the skin around his eyes crinkled giving a warm glow to his face. ' Sure. I bought them in New York. Everything is cheaper than in Israel.' He spoke English with a soft American accent, strongly interlaced with harsher Hebrew tones. The mixture was very attractive.

'Have you finished the army?' asked Judy.

'Oh yes, four years ago. I just do ninety days a year, *miluim*, like everyone else.' He had a habit of fixing his eyes carefully on the person he was talking to, but in a quiet unassuming way.

'That's a lot of army,'

'You're not kidding. I didn't miss it when I was in America. But I didn't want to stay there.'

Dani was pulling pieces of meat off the skewer. Eve watched his long slender fingers work gently on the meat, the backs of his hands and his narrow wrists covered with dark hairs. I wonder if all his body is covered with hair, she thought, She had never found body hair attractive on a man. Hairy chests and medallions, she couldn't help thinking, on crowded beaches. Her eyes went automatically to the open neck of Dani's shirt. There was hair but no medallions.

'Why didn't you want to stay in America?' Judy asked.

'I have a lot of family here. But I might go to Hampstead next year. My father has business connections in Hampstead. You know Hampstead?'

He pronounced it Humpsteed. Eve laughed, 'Everyone knows Hampstead. It's like Dizengoff. It's not far from where I live. If I'm back in England you must come and visit.'

'Bloody 'ell Eve,' cut in Hilary, 'What a load of crap you're giving the poor bloke. You ain't going to leave this place. You'll still be 'ere when the bloody Arabs nip back!'

It was June. The perimeter road running past the *moshav* was completely deserted. Not even the army went past. Norbert and Hilary waited for a car to take them down the mountain for the next two days.

'This is ridiculous,' said Hilary, as she threw herself onto Judy's bed and lit a cigarette. 'We'll be 'ere forever. It's a thousand miles to bloody India. Gawd knows why 'e wants to go there.' Judy laughed. Hilary's face softened. 'One thing's flipping obvious. 'E'll never get there without me!'

They set up a card table and chairs made out of wooden crates on the road outside Eve's house, the lowest point on the moshav. 'We'll 'ave to do something or we'll go stark staring raving bonkers. You to deal Norby.' They played for two days, volunteers, soldiers, moshavniks, drifting in and out of the game.

On the third morning Eve walked back down the road from the kitchen at midday to find them gone, the crates lying forlornly on their sides in the road. She felt the sudden prickle of tears in her eyes. Alone again, she thought.

She went with Judy to Moishe's house in the evening. Zoar and Dani were there eating huge slices of cheesecake , drinking white wine and beer.

'So they go at last,' said Zoar, a smile on his face. 'Who next?'

'Nobody,' said Moishe in a loud voice. He looked round the room. 'You all are to stay. The *moshav* need good workers. *Nu*? Etty?'

Etty nodded as she knelt on the floor opening packets of crisps, filling bowls. 'Sure we all stay, build the land.'

'Like in the song,' said Dani his voice soft in the noisy room.'

'Which song?' asked Judy.

'It doesn't matter, they're all the same. We are pioneers, workers, we must go forward. All that stuff.'

Eve felt a stab of pain as everyone laughed. They were laughing at the Zionist songs, the songs of her youth, the songs that had echoed in her ears as she worked her way around this crazy country.

'Those songs are very important. They bring people together. God knows there's little holding Israeli society together now.'

'But it is not 1948 anymore Eve.' Dani replied, his voice suddenly more forceful than before. 'It is 1976. Israel is not the same. Who comes here now?

People come, they have a holiday, go home. That's it!'

'No!' cried Moishe. He held up his hand, thumb pressed on his middle finger, shaking it for attention, 'Listen to me...'

'*Nu*, Moishe,' laughed Zoar. 'You wait, Dani is right. What is there since the Yom Kippur War? Army , army. Ninety days each year we must to go. Everybody sick, Judy. You know what is ninety days? We don't want songs. We want action. The government are old men.'

'And they are all Ashkenazi,' nodded Dani, his eyes grim behind the glasses. 'They shove the pioneers at us, they howl about the *Shoah*, the holocaust Eve, right?' Dani pointed to his chest, 'My family weren't in the *Shoah*. We come from Baghdad. We are sorry, of course. But fifty per cent of Israelis are from the Arab countries. We don't want pioneer songs, we want a place in government.'

Eve felt a shock run through her as she heard Dani dismiss the holocaust as outside his experience.

Moishe nodded vigorously. 'Yes yes, you are right. It must be more equal. But still we need more *Olim*, more immigrants. You know Eve... ' He fixed her with a hard stare, his arms bare to the shoulders in a crisp white singlet. She felt a little jump inside her. She had to prise her eyes away from the long stretch of his skin. 'The Arabs they have big families, lot of childrens. Soon there will be more Arabs than Jews in North of Israel.' He ticked of on his fingers, 'Nazareth, Bethlehem....'

'Moishe, Moishe,' put in Zoar,' there is a life outside Israel. You should go and look. Hey Dani?'

Dani smiled and nodded. 'Some guys like Herzl will never go outside.'

'Why's that?' asked Eve.

'Because they can't take their guns,' said Dani. ' Many Israeli guys are the same. They are not used to going anywhere without their guns.'

Etty laid a hand on her husband's arm. 'That is not why Moishe wants to stay.'

Stars filled the wide sky across the huge bowl of the Huleh valley as they left all together. The moon was behind them. Now and then torches flashed in bushed on the hillsides. The night patrol were checking for terroists.

'Are the skies like this in New York?' Eve asked Dani.

Zoar and Judy had disappeared. They were alone on the rough pitted road. Alone except for the stars and the Golan.

'It's not the same. There are the street lights, they blot out the sky. And the pollution.'

He took her hand and they walked on in silence. There was just the bark of a dog, slither of her sandals on loose pebbles. It was so quiet she began to hold her breath.

They walked on past Eve's house, and beyond the last lights of the *moshav*, down the road towards the valley, deeper and deeper into the endless black and stars of the Golan night. I'll stay here forever , she thought. Her mind skittered and slipped over words, thoughts, pictures. Dani's hand felt cool and comfortable. It was a firm strong hand with a long palm . We're just holding hands. Under the sky. It's very beautiful.

They began to talk in quiet voices. He asked her about England, the weather, her family. He told her his family were Iraqi Jews from Baghdad. He had three brothers and sisters and fourteen cousins. They all lived close to each other in a suburb of Tel Aviv.

She felt awed and jealous. All those people to share your life with, swap impressions. There can't be secrets in such a big family, she thought.

When they arrived back at her house he leant down and kissed her lightly on the lips.

As she lay in bed she thought about Dani and his big family, sitting all together in large living rooms, passing huge plates of food and laughing.

*

'More tea Mrs Stone?' Betty Freedman lifted the silver teapot and reached out for May Stone's cup. The living room was very quiet. Jack and Deborah sat on dining chairs near the table which was pushed up against the wall. Jack's parents were on the plaid three seater in the bay, silhouetted against the sunshine beyond the netted windows. Morris leant on the mantelpiece, pulling on his pipe, his eyes fixed longingly on the door. He'd rather be in the workroom, thought Jack.

May had already removed a pack of cards from her husband as they arrived at the front door and snapped at Jack to comb his hair once more. She now sat straight-backed in her red crepe de chine, pleated from the waist down, her fur stole on her lap. She was thinking that this was a plain dark room and Mrs Freedman could do with more rouge on her cheeks.

Solly was in poor spirits. He'd been challenged by Cyril Rainow to a game at the club that afternoon and he knew he could have beaten him hollow. He was trying to catch Morris' eye to see if they could sneak off to the workshop. He had a spare pack of cards in his trouser pocket.

'So Jack and Deborah want to get married,' said Betty suddenly in her thunderbolt-from-the-blue tone.

Jack sighed inwardly.

It had been Deborah's idea to get the two sets of parents together. It was already June. After Simon had been sentenced to ten years in Wakefield prison for carrying explosives, the cell had gone to ground. Jack was aware Deborah was guessing about his involvement. She was probably too frightened to ask in case she got him into trouble.

'It's time we thought about wedding plans Jack. If you still want me,' she had said playfully on a Sunday afternoon picnic in Hertfordshire.

He looked up at her from the blanket where he lay stretched out in the hit sunshine. 'What do you mean? Come here. ' He pulled her down covering her lips in a fierce hard kiss.

'All right Jack,' she laughed pushing him off and straightening her dress. ' Message received loud and clear. So we'd better get the two families together hadn't we?' She cocked her head, her tone pert, teasing.

Jack groaned. He'd been dreading this moment, her mother and his father. He couldn't imagine them in the same room together. 'If we must.'

Betty Freedman fixed her eyes on May Stone. Jack could see the battle lines forming. 'And what do you think about this Palestine nonsense?' That's it, thought Jack. The first wave over the top and no time for laggards.

May replaced her cup on its saucer, her head tilted to one side as she pursed her lips into her 'polite' smile. Nice bit of china, she thought, but there's no joy in this house. 'Well I think it's a good thing,' she replied.

Her Yiddish tones grated on Jack's ears. He felt aware for the first time of the gulf between the two families. I assumed it was enough we're all Jews, he thought.

His mother was still talking, 'Palestine needs young people. Lieutenant Levy came to my house for dinner you know.'

Jack shifted his knees under his saucer and gave Deborah a knowing look. His mum wouldn't let this lot trample on her.

'Morris and I are in complete agreement, aren't we Morris?' Betty glared at Morris. He gave a slow nod, his lips pressed together.

They've rehearsed this, thought Jack.

'Palestine is no place for our little girl. We would be against this marriage if....'

The room broke into an uproar. Deborah threw herself to her feet crying, 'Mum! How could you!'

Morris carried on nodding saying loudly, 'Yes! yes! yes!'

Jack, desperate to calm the situation, put his arm out and tipped over his cup.

'Jack! Look what you done. All over Mrs Freedman's best floor. *Oy vay*!' His mother was down on her hands and knees scrubbing with a napkin. She looks so tiny, Jack thought with a stab. This is crazy.

Then Solly stood up, adjusting his tie, his smooth face, golden against the fine silver of his hair, still handsome in his fifties.

'Now then, let's all sit down. *Hodje* Jack! *Hodje*!' Their eyes met as Jack obeyed the command of his childhood.

'*Nu*? What have we got here?' Betty opened her mouth to speak but Solly cut her off neatly. 'Two young people. That's all.' His voice rose in mock surprise. 'Like us. Before the war.' He nodded solemnly. 'Before the First War. We got married didn't we? No-one tried to stop us. They are not children anymore. *Nu?* Morris? What d'you say?'

Morris shook his head. But then as he saw his wife arching again he said hastily, 'I suppose you're right. We did some crazy things and look at us now. I was in the trenches you know.' He wagged his pipe at Jack.

'I know,' said Jack quietly. 'Deborah told me. Look we don't want any of you to be upset. But Deborah and I want to get married early next year, once she's got her exams. And then we are going to Palestine. We'd rather go with you're blessing.'

The wedding was set for the end of February. 'We go the following week then,' said Jack as they walked across the park after tea. 'I'll tell Michael.'

'That's fine,' said Deborah her face content. 'I'm so glad they agreed in the end Jack. I didn't want to go against them.'

'I know,' he said.

But time seemed to drag for Jack as events in Palestine entered a new phase of intensity. Three more Irgun prisoners were sentenced to hanging for their part in the great Acre prison escape. The Irgun were searching the streets of the Mandate for hostages, repeating their threat of a hanging for a hanging.

Jack went to see Fitz. 'If I were there I could do something!'

'No Jack! ' Fitz's eyes filled his face as he pulled off his thick glasses and leaned forward in his chair. 'We need you here.'

Jack shook his head. 'Sometimes... I just feel so useless.'

Fitz was pacing the floor now as if trying to transmit his energy to Jack through the floorboards.

'You are doing a lot Jack, listen! You know how it is for the Irgun out there. The Haganah betray our boys to the British. The British torture and murder them. Numbers are still small. Recruitment from England is our priority.'

'Anyone could do that.'

'No Jack. They look up to you. You were a commando.'

Sometimes he wished he wasn't. Sometimes he wished he were just nineteen. Like the lads he marched in the woods. Innocent, free, untrained, unblemished. Then they would take him, by God! They would grab him with greedy arms, pass him from train to boat across the unseen dark of Europe, to the ragged beaches of Palestine. They would give him a weapon, expect from him deeds they would never allow on the dusty streets of London.

He felt like an outsider as June turned to July. Suddenly the newspapers were full of the kidnap of Martin and Paice, two British Sergeants in Palestine. Irgun radio announced they would not be released until the three Irgun prisoners had their sentences commuted.

Tension rose in the training groups. Jack drilled them at midnight because the summer evening were so light. As they marched , turned, lined up smartly, their arms bare in the warm summer air. Jack could sense their urgency. To be there, to help, to carry a gun.

The Vanguard printed transcripts of the Irgun radio messages, warnings, threats.

'Keep up the pressure, right Jack?' Michael kept saying.

Jack nodded as he proofread articles.

'The thing about the British I learned in the commandoes,' he said one morning. 'They hate to think their very own Tommies can be violent. So we keep shoving it under their noses.'

Numbers swelled on Sunday mornings at Speakers' Corner.

Early on the morning of July 29th the three Irgun prisoners were hung. The Irgun in Palestine knew they had to carry out their threat, gallows for gallows. The bodies of the two British Sergeants were strung up in an olive grove outside Netanya. A wave of anti-semitism was unleashed across England.

Michael stood up in Hyde Park the following Sunday before a large crowd. The mood was ugly. The Hammers were gathered round in full force. The police stood two deep along the edge of the crowd.

Michael held up a copy of the Manchester Guardian with the headline, TIME TO GO! blazoned across the front page. 'Listen to your own counsel,' he cried above the shouts of ' murdering bastards' and threats of retaliation. 'It is not just anger against the Jews which has emerged this week. The English people are sick to the stomach with the brutality of their own forces in Palestine.' He stood holding the paper high as the crowd roared and pushed.

As the noise subsided he continued, 'Look at the refugee ship the Exodus. Four and a half thousand refugees herded into British prison ships, turned away kicking and screaming form the Promised Land. People who have already survived Auschwitz.' He waited for the word to sink into the restless crowd.

A bottle flew through the air and smashed behind the Hammers. The police elbowed into the back of the crowd and dragged away a man. For a few seconds a hush fell. They're angry, thought Jack. But they know he's right.

'The British have no right in Palestine, no business there. It is not their country and it is time they left! Let me tell you my friends, the British will never hang another Jew in Palestine!' His words thundered on the air like an ancient prophecy.

Jack felt increasingly restless. It was time for some action and he felt he had a fool proof plan. He arranged to see Fitz at the beginning of September.

'I have an idea.'

The nights were drawing in and Fitz had lit the standard lamp. To Jack it felt like the old times, before Simon was caught, when they were an Irgun terror cell, gathered round the wooden table.

Fitz leaned back in his chair, his eyes small, disinterested. 'What is it?'

Jack pressed on determinedly, 'We went to visit my cousin in Portsmouth in the summer. He took me down to the harbour. The navy has a destroyer there. Listen Fitz,' Jack wanted to grab him by the lapels, make him care. 'It's the destroyer that escorted the Exodus refugees back to Hamburg.'

Fitz moved slightly, his eyes beginning to focus more keenly on Jack. 'You are certain?'

'Oh yes,' said Jack in a low tense voice. 'It's the one. We went to the local pubs. Drank with the sailors. Some of them even talked about it. Sending the Jews back to German soil, in German camps, guarded by German police.' The light was up in Fitz's eyes as both men remembered that vision of hell. Concentration camp survivors beaten unconscious as they struggled, hauled back thousands of sea miles by the British to the land that reviled them.'

'So?'

'We blow it up.'

'Fitz gave a short explosive laugh. 'We do what?'

'Listen, just listen will you. I watched the ship over several days. It's not really guarded. Why should they bother? We pick up uniforms from government surplus, get on board and plant a bomb. Right in the engine room.'

There was silence in the dim dank room. Fitz took a cigarette carefully out of a new packet and lit it. Jack's muscles felt locked in tension. He had gone over the plan so many times in his head. He knew it was foolproof.

'I will think about it Jack.'

'Think about it! What the hell is there to think about? It's time to do something for God's sake. I thought this was an active cell.'

'I said I will think about it.'

There was nothing more to be said. Jack went home and tossed restlessly all night.

They met five days later. Fitz came straight to the point. 'The Irgun command is against the plan.'

'But why for God's sake?'

'There would be too big a loss of life. It would work against us right now. Also, it is too dangerous. One of our cell has already been caught. Maybe next time it will be me. I am the link here. I must to stay free.'

There was nothing else to be said.

Four months, thought Jack impatiently, as he walked home. Then Deborah and I will get married and we'll be off. They won't be able to stop me then.

He knew Fitz was right. The individual must not jeopardise the cause. But in his mind he had seen the ship ablaze, the sufferings of the refugees avenged, the British sailors running along the dockside in disarray.

CHAPTER SEVENTEEN

'You see!' Jack held up the transcript of an Irgun broadcast. 'It's open warfare. The British will give them all the best positions as they pull out. Bastards!'

'Predictable though,' said Michael as he lit a cigarette.

They were in the office, snow piled thickly outside on the kerb. The Government had announced they would leave Palestine in May. It was the signal the Arabs had been waiting for.

'We'll have to fight for every inch now. Funds and recruits, that's the priority.'

Jack nodded grimly, 'Trouble is we're running out of time rapidly.'

They had booked the wedding for the last week in February. They would leave for Palestine five days later.

Jack settled down to wait. He had waited before. It was in his blood. Instilled through long years of war. Just a cog in the wheel of the cause, he told himself. More expendable than Fitz. Less expendable than Simon.

Deborah made wedding lists. 'We'll invite everyone. We may never see them again.' Her mother alternated between dry-eyed sobbing fits and days of martyred silence.

His days were filled with fund-raising, recruitment. At night he trained group after group of eager teenagers.

In spare moments he visited government surplus stores hunting for the best equipment to take with him. He would have liked to take weapons or explosives. He still had some in a friend's garage.

Michael had asked him to look after a few parcels for him, 'just until they're needed,' he'd said with a wink. Jack didn't ask any questions but when he had emptied the boot of the car and stacked the four square parcels in a corner, he opened one. Sticks of gelignite were packed neatly, two deep, six to a row. But he knew he was likely to be searched at Calais, if not Dover. It wasn't worth the risk.

They trained right through the long dark winter, in frost filled woods, often ankle deep in snow. Jack drove them hard, bludgeoned them with slogans, messages, history. Shoved, pushed and bullied them for the cause.

Fitz came to talk to them, in between racing round the country on desperate recruitment drives, from Glasgow to Portsmouth. Jack watched the young faces stare wide-eyed as Fitz stirred their fantasies, their heroism. He will give them the war they crave, he thought.

Deborah passed her nursing exams and they went out to celebrate. Her face shone with excitement by the light of the candle on the restaurant table, as she spoke about hospitals, settlements, pioneering new methods in a new country. It was the week before the wedding. She's lovely, thought Jack, a great stirring of emotion inside him.

'And children Jack. We'll have to have lots. To help build the land. How many do you think, three, four?'

'Oh six at least,' he laughed. 'We'll have to get working.'

She blushed slightly and reached out for his hand. He stroked it gently. 'Feeling shy?'

'A bit.' But then she raised her chin in the familiar determined line towards him. 'But it'll be fine Jack. I'm not worried.'

He wasn't either. The wedding next week and then they'd be off, to a new life. Jews in a home of their own at last. He felt a burden lift from his shoulders as the last few days slipped easily past.

Jack enjoyed the wedding, which surprised him. Afterwards he decided it was because of the atmosphere of departure. It was more like a farewell party. Everyone was there, friends from the Hammers, the army, schooldays, as well as every member of the two families that could be persuaded to gather together. Michael came with a tall elegant young woman they had never seen before. 'Oh, Anna and I go back a long way,' he said casually when Jack raised a querying eyebrow.

There were speeches and telegrams. Deborah and Jack's parents poured champagne into each other's glasses. 'My mother is making a big effort,' whispered Deborah to Jack as they took the first waltz.

'Much appreciated I'm sure,' grinned Jack.

Everyone came up to say goodbye. Many pressed money into their hands. 'If you don't need it, someone out there will,' said Michael when Deborah tried to refuse.

Then it was over and they were in a train rushing towards Sussex and a honeymoon in a friend's cottage. Jack felt a great flood of freedom as they sped past fields and woods. Freedom from parents, the cause, Fitz. He could choose now, he was married, they were a team.

They made love by candlelight on the first night. There was no electricity. Afterwards she said, 'Now I know the touch of your skin.' He felt they had known each other for ever. This is how it should be, he thought and yet he felt privileged to have been touched so deeply.

They arrived back in London on a wet Friday morning and went straight to the Stones' flat. Deborah wanted to unpack, wash her hair. Jack felt restless. London seemed claustrophic after the countryside. He went to see Michael.

'Glad you came over Jack. I was just about to telephone you.'

'What? In Sussex?'

'If necessary, yes.' Michael's eyes crinkled with amusement. 'Fitz wants to see you.'

'Why for God's sake! We're leaving next Tuesday. I'm going to see about the boat train today.'

'He said it was urgent.' Michael's stare was cool, penetrating.

How much does he really know? thought Jack . There was a silence. Then Jack said,' I'd better go round.'

'I should if I were you.'

But you're not, thought Jack impatiently as he walked rapidly round to Fitz's house.

'Come in Jack. I was hoping to see you today. Good honeymoon?'

'What is it Fitz. I'm busy.' Jack paced the room as Fitz sat down on a chair by the table.

'I have to go to Palestine. It's urgent. Just for a few weeks. I need you to take over Jack...'

'You what!' Jack spun round to face him. 'What on earth are you saying.'

'Wait Jack, please. Sit down.' Fitz's voice echoed in the small room as if he were speaking to a crowd in a synagogue hall. Jack remembered the power of that voice.

He sat down, suddenly tired from all the emotion of the day and the long journey back to London. 'Fitz, I have to go now. We've planned it for God's sake, we're ready...'

'We need you still. We only ask that you decide.' Fitz's voice cut through Jack, slicing holes in his anger. ' You are part of the cause. We need you now more than ever. I have to go and there are forty kids waiting to be trained and sent on their way. Only you can do it of all the men I have in London today. Do you understand me Jack?'

Jack shook his head slowly from side to side, too weary to speak. He could go, he knew it, Fitz knew it. He could stand up now, without another word and walk out. Buy the tickets, pack, take Deborah and sail away, as if.... as if none of this had ever been; the Hammers, the Irgun, the cell, Simon, the rallies and the speeches and the long cold nights in the woods.

But he wouldn't, couldn't do it. He was their man and he would follow their wishes. Fitz knew it, knew he could ask him and damn the disappointments, the broken plans.

'How long?'

'Just a few weeks. Really Jack, maybe four or five.' There was a pause. Fitz's voice dropped, softened. 'I know Jack. I know. But you will go. When I get back, you can go. The very next day.'

On the bus home Jack stared out of the window, numb. There was no anger, no impatience, just a dull emptiness instead of the great well of excitement that had been building for months.

Deborah was furious, slapping outstretched hands on the kitchen table and crying, 'Why now? Why are they asking you to stay when it's so important to us to go!'

'Hush darling,' said May soothingly, her face bewildered. 'Nu Jack. Why don't you ask Lietenant Levy, such a nice young man. He'll sort everything out.'

'No mother,' said Jack quietly. 'He can't. It's nothing do do with him.'

Deborah's head jerked up, her face red, skin stretched tight across the cheekbones, 'What do you mean? If it isn't Michael then who?'

Jack stared at her. His mother looked from one to the other and then picking up a bin by the sink muttered, 'I take out the dust now.'

When she had gone Deborah said,' I want to know. I have a right to know who is spoiling our plans and why.'

Our first real crisis, thought Jack and what if...? His mind couldn't voice the fear. He let the awfulness drift away. Fitz's voice drummed in his ear, 'You tell nobody. Not even your dead grandmother.'

'No Deborah. I'm sorry. I know it's hard for you to understand, harder even for me to say it. But you don't have a right. I have a job to finish and we will go when it's done.'

She leaned back against the sink, arms folded tight across her chest, eyes bright with anger. Then she ran out of the room. Jack heard the slam of the bedroom door a second later.

After a few minutes he went in and lay down beside her. She turned over towards him, face running with tears and said, 'It's not just that we can't go yet. It's so many things. All the secrets between us, I know I shouldn't ask but sometimes I just can't stand it.' She sat up and reached out for the cigarette packet. He took it from her and lit two, handing her one.

'What else?' he asked, not sure he wanted to hear more.

She hesitated. In the silence of the little flat they heard May come back and lock the front door. Then she unlocked it again to put milk bottles out, grumbling to herself in Yiddish. The familiar tinkling of glass was comforting in the tense dark bedroom.

'The longer it takes to go the more room there are for doubts Jack.' He moved as if to speak but she said hurriedly, 'No, let me finish. It's not just my doubts, it's mum and dad. I know they agreed, but when I tell them we're not actually going yet, well you can see can't you? '

Jack nodded, his face dark behind the glow of the cigarette. 'We'll talk to them together. It's our life, we make the decisions now, right Mrs Stone?' He could fell her soften in his arms and he found her lips and pressed hard against them. Just a few more weeks, he thought. Oh God.

Jack had given up his job and so most of the days were spent at the office in Avery Row, helping Michael to put out The Vanguard. At night he trained the groups hard to be sure they would be ready to leave on time. He wanted no further hitches once Fitz returned.

In the second week in April a message came from Fitz to say he would be back in a week. Jack raced home a large bunch of daffodils in his hand.

When he arrived at the flat Deborah called him into the bedroom. 'Next week love,' he called excitedly as he stood in the open doorway. 'I've had word. We can book the boat train.'

'Come in Jack and close the door.' Deborah's voice was tight, strained, her face pale.

'What is it?'

'I'm late.' She saw the lack of comprehension in his face and dragged a hand across her eyes. 'I'm late Jack, don't you understand. I'm never late, it's always the same date, same time, between three and five in the afternoon.'

'What do you mean Deborah? What is it?' His mind was confused by her reaction to his news. All he had thought about on the way home had been her excitement, how she would throw her arms around him, drag bags out from under the bed, talk endlessly about hopes and plans and their future together in Palestine. He couldn't understand what was wrong.

Then slowly it dawned as she carried on more impatiently, 'For Heavens sake Jack. I think I'm pregnant.'

For a second he was stunned. He had never thought, never realised. It was so quick. Then his face broke into a wide smile. 'But that's marvellous. Why didn't you say so. Are you sure? What does the doctor say?'

'I haven't been to the doctor.' She sat down heavily on the bed, shoulders hunched as tears began to trickle down her face.

'Why not?' He didn't noticed how upset she was. He began pacing the tiny room, bumping into furniture, his mind a whirl of added preparation.

'Don't you see what this means Jack? For God's sake sit down a minute and think.' She looked past him at the wall where she had pinned up photos of their wedding. Then she said very carefully, 'We can't go. Not now. Not pregnant. My mother...'

'You're mother! Have you told her already?'

She nodded, her face frightened. He couldn't believe it, she had told Betty before her own husband. He didn't trust himself to speak. Then he was gone from the flat, tearing through the warm spring streets, thoughts crashing round inside his head, mercilessly.

When he returned Deborah was sound asleep on top of the eiderdown. He covered her with a blanket and lay down beside her.

When he woke it was after nine and he was alone.

His mother came in with some tea. 'Where's Deborah mum?'

She didn't answer but began folding clothes, opening drawers. 'Leave all that. You know Deborah doesn't like you to do it.'

She straightened up, a pair of trousers hanging over her arm. Her face was strained, '*Oy* Jack, what you doing to that poor girl? She's gone to the doctor.' She shook her head clicking her tongue.

'Did she tell you she thought she was pregnant?'

'Yes. At times like this a girl needs her mother darling. Be patient.' His mother shook her head and went out.

He was waiting in the kitchen when Deborah returned. She took the cup of tea he poured and sat down.

'It's almost certain.' He nodded, his face stiff, numb. 'We can't go Jack. In the middle of a war. How would we cope?'

He said nothing. She talked on and on, her mother's cliches interlacing the reasoned arguments.

'...won't stand in our way but...'

'*Nachas* from your children....'

'I know it's disappointing but we should count our blessings. That's what mum always says.'

She stopped and dropped her eyes.

'Well at least I know what your mother thinks,' he said quietly.

She opened her mouth to speak but May came in with a bag of shopping. 'Deborah darling, what's the news?'

'Almost confirmed.'

'*Mazel-tov!*' but there was an anxious look on her face.

She understands, thought Jack.

Deborah stood up, tucking her handbag under her arm and said, ' I think we should go and talk to mum and dad Jack.'

May nodded as she dumped bags of vegetables onto the table. 'That's right. Go see them, sort it out together. We don't want bad feeling. Tell them you go later.' She waved a hand in the air and began opening cupboards behind them.

As they stood at the bus stop Jack put his arm round her and pulled her head onto his shoulder. Two women turned round and eyed them disapprovingly. In Palestine they are dying, thought Jack. And we are going to be parents. What the hell do I do?

In the dreary living room Jack sat and watched Deborah slide back into childhood. Betty stood behind her chair, fingers gripped to the cream anti-macassar.

'They've got malaria, disease, heat, flies,' Betty listed.

'No water, little decent food, just a tent,' continued Morris.

Like a double act, thought Jack.

'And then there's the war. You must see you can't take a pregnant wife out to all that. I always said, didn't I Morris?' Morris nodded. 'That it would get worse and I was right.'

'We all knew that Betty,' said Jack a sarcastic edge to his voice. 'But I agree.'

Betty let out a surprised,'Oh.'

Morris nodded as if he had read Jack's mind all along.

'We'll just have to go later. Right Deborah?'

Deborah looked up at her mother. In that moment Jack felt lost, stripped of his role of husband. As if because of some strange misdemeanour.

'Mum suggested we move in here. There's more room and I want to be near her for the baby.'

Jack stared into Betty's face. A look of triumph flashed in her eyes. As if this is all a game, he thought. Well, it's not over yet. 'If that's what you want,' he said.

'It is.'

Jack's parents were content to let Betty decide. The coming of the baby moved all the goalposts. But after May had gone to bed that night Solly said to Jack, 'Won't be forever. These things happen when you get married. Go when the baby's born. Don't have to stay with that lot forever.' He gave Jack a knowing wink.

They moved into the Freedmans' house at the weekend. Michael helped with their things, running up and down with huge cardboard boxes, calling to Jack, 'Shall I put it here? Where does this go?'

Betty cleared out two of the bigger bedrooms, one to be used as a sitting room. They could hear the whir of the sewing machine below as they paused for a cigarette.

'I'll make some tea shall I?' Deborah's face was worn with fatigue and the excitement of the move.

'Call when it's ready,' said Jack. 'I'll come down for the tray.'

When she had gone Michael stared across at him from the open window. There was a stiff breeze which blew back the cigarette smoke into the room.

'Regretting it now?'

'What! Marrying Deborah? Don't' be crazy.' Jack bent over a crate and began unpacking ornaments, his face closed.

'Good, good.' Michaels' voice was light. 'You'll go later Jack. It'll still be there....'

'I'm needed now!' snapped Jack.

'You're wife needs you more.'

Jack said nothing. The room was silent except for the rustle of paper. Betty went into the garden and began hanging out washing. She was singing quietly.

'She's happy anyway.'

'And so should you be. A beautiful wife, your first child on the way.'

'Bloody hell Michael!' Jack threw himself to his feet and stood facing Michael. 'I never thought in a million years! We should be there by now. What is there left to do here. You know what will happen when they declare independence.'

Michael was looking over Jack's shoulder. Jack turned round to see Deborah standing in the open doorway, a strained smile on her face. 'The tray's ready.'

Jack stared at her as if waiting for her to say something more. Then he brushed past and down the stairs. It's as though she's sunk into another world, he thought furiously in the kitchen.

The State of Israel was declared on May 14. Immediately most of the members of the Hammers left to join in the fighting. Fitz met Michael and Jack the night before he left and demanded the Hammers funds to take with him.

'Not at all Shlomo,' smiled Michael. 'Those funds are my responsibility.'

'You crazy Michael!' stormed Fitz. 'That money is the Irgun's. I want it now. I leave tomorrow.'

'There are certain outstanding expenditures....'

'What! What rubbish you talking to me now!'

Jack had never seen Fitz so worked up. His round bald head seemed to swell in the soft light of Michael's living room, as he walked furiously round the furniture.

'What do you say Jack?' Fitz's eyes rolled behind the thick glasses as he bent towards Jack.

'It's up to Michael. You know that.'

Fitz exploded into a stream of Hebrew and stormed out of the flat. Michael poured himself a drink, a thin smile on his lips. 'Always a man who wanted his own way.'

'Didn't we all,' said Jack wearily.

Fitz was killed in the battle around Jerusalem along with two other members of the Hammers. Michael was given a commission in the newly formed Israeli army, but not at the level he expected.

'Ben Gurion is prejudiced against the Irgun,' he wrote to Jack. 'I don't think they'll ever acknowledge how vital our work was. Pig ignorant of them. Shame about Fitz.'

One warm September night Jack drove with Deborah to the garage where the gelignite he had stored for Michael was still kept. They loaded the car and drove to the river beyond Greenwich. Jack stripped down to his underpants and swam out with armfuls of the explosive. Deborah stood on the bank, her profile swollen now at seven months pregnant and kept watch.

He was about ten yards out, during his second trip when a police launch suddenly came round a bend, lights sweeping the water.

Shocked, Jack dived beneath the surface, still holding the gelignite. When he came up Deborah had gone. He could just see the outline of her head in the car.

'That was close,' he grinned as he stood by the car door dripping.

She gave a little shiver. 'Imagine being caught now. They'd probably deport us.'

'Would that be so bad?' he said and turned abruptly back to the river.

When the last sticks had drifted away from his hands to the muddy riverbed below Jack felt a deep desolation. I've cut the last ties, he thought. It's over.

On a Friday in November Jack came home from work to find Betty waiting for him.

'Deborah's not well. She's had a headache all day.'

'Oh?' Jack put down his bag and took off his hat. It was a damp foggy night.

'I think we'll stay in.'

Jack's heart sank. Betty and Morris were invited to Shabbos dinner with friends in south London and they were planning to stay the night. Betty hated the bus ride home. She maintained London wasn't safe anymore since the war. '... and she lived through the Blitz,' Deborah would laugh.

Jack had been looking forward to an evening alone in the house with Deborah.

'I'll go and see how she is,' he said hurriedly. 'Don't decide yet.' He ran upstairs.

Deborah was listening to the radio in their sitting room, knitting a little jacket.

'How are you love?'

She gave him a tired smile, ' All right. Chicken for dinner. Mum and dad'll go soon and we can have it alone for once.'

Betty called upstairs, 'We'll stay then shall we?'

'No mum. I'm fine, honestly. Jack's here now.'

Her mother frowned at the bottom of the stairs. Then Morris said, 'Come on Betty, leave the young people alone.'

'Well, all right,' she said reluctantly and pulled on her coat, buttoning it up slowly and calling to Jack, 'The doctor's number and Freda's number are on the pad by the phone. Call me! Even if it's two in the morning.'

'I will,' said Jack trying to sound reassuring. He held his breath until the front door shut and he heard the click of the garden gate.

Then he turned to Deborah, a broad smile on his face, ' Alone at last.'

She ran a hand across her forehead in a tired gesture and smiled back, 'Lovely. Let's eat. You must be starving.'

But she ate very little saying, 'I'm just sleepy. Still six weeks to go.' She patted her swollen abdomen. ' It's a long business.'

'Haven't felt a kick for a while.' He smoothed his hand over the bulge.

'It's a bit quiet at the moment.' Seeing a look of anxiety on his face she laughed,' That's perfectly normal Jack. Now be a love and wash up. We can chat in bed.'

But when he got upstairs Deborah was already asleep, her hair covering her face. He looked at his watch. Just nine o'clock. She must be tired.

He was in a deep sleep when he heard Deborah's voice, 'Quick Jack. Get the doctor.'

He forced his eyes open and switched on the bedside light. It was one o'clock. 'What is it?'

'Baby's coming.' It sounded as though she was choking. As his eyes adjusted to the light he could see Deborah's eyes bulging from her head. Her hair was matted and damp and she was breathing heavily.

When he threw back the sheets there was a damp stain between her legs. 'Blood,' he whispered. Panic rose in him as he stared at her.

Then she began to moan over and over, 'Mum, mum.'

'It's all right love, I'm here. ' But his voice shook. God! What do I do? The telephone's downstairs, but how can I leave her in this state?

She didn't seem to notice him, but carried on rolling around, calling for Betty. He got up and stood in the doorway for a second. Then he made a bolt for the phone.

'Send for the doctor!' he screamed to the voice on the other end of the line. He was sure she was going to die.

As he arrived back up at the top of the stairs there was a power cut. The whole house went dark. Deborah began screaming. He called out to her and groped back down to the kitchen for matches and candles. It can't come yet, he told himself. Babies take hours to be born. The doctor will be here soon.

When he got back to the bedroom and lit a candle he couldn't believe his eyes. The baby's head! He could see the black down of its hair. Deborah had been sick and the sheets were a wet mess of blood.

Afterwards he couldn't say how the baby had been born. He kept yelling Push! Deborah screamed and then her face began to twitch. Suddenly the baby slipped out. The twitching became very violent and then Deborah went rigid. When he bent over her she was unconsciousness.

The baby lay on the sheet very still and silent. He could see straight away it was a boy. Then he heard the doctor banging on the door and he hurled himself downstairs to let him in.

'*We called him Noah,*' he wrote to Michael weeks later.

'*Deborah never even got to hold him. It was high blood pressure, toxaemia the doctor called it. We hadn't realised and that shut off the supply to the baby. No oxygen, poor little mite. Deborah was taken into hospital and we buried him on the Sunday. Didn't even have him circumcised.*'

*

CHAPTER EIGHTEEN

'Telephone for you Eve. In reception.'

Eve was washing up in the kitchen when Etty called through the open window. She frowned. Who on earth was ringing her up here? Must be Bud, she decided. She wiped her hands on a towel and called out, 'Coming.'

It was *Shabbat*. A bus load of Americans had descended on the guest house for lunch. She had gone out to greet them with Judy, teacloths tucked into the waistbands of their jeans, sleeves rolled up, tennis shoes crunching on the gravel.

'Gee, you're all the way from London. You girls must be having a wonderful time up here.'

They flashed wide grins, nodded their heads casually, conscious they blended into the rugged background. The remote *moshav*, the rough unmade road, their hair tangling in the breeze.

The Americans were all middle-aged women. They wore flowery dresses and flimsy white sandals. 'You been here that long? Heck you must be sabres by now!'

'Not quite,' laughed Judy. 'We're working on it.' They ushered the group into the dining room, ran in and out with plates of food.

'That one reminds me of my mum,' said Eve in a low voice nodding to a woman on the end table.

'They all remind me of my mum,' grinned Judy. 'You realise this is the most exciting event since Norbert and Hilary left.'

The moshav is very quiet, thought Eve as she walked round to reception to take her telephone call. Perhaps I can persuade Bud to come up for a visit. Dani and Zoar had gone to the Red Sea for a week scuba-diving. She felt lost without them.

Etty held out the phone to Eve with a flourish.

'Did they give a name?'

'No,' smiled Etty.

Eve perched on the corner of the desk and held her hand over the microphone. 'Male or female?'

'Male, not young, English.'

'Oh.' Eve removed her hand and said cautiously, 'Hello. Eve speaking.'

'It's dad.'

'Dad! This is great. How are you, how's mum? Are you thinking of coming over for a holiday?'

'I'm here already love. I'm in Jerusalem.'

Her heart missed a beat. Here! 'I don't understand....'

'I've come for a little holiday Eve.'

'But, look dad, I mean you didn't say anything.' After all these years! She thought. My God! He's finally made it. Noah! The word entered her head automatically.

'That's all right isn't it? Just came on the spur of the moment. Can you get down here, or shall I come up to you?'

'No,' she said quickly. She suddenly felt the need of neutral territory. 'Give me the name of your hotel and I'll come to you. It won't be before tomorrow afternoon. There's no transport on *Shabbat*. Where's mum?'

He hesitated and then he said, 'She didn't want to come.'

'Bad news?' Etty's face was concerned.

Eve realised she was frowning and shook her head, 'No.' She walked out into the bright sunshine her mind whirling. Why didn't he write and tell me? Where's mum? Why didn't she come too? God! Where do we begin? She felt suddenly afraid and then stupid and laughed at herself. It's only dad. But the fear lingered, permeating the rest of the day and the bus ride to Jerusalem the next day.

Jack sat in the hotel lobby on Sunday afternoon waiting for Eve, chain smoking a pack of duty frees. He had tried the Israeli beer but found it too weak. The sun was hotter than he had imagined, but he had put on the brown cord trousers he had left England in the day before. An open neck short sleeve shirt was his only concession to the heat.

Israel. He still had to resist a desire to call it Palestine. When had he decided to come? Was it really only a month ago? Or had he made up his mind the day Eve had come home with the ticket.

'I'm going to Israel next month.' She hadn't smiled or looked excited, her face was almost defiant. Did he think he would try to stop her?

He had replied in cool neutral tones, 'That's nice love. How long will you be away?'

She had stared deep into his eyes for an instant and then turned to go. 'Couple of months,' she threw over her shoulder.

Deborah wouldn't talk about it. From time to time he made the odd comment to see if she would react. Once he said, 'We could pop over for a week. Visit.'

She had lifted her head from her book, her eyes wide, 'To Israel? What for?'

He hadn't shown Deborah the letters. He had been surprised, almost shocked when Eve had written demanding to know about Noah. He couldn't remember putting anything about him in a letter. Once she started she didn't stop. It felt like a flood pouring through him, flushing out all the dark secret corners of the years. He felt invaded, guilty, impotent. We made a mistake to keep it secret, he thought. But I never wanted her to feel tied to us.

A phrase came into his head, 'Knowledge is freedom.' Who said that? Then he remembered. It was Michael. All those years ago in a synagogue hall. 'Knowledge is freedom. Don't take the words of Ben Gurion as the one and only truth. Keep asking yourselves, Why is it taking so long?'

Michael had emigrated to New York after ten years in Israel. They'd lost touch over the years.

Wonder what he'd make of this place now, thought Jack with an inward laugh. Feels like every man for himself on the streets, everyone pushing and those drivers! He shook his head and lit another cigarette. They honk if you even think about leaving the kerb.

The heat was overwhelming but at least people spoke English. Jerusalem felt strange, so many Arabs. Hard to feel Jewish here. On the bus ride up from Tel Aviv he had seen the burnt out jeeps left over from the '48 war. Some sort of memorial, he had thought. This is where Fitz slugged it out alongside all those kids I trained.

He had expected to feel some sense of return, of belonging, perhaps to have had it recognised by the Israelis he met in the cafes. I worked for this, he wanted to say. For your freedom, to go on living and fighting and dying here. But inside his head he could hear the irrelevancy of his words. Time had swept on past him, they would just shrug and carry on down the street.

He looked up as Eve entered the hotel lobby.

His first thought was, She's changed so much. Her body was leaner, her legs dark brown beneath faded cut-off jeans. Even her toes were dark in the worn leather sandals. She had plaited her hair and pinned it to her head. Elegant, he thought approvingly. Boyfriend? Or maybe just the way they wear it here.

She was gazing round for him, a small rucksack slung over one shoulder, arms bare in a blue singlet. Round her neck hung a gold Star of David. Solly had given it to her when she was thirteen, 'Because you won't have a barmitzvah,' he had said with a knowing wink.

She looks tough, he thought. Independent. The life out here suits her.

The last thing Deborah had said at the airport was, 'Ask her when she's coming home.' He had gazed into her wide brown eyes brimming with tears. Just like Eve's, he thought. 'Don't let me lose her Jack.'

He had nodded and said comforting words. But inside he felt annoyed. I'm not going out there to dictate to her, he thought firmly.

'Dad!'

He stood up and she dropped her rucksack and flung her arms around him. Then she stepped back, suddenly awkward in the hall of the hotel.

'You're looking wonderful love. Do you like this heat?'

She shrugged. 'I don't mind, but it's cooler on the Golan. How long are you here for?'

'Just a week. Your mother doesn't like to be alone for long.'

He flicked his eyes away from her when he mentioned Deborah.

Eve noticed but said nothing. He's the same, she was thinking. Same brown hair, heavily laced with grey, the nobbly scar on the cheekbone where he was hit by flying shrapnel in France. The skin on his chest and arms was already beginning to tan.

I thought he would look so different, but he doesn't.

'Shall we go out? Are you tired?'

'Me?' she laughed. 'No, just let me dump my stuff in the room.'

They went to the Old City and down through the *shouk*. Jack stopped at every shop and Eve showed off her haggling talents, using tips she had picked up from Steve. 'Never show interest in the things you want, ' she advised him, a grin on her face. 'It helps if you know a couple of choice Hebrew or Arabic phrases.' Her face was flushed with success as she dropped bargain after bargain into her father's arms. I can do this better then him, she thought.

They passed the steps to the Armenian woman's hostel. Some baskets hung on the wall alongside the steps. 'Let's take a look at those,' said Jack.

Eve felt a sudden fear that Jenny would appear. What the hell would I say to her? She thought angrily. She fingered the scar on her hand. It stood out, a long white line against her tanned skin.

'What happened?' Jack took her hand, his face concerned. So many things I don't know about her now, he thought.

She smiled and shook her head. 'It's nothing. An accident in the kitchen. There's another shop further down, better than this one.'

They walked on until the *shouk* ended and they approached the Wailing Wall. All through the narrow streets Jack thought of his friends who had died fighting for Jerusalem. At the barrier between men and women they separated. Jack found himself surrounded by men muttering prayers, touching the huge stones.

Fitz died fighting for this. What did I know about him? He never talked about his home, his family. No hint of the man, just his ideals, his total committment. He sucked us in, pinned us to that map in his house. He could make us do anything. A low deep feeling of regret welled in Jack as he remembered the lost chances. It's because of Fitz I never made it. If we had gone straight after the wedding, she would have had the baby here. Maybe he would have survived.

He ran a hand over his eyes and shook his head. No use thinking like that. Not Deborah's fault anyway, or even her mother's. A sarcastic grunt sounded in his throat but it didn't sound out of place in the middle of all this prayer. He stood on tiptoe and could just see Eve wandering around. What can I say to her? He asked himself and felt the tension pull his muscles.

They had dinner that evening on Jaffa Road in the new city. Eve had changed into a white *jellabah*, embroidered at the neck and wrists. Round her neck hung a black pouch on a long string, heavily embroidered in bright colours on the front. 'Bedouin women make these,' she said.

'It feels very Arabic here,' said Jack. 'More than I expected.'

'You're in the Middle East now dad. Not Golders Green on a Sunday morning.' She laughed. 'Jerusalem takes a lot of getting used to.'

They ate shish kebab and salad drinking glass after glass of iced coke. She felt herself freezing up inside as she thought of all the things she wanted to hear him say. The silence deepened between them until she thought it would never be broken. It would have been better if he had never come, she found herself thinking desperately.

Then Jack said, 'Grandma and Grandpa Stone send their love. They keep asking when you're coming back.'

She nodded. A safe subject. 'What did you tell them?'

'I always say the same thing. You'll come if and when you want to.'

Eve picked at her salad miserably.

Jack watched her. So much to talk about, he thought and I don't know where she wants to start. But he realised this was just an excuse. 'You're mother is worried you might not come back.'

Eve looked into his eyes, a long penetrating look brimming with questions. 'All the more reason for her to come and visit me.'

He moved his glass and stared at the round wet mark it had left on the Formica. A waiter came up, a young Israeli in a T shirt advertising Coca Cola. He gathered the plates clumsily and walked off shouting down the restaurant in Hebrew, his feet dragging in slip-on sandals.

'It you stay...'

'I don't know dad,' she cut in impatiently.

'Plenty of time,' he said quietly.'

The next morning she took him to Yad Vashem, the memorial museum to the Holocaust. As they reached the door a crowd of American teenagers in front jostled and laughed, tossing gum between them. The inside of the museum was dark after the bright sunshine and as Eve and Jack stepped inside a silence fell over the rowdy group. When Jack looked around him he could see why.

Afterwards he said to Eve, 'I thought I knew it all.' His face was grey. She nodded.

'That child's shoe at the end.' He lit a cigarette and pulled on it deeply. 'Says it all.'

They walked down the path in silence. I'll never go again, she thought in anguish.

'No-one would listen,' Jack said. ' But we didn't really know. We heard things. But it wasn't until the Belsen newsreel that the real horror came home to us.'

'What then?' she asked almost holding her breath. Is this it? She thought. Are we about to really talk?

Jack shrugged. 'You learn to live with it. Every Jew has to. Always will now.'

His eyes were guarded, his face closed with the pain of seeing the museum.

He's not ready, she thought. But she felt more certain that he wanted to talk.

'I want to take you to my kibbutz, ' she said.

A look of relief crossed his face. Safe ground again. 'Fine, how about tomorrow?'

Bud was overjoyed to see her, lifting her off the ground in a bear hug. Then he stood hands outstretched crying, 'Jeez Eve! This is almost terrific!' He shook Jack's hand vigorously. 'Pleased to meet you. Any father of Eve's is a friend of mine. Wanna see round?'

He dragged them through all the animal sheds, along the edge of the cotton fields and then to the dining room.

'Are you still in the same hut Bud?' asked Eve.

'Are you kidding? I'm a candidate now. Got a real cool pad.'

The word candidate hit her hard. Before she could adjust to it she had to explain it to Jack. 'It means they're considering him for membership to the kibbutz. Bud's been studying Hebrew,' she flung him a glare, ' jammy bastard.'

'The what?' shrugged Bud with a grin.

She gave him a thump. 'Anyway, he's become a new immigrant. I suppose they'll give you a gun next, you great lump!'

'Yeah, I'll have to do the army as well. But it's not forever.'

That pleased her. I couldn't have stood it if Bud had gone macho, she thought.

Bud had a new bungalow in a row which the kibbutz had just finished building for single people.

'It's beautiful Bud,' said Eve admiringly.

There was a small kitchen unit, with a fridge, a bench and a built in table. This opened into a large sunny sitting room. A door in the wall lead to a bedroom.

'Big enough for the double bed,' grinned Bud.

'Still going with Shula?' asked Eve as Bud took beer and coke from the fridge.

'He shrugged again, 'On and off. How 'bout you?'

She glanced at her father. He smiled and passed around a packet of cigarettes, a quizzical look on his face.

Bud neatly changed the subject. 'British cigarettes. Haven't had these before. Benson and Hedges,' he read off the packet.

'Better than Marlborough,' said Eve.

'Like hell!'

On the bus back to Jerusalem Eve felt close to tears. Bud was a candidate, he'd taken the plunge. What about me? Her mother was still in London, too afraid to come to Israel. Her father hadn't mentioned Noah or the letters. Only three more days left. If he goes away without speaking.

'Living here there seem to be so many decisions to make,' she suddenly said.

'It's the same everywhere,' said Jack staring out of the window. 'Perhaps here it's the first time you're really confronted with being a Jew.'

'I was always a Jew in England.'

'Always?'

Andy's name floated silently in the air between them. The bus jerked round a bend, the driver leaning on his horn. It was two o'clock. Everyone stopped talking as the news came on the radio. The driver turned the volume up to full power. The entire country stops for the news, thought Eve. Sudden images flashed in her mind, workers frozen at their work benches, in the fields, in kitchens coffee cups half raised to housewives lips. Like clockwork models run down.

'It's since the '73 war,' she explained to Jack. 'No-one wants to be caught out again.'

Jack nodded. 'Did you come out here because of Andy? Something he said?'

She had never told her parents, too ashamed that Andy could sink so low. But it didn't seem to matter anymore. 'He said it would never work. I was Jewish. Then we split up.'

'I'm surprised at Andy saying a thing like that,' said Jack quietly.

'So was I.' There was a pause and then she said wearily, 'But it was over before that dad. I just wouldn't admit it. It did have something to do with me coming here, but not everything.'

'What else?'

She hesitated, not sure what to say now the moment seemed to have arrived. Two soldiers climbed on the bus and sat down in the seat opposite, guns balanced between their legs. One of them fiddled with the safety catch, flicking it up and down. Eve tried to imagine squeezing the trigger. All the way back until the explosion. She closed her eyes and then opened them again.

'What else?' Jack repeated. His words swung in the air as though on a wire, testing the tension.

'I should have been born here.'

Jack felt a ripple of shock run through him. He stared at her face, suddenly very small and pinched. She looked vulnerable, a little girl again. Is that what drew her here, Deborah's stories? I never thought we said that much. I never told her anything. His mind was struggling with Eve's words, I should have been born here. That's how she sees it, whatever I say now. He felt suddenly helpless, as if they were strangers on this bus.

'There's so much I want to know dad. It's important to me.'

He could almost touch the hunger in her voice, as though it was a tangible thing she put in his hand. Then the bus ground to a halt and they were struggling through the crowds onto the pavements. They walked in silence back to the hotel. He longed to put his arm round her, but her shoulders were tense, closed.

When they reached the lobby of the hotel she turned to him and said, 'I'm tired. Let's have a rest before dinner.' He nodded and then bending over kissed her lightly on the cheek.

In the room Jack pulled down the blind and stripped down to his underpants. It was mid-afternoon and very hot. He stood in front of the mirror. Getting a waist, he thought. But the rest was the same. Muscles hard, shoulders still straight. I'm 53. Noah would have been 27. Married with kids.

He lay down on the bed and pulled a sheet to his waist.

Or dead in some Israeli war.

He tried to imagine himself and Deborah working together on a kibbutz, Noah and Eve tumbling in the dust outside the childrens' house. But the picture wasn't clear, like bad weather in his mind causing the image to crackle and fade. It's too late to think about all that now, he told himself and slipped into a deep sleep.

In the evening once it was dark they walked to Jaffa Gate. 'There's a cafe just inside the Old City which makes the best falafel,' said Eve.

She was dressed in shorts and a T-shirt. The air was still very hot and Jack felt relieved the sun had gone down. As they moved through the streets the silence between them deepened. Jack thought of things to say and abandoned each one.

They sat at a table on the pavement. The *shouk* was closed but groups of tourists wandered past their flashlights bursting into the still air.

'Some people will snap anything,' said Jack at last.

Eve picked up a falafel ball and broke it in two. She said nothing. Two Americans walked past laughing loudly,'...no kidding, only two dollars. These A-rabs know nothing about doing business.' They snapped each other in front of the Gate.

Eve snorted,' I hate the way someone always has to be in the picture.'

Jack eyed her uncertainly. 'Do you want to talk about our letters?'

She looked at him startled, as if this was the last thing on her mind. Maybe I'm wrong, thought Jack wildly. Maybe all this moodiness is over a boyfriend.

He was about to ask about Bud when she suddenly said, 'You never talked about those things! All my life you and mum and grandma and grandpa never said.'

Her tone changed abruptly, more accusing, as if she had to force out the words. 'Treated me like a kid or an idiot or something!' She tapped her chest hard. 'I found the death certificate! ' I knew about Noah for Christ's sakes! He was my brother dad and you never....' She broke off, serviette gripped to her mouth.

Jack felt numbed by the intensity of her outburst. He picked up a glass of water and sipped, his eyes fixed on her.

'Do you have a photograph? Of the baby. Of Noah.'

A look of horror crossed his face. 'Have you gone mad?'

She shook her head sharply as she stared at him, eyes wide, skin stretched across her cheekbones. 'I read about it in the paper. A couple decided to abort their baby, it was deformed of something. Afterwards they held it for a little while and photographed it. Ever since I wanted to ask you if you had a photo of Noah.'

Jack couldn't speak, his mind pouring back twenty-seven years to the blood stained sheets and the tiny crop of hair on his dead son's head. She doesn't understand what happened, he thought angrily. God! How could she. We never talked about it. Never.

In a voice which cracked with emotion he said, ' Noah wasn't deformed. We didn't realise....'

'You should have! I told Susan Parker!'

'Told her what love.'

'I told her I had a brother.' Eve looked away as the tears finally broke through, streaming down her face. 'She laughed at me.'

That baby, thought Jack. Tore us all apart. He wanted to reach out and comfort her, but she seemed so remote, bent over the table as the tears flowed into her serviette. A boy came and cleared the plates. He said something in Hebrew and she shook her head and waved him away. As he walked back in the cafe he shouted in Arabic and someone gave a roar of laughter. Eve looked up and wiped away the last of the tears. 'Was I a mistake?' Her voice was hoarse.

He flinched.

'Amistake, you know dad. An unplanned pregnancy. Result of a fling, or...'

'That's enough Eve!' snapped Jack. She stared at him defiantly. 'You were a pleasant surprise.'

She stirred her coffee, watching the froth swirl round, her mind confused, tired. Why on earth did I ask him that? What the hell does it matter now?

But it hurt that her mother hadn't longed for her. She suddenly realised she was jealous of Noah and gave a short laugh.

'What's funny?'

Her face was surprised, as if she had forgotten he was there. Then she said in a slow controlled voice, 'Why didn't you tell me about Noah?'

'Because,' he stopped. She was staring into his eyes and suddenly it was Deborah, before the wedding, before the baby. He stared back, savouring the moment and then he said, 'Because it all happened years before you were born Eve. It was a very unhappy time and we all tried to forget about it.'

'And after I found the death certificate. Didn't you think then was the time?'

He shrugged helplessly. 'No. I don't know...' He looked away. 'No. We talked about it....'

'I know.'

'Really? How did you know?' His tone was hurt as if it had happened yesterday.

She felt annoyed. He's treating me like a little girl again, she thought.

'I sat on the stairs. Listened to you all talking. I remember grandma saying something about me not understanding.'

Jack gave a grunt. 'She always thought she knew best. It wasn't easy you know living with my in-laws all those years.'

'I know dad. I could see. So why didn't you move out?'

Some Arab boys ran past shouting to each other. One of them threw an empty can on the ground and kicked it ahead of him. They could hear the clatter of the can long after the boys were out of sight.

Jack sighed. 'What you have to understand is that your mother was very ill after Noah's birth. She had high blood pressure. He died because the blood supply was cut off. Mum was well, depressed for a long time after. Even after you were born she wasn't really back to normal. ' He looked away down the narrow winding street into the *shouk*. It was almost deserted now. Eve passed him a cigarette and they smoked in silence for a minute.

'We became trapped. Your mum needed grandma and she was absolutely marvellous when you came along. I just couldn't prise your mother away.'

Eve felt a stab as she saw the helpless look on her father's face.

'It was nobody's fault Eve. You never know what's round the next corner. Just try to keep a hold on your life. I let mine slip away.'

She could hardly bear the sadness and longing which permeated his words. She put her hand out and covered his outsplayed fingers. 'And Palestine? All those dreams to build the land?'

He squeezed her hand and smiled. Then he shook his head. 'We never made it.'

'It would have been easier if I'd been born here,' she suddenly said fiercely.

'Would it?' Jack indicated the street with his hand. 'All these people here, all the sabres. They find it easy do they?'

She was silent.

'After the war I felt like you.' She looked up with interest. He could feel the pull of her hunger again. How much do I say? He thought. 'You tell nobody,' Fitz had said. But it was all so long ago. What did it matter now?

'I was angry, confused. I joined a group called The Hammers. We raised money for the Irgun.'

Her face was alight, eyes wide. Like the kids I trained, he thought. The same desire.

'God! What did you do?'

'We had a stand at Speaker's Corner every Sunday, sold a newspaper, fought off the Blackshirts.'

They had leaned closer to each other across the small table, elbows resting on the plastic cloth. Without realising it they had lowered their voices.

He's holding back, she thought. That's not the whole story.

Jack lit another cigarette, his face set, eyes staring into the middle distance. The waiter came back. She ordered more coffee, swirled the ash from her cigarette round in the saucer with a matchstick. She was trying to remember something her mother had once said. Got it! she thought.

'Mum said one of your friends went to prison, caught with explosives.'

She held her breath. He was gazing at her , his eyes keen, penetrating, as if weighing up how much he could trust her. Come on, she thought. Don't go silent on me now. This was the most they had talked in her whole life. He can't stop now.

'Simon,' he said.

She felt a thrill of triumph.

'Simon Block. We were in an active cell together.'

'Terrorists,' she breathed. A crease of uncertainty lined her forehead.

He nodded and pulled on his cigarette. 'I was recruited by the Irgun to train groups for military action in Palestine. Later I became part of an active cell which planned an explosion on an MOD yard. But Simon was caught before we could carry out the plan.'

He looked at his watch. It was after ten. 'Come on love. Let's go back to the hotel and have a drink.' He smiled at her, the smile from her childhood, familiar, slightly crooked, the scar on his cheekbone standing out thick and white.

'Ok.' As she stood up she felt the tension of the past two days slip away. I can ask him anything now, she thought. Years seemed to stretch ahead of them.

At the hotel he pulled a bottle of vodka out of his suitcase. 'Duty free. I'll just nip down to reception, see about some ice.'

My dad, a terrorist, she thought, after he had gone. My God! Dear old dad, always so quiet and gentle. What on earth did he get mixed up in? Images of IRA bombings and sectarian killings filled her mind.

He came back through the door carrying a bottle of lemonade and a bowl of ice cubes. 'Why?' she said.

He looked at her bemused. 'Why what?'

'Why become a terrorist? What about the King David bombing? That was so awful.' Her face screwed up in distaste.

Jack went to the bathroom and returned with two glasses. He poured out a generous measure of vodka and mixed it with lemonade and ice. 'Lehaim,' he grinned.

He stood by the window drinking staring into the street below. He could remember every minute in the cell, Fitz and Simon arguing philosophy, Harry checking equipment, those huge shoulders hunched under the standard lamp in Fitz's dingy room. He could remember every word they spoke, each tiny nuance, every detail, every item repaired on the Lost Horizon. Another failure, he sneered silently. What a shower! Couldn't even collect the stuff for a bomb without getting caught. He felt a sudden passionate longing for those deep November nights, the smell of fog as it penetrated Fitz's curtains. I'm here now, he called silently to Fitz and it's so different you wouldn't believe it mate!

'Dad?'

He turned. She was sitting on the edge on the bed holding her glass in two hands as if to warm them. Well at least I haven't failed there, he thought.

'I'll tell you why Eve. Total dedication to the cause. That's what drove us on. I would be horrified today about the bombings but in those days the only thing that mattered was the Irgun. Do you know what our motto was?'

She shook her head.

'*Rach cach*. Only this way. If it hadn't been for the military action of our boys the State of Israel would never have been created.'

As she stared at her father Eve realised for the first time what the coming of Noah had really meant to him. What he had lost and the struggle he must have gone through fighting to come to terms with it. His words from the first letter echoed in her head, 'Noah. Our Ark who sunk us all.'

'You must have loved mum very much not to leave her and go after such a committment to the cause.'

'I did,' he said quietly.

Part Four

Raid!

CHAPTER NINETEEN

July 3rd 1976.

'Its thirty-five degrees in London. There's a drought.' Judy tossed over a copy of NEWSWEEK. 'Crazy isn't it?'

'Dad said the back lawn has all gone brown.' Eve flicked through the magazine. There was a picture of secretaries sunbathing in bikinis in Hyde Park. 'Any news of the hi-jack?'

'I didn't listen to the news this morning.' Judy yawned and stretched her legs.

A sudden blast of pop music broke out in Meni's room. Judy groaned. 'Not the Byrds again. That's the third time this morning.'

'Bored?'

'As ever.' Judy stood up and spat a wedge of chewing gum over the balcony. It was a hot bright morning, but a breeze made the sun bearable. The road wound still and empty down the mountain. 'It's like a desert island up here.' She turned and grinned at Eve. 'We should choose our discs.'

'Times They're a Changin"

'Acker Bilk, Strangers on the Shore.'

'Your kidding! Moody Blues, Dear Diary.'

Judy put on a BBC voice. 'We are sorry to inform you that your choice has been cancelled due to lack of interest.'

They both started laughing. Meni wandered in dressed in Stars and Stripes underpants. 'What funny, hey?' He blinked behind his glasses and stroked his beard, grinning.

'Nothing,' said Judy. 'You thinking of going AWOL and emigrating?'

'Why?'

'The pants. Do you honestly think America would have you?'

He answered with another question. ' What you do tonight?'

They looked at each other and shrugged. 'No idea.'

'Ok. We go to hunt.'

Judy pricked up, her eyes keen with interest. 'Hunt what?'

'Pig.'

An hour later Eve walked up the road to the guest-house. There were only three or four people staying on the *moshav*. Herzl had asked her to make lunch. She loved this walk, knew every hole and gulley driven by the winter rains. I must have walked up and down a thousand times in the last few months, she thought.

She could see the plum orchard at the back of the stables where she had gone to pick plums the evening before. The sun had already settled pink across the hilltops as she entered the little grove. She had to strain in the dim light under the trees, to see the ripe golden plums, so sweet and juicy with that tart sour kick around the stone. The evening air was cool and mountain clear. As she swung back down the stony hillside, plastic bag bulging, clouds puffed on the horizon, turning blue. Her body swelled with emotion and all she could think was, I want to stay, I don't want to leave.

I have thought this so often in the Golan, she thought now as she walked into the kitchen. I just couldn't get it over to Dad. He should have come up here. Then he would have understood.

It was almost two weeks since her father had gone. They had talked for days, breaking the silence of her childhood. But his going had left her lost. A deep well of pain hung inside her, tunneling into her thoughts as she remembered how they had talked.

'Why did you lie to me?' she had shouted one morning, in a sudden rage towards him.

'No-one lied to you Eve! Don't be ridiculous.' Jack's face creased in irritation as he stood by the basin, running an electric shaver over his chin.

'It was lies! Lies by omission! Mum told me the story over and over again. But she never finished it. Never said why you didn't come.' She flung out an arm in his direction. 'And neither did you!' Inside she felt the bubble of hysteria rise. In a minute I'll roll on the floor and scream, she thought in horror. Like a kid throwing a tantrum.

He rubbed a hand over his chin, checking for patches of stubble. 'I didn't want to talk about it.

"Then why are you now?'

The buzz from the shaver ceased. She felt a sharp rush of fear.

He turned, eyebrows furrowed, mouth slightly open. 'Because you asked.'

'I asked before.'

'Not like this.'

'Like what?'

'Like an adult.'

She felt desperate to peel back the layers, evoke a reaction. She changed her mind about him continually. He was weak, easily dominated. He loved her mother, couldn't bear to upset her. He was a martyr, a bereaved father. He was none of these.

She felt more and more like the little girl bewildered at home, observing conflicts, broken-off sentences, eyebrows raised in warning.

'Grandma always said mum was filling my head with nonsense.'

Jack looked up from his plate. They were eating lunch in The Old City near the Fourth Station of the Cross. A group of pilgrims walked past, massed close together, Bibles open, fingers running along the page as they read aloud in Italian.

'Grandma was against us going from the start,' he said. 'But I didn't know she said that in front of you.'

'What did you know?' she challenged.

'That's not fair Eve!'

The pilgrims broke into song. Their voices sounded operatic in the narrow street.

I'm just being petty, thought Eve miserably.

One evening she took him onto the walls of the Old City to clamber about the broken stones. The moon was full, running a long blue path to their feet. They lit cigarettes and sat down. A church bell rang the hour.

'So much religion here,' Jack said. 'Religion and blood. I read somewhere this city has been conquered eleven times.'

She nodded absently, 'Something like that.'

Jack was quiet, aware she was not interested in history at that moment.

Then Eve said,' Did you know I had trouble breathing sometimes?'

'No.' He looked worried.

'Oh it's nothing,' she said briskly. ' I asked the doctor at college. He said it was psychosomatic. Because we didn't communicate at home.'

She turned to look at him her eyes wide with meaning. He stared back and then lit another cigarette from his glowing stub.

That hit home, she thought. It gave her a perverse feeling of confidence to say it now. 'We didn't communicate.' She kept on thinking of ways to bring it up.

'Andy used to say I was secretive.'

'In what way?'

'You know, if something happened, like I got a good mark for an essay. Or...you remember Karen?' He shook his head. 'It doesn't matter. But she got pregnant and had to leave.

'Eve picked up a newspaper from the bed and laughed at a cartoon on the back page. Jack was folding socks which had been drying on the balcony wall. Sun flooded the hotel room leaving clear demarcated areas of black and white on the tiled floor. How many floors did I wash like this on kibbutz? she thought.

She continued talking, 'I wouldn't tell him until long after things happened. I couldn't. Used to make him furious. 'Shit Eve! You should have said!' She laughed as she mimicked Andy's Manchester accent. ' I couldn't. I was used to not talking about things.' Her voice dropped as she eyed Jack, his hands still now, a black sock draped over one wrist. 'Like at home.'

An arrow of pleasure ran through her as she saw his eyes narrow in pain.

Alone in her room late at night she made notes, terrified she would forget things.

He wasn't at Belsen. Thank God! Ever since I was twelve I was convinced he had been there when they found the camp. He wasn't even in Germany by then. His face was amazing when I asked him. I think he's horrified by my thoughts. I won't keep anything from my children. (If I have any.)

One morning he opened his suitcase and pulled out a box of photographs.

'You never said you had these!' She fell on her knees, rifling through, spreading them out all over the floor.

He smiled at her excitement.

'You. Uncle David and, ' she screwed up her eyes. 'I think that's grandma. Where is it? Brighton?'

'Margate. We used to go for the day on the train.'

She snatched a faded sepia picture. 'Grandpa. In the Russian army. This is brilliant dad.'

He knelt down beside her, infected by her enthusiasm. 'This is mum and I soon after we met. I was already in The Hammers and we were doing up the boat. I had a picture somewhere...'

'What boat?'

Their eyes met, hers' wide with questions. For a moment they stared at each other, pupils locked and then he turned away.

'Didn't I tell you? We bought a boat. We were going to do it up for battle, sail it out to Palestine for the Irgun.

'Christ!' she breathed. 'What happened?'

'Fell through. Like a lot of things in those days. ' He looked at her expectantly.

But she had picked up another photograph and was staring at it. Deborah, heavily pregnant, hands folded over her swollen abdomen.

'Noah. Or me?'

'Noah.'

'Can I keep it?'

He looked as if he would say no. She tightened her grip on the picture. Then he said, 'If you want.'

In her notebook that night she wrote, *'I have the nearest thing to a picture of Noah. If anyone asked me I couldn't say why he's so important. Perhaps it's just that I was denied him. As though he was a lie or a figment of all their imaginations. Dad called him, 'Our Ark who sunk us all.' Launched himself into our lives. Even mine before I was born. But if I had known about him I wouldn't have felt sunk. Only diverted.'*

'Are you coming tonight?' Dani put his head round the kitchen door.

Eve was chopping onions, her eyes streaming with tears. She clutched a teacloth to her face. I must look awful, she thought and ran a hand through her hair. 'Well Judy certainly is. She's pulled her army trousers out of the wash.'

Dani laughed. 'She should join.'

'I think that's what she's planning.' Eve filled a saucepan with water and put it on to boil. 'Coffee? We do espresso style here, bang in coffee, sugar and milk and stir vigorously for five minutes.'

'Sounds good. So, you think you won't come?' There was a hint of anxiety in his voice.

'I don't want any trouble with the guns.' She looked up and grinned. 'But it sounds like fun.'

'It will be ok. Zoar is going and I am and Meni also. It would be good if you came too.'

'Even up the numbers.' He looked puzzled. 'Two girls, two boys.'

'Oh yes. And Meni.'

'He doesn't count,' and they both laughed.

After Dani had gone Eve wandered restlessly round the kitchen picking up vegetable peelings, stacking plates.

The big kitchen window was open. She could see a herd of goats on the road beyond the *moshav*. A Druze boy came into sight round the bend of the mountain throwing stones at the goats in front, shouting in harsh high-pitched tones. In the winter she had stood with Judy and Mick on the rough lane through Ein Kenye, the Druze village below the *moshav* and watched the goats wander home. The Druze built their houses on concrete stilts, with shelter for the animals beneath the living quarters.

I like Dani, she thought, leaning on the damp work surface sniffing the warm midday air. I like the way he wears his jeans. Not hugging his crotch like a come-on. She laughed out loud and looked round embarrassed to check she was still alone.

When she had returned to the *moshav* from Jerusalem, Dani and Zoar were still away in Eilat. 'They're staying another week,' said Judy in a subdued voice. 'They phoned Avram yesterday.'

'Missing Zoar?'

Judy shrugged. 'A bit. He's such an oaf.' She laughed. 'What the hell are we going to do without them?'

'There's always Luke.'

'Oh God!'

Judy didn't ask her if she missed Dani. Eve was relieved. Its not like that, she thought. Not yet. But she could still feel the cool length of his palm as he held her hand under the Golan stars.

They had a party in Meni's room when Zoar and Dani returned, tanned almost black from the desert sun.

'We dived every day,' said Zoar. 'And lay on the beach watching bikinis.'

'I'm surprised anyone was wearing them,' said Judy and gave Zoar a shove.

'Only the boys,' grinned Dani.

Meni's room was very small. Eve sat on the floor next to the record player, Dani squeezed in beside her.

'Are you comfortable?' he asked.

'No.'

'I'll move.'

But she put her hand on his knee. 'It's ok.'

'I feel like tomato,' said Meni as he rolled a joint.'

'What on earth do you want a tomato for Meni?' said Judy.

'Two boys, two girls and me!' he tapped his chest with a grin.

'He means gooseberry,' said Eve and they shouted with laughter.

'In the Yom Kippur war we kill a pig. When we cut it open there is a hand inside.'

'Revolting,' said Eve.

Zoar lit a cigarette. 'The pig eat the dead Syrian soldier.'

They were in Zoar's house waiting for Meni to bring the tractor round. Judy was dressed in her army trousers and a black singlet. Her hair was pulled back in a scarf, head band style across her forehead. On her feet were a battered pair of brown kibbutz boots.

She looks like a terrorist, thought Eve.

They heard the loud roar of an engine on the road. 'It is Meni.'

Outside it was very dark. The huge wheels of the tractor rose like a mountain above Eve's head.

'You hold the torch Eve.' Dani handed her a heavy metal torch. She switched it on. The powerful beam reached across the road into the darkened bushes.

Zoar was checking his gun. He pointed it into the air and fired. Eve jumped back shocked by the noise, the great length of flame piercing the night.

Imagine a war full of this, she thought. Hours, days, years. That small viscious piece of metal entering her soft unmarked body. Gaping abdomen, shattered breast, oozing face. The sense of pain was meaningless. She could not begin to imagine the long shards of agony which would rip through her sensory system.

She looked round at the little group. Their faces were expressionless. Then Zoar said, 'Let's go.'

They clambered up onto the tractor. Eve sat on the hub of one of the wheels, clinging to the sides as they bounced off up the road. Meni was driving. Suddenly he swung left into the scrub and headed down a wadi.

Eve looked across the hillside rising ahead of them. Further along, back towards the *moshav,* lights flashed in the bushes. Soldiers checking for terrorists, she thought.

How many days have they been in Uganda? She had watched the evening news, Idi Amin, fat and jolly filling the screen. Those poor bastards. God knows how they'll ever sort out that mess.

'Ok?' Dani's hand pressed her thigh.

'Great. This is really exciting.'

'I told you it would be!' cried Judy. She was sitting on the opposite wheel hub, boots resting on Zoar's lap.

Zoar was smoking a cigarette. Eve watched the red glow as it moved to and from his face. The night air was warm. She was wearing shorts and a t-shirt. The air felt good against her skin.

Dani's body was very close, its weight filling the space between them, his hand still on her thigh. She could feel each finger separately and the heat of his palm spreading outwards. Then he began to move his thumb slowly across the soft thin material of her shorts, insinuating down towards the under part of her leg.

The gears crashed and the tractor jerked to a sudden halt.

'What's happened?' asked Eve.

'We are here.' Zoar took the torch from her and switched it on. 'You point it around. We listen for pig. When we see him you keep still the torch. We kill. Ok?'

She nodded and took the torch. Judy was very quiet on the other side of the tractor. They all settled down to listen to the sound of pigs scuffling and snorting in the undergrowth.

'How long?' she whispered to Dani.

He had taken his hand away and picked up his gun. He shook his head. 'I don't know.'

While they waited she thought about Dani, his thumb stroking the soft flesh on her leg.

Before they had walked up to Zoar's house that evening Judy had said, 'I'm sleeping with Zoar tonight.'

'Oh. Where? Do you want the room?' I'll have to sleep in Norbert and Hilary's old room, thought Eve.

'No it's ok. I'll go to his house.'

'What about Dani?' The words slipped out. Eve felt annoyed. She avoided Judy's eyes.

But all Judy said was, 'They have separate rooms.'

She thought about Dani's room now as they sat in silence, ears straining like practised hunters. Would he have a double or single bed? Single probably. Too narrow for two. If you were actually sleeping of course. Do I want to sleep with Dani? she wondered, the idea slowly taking root in her mind.

'How do you feel?' whispered Dani.

'Bloodthirsty,' she hissed. 'And my backside's numb.'

'Want me to rub it for you?'

She couldn't resist a slight giggle.

'Ssh!' grumbled Zoar. 'We frighten the pig.'

They sat in silence, the white lip of the moon in the sky. She slipped into a fantasy about hunting, running barefoot through a jungle, knife in her hand, following the animal scent. Then she thought of her father in the war, face blackened, the long commando knife he had hung on a nail in the shed, fastened to his belt. Creeping forward across wet muddy fields, separated from his friends.

I would hate it, she thought. It would be absolutely awful.

She tightened her grip on the torch and looked down. It was a long black drop. Like the hole Herzl had dug the week before outside reception. Moishe had run a tractor over a pipe and cut the water to the *moshav*. She had walked up from her house in the clear morning light, the mountain tall and cloud free in front of her, her feet feeling loose and strong in her boots.

She was thinking about Bud on his kibbutz, the decision to stay behind him when Moishe cried out, 'Now we need to melt the snow!'

'What on earth's happened!' Herzl was at the bottom of a huge hole, his black curls laced with dust, pipes everywhere. 'No water!' shouted Herzl, grinning like a wayward schoolboy and wiping a muddy hand across his face.

'Well don't ask me mate, I'm just a volunteer!' and she had stood laughing over him as he struggled with a knot of piping.

What is it about this country that makes everything into a mad adventure? Thought Eve. Even a cut to the water supply!

'*Shama*! There!' Zoar pushed her hand holding the torch over the side of the tractor.

The beam shone deep into the valley. She could hear the safety catches release behind her. Then there was a scuffle and suddenly a gun barrel landed heavily across her lap.

'Judy!' Eve looked up into eyes wild with excitement.

The gun exploded. She heard Judy yell, 'Bullseye!'

Then she fell, racing down from the great height of the tractor wheel, the torch already lost in the wadi. As she screamed there was a terrible crashing in the undergrowth. A huge pig, tusks flashing, broke through beneath her.

When I hit the pig! whipped across her mind. Above her, a blur of shouting, Hebrew and English. Then someone grabbed her legs, hauled her back as if through hundreds of feet, as the deep thick stench of pig slammed into her mouth and nose.

Another gun shot and Meni jumped past her, whooping, closely followed by Judy. Eve sat rigid in Dani's arms.

'Eve! Are you ok Eve?' Dani's voice was edged with panic.

'She is ok,' growled Zoar. 'Why she drop the torch? She hear the gun before?'

You bastard, thought Eve.

Then Judy shouted up to them, 'I killed mine, I really did!' She held Zoar's M16 rifle high above her head.

The wadi was pitch black. No horizon of light, the moshav out of sight over the ridge. There were only the flashes of torchlight from the night patrol down the valley.

'Ok, we move!' said Zoar and jumped down with a rope. They lashed the pig to the back of the tractor. Then Meni drove off up the wadi shouting wildly in Hebrew and English to Judy.

As they reached the road, Judy turned to Eve, the whites of her eyes gleaming in her darkened face, 'You ok?'

'Of course,' said Eve in a quiet voice. 'And you?'

But Judy just laughed.

She's gone mad, thought Eve, her mind overloaded with fright. They're all mad except for Dani. Christ I nearly got killed and all they can do is tick me off for dropping the torch. Crazy, all of them.

Meni ground to a halt in front of Zoar's house. They jumped down and stood staring at the pig. It was a huge black beast with long coarse hairs all over its body. Blood seeped from a deep hole above one eye.

'What will they do with it now?' asked Eve.

'Sell it,' said Judy.

Eve eyed her uncertainly. She had slung Zoar's rifle over her shoulder, one hand held onto the strap, legs slightly apart, jaw set. Ready to fight? thought Eve.

'Better not let Avram see you with that gun,' said Eve.

Judy's face broke into a wide grin, 'Who gives a shit! It was a great evening.'

'Judy, just don't...'

'Don't what Eve?' Her voice was almost menacing.

Meni drove the tractor away, the last stench of dead pig filling their nostrils as it lurched forward.

'We go inside, drink something,' said Zoar. He took the gun from Judy and propped it behind the door.

As Judy walked into the living room Eve thought, What the hell's happened to her? Blood had splashed onto the leg of Judy's army trousers and her hair had come loose, falling around her face. She pulled it back in swift strong movements, tugging it into an elastic band, her eyes fixed in an intense stare ahead of her.

Dani caught Eve's hand, 'Coffee?'

'Not here,' said Eve, flicking her head in the directing of Judy and Zoar. 'Come and have coffee in my house.

As they walked down the road Dani said, 'Are you angry?'

'Yes. With Judy. It's all gone to her head tonight.'

'I don't understand.'

'The gun. I think she's been dying to shoot something or someone for months.'

Dani nodded. 'Its not unusual. Put a gun in a man's hand and he thinks he's Superman.'

'But you have to resist those feelings. I get them too. We all do living up here. Judy's taken it too far.'

'It's only a pig Eve.'

She hesitated and then she smiled, 'You're right. Maybe I've taken it too seriously.'

'You're the one who fell.'

The house was empty and dark. Eve walked through the living room to the kitchen switching on lights, a slight quiver of expectation in her abdomen.

Dani leaned in the doorway watching her as she filled a pan with water. Mud had splashed onto the front of his shirt and his jeans were creased. It was the most untidy she had seen him. He looked down at his clothes and grinned, 'It's like the army.'

She nodded smiling absently and lit the gas under the pan. Her mind was weighing up the rest of the night.

'Sugar?'

But he was gone. She could hear him in Meni's room fiddling with the record player. The heavy tones of Leonard Cohen, 'Bird on a Wire' meandered through the silent house.

Neutral territory, she thought. A good place to start. She took the coffee into the room. They sat side by side on the floor, backs against the wall opposite the bed. The window was open and a cool fragrant breeze washed around their heads.

As she leaned forward to sip the coffee Eve could see the outline of Meni's Kaloshnikov rifle under the bed.

'Look at that,' she nodded in the direction of the gun. 'He didn't even bother to get it out for the hunt.'

Dani smiled, his long tanned face creasing along lines that were becoming familiar. 'The army gives him a hard time.'

'I'm sure it's a two way process,' said Eve wryly.

The track ended. They listened in silence to the next one. Tea and oranges, thought Eve as she followed the words of the song. 'That would give me indigestion.'

'What would?' Dani murmured. He had moved closer and was stroking her bare leg below her shorts.

Her mind was beginning to concentrate on the movements of his hand as it traced ever widening circles on her leg. She became absorbed in the parts she wanted him to touch next, willing him to discover them for himself.

'What?' he said again.

'Tea and oranges.' Her voice was barely more than a whisper, husky and beginning to crack. 'I don't like the two together.'

He blew in her ear. Her legs weakened on the length of the floor and began to move apart. She suddenly longed to be naked. 'I like this combination,' he said and his tongue reached into her ear in hot wet movements.

She was surprised he knew such a complicated word. She covered his mouth with her's and then rolled on top of him pulling at his jeans.

'Hey, hey!' he laughed. 'You are feeling strong now.'

'Very. The hair on your chest is so soft.' This is all because of Max, she was thinking with joy, as she undid the buttons of his shirt. He gave me all this brazen confidence!

Dani had loosened her bra and she could feel the delicious pull of her breasts as their weight fell forward.

He raised her T-shirt along her back and together they pulled her free. Then in one movement downwards she was naked. The breeze blew fresh across her body, whipping her desire as he kneaded her large round buttocks and then pulled minutely on the tiny coarse hairs.

I'll come too soon, she thought, as waves of pleasure roared through her. Her hips were already in rhythmn and then his hands moved to her breasts.

She calmed slightly and began to unzip his jeans. He wore spotless white under pants, already bulging. She loosened his erection and muzzled it against her pubic hair. Her breath was coming faster now. Then he suddenly grabbed her and moaned, 'Inside.' She guided his penis into her flooded vagina and felt the huge soar of orgasm as he gasped against her breasts.

As she lay on his body listening to the rapid beat of his heart she heard a slight movement by the door. Pushing her hair back from her face she turned her head to see Meni standing a few feet away, an amused grin on his face.

She opened her mouth to speak but he raised his hand in a half salute, two fingers open in the peace sign. Then he disappeared and she heard the click of a bedroom door at the end of the corridor.

All she could think was that he had seen her naked. Then she burst out laughing. Dani joined in. 'No, you don't understand,' she cried, waving her hand in the air. 'I wasn't even embarrassed we were having sex. Just that he saw me naked. And in his room. Isn't that ridiculous?'

'No,' laughed Dani. 'Sex brings out the silly side of people. And now the first part is over you can show me what you really like.' He rolled over covering her with soft gentle kisses.

CHAPTER TWENTY

'Did you hear the news?' Moishe cried out in English as Dani and Eve walked into the guest-house early the next morning. Moishe had an Uzi sub-machine gun slung over his shoulder.

Strange, thought Eve. He never carries a gun.

Dani called out a greeting in Hebrew and then said, 'What news?'

'The hostages are free! The Israelis went into Entebbe last night and got them out!'

Herzl ran in, shouted something in Hebrew and ran out again. Everyone followed him into reception. Judy was there with Zoar and a crowd of moshavniks.

Eve grabbed Judy's arm, 'What the hell's going on?'

But suddenly the excited hubbub in the room stopped and Zoar turned up the radio for the seven o'clock news.

My God! thought Eve. What kind of people are these Israelis? We go to bed last night and all the hostages are still there, in the massive heat of Entebbe and by the next morning they are gone.

'Come on!' said Dani. He was pulling her arm. Everyone was pushing out of the door, shouting, laughing and clapping each other on the back. Eve realised all the men were carrying guns.

'Where are we going?'

'First to my house to get my gun,' said Dani.

'Why?'

'There is an order. Every Israeli must carry his gun now because we are afraid of terrorist attacks. Then we go to watch television in Moishe's house.'

As they walked rapidly down the road Dani began to talk in an excited voice. 'They got them all out. One Israeli officer was killed and I think some hostages were hit.'

'It's incredible Dani. I just don't believe it!'

'Nobody believes it! The whole country's gone crazy. Like we won a war!'

That's it, thought Eve. That's what feels so different. She thought of the *moshavniks* faces as they shouted the news to each other. The electric feeling in reception as they crowded round the tiny radio. Just like a war. A war that's been won.

Dani collected his gun and then they raced hand in hand to Moishe's house. All round the *moshav* they could hear shouts as people yelled details to each other, out of windows and across brick walls.

'Everyone is greedy for news. They want more and more,' laughed Dani.

He's like a kid let out of school, thought Eve. This is just what Israel needed. They've all been walking round like old aged pensioners since the Yom Kippur War.

'Just what the doctor ordered,' she cried as they leapt a pothole.

'What?'

She waved her hand. 'Doesn't matter.' But it is, she thought. How the hell did they manage it?

In Moishe's house the television was on full blast. Moishe and Etty sat on the floor, Zoar and Judy next to them. Two soldiers, guns balanced between their knees crushed together on the sofa. When they saw Eve they squeezed apart and Dani nodded to her to sit down. He knelt behind her and murmured translations.

The army was holding a press conference. Dani told her everyone was still waiting for the planes to land from Entebbe. A colonel was describing a model of the hanger at Entebbe airport where the hostages were held, pointing with a long cane.

'We built that,' said Dani in Eve's ear. ' When Israel was friendly with Uganda, we helped them with the airport. So we have all the plans. The army built a mock-up of it and started rehearsing the rescue three days ago.'

Moishe looked over his shoulder, a broad grin on his face. 'It took them just 36 minutes Eve. Think about it! 36 minutes. They kill everyone, all the terrorists, 100 Ugandan soldiers, and bomb their planes too.'

'Ssh, listen to this now,' said Etty.

There was a shot of Ben Gurion airport. Thousands of people had gathered, spilling onto the runway, defying all security. 'Now they wait for the plane,' said Etty.

A stream of Hebrew came from the commentator. Eve looked at the huge Golani soldiers in full combat gear. A swell of emotion filled her as she watched their absorbed faces. They must feel so tremendous, she thought. What an incredible country!

'That is a picture of Yonatan Netanyahu, the soldier who was killed,' said Judy pointing to the screen. 'It's amazing, they only lost one man. He was a Lieutenant Colonel. Nice looking bloke.'

'Did they say how many soldiers took part?' asked Eve.

'90. They used a Hercules plane and glided in behind a British scheduled cargo flight so they wouldn't be spotted.'

Everyone was eager to swap information, searching out the English words for Eve.

'They decide to go and they go, but the cabinet, they still talking, shall we? Shan't we? But still the soldiers go,' laughed Moishe.

'Yes, but they could have turned back,' reasoned Judy. 'If they hadn't have gone it would have been too late.'

'The pilots they never fly so far before,' said Zoar.

One of the soldiers turned to Eve and shook his hand, his thumb pressed onto his middle finger. When he spoke he had a thick rough voice, ' Every man take 45 seconds to find his place. They practise for three days.'

The picture on the screen changed to a group of Israeli teenagers dressed in the khaki uniform of the National Youth movement. They were grouped in formation round the blue and white flag, singing with earnest looks on their faces.

'God! I hate this kind of stuff,' groaned Judy. 'Reminds me of the Hitler Youth.'

'They have to fill in with something between news,' laughed Eve.

'Coffee!' called out Etty. She came in with a tray loaded with coffee and biscuits.

Eve stood up feeling cramped on the sofa. The two soldiers immediately spread into the space she had left and started to argue in loud voices. Judy had moved over to the dining table where the tray stood. She was stirring sugar into a steaming mug. Eve watched her for a minute and then walked over and threw her a cautious smile.

'Exciting isn't it?'

Judy put down her spoon and sighed, 'I never seem to be where the action is.'

'You mean you wished you'd been hi-jacked?'

Judy laughed. 'Shit no! Just, oh I dunno. Somewhere.'

'Other than here?'

Judy eyed her carefully, 'Like you last night?'

'How do you mean?' Eve felt uncomfortable. Not a row. Not here, she pleaded silently.

'Didn't you wish yourself miles away? You must have been terrified. I felt awful for you.'

'Bloody funny way you had of showing it,' said Eve gruffly.

'Oh come on Eve. Zoar was being an absolute sod. I didn't want to make a fuss or they would have all ganged up on you. No feelings these Israeli men!' She threw Zoar a meaningful look. He was deep in conversation with Dani on the other side of the room.

Eve looked into Judy's face. So I was wrong, she thought. Judy wasn't down on me at all. Just the heat of the moment, I suppose. She felt a warm rush of feeling for her friend. We've been through so much together. Can't let this come between us.

Judy was smiling at her over the rim of her mug. 'Actually I'm crazy about Zoar. But he needs some educating.' She nodded in Dani's direction, a gleam in her eye. 'Cracked it there haven't you?'

Eve grinned. ' He's off to the army next week. 20 days *miliuim.*'

'Good God Eve! What're you going to do?'

Eve shrugged. 'We'll see when next week comes.'

'Eve!'It was Dani calling her. 'Come and see Idi Amin.'

They hurried back to their places, the two soldiers insisting Eve squeeze between them again. On the television there was a clip from a film of Amin made by the French a couple of years earlier.

The Israelis hooted with laughter at the sight of the African leader, in the uniform of a Field Marshall rows of medals bouncing on his large chest.

'Fat bastard, hey Eve!' yelled Zoar.

She nodded and grinned, thumbs up.

On the screen was a tank and two foot soldiers. Amin walked beside the tank through the scrub of the Ugandan countryside. Suddenly he brought his arm up and then lowered it quickly, a big grin on his face.

'Fire!'

The tank fired and the camera panned in as the shell exploded onto a low hummock in the distance.

'There!' cried Amin. 'I take the Golan Heights!'

The room exploded. The Golani soldiers roared so much Eve was terrified they would let off their guns, The great fat face of Amin filled the screen as the Israelis hurled insults and waved their arms at him.

'What you think Eve!' cried Moishe. 'Idi Amin Dada come and take the Golan Heights?'

'Not a chance!' Eve yelled back over the noise in the room.

She pulled herself to her feet and walked round to Dani behind the sofa.

'This is a great day Eve,' Dani said and took her in his arms, pressing his lips against hers. One of the soldiers gave a wolf whistle and Eve began to laugh against Dani's lips.

Dani pulled away grinning. 'Let's go. I want to see Avram. He will be in reception now for the guests.'

'I don't want to miss anything,' said Eve. But the youth group were back on the screen. 'Oh, ok. We'll come back in a while.'

Outside the air was hot and bright.

'American Independence Day. July 4th,' said Dani.

'Most suitable. What do you think the Americans feel about the rescue?'

'Oh they are very pleased. All over the world Israel is getting congratulations. Except from our enemies.'

'Who are also all over the world.'

'*Bidiouk*. Exactly.' Dani's face narrowed, a note of sadness in his voice. 'It's hard to be an Israeli all the time. I think you need a rest from it sometimes.'

'Would you rather be an Iraqi?'

It was the most personal question she had ever asked him.

He hesitated as if unsure of her reaction. Then he nodded. 'Of course. All my family were born in Iraq.'

He had stopped and was standing a little way ahead of her on the stony road, his eyes on her face, wary, uncertain of her reaction. ' I like Arabic music, Arabic food, I like to speak and hear Arabic...'

'And Arabic women?' Now's the moment of truth, she thought and was surprised how much it meant to her.

He shook his head quickly. 'No. Well, yes.' He gave an embarrassed laugh. 'I like them But I don't have to just be with Iraqi girls. It is enough that you understand what I feel.'

'I think I do,' she said and they walked on up the road in silence.

In reception Avram was on the phone. As soon as he had finished another moshavnik rushed in and picked up the telephone. As he shouted at the person on the other end of the line Dani laughed.

'The first thing everyone says is, ' Did you hear the news?' Not, 'Hello how are you?' or 'This is Chaim, can I speak to Avi.' It's very funny Eve.'

Dani started talking to Avram in Hebrew and Eve sat down. A constant stream of people came in to use the phone. She began to recognise the phrase, *Shamaht et ha hadashot*? Did you hear the news?

Just like in the Beiliss case! she suddenly thought. 1913. Russia. Beiliss was put on trial for a Blood Libel, accused of killing a Christian child to take his blood for matzos. She remembered her history tutor at college telling them to read it up. 'The worst aspect of the case for the Russian intelligentsia,' he had told them, ' was that it clearly showed how backward Russia was compared to the rest of Europe. They were absolutely horrified.'

It was the telephone girls who spread the news round Moscow. 'Acquitted!' they all cried before they put calls through.

Eve looked up. Avram called over to her, 'My friend was on the rescue team Eve.'

'Really?' Eve was impressed. ' Did he tell you? I would have thought it was a big secret.'

Dani laughed. 'Zoar says the same. His friend from kibbutz he also thinks went to Entebbe.'

'No, really Dani.' Avram's face was serious. 'Yossi, you know Yossi Cohen? He went from his home before three days. Nobody knows where he gone. They practice for three days, each man taken by hand by the army. You know Yossi, he is the best.'

Dani nodded. 'Ok maybe Yossi went, maybe Zoar's friend too. You know this country. The whole place is one big kibbutz. Everybody will know somebody who went.'

Eve grinned. 'Must be rumours flying everywhere today.' She looked at her watch. It was nearly nine o'clock. The water must be hot enough by now, she thought. The thermostat had been playing up again in her house. She touched Dani's arm. 'I'm going to take a shower. Where shall I see you, for the next installment?'

'I will go to Avram's house. Don't be too long. We should watch them land.'

'Of course.'

She swung down the road, exhilarated, her skin tingling, her mind racing over the morning's events. In the distance she saw Luke stroll out of a house near one of the shelters.

Wonder who he's screwing now? she thought with a grin. He gets more gorgeous every day. Her eyes followed Luke's long slim body as he loped up to the guest house, his smooth hair bleached white by the sun. California will love him when he gets home.

Home. The word struck a deep hollow chord inside her. Her father had been home almost three weeks. But he hadn't written.

Had she made him angry? There wasn't enough time to say it all and then put it right!

She pushed open the door of the house. It was quiet. Everyone had gone to watch television. In her room she stripped off all her clothes and walked naked across the corridor into the shower. She pulled her hair loose from an elastic band and stood under the powerful jet. She felt sore between her legs from lovemaking. It was beautiful, she thought and rubbed her limbs to loosen her tired muscles.

'I have six more days Eve, ' he had said. ' Then I won't see you .' His face elongated with sadness. 'We are just beginning.'

'I know,' she said with a sigh. 'Let's just be together now. I don't want to think about the future.' She leaned over to her bedside table and scribbled on a piece of paper.

'What's this?' he said blinking in the dim light.

'My address in London. In case we lose touch.'

There is so much future to think about, she thought as she squirted shampoo onto her hand. The next few days before Dani goes to the army. The next few weeks, months. The next time I see Dad and Mum.

She had said goodbye to Jack at the hotel. 'My bus leaves soon and anyway I hate airports,' she had said.

He stooped to pick up his passport from the bedside table and she suddenly noticed how grey his hair was, the wrinkles mounting across his neck. She watched his hand close round the passport. The same hand which had held her safe from roads and big dogs as a child, a broad flat hand, flecked with the dark brown freckles of middle-age. She felt a lump rise in her throat at the thought of parting but the fresh glow of anger still burned inside her.

We don't understand each other, she thought bleakly. Nothing's changed.

Then he turned and in his eyes there was the same calm gaze which had been there since his childhood. Even though I didn't know him then, she thought. On an impulse she put her arms round his neck, interlacing her fingers behind him and smiled up into his face. Like lovers, flicked across her mind.

'Well, bye then dad, have a good trip home.' She kissed him on the cheek, breathing in his smell she had called, 'special Dad' since she was six.

Maybe we don't have to understand each other, she thought, as she adjusted the shower head to increase the spray. Let's take a rain check, as Bud would say. I just want to concentrate on Dani right now. And Entebbe! she thought with a start. Mustn't miss the landing.

She dried herself hurriedly and dressed, leaving her damp hair loose. It was already nine-thirty and they would be landing soon.

When she arrived at Avram's house the front door was wide open. Inside it was very quiet. Chava, Avram's wife sat on the sofa in the living-room alone. The television wasn't on.

'Shalom.'

Chava looked up, her round dark face etched with sadness. Deep black shadows hung under her eyes. She nodded wearily and patted the sofa. 'Shalom Eve. Come, sit.'

Eve sat down feeling awkward. Where the hell's Dani? she thought. What's going on? Her mind began to turn over possibilities.

Chava was dressed in shorts and an old T-shirt. There was a hole in one sleeve and her hair was beginning to fall away from the pins on her head.

She's always so slick, thought Eve. Like Avram. They're the smartest pair on the *moshav*. 'Peacocks!' Meni would laugh when they swanned into the guest-house at dinner, Avram in his white suit, Chava in six inch heels and a skirt designed to accentuate her beautiful legs.

'Not watching TV?' Eve asked.

Chava shook her head slowly.

'Something up?'

Chava drew a king-size cigarette out of a pack on her lap, 'You want Eve?'

Eve nodded and took a cigarette.

Abruptly Chava started to talk. 'Today is the first anniversary of the death of my friend and her baby.'

A shock ran through Eve. What's this got to do with Entebbe, she thought confused.

Chava was still talking. ' Terrorists jumped the border and ran down past the moshav to her kibbutz in the valley. The men were all in the fields when they heard the shots. They had to run home to get their guns. Nullah and the baby were already dead. The terrorists killed them in cold blood.' Chava stopped as abruptly as she began.

Like someone pressed the off button, thought Eve horrified.

Voices sounded at the open door. Dani and Avram came in.

Avram was chewing a bread roll. His mouth full he nodded to Eve, walked over to the television and switched it on.

'Sit, sit,' he motioned to Dani.

Dani sat down next to Eve on the sofa. Chava , cigarette forgotten in her hand, continued to stare into space. Avram slumped down in an armchair, eyes fixed on the TV, his teeth gnawing on the bread.

Yellow teeth, Eve thought. Smart suits, Brut aftershave, but he doesn't clean his teeth. She looked at Chava and back at Avram. The silence between them was like a wall.

Dani didn't seem to notice. He took Eve's hand, his face on the screen and said, 'Ok? Good shower?'

'No,' muttered Eve, her eyes on Avram. 'Let's go.'

Dani looked at her, eyebrows raised. Then seeing the look on her face , he nodded briefly, said something in Hebrew and stood up. Tugging gently on her hand he led the way outside.

'Did you know about Chava's friend?' Eve burst out, relieved to be in the open air.

Dani shook his head. Eve told him the story finishing with, 'And what about Avram? I know he fancies himself but he's just so insensitive!'

'I don't think those two talk very much.' Dani put his arm around her. ' Or do anything else.' He gave a wicked laugh and squeezed her breast.

'Wouldn't surprise me,' Eve laughed back.

They hurried up the road to Zoar's house, suddenly afraid they were missing something. Zoar and Judy were glued to the TV set, arms locked around each other's waists.

There's something different here, thought Eve when she saw them. But her attention was caught by the wild scenes on the screen.

'They've landed!' cried Zoar. 'Look at all the peoples go crazy.'

The runway was packed with cheering crowds, jumping up and down, waving arms, flags, small children balanced on shoulders. Eve felt close to tears and turned her face away embarrassed. She felt Dani squeeze her arm. Maybe he feels like crying too, she thought. But when she looked into his eyes they were dry.

Streams of Hebrew came from the excited commentator. Dani said in English, 'You hear that, about Kenya?'

'What?' said Eve tugging at his sleeve.

'They were supposed to refuel at Entebbe,' said Judy. 'But there wasn't time. President Kenyatta let them land at Nairobi airport. They didn't know he would let them until they left Entebbe.'

Zoar turned round, 'The man just say they kill one hundred Ugandan soldiers. But three passengers were killed and some wounded when the Israelis kill the terrorists.'

'And they left a woman behind,' put in Judy.

'God! Who?' said Eve.

'Someone called Dora Bloch. She was ill and the Ugandans had taken her into hospital. Amin is bound to release her now.'

A silence fell over the room. Judy moved closer to Zoar. Eve felt a chill creep through her. What if he doesn't let her go? The picture of Chava's friend and her baby filled her mind. It's always the weakest in the front line, she thought.

They watched for almost an hour as the planes taxied to a halt and the passengers were unloaded. The identity of the soldiers who took part in the rescue was kept secret.

'See your friend anywhere Zoar,' teased Eve.

'Not yet, soon,' laughed Zoar.

Eve felt her mood swing from elation to tears and back again as she watched hugging, kissing and crying flash to and fro across the screen. It's an enormous day, she thought. After all the dead and wounded of the '73 war. A day to shout and laugh about. This is such a mercurial place to live.

'How about some food?' Judy had disentangled herself from Zoar and stood over Eve smiling.

'Great, I'll come and help.'

It was a relief to move about after sitting crouched over the set for so long. 'I haven't watched TV so much since the first moon landing,' said Eve , as they walked into the kitchen.

Judy nodded and began slicing bread. There was a silence and Eve began to wonder whether they had really smoothed over the upset of the previous night.

Then Judy said, 'I moved in with Zoar last night.'

'Oh?'

'For good Eve. I'm staying...' Suddenly she was talking in a rush, words tumbling out, '...I'm going to become a candidate, Zoar's already a member so it'll just be a formality and we'll get married...'

'Married! Hold on Judy. I mean, have you thought this through?'

'We talked all night Eve, it was so wonderful!' Judy's eyes were shining.

With love? thought Eve. Or something more? Its not just Zoar she loves.
If she really does. Its Nevae Ativ, the Golan, the mountain, the Druze. And
the danger. Zoar is the key to all this.

Judy was still talking, '...I never felt like this before about anybody. We've
made so many plans. And you Eve. You must stay too. And persuade Dani.
Zoar wants him here so much.'

'Dani!' Eve laughed. 'A *moshavnik*! You must be joking. He's a business
man. Zoar should know better than that.'

'Oh come on Eve. Its what you've always wanted. To stay here and build
the land.'

The old slogan rippled through Eve. And the echo? She searched for it in
her mind, the sound of her mother's voice, the special look on her face when
she said , 'You could have been born in Israel.' It's not there, she thought.
Faded away.

Judy's voice slid between her thoughts, 'Admit it Eve. It's what you've
always wanted, to stay.'

It was then Eve realised. And knew for sure that it wasn't the first time,
but part of the process she had gone through. Couldn't be avoided in fact. No
process can truly be avoided if it is allowed to run its course. That's the risk,
she thought. She felt sad and yet free, relieved of a burden and already
grieving at the loss.

'Eve? What do you say?'

Eve shook her head slowly. 'No Judy. You're wrong. This is not what I've
always wanted.'

'But you and Dani...'

'It's not me and Dani, not the way you and Zoar have decided anyway. We
hardly know each other. He's going into the *miliuim* and I'm going home.'

The word resounded through her mind as she turned and slipped out of the
house, blotting out Judy's cries of, 'Hey, wait a minute!'

Outside the road was empty. Sunshine filled the hills and the valley, the
clear air still and warm. Tears filled her eyes at the thought of leaving all this
behind. Love for the Golan coursed through her, an almost unbearable ache.
I'll have to visit each corner one more time so that I never forget, she thought,
brushing tears from her cheeks.

Someone called her name. It was Moishe on his balcony. 'Did you see
them land?'

'Yes,' she nodded, hoping he hadn't seen her crying.

'Come for coffee.'

His long muscular arms, bare to the shoulders, leaned like tree trunks on the low wall. Eve looked up into his eyes, wide and clear, reflecting all his feelings for his country, all his dreams. This is the true sabre, she thought. The sabre of the posters, the songs, the camp fires. Without sabres like Moishe this country would die. And God knows that's what the world expects Jews to do, she thought with a sudden surge of bitterness.

'Ok,' she waved and walked up the hill.

Leaning against the wall in Moishe's kitchen Eve asked, 'Where's Etty?'

'The children they need to run a little now. We watch TV since six. So what do you think now of Israel? You make it your home?'

The second time in ten minutes, thought Eve with a pang. Her body tingled with nerves, expectation of the conflicts ahead. So many people to tell, all they way back to Bud.

She took a deep breath and shook her head. This is not going to come out as an apology, she thought grimly. 'No Moishe. I'm going home.'

'What! Why Eve? I thought you happy here.'

'I'm not unhappy of course. But...this is not my home. Home is where you feel at home. Not an outsider.'

'But you are Jewish. All the peoples here are Jewish.'

'All?'

'No. Of course not all. But this is the Jewish Home. After Hitler it must be.'

'Oh yes. I agree. After the Holocaust there was no other way forward. We Jews need our own homeland. But I am an individual Moishe. Not a cog in the wheel of a cause. I must be free to make my own mind up.'

'So what you decide?'

'I am a Jew of the Diaspora. That is a perfectly valid identity. Just as valid as being an Israeli Jew. I was born in England and that is where I feel at home. That is where I want to make my life.'

'So you leave us Eve. You leave the Golan and all your friends.' Moishe's face was lined with sadness.

He takes this as a personal failure, thought Eve. 'I don't go empty handed Moishe. I know what it means to live in Israel, the struggles and the fears and the hopes of the Jews of Israel. But Entebbe is your victory. I am the foreign visitor who was privileged to share it with you. Entebbe is a direct product of the strength and creativity of the State of Israel.

"You will be back.' Moishe's eyes were liquid with passion.

'Yes, to visit.'

'No Eve. To live. When they say they give back the Golan you will come.'

Part Five

War!

CHAPTER TWENTY-ONE

January 22nd 1991.

'And the family? Everyone's safe?'

'Oh yes. Dani's on the phone all the time.' Eve swung round to grab Benji's arm as he swiped at the cat. 'Just a moment Sally. Crisis looming.' The cat nipped smartly out of the flap in the back door and Benji roared off into the playroom, arms out, banking like a bomber.

'Sounds like he's well into it,' laughed Sally.

'A bit too much,' said Eve. 'One of the Scuds at the weekend landed in the park near where Dani's mum lives. Sam was quite upset. We've stopped watching TV with the kids around.'

'Shouldn't Benji be at nursery?'

'He's recovering from a cold. Look I'd better go. There's so much to do....'

'I always said you were crazy to have four. Heard from the Guardian yet?'

'They're taking that article but they want another. I just haven't got the time. I'm between au pairs and Dani's up to his eyes getting the new deli opened on time in Golders Green.'

'Problems, problems. Same time on Thursday for lunch?'

'Oh God yes. I need an oasis.'

Eve clicked off the cordless phone and went to check on Benji. He was playing with a huge army of toy soldiers Sam and Gidi had set up on the floor. He looked up as she came in and gave her his 'naughty' grin, nose running. She swooped down with a tissue, cleaned him up and said, 'For Heaven's sake don't mess this lot up Benji. Sam will go mad.'

'I won't.' Benji sprawled back across the carpet, his tiny legs beating up and down as he made staccato gun noises.

He's still small for his age, thought Eve. The other four year olds look like giants next to him. She made a mental note to get the doctor to check his height again and went back into the kitchen to load the dish washer.

It was Tuesday. Shelley on the other side of the close was doing the school run. Sam and Gidi needed haircuts....

The phone rang. She dropped a glass. The glass smashed into vicious shards on the tiled floor. For a second she felt herself shake. We're so much on edge, she thought. Every ring of the phone threatened bad news.

'Hello darling, it's me.'

'Oh good.'

'Why? Do you need something?'

'No, no it's ok.' She tried to inject a casual note into her voice.

'Well we've set the opening date for the new deli.'

She relaxed. It's just a business call. 'That's great news. I'll have to get a new outfit.'

They laughed. 'Any excuse,' said Dani. 'Will you have time to start your article?'

'Not with Benji under my feet. I must get another girl. I miss Corinne so much.'

'Try the agency today. I want you to come with me to the restaurant in Hampstead to look at decorations. Jewish food is getting bigger and bigger.'

'War gives people an appetite. Did you hear about the holocaust memorial in Hyde Park?'

'No. What happened ?

"My dad said someone smeared red paint all over it. He went to have a look.'

'Bastards! Like the poor the antisemites are always with us.'

She could picture his face as he spoke, eyes serious behind Ralph Lauren glasses, hair just beginning to throw up grey strands as he turned forty. Dani liked an expensive but casual lifestyle. They had a six bedroom house on the edge of Hampstead, opposite the Heath Extension, but the kids went to the local primary school. Holidays were usually with family, his brothers and mother in Tel Aviv or with his sister in Los Angeles. The children were at home in both places, speaking fluent Hebrew which Dani had spoken to them from birth.

I nearly missed him, thought Eve, as she swept up the glass after Dani had rung off. Me back in London in '76, drifting, out of work. Dani in the army and then sent back to America for four months by his dad.

Sally and Pete were engaged by the time she returned. 'Then we're off to New Zealand for two years, 'Sally told her. 'The company wants Pete out there and I'll get a teaching job. Andy's in Hong Kong.'

Eve shrugged, aware of Sally's eyes on her. 'Good for him.'

'Didn't meet anyone in the Promised Land?' Sally grinned as she swirled gin and tonic in her glass. They were in a London pub, punk music crashing on the juke box. Eve had been back three weeks and ached for the Golan.

'No-one special.' She was searching in the pockets of her jeans for change. 'You'll have to lend me a couple of quid Sal. I didn't need money on the Golan, got out of the habit of carrying it.'

Sally raised her eyes to the ceiling, 'Sounds like a right dump. What on earth did you do out there?'

More than I've ever done before, thought Eve. She shrugged again, 'Washed dishes.'

'A great training for life. And what now my ageing hippie friend? A dazzling career in Woolworth's?'

'I'm only twenty three,' laughed Eve. She sipped her drink. 'I'm writing, trying to break into journalism. The dole covers all my needs.'

Sally leaned forward over the damp tabletop, her engagement ring glinting on her finger. 'What you need is a bloke.'

'Maybe. But right now I have to settle into the flat and fence off mum and dad and my grandmother who keeps force-feeding me with chicken soup.' She stood up and looked at her watch. It was ten o'clock, a warm August night. At least there's a heatwave, she thought. 'I must go Sally. Got an early start tomorrow.'

Sally slapped a five pound note into her hand. 'It's not a loan. For old times sake, ok?'

Eve looked at the money and then nodded. 'Ok. I'll do the same for you when I'm rich and famous.'

On the bus home to her flat in Lewisham she thought, Does Dani feature under the category of blokes I met in Israel? She was glad she hadn't said anything to Sally.

Her eyes panned over the narrow streets and grimy buildings of South London. A boy on the plane back to England had said, 'It takes six months to adjust after living in Israel.'

Orange street lights blotted out the stars. The air was filled with car fumes. On the Golan now, she thought, it would be full moon.

The heatwave stretched into autumn. A woman's magazine took one of her articles. Grandma Stone turned eighty and her parents made a party. As the winter began Eve still thought about the Golan every day.

One chill morning, rising late her flatmate already gone to work, the telephone rang.

'Eve? This is Dani Gabbay. You remember me from Nevae Ativ? I am in Humpsteed.'

'Dani! Of course I remember,' she had laughed. God! He still can't pronounce it. 'Let's meet.'

Time for a coffee, thought Eve, as she scooped powder into the dish washer. She stilled missed cigarettes, but they had both given up with her first pregnancy. 'We'll give their little lungs a chance, ' she had said as she drew in the last stretch of nicotine.

But the last few days since the first Scud attack had been harrowing. She found herself longing for a cigarette. The children spent the evenings dive-bombing off the sofa and pelting Dani with questions.

'Were you a pilot dad? Was grandpa?'

'Were you in the same war?'

'Grandpa's old stupid. They couldn't be in the same war?'

'I'm not stupid dumbo. You're stupid!'

'Boys, that's enough!' Dani's voice was calm, level. 'No-one is stupid. But you remember, this is a real war, not a game. People are getting hurt.'

They were quiet, Sam and Gidi silently kicking each other on the sofa, seven year old Jake sucking his thumb, Benji stretched out on the floor with his toys.

'My brothers have put the children with friends in Jerusalem, ' said Dani, his eyes fixed on the screen.

'Why dad?' jumped in Sam, always alert.

'They don't think Saddam will bomb Jerusalem because of the Palestinians living there.'

The TV showed sniffer dogs, trained in earthquakes, padding over severed slabs of concrete, searching for bodies.

'They bomb in Ramat Gan,' said Dani. 'Where the Iraqi Jews live.'

'Why Ramat Gan dad? Because Savtah lives there? Dad? Why?' Sam's voice was insistent.

Dani focused on Sam and smiled. 'Ramat Gan is where all the Iraqi Jews live. That's why Savta, your grandma lives there. People in Israel call it 'Little Baghdad'. Before the Gulf War they laughed and said Saddam will never bomb there. Now we see what he does.'

Jack and Deborah came to tea on Sunday afternoon, four days into the war, their faces lined with anxiety. Scores of Israelis had already been injured, hundreds of buildings damaged.

'How's the family,' asked Jack.

'They are all ok,' Dani gave a little tense smile. 'They will be all right. Not too many bombs have fallen and they are putting in the Patriots this week. The Iraqis are not very accurate.'

'Its the threat of gas which is so terrifying,' shuddered Deborah.

Eve shook her head and went into the kitchen. This was her waking nightmare. Ramat Gan awash with gas, the whole family wiped out, Dani a screaming, hysterical mess, the children wailing. What the hell would I do? She thought for the hundredth time.

She filled the kettle and switched it on. Jack came in. 'Need any help? Mum's playing Snake and Ladders with the kids. Dani thinks they've watched enough TV.'

Eve nodded and swallowed, her eyes on the kettle.

'I know this sounds crazy dad, but I want to be there!' she suddenly burst out. 'Put on my gas mask, tape up my windows and sit in my sealed room. Another Jew in Israel, two fingers in the air to Saddam bloody Hussein. What the hell am I doing here!'

Jack opened a cupboard and started taking out mugs one at a time, lining them up on the worktop. She could see the tension in him by the tilt of his head.

'I know love....'

'You just never get over the feeling for Israel! It's incredible!' She stopped, a lump in her throat threatening to choke her. Moishe's last words echoed in her mind. 'You will come. When they give back the Golan.'

I never took him seriously, thought Eve. Just wanted to get back to London, get on with my life. Now they might take the Golan! The thought pressed on her like a weight.

'No-one's asking you to get over it,' said Jack as he poured milk into cups. 'It's just you have different priorities.'

As Eve sat in the kitchen, sipping her coffee, the dish washer whirring, she thought about her father's words.

Everyone on the *moshav* had priorities. But they all hinged on fantasy, it seemed to her now. Avram wanted to get rich quick, Judy wanted legitimised violence, Moishe wanted to be an old style pioneer.

And me? What did I want? I wanted my mother's words to come true. I wanted to be able to say that I was a sabre.

'Lunchtime mum.' Benji pulled himself up onto her lap and started to push her hair back from her forehead. She found it soothing and let him continue for a moment.

Then she smiled and said, 'Ok big boy. Chips or pasta?'

'Both,' he grinned, clapping his hands. 'And ketchup mummy. Please, please.'

'You're so naughty,' she laughed picking him up and cuddling him. Kids! They really ground you when things are tough.

While Benji was playing with the food on his plate, sorting it into 'goodies' and 'baddies', the telephone rang. It was Dani again.

'Ofer just phoned.' Ofer was Dani's eldest brother. 'He decided my mother should come to London and he's managed to get her a flight out on Thursday morning. It's the earliest one they could get. All the flights are heavily booked. Will you cope?'

'Of course Dani! God! I'm so pleased! Anyone else want to come. I'll sling mattresses down in the living room if necessary.'

'No Eve. No-one else wants to.'

His tone was cool, critical. Most people wouldn't leave, she reminded herself. Israelis have seen all this before.

'So it's ok?'

'Yes, yes,' Eve repeated. 'Sharona must stay until the end of the war. She must be terrified. ' She tried to picture her mother-in-law in a gas mask and failed.

'She can't move quickly enough when the sirens go. I think that's the main problem. Anyway gives you a couple of days to get the spare bedroom ready. Pity it's turned so cold. I hope it doesn't snow.'

'Savta's coming to stay,' Eve smiled at Benji as she put the phone down.

'Goody, goody,' laughed Benji, his face covered with ketchup. 'Savta, Savta.'

Eve put Benji down for a rest after lunch and went to check the spare room. It was a large sunny room on the first floor, between Sam and Gidi's bedrooms. They had put in a double bed, wardrobe and dressing table when they moved in.

'My parents can come and stay and if my brothers and their families come there is room for camp beds for the children,' said Dani.'

'The kids will probably all bunk in together,' laughed Eve. But they had bought a folding z-bed just in case.

Maybe Sam will sleep in here with her, thought Eve. She will feel so lonely away from Israel. Dani's father had died the year before and this would be the first time Sharona had visited England alone. And it's winter, thought Eve. She hates the cold so much.

'Come and live in Israel Eve, the sun shines every day. Even in winter,' Sharona said every holiday.

'The business is doing so well,' laughed Eve. 'And the children are settled in school. I can't see us moving now.'

'You will come when the boys go into the army.'

Eve felt a chill ripple through her. 'They don't have to,' she said quietly. 'They have dual nationality. I asked the Israeli embassy. They are exempt.'

She knew Dani didn't want them in the army either. 'When Ofer's son is eighteen he'll send him to England. He'll never let him go to the army,' Dani often said.

Dani and his three brothers had all been in the Yom Kippur War at the same time. 'We were all front line soldiers. When I came home to visit my father burst into tears,' Dani had told her. 'We have given enough. My sons are British.'

Eve spent the afternoon cleaning and was still tidying the front room when the boys arrived home.

'We played bombers all lunch play,' cried Gidi breathlessly.

Sam grabbed at a packet of crisps on the kitchen table.

'Mine, mine,' howled Benji. Sam tossed him the open packet and crisps showered onto the kitchen floor.

Gidi jumped on them yelling, 'Air raid! Air raid!'

Benji howled even louder.

'Stop it right now you lot, or up to your bedrooms!' Eve stood in the doorway, hands on hips, her ferocious 'Watch out!' look on her face.

The kitchen became quiet. Benji wiped his eyes, Gidi stood still looking sheepishly at the mess.

'Sorry mum,' said Sam. 'My fault. I'm starving.'

'Then clear up this mess and I'll organise a proper snack.'

The floor swept, the boys sat round the table devouring sandwiches. Eve smiled as Sam shared a packet of crisps with Benji.

'You can have them all Benji.'

'No Sam Sam. You have some. We're sharing mummy,' smiled Benji sweetly, basking in the attention.

'Good boy,' nodded Eve. 'School ok Jake?'

Jake shook his head, thumb in mouth and burst into tears.

Eve drew him onto her lap and pulled out a tissue. 'Jaky? What is it?'

'Steven Pett said everyone in Israel is going to die in the war,' said Gidi. 'Everyone knows Steven Pett's a wally, but Jake won't listen.'

'Its all rubbish Jake,' declared Sam. 'They said on Newsround last night that the Americans will have the Par... Part...'

'Patriot,' put in Eve.

'Yeah that's it, them missiles ready by today. So when the Iraqis send a bomb Pow! They'll smash it up!'

'Yipee!' yelled Benji, excited by Sam's voice. He zoomed off into the playroom pretending to fire a machine gun.

'He's mad,' laughed Gidi.

'Can we watch Newsround tonight mum?' asked Sam.

Eve hesitated. The children were both entranced and unhappy about the war. She and Dani had agreed not to watch the news until they were in bed.

'I'm not sure...'

'Come on mum, everyone watches it so they know about the war.'

'The teachers do it in school,' said Gidi slyly.

'Do they? Well. I suppose it's all right. But perhaps Jake you help mummy lay the table.'

'No,' mumbled Jake past his thumb. 'Want to do the same as Sam and Gidi.'

When Dani arrived home at six the boys were all playing together with the soldiers on the playroom floor. He looked in for a minute to say hello and then went into the kitchen.

'Something smells good,' he said as he bent to kiss Eve.

'Beef stew, a la Eve. The kids have already eaten, so we can have ours in here.'

'Good.' He reached out and switched on the radio for the news.

Eve wished he hadn't. She craved a break from it all. They watched news all evening. Hours and hours of terror and tension. The living room was strewn with newspapers in Hebrew and English.

'The Patriots are in place,' said Dani as they ate. 'And my mum will be here the day after tomorrow. Things will be ok.'

Eve nodded. 'I'm sure,' she mumbled, her mouth full.

At nine o'clock the news reported another Scud attack on Tel Aviv. Dani scanned the pictures anxiously.

One pile of rubble looks just like another, thought Eve.

'It doesn't look like our area,' said Dani, rubbing his tired eyes.

They sat through Newsnight and then Eve stood up and pointedly turned off the set. 'Enough's enough. Time for bed. You look exhausted.'

Dani smiled wearily. 'You're right.' He made a grab for her legs. 'Do we have time for some fun?'

'Oh ho! I see,' she grinned.' 'Not too tired for that.'

It was past eleven before they turned out the lights. Eve rolled over to face the window and patted Dani's behind. 'Same time tomorrow night,' she mumbled. He didn't reply.

The telephone rang. It was pitch black except for the red numbers shining on the clock. 1.17 am. Eve fumbled for her bedside light.

Dani picked up the phone. '*Ken? Mi zeh*?' He always reverted to Hebrew if he was half asleep.

Then his voice changed as if someone was slicing his throat. 'God! Oh God! When?...Yes!...No! The apartment?... All of it...?'

Eve felt gripped with terror. Who was it? What had happened? Dani's voice droned on, staccato noises like an animal in pain. After nearly ten minutes he put down the phone tears on his face.

Sam padded in rubbing his eyes. 'What is it? Why is daddy crying?'

'It's all right Sam. Don't worry.'

'Dani? What's happened?'

Dani began talking, his eyes glazed, unfocussed. 'That bomb, it fell on my mother's apartment block. That was Irit phoning from Los Angeles. They saw it all on TV. We didn't get the CNN pictures here. She saw our mother being carried out on a stretcher, but she can't get through to Israel yet. One child in the block was killed.'

Eve's chest contracted. This isn't a TV war anymore! she realised. It was here in their home, booming over the rooftops, threatening their lives.

'We must try Israel,' said Eve. She took the phone and dialled.

Gidi joined Sam on the end of the bed. Eve couldn't get through and put the phone down. 'I'll try every few minutes Dani,' she said desperately. 'I'll get through.'

Dani blew his nose loudly and wiped tears from his eyes. 'I can't believe it,' he said weakly. 'I just can't believe it. All the way from Iraq and they bomb my mother.'

Sam said , 'Are all the family coming here from Israel to stay? If they don't they'll all be dead.'

No-one answered him. Eve looked at the frightened children. How can I protect them from all this? Their grandmother injured in a bomb, their father in agony. It's always the old and the weak, she thought ferociously.

She went down to make hot drinks for everyone. Fortunately Jake and Benji didn't wake up. After the boys had finished their milk she said, 'Come on, let me tuck you up again. There's no more news for now.'

'Can Sam sleep with me mummy? I'm frightened.' Gidi clutched his brother.

'Of course sweetheart. I'll make you a cosy bed right next to him.'

She had to sit with them for an hour before they fell asleep. Through the rest of the night she heard Gidi mumble from time to time in his sleep, a mixture of Hebrew and English.

Pictures started coming through on television at six. 'I think that's the kitchen,' murmured Dani. He was wrapped in a blanket, a hot water bottle clutched on his knees.

He looks like an old man, thought Eve as she gazed at his face, the eyes wide as they stared at the screen. She began to cry silently as she looked at the appalling wreckage, taking care not to let Dani see.

The commentator was reviewing the attack. 'It appears the Scud came over at about 8.37 p.m. Israeli time last night, January 22nd. It was intercepted by a Patriot missile, but was only knocked off course. Not exploded. The bomb fell in Tel Aviv and reports are that more than ninety people were injured, one killed and two old people died of heart attacks. Several apartment blocks were totally destroyed and hundreds damaged.

People living in the blocks will be allowed back for a few minutes this morning to gather belongings. Then the wreckage will be completely bull - dozed.'

The scene changed to a woman standing in front of a mound of twisted concrete. 'My street looks like an earthquake hit it. It's completely different when the war enters your own living room.'

'I know just how she feels,' said Eve as tears welled up again. Dani was silent rocking himself under the blanket.

An elderly man spoke into the microphone. 'I was in Auschwitz. I saw people gassed. What more can they do to me?'

It was almost seven o'clock and beginning to get light. Eve turned round to see Sam leaning against the wall. How long has he stood there? she thought with a shock. What has he seen?

She switched off the TV and frowned at Dani. He looked over his shoulder and nodded.

'I'll try Israel again.'

'I'll get the children ready for school.' Her body felt stiff with cold and shock as she stood up.

While she was dressing Benji she could hear Sam and Gidi arguing in low voices in the bathroom.

'Bet you!'

'Bet you!'

'Go on then, prove it!'

'Ask dad if she's dead. He said she was!' Gidi's voice was getting higher and higher.

'I will! I'll go and ask him right now!' Sam yelled.

Eve pushed open the bathroom door and grabbed Sam as he tried to rush past her. He struggled a little and then burst into tears.

'What is it? What's going on?'

'Nothing,' said Gidi sullenly. He pulled a face at Sam. 'You pooh!'

Sam lunged for him. Eve pulled him down. He was so tall now, past her shoulder and powerful for his age. Gidi was smaller and slighter. The last time they had a serious fight Sam made Gidi's nose bleed.

'Now look,' said Eve firmly. 'Daddy's very upset. We should be able to rely on you in a crisis to be sensible with the little ones.'

'You always keep it a bloody secret!'

'What secret Sam?' Eve asked too surprised by the force of his accusation to tell him off for swearing.

'You know, bloody, bloody! The war. You switch off the TV. Daddy's hurt and I don't know where! Gidi says Savta is dead, been gassed in Tel Aviv. He's bloody lying!'

She had to sit on him this time, pin his flailing arms to the floor. He rolled his head from side to side and roared at her.

Then she was soothing him, stroking his head, pulling him into her arms. Haven't done this since his rat died, she thought, amused in the middle of their pain.

Have we kept it a secret? But we were only trying to protect them from all this horror. I sound like my grandmother, she thought.

Suddenly she realised how they felt. Noah! The secret they kept from her. She had to prise it out of her father when she was in her twenties. She remembered her declaration that she would tell her children everything.

And I always have, she thought. Oh God! I mustn't make a mistake now.

'Right,' she said. 'We'll all go into Sam's room. The little ones as well. And I'll tell you everything. It's not a secret Sam.'

'Promise?' His face streaked with tears and dust was two inches from hers'.

'Promise. Cross my heart and hope to... Well never mind. Absolutely everything. From now on we'll watch the news together and I'll answer any questions you ask.'

After they had talked Eve went down to make breakfast. Dani was on the telephone in the living-room, speaking Hebrew in low rapid tones. She moved quietly round, her heart beating fast. Israel or America? Is Sharona alive or dead?

Then Dani appeared in the doorway, his face ashen. 'My mother is in intensive care. Pieces of rock entered her brain. Her hearing might be affected. Ofer, Nili and the boys were also in the apartment. They were all hurt, but not seriously. Nili is in deep shock.'

'Oh Dani.' Eve was crying freely now, unable to hide it from him anymore.

Dani pulled out a chair and sat down, hand running through his hair.

'That was Miki on the phone. He was at home with Gila. Ofer rang him from the hospital about an hour after it happened. He's only just been able to get through to me. It's not good.'

She shook her head and put her hand over his. She had never felt so helpless. 'It's such incredibly bad luck Dani! Hardly anyone's been hit. If the Patriot hadn't been fired and hit that Scud....but then someone else would have been bombed...' she tailed off uselessly.

'She's seventy-two. An old woman.'

He stood up and pushed in his chair slowly. 'I'm going to take a shower.'

The boys were very subdued at breakfast. Eve told them about their grandmother and they all listened wide-eyed. Even Benji seemed to understand this was not a time to be silly.

She drove them to school and dropped them off at the gate. 'Sam, you're in charge. See that your brothers are ok. Take Benji right into the nursery and don't leave him until you see Mrs Lever.'

'You can rely on me mum.'

She drove away with relief, glad she didn't have to face the other mothers. It's as though we're shut in a world of our own, she thought.

Dani was in the kitchen sipping tea.

'Are you going to work?'

'No.' He looked into her eyes. 'I'm going to Israel. I've booked an El Al flight from Heathrow at midday.'

She stared at him and then looked away afraid he would see the terror spreading through her. Dani in a sealed room, gas mask over his face. Dani gassed. Dani buried alive. Dead. She could hardly bear to listen to herself.

'I'll come with you. My parents will move in, look after the ....'

'No! The boys need you. You have to stay.

'Her mouth was dry with fear. How could she let him go? How could she ask him to stay?

'What about the children? They will be upset they didn't say goodbye.'

'I'll phone every day, every few hours. It'll be ok Eve. The hospital is safe. I won't roam the streets. I'm used to gas masks. I was a soldier, remember?'

'I'd better pack.' Lists ran through her head. Shaving stuff, underwear, shirts, soap.

Her body was moving slower and slower, as the dull weight inside her surfaced.

Don't think. Not now.

Passport,cash.

The weight moved up another inch, pressing on her lungs. The familiar struggle for air. This is how I always dealt with pain, she thought. I have to manage now.

They drove to Heathrow in silence. Dani was wearing the blue sweater she had given him on his last birthday.

I couldn't bear it if.... She shut off the thought. His mother could be dying, she told herself. I'd do exactly the same in his position.

Her last view of him was his smile and the blue sweater bobbing through the double doors.

She telephoned her parents when she arrived home. She felt exhausted and desperately alone.

Jack answered the phone. 'Why didn't you tell us before? We'll come straight over.'

'No dad. It's ok. I couldn't tell you until now. Dani's been on the phone non-stop. I'm just so angry, God!...' her voice broke as the pent up emotions broke through.

'It must be awful love. My friend's house was bombed in the Blitz. There was nothing there when I went to look.'

'Its not just that,' she forced out between sobs. 'Its...God dad!...They were all thrown out in 1950 by Iraq and now two decades later the Iraqis make them homeless again. It's so bloody unfair!' The impotency of the word drove her mad.

'Oh Eve. We're so terribly sorry. But look, don't worry. You know Dani. He can take care of himself.'

'So can Ofer and look what happened to him,' she said bitterly. 'If it weren't for the children I would have gone too.'

'Of course. But you have to stay Eve. The children need their mother now.'

She sat up late that evening after the boys had gone to sleep. They were so good about Dani going, she thought. Only Benji cried at bedtime, ' Want my daddy, want my daddy,' until exhaustion overcame him and his eyelids dropped shut.

There was a movement behind her. It was Sam. 'Come in darling,' she smiled.

'Can I sit with you mummy?' His voice was cautious.

'Yes. I could do with some company. How about a cuddle?'

He crept into her arms and she held his soft weight against her, absorbing its heat, like an amulet against the fear and the loneliness. Thousands of miles away Dani sat at his mother's bedside, gas mask at his feet.

She thought about his brown suitcase, neatly packed, sitting open on their bed before he left. All that I could do for him, she thought.

Thinking of the suitcase reminded her of a programme she had watched on TV about an Austrian Jew who had married the daughter of a former concentration camp guard.

In one scene the parents and the young couple were having dinner together. The camera moved over the uneasy face of the camp guard. Eve had scanned his face, searching for a reason, an explanation.

Then the voice of the Austrian Jew came over, 'In Austria the Jews have always lived with bags packed.'

GLOSSARY

Aliyah	emigrating to Israel
Amod dom	stand to attention
Amod noach	stand at ease
Bidiouk	exactly
Boi ha regah	come here now
Challa	plaited bread
Chalutz	pioneer
Chaltuzim	pioneers
Eretz ha vad chalav	land of milk and honey
Fedayeen	Arab guerrillas
Garin	soldiers on a settlement
Hodje	quickly
Irgun Zvai Leumi	Irgun National Army
Jellabah	a long robe
Kadimah	forward
Khefiya	scarf
Lehaim	to life
Lehitrayot	see you
Lokshen	noodles
Loul	chicken shed
Meziah	a bargain
Meshugganah	fool
Miluim	army reserves
Moshav	collective settlement
Moshavnik	members of a Moshav
Nach tig a tog	night into day
Nu	well
Od mayat	in a while
Oy va voy	oh yes
RACH CACH	only this way
Rak b'eretz	only in Israel
Shabbat, shabbos	Sabbath
Shalom	hello/goodbye
Shema Yisrael adonai eloyhanu adonai ehud. Baruch shem cvod…	Hear O Israel, the Lord is our God, the Lord is one. Blessed be his name….
Sherout	shared taxi
Shil shul	diarrhoea
Shiva	mourning
Shouk	bazaar
Shukran	thankyou
Smoalah	left
Ulpan	Hebrew course
Yallah	come on
Yamina	right